MARY CHAMBERLAIN is a novelist and historian. Her debut novel, *The Dressmaker of Dachau*, was published in eighteen countries. She is the author of non-fiction books on women's history, and Caribbean history including *Fenwomen*, the first book published by Virago Press. She lives in London.

Praise for *The Hidden*

'Recent novels such as *The Guernsey Literary & Potato Peel Society* have taken the occupation as their subject, but none so potently as Mary Chamberlain's *The Hidden*... As Chamberlain's narrative moves between past and present...the realities of life under a ruthless occupying power are slowly, skilfully revealed.' *Sunday Times*

'A fascinating and powerful story of love, endurance, betrayal and guilt.' Anna Mazzola, author of *The Unseeing*

'A heart-breaking yet hope-filled tale.' *Woman's Own* Magazine

'A powerful story, well told.' *Choice*, book of the month

'[Chamberlain] has a wonderful knack for slowly and skilfully peeling back the layers as the narrative moves across past and present... This compelling and heart-rending novel is a potent reminder that the horrors of war aren't limited to the battlefields.' *Herald Scotland*

'A riveting World War saga.' Cecilia Ekbäck, author of *Wolf Winter*

'Hauntingly atmospheric, historian and author Mary Chamberlain takes the reader to the dark days of the Channel Islands under German Occupation, and tells a hugely moving tale of love, survival *Bookbag*

ALSO BY MARY CHAMBERLAIN:

Fiction

The Mighty Jester

The Dressmaker of Dachau

Non-fiction

Empire and Nation-building in the Caribbean: Barbados 1937 – 1966

Family Love in the Diaspora: Migration and the Anglo Caribbean Experience

Narratives of Exile and Return

Growing Up in Lambeth

Old Wives' Tales: The History of Remedies, Charms and Spells

Fenwomen: A Portrait of Women in an English Village

THE HIDDEN

Mary Chamberlain

A Point Blank Book
First published in Great Britain and Australia by Point Blank,
an imprint of Oneworld Publications, 2019
This mass market edition published 2019

A CIP record for this title is available from the British Library

ISBN 978-1-78607-662-5
ISBN 978-1-78607-506-2 (ebook)

Typeset by Fakenham Prepress Solutions, Fakenham, Norfolk NR21 8NL
Printed and bound in Great Britain by Clays Ltd, Elcograf S.p.A.

Oneworld Publications
10 Bloomsbury Street
London WC1B 3SR
England

AUTHOR'S NOTE

The German invasion of the British Channel Islands began on 30 June 1940 and was completed with the surrender of Sark on 4 July 1940. All but twenty of the residents of Alderney had been evacuated to mainland Britain, along with many men of military age, and some women and children, from Jersey and Guernsey. The islands were not liberated until 9 May 1945. They were the only part of the British Isles to be occupied during the Second World War.

The governors of Guernsey and Jersey had been recalled to London shortly before the Germans invaded, and their responsibilities handed to the bailiffs, Alexander Coutanche in Jersey and Victor Carey in Guernsey, with instructions to continue administration of the island under the German authorities.

Between September 1942 and February 1943, residents who had been born in Britain were deported to internment camps in France and Germany. They did not all survive the war. Those Jews remaining on the islands (most, but not all, had been able to evacuate before the German invasion) were also deported in the same period to France and then to concentration camps in Germany or Poland, where many were murdered.

With no hinterland in which to hide and no assistance from London, resistance in the Channel Islands was limited to protests and acts of defiance. In Jersey there was a clandestine network of safe houses for escaped prisoners, organised by Norman Le Brocq, a member of the Communist Party who also distributed leaflets encouraging mutiny within the German forces. Some individuals engaged in clandestine protests like the 'V for Victory' daubings, or secreting notes disclaiming Hitler into German possessions, and a few clergymen protected members of the outlawed Salvation Army church; Charles Rey, the Jesuit priest, used his geological collection to manufacture crystal sets after the confiscation of wirelesses in 1942.

Islanders charged with resistance were also deported or, after August 1944, imprisoned locally.

PROLOGUE

St Helier, Jersey: June 1985

The chequered marble floor needed a scrub. Her heels clicked as she crossed it, echoed in the hollow house. The vast oak staircase was still there, though the balustrades were dull and dusty, the ruby carpet threadbare on the tread, the stair rods covered in verdigris. To her left was the officers' bar, where she'd first heard 'Lili Marleen' being played on the gramophone.

Dora opened her mouth. The verses swirled in her head. She knew the words off by heart, even now, after all those years. She walked along the landing, up and into the attics. Her fingers were shaky as she turned the door handle. She was all alone. What if the door slammed behind her and she couldn't get out? No one knew she was here and her cries would not be heard. But something was drawing her in, churning flashbacks into compulsions. *Come closer.*

CHAPTER ONE

DORA

London: a few months earlier, March 1985

Please forgive this letter out of the blue, but I am trying to trace a Dora Simons, or Simmons, last heard of in 1943 in Jersey. I believe she worked as a midwife...

It was dated 24 March 1985, written on headed notepaper, the Huntingdon Bed & Breakfast, Bloomsbury. Dora knew the kind of place well. Swirling carpets, nylon sheets, full English breakfast. Cheap.

Mr Joseph O'Cleary, of La Ferme de l'Anse, St Martin, Jersey, gave me this address...

Dora folded the letter in two and sat down hard on the kitchen chair. Her chest tightened, making her breathless. She had no idea who Joseph O'Cleary was. It stood to reason that someone else would be living in the farm after all these years, but how he had come to have *her* address was anyone's guess. She'd given no one her details when she left. Nor had she met any Irishmen, or if she had, she'd forgotten. Whoever O'Cleary was, he'd got her name wrong. She was Simon. Not Simons. Or Simmons. An easy mistake, if you didn't know her.

This could be a hoax. She'd reply and then be lumbered with a subscription to *Reader's Digest* or some cookery club that she had no interest in. She received those letters all the time. *Congratulations!*

You have won first prize in our million-pound draw. To claim your prize, take out a year's subscription to…

Dora screwed up the letter. Walked over to the sink and filled the kettle. A cup of tea. Just the thing. How very *English* she'd become over the years, drinking tea through every crisis. She'd grown to tolerate it with milk. She turned on the radio. Something sharp and discordant was being sung. She reached for her cigarettes, eyeing the balled-up paper on the table. Whatever they were playing wasn't music in her book. No melody, only episodes that jarred, upside down, back to front.

She opened the letter again and spread it flat, ironing out the creases with her fingers.

> *…although, as he indicated, it may not be current. If you are not Dora Simons (or Simmons), I wonder whether you would be so kind as to reply and let me know, so I can eliminate you from my searches.*

She stood up, holding onto the back of the chair for support.

Yours sincerely, Barbara Hummel.

The writer gave no clue as to why she wished to contact Dora. It wasn't a name Dora knew. Perhaps Barbara Hummel was one of the babies she'd delivered. She rarely learned what they'd been called. That all happened later, at the christening, and no one invited the midwife to one of those. Nor was Hummel an English name. More Scandinavian, perhaps. Or German. The English was perfect, but then, she thought, the continent was so much better at teaching languages than England. *The continent*, as if England was not part of it. As if she was not part of it.

Hummel could be a married name, of course.

She'd deal with the letter later: *Dear Barbara Hummel. Thank you for your communication dated 24 March 1985.*

Or ignore it, pretend it had never arrived, scrunch it up again and throw it into the bin. It could be a made-up name. It could be a criminal syndicate. What if they blackmailed her? She switched off the radio.

It was raining outside, and windy with it. The kettle turned itself off with a click and Dora poured the water into the pot. At least she hadn't succumbed to the teabag. She wasn't *that* English. She still used tea leaves, proper leaves that swelled in water and made good compost. She'd drain the dregs into a tidy in the sink, then add them to the bucket in which she put her peelings and apple cores and empty it all on the compost once a day. Her garden was her pride and joy. Uncle Otto'd had no interest in it. He'd been glad for Dora to take it on, *Save me paying,* he'd said. But that wasn't the reason. He saw it as therapy for her, and he'd been right.

It had taken her years to knock it into shape. The shrubs were thick and tall now, the herbaceous border lush and colourful and the cherry tree – her father's favourite fruit – mature and productive, even if the birds ate the fruit before she could. It wouldn't be long before the cherry blossomed. It always came with the camellias, after the magnolia, a waterfall of pink that filled the garden from week to week. She'd planted clematis and climbing roses, wisteria and hydrangea, and as the season progressed, they spread a floral palette and filled the garden with the sweet nostalgia of scent.

The daffodils would flower soon, too. Tough, were daffodils. She watched as the wind bent them over and the rain pummelled the buds. The cloudy sky indicated no let-up. She'd have to brave the elements, put on her mackintosh and waterproof hat, her stout walking shoes. She'd be dry enough. She'd shake off the water and bounce right up, like the daffies. Couldn't abide umbrellas. They took up space and blew inside out.

Perhaps she could write to this Barbara Hummel and ask her why she wanted to trace Dora Simon. Could she do that without admitting who she was? *I am in contact with Dora Simon (please note the correct spelling) who has requested me to ask you why it is you wish to trace her.*

Enough. She was fine. Breathing normal, hands calm, crisis passed. There was nothing to this letter. She twisted it up again and put it in the bin. She pulled her shopping trolley out from the cupboard under the stairs, checked she had her purse and keys and looked into the hall mirror to make sure she looked presentable before she set off.

Since when had her hair become so white? It was still thick and wavy, but its rich summer colours had long turned to winter. Like an Arctic fox or a mountain hare. Perhaps she should colour it. Nothing too brash, too brassy. A rinse, perhaps, a soft shade that would tone in. Her crowning glory. She kept it in a bun now, away from her face, curls pulled flat and taut. It made her look strict, stand-offish.

'People think you're hard to get to know,' Charles told her once. 'Detached. Forbidding.'

'Easy on the budget,' she'd said. How could she afford a regular hairdresser on her pension from the university? She could have applied for promotion, but she'd never had the confidence. Been happy to stick at the top of her grade for her entire working life.

Her heart had died in the war, she knew that. Her body had lingered on, but the years had caught up with her now. She looked old. Would it suit her short? Release the curls? A good cut could last months. She sucked in her cheeks, turned to one side, looked at herself from the corner of her eye. It would take years off her.

She was rigid in her ways, she knew. Charles told her that all the time.

'Plain stubborn.'

'I have routines,' Dora said. 'They're different.'

But she'd never had to adjust to anyone else, to accommodate their needs, not after Uncle Otto died.

She pulled on her rain hat, turned down the brim. Dora paused, eyeing the bin where the scrunched-up paper was. That letter was tugging her back into a place she thought she'd never have to visit again. It made her uneasy. She didn't like to be discombobulated. Now *that* was a word. Worthy of German, in its way, with all those syllables. Tipped off balance. She'd kept a tight rein on her life since the war, but restraint was a flimsy prison, its bars soft as a spider's web. No wonder she wanted to change her hair. Why not get a fake tan while she was about it? Or a facelift? Escape into somebody else. Was she really so forbidding?

Library books. She checked the shopping trolley. Of course she'd put them there once she'd read them. Habit of a lifetime. She must be getting old. Forgetful. She had strategies against that. She kept herself busy, especially now, after retirement. 'Never be bored,' her father used to say. 'But don't be afraid to be idle.' He was full of sayings. She thought of him every day, even though it was more than fifty years since he'd died. That's how the dead lived on, became immortal. Who would remember her? She had no children of her own. 'Dust to dust.' That was what her father used to say. 'Science gives us the answers. Who needs rabbis and priests?'

She played bridge competitively, practised compulsively, dealing herself tricks on the kitchen table and going to the club three nights a week. Trips to tournaments in Eastbourne or Scarborough. Choir every Thursday, taking the bus to Tufnell Park. She practised the clarinet, too, bought sheet music from Boosey & Hawkes in Regent Street. Dinner with Charles once a week when he came up from Kent, her place or a restaurant.

'Why don't we just live together,' he'd say. 'You don't have to marry me.'

'I like things the way they are.'

And her garden. That was her true joy. Weeding and pruning and cutting and trimming. It looked wild, but it wasn't disordered.

La Ferme de l'Anse had wisteria, a gnarled, seasoned plant that hugged the front of the house and crowned in May. She could see it now, the magnificent scented pendants in shades of amethyst and purple. Roses too. Wild pink climbers in the hedgerows, standards in the border, white or burgundy with a heady perfume. She'd never recollected it before. She could feel the sweat under her arms, her trembling legs and hands. She gripped the edge of the table. Steady. *Steady.* Breathed deep. *Pull yourself together.*

Had her unconscious been trying to recreate it? A stem memory? Frail and unformed, now multiplying and morphing like a cancer cell. Was her garden nothing but a *memento mori*? Of what? A time?

A love?

§

A whole week had gone by. The scene at the front of the house could have been Brighton beach after a bank holiday. Pizza delivery boxes, scraps of tin foil, orange peel, juice cartons. Newspapers. Empty wine bottles. They were now required to put out their rubbish on the pavement, which meant the foxes had first pickings, before the dustmen came. She'd told her tenants again and again not to put unwanted food in the garbage. But they did. This was what greeted her every Wednesday morning. It was always Dora who had to clear up the mess.

She wore a pair of rubber gloves and carried a large black plastic sack. Scooped up the detritus and the ripped bags, crammed them into the new one. The foxes had been particularly active that morning. Every dustbin had been tipped over, including, Dora saw, her own, even though she was meticulous in making sure there was nothing to tempt the animals.

And there it was again. Dora picked the letter off the forecourt, was about to ram it into the bag. Pocketed it instead. She'd have one more look at it. She stood up, heard the rumbling of the dustcart, secured the top of the black bag tight. She'd have a word with the dustmen when they came. Ask them to clean the mess in future. What did she pay her rates for, if it wasn't to clear the rubbish and light the streets?

When she thought about it, this woman was looking for Dora, *last heard of in 1943.* So she must only be interested in the time before. La Ferme de l'Anse. She could talk to her about those days. A wartime affair. *You know how these things go.* Flash in the pan. Whirlwind romance.

She'd write to this Barbara Hummel after all. Though she may have left the hotel already. It was not the sort of place you stayed in long term. That would be the best of all worlds. Dora would have replied, the woman would never have known.

Dora smiled, stepped onto the pavement, flagged down the dustmen.

CHAPTER TWO

JOE

Jersey: May 1985

Joe fingered the halter in his hand. The air was still, save the melody from the fields, the rustle of the grasses as the mice and the beetles scurried about their business, the hum of the bees as they dipped inside the clover blossoms.

He pulled the letter out of his pocket. It had been sitting there for a couple of days, forgotten. He was getting absent-minded. It had a Jersey postmark and the sender's address written on the back of the envelope. *B. Hummel, c/o Hotel de France, St Saviour's Road.*

> *Dear Mr O'Cleary,*
>
> *Thank you for your help. I am pleased to report that I have traced a Dora Simon (not Simons, or Simmons). I am hoping that I may be able to meet her in London next time I visit and will be able to report back more about your friend.*

Dora Simon wasn't a friend. Not even an acquaintance. It was forty years since he'd pushed himself into the scrum surrounding her that day as she'd crouched on the ground with her dress ripped and locks of red curls lying on the paving stones like boiled shrimps. It was the Red Cross that had given him her details, and he'd kept her address, at the time, meaning to write. But he never got round to it and then forgot he even had her details, until a couple of months ago.

Still, he was glad to hear that the woman was still alive. He presumed she was well, though none of them were spring chickens anymore. He'd be seventy himself this year. Fit as a fiddle, mind.

I'll be back in Jersey in early May. If I may, I'll drive up to your farm to make your acquaintance.

Why would she want to do that? He'd written to her once already, c/o the PO box number she'd given in the paper. *The photograph is that of Dora Simons, or Simmons, a midwife. Last known whereabouts, Jersey, 1943.* That's what the old man had told Joe. What more did she want?

'No.' Joe said it out loud. He didn't want to make the woman's acquaintance. It was hard enough living with himself as it was. *A bit of a recluse*, that's what they said about him. *A bit of an eccentric.* Well, that suited him fine. He had the farm, he had the birds, he had fresh air and food. He kept himself clean, if not always tidy. His trousers were old and held up with binder twine, but there was wear in them still. His jacket was torn, but he had another for town and a black tie for funerals. He shaved twice a week and that was enough. He didn't want any more company than he had already. Spying and prying. Busybodies. *Ghouls.* He did *not* want to meet a stranger who'd stir up memories.

But he owed it to Geoffrey.

For how had this Barbara woman come across Dora Simon's photograph, if she didn't have something that might be of interest to the old man?

He heard a car slow, change gear, turn the corner, enter the end of the lane. He looked at his watch, a newfangled digital Casio which showed the date as well as the time. It was too early for Pierre. He cupped his ear towards the distant murmur. He used to know the make of every car from the sound the engine made. But this car. He listened hard. It was one of those cheap imported jobs, from Italy or Japan. Ran on wound-up rubber bands, sniggered. Pierre had a Land Rover, a sturdy diesel number that brayed like a deer in rut. Nor was it the inspector's car. That was a Ford. He didn't want the inspector out, not today. Besides, it was a Sunday. No inspector worked Sundays.

The cry of a curlew broke the quiet. Joe dropped the halter, lifted his binoculars, trained them to the cliff edge, left, right, up, down. Crou-eee, crou-eee, the bird was howling like a pup. Curlews were common enough round here, but he still thrilled to see them. There she was. Silhouetted, and the sky full of tubby clouds with blown-out cheeks. Fair weather. Some clouds were angels, high in the icy heavens, willowy and graceful, others puckered like wet skin. But cumulus, they were his friends, even when they blocked the sun and shrouded the blue. They were no threat.

He followed the bird as it glided across the sky. Up there were thermals that wings caught and floated on. Did they swim in the air for joy, for the pleasure of the wind blowing through the dappled feathers, stroking the skin? The curlew's long, curved beak and its outstretched legs made a crescent in the sky, but on land its beak looked too long for its head. Like Pinocchio's nose. Was a curlew a liar too?

Joe had watched the birds for as long as he could remember. Awake with the light, he'd gazed through the attic window from the bed he shared as a child with his brothers and sisters until the girls got too old. They'd shove him close to the glass so he caught the draughts, but it was worth it. He had a ringside seat of the Owenmore estuary as the gannets and the petrels dipped and circled, their cries like the calls of old friends. He knew who was out there and why. He cherished those dawns.

'Just look at you,' little Bridey, the sister nearest to him, said. 'No bigger than a sparrow yourself. Would you want to fly away with them?'

Yes, he wanted to say. *Yes.* Their *daidí* was a hard man. Never gave a thought for Joe, unless there was a fist behind it.

The bird dived below the cliff as Joe trained the binoculars on the house. The car came into view, bumped across the pitted farmyard and stopped outside the front door. From where he stood on the slope, he couldn't be seen. Handy, he could check the visitor before he need show himself.

It was a while before the door opened and a woman stepped out. Her back was towards him but he could see that she was dressed in a plaid coat and a purple beret. Not from round these parts. She went into the porch, knocked at the door. *You're wasting your time.* He used to hope little Bridey would come knocking, but now, after all these years, if she did, he'd say the same to her. You're wasting your time. The woman was bending low, peering through the letter box. Much good may it do her. The plywood he'd nailed over the opening stopped the busybodies as well as the draughts. She wouldn't see a thing. Besides, local people knew that they never used the front door, hadn't since the war. Knew also that the old man inside was as deaf as a post.

The woman turned back to the car. It had to be that Hummel woman. If it was him she was after, she'd have to come back another day. Now was not convenient.

She walked away from the car, through the farmyard. There was a path at the end that led down the cliffs onto the beach below. Strange to be dressed up with a hat and all, to go walking on the beach. He hoped she wouldn't be long. Pierre would be here soon. They'd wake up the old man and get the business started.

Betsy was grazing, pulling at the grass so it screamed, flicking her tail over her dun, worn hide. She jumped as he came close, kicked up her hooves and skittered away.

'Betsy girl,' he said. 'Don't make it hard.' He fished in his pocket for the lump of salt and held out his hand. She walked towards him, one slow hoof at a time, smelled him with wet nostrils, curled her tongue and rasped it over his hand. She bucked as he pulled the halter over her, tried to run away, but he held firm.

'I may be small,' he said. 'But I'm still strong.' For wasn't he the bantamweight champion of Ireland, even if it was before the war? But what would Betsy know of that?

He led her down the field and through the gate. He'd get her bedded down before Pierre came, calm and quiet so fear didn't taint her meat. Pierre wasn't due for an hour or so, and the woman would be gone by then. And even if she wasn't, Pierre liked his drop of Jameson before he did his business, as well as after, and the old man always had a nip with him, so she had time to walk to St Brélade's and back for all he knew.

It was inconvenient of the woman to leave her vehicle here, as if it was a public car park. He led Betsy past her car, into the barn. He'd prepared her stall, the single chute at the end with the head gate that he used to keep a cow steady for impregnating. Nothing was done nature's way anymore and though it was a messy job, sticking your arm up the animal's backside and feeling around inside, he had to admit it had more chances of success than running a randy bull with an unwilling cow. He'd secure Betsy later, when Pierre was here. For now, she had the freedom of her stall, with fresh hay to eat and water to drink, clean straw to bed on and the familiar smells and sounds of home.

She'd be content there. Betsy had served him well, and hadn't he been kind to her? He owed her this. He'd learned how to slaughter from his father, and butcher the beasts. He put up a new salt block. She walked towards it and curled her tongue around its edge, licks rough as a file, a line of drool falling from her mouth.

'Enjoy it, Betsy,' he said. 'Enjoy.'

He walked back out and over to the car. A Toyota. It was hired, he could tell by the number plate. He tried the driver's door. It opened. Inside was empty and clean, freshly valeted. If she had a bag, she'd taken it with her. He leaned over and opened the glove compartment. A duster. A log. He pulled it out. Avis, service history. If she didn't come back soon, he'd give them a ring, tell them it was causing an obstruction.

He slammed the door shut and set off towards the cliff. There was still some time before Pierre was due. She was most likely on the beach. He'd ask her to move her car somewhere else.

Most of the path had eroded into scree, slippery unless you knew how to walk it. Joe took firm, even steps, flat onto the sole of his boot, like he had done as an altar boy on the Saints' Road, up the Brandon Mountain, *Holy Mary Mother of God.* The voyagers' saint was Brendan, a Kerry man.

His binoculars hung round his neck. Zeiss lens, picked up at the end of the war, victors' spoils. He'd had them now for over forty years, and they weren't new then. Best glasses he'd ever had, even better than the Dollands. They'd see him out now, the adjuster as sensitive as ever and the lenses pristine, without a scratch.

He jumped the last two feet or so onto the rock – how that woman got down was anyone's guess – and strode out across the sand. Strange that he couldn't see the woman anywhere. She must have walked fast, and far.

Joe clambered back up the cliff and walked behind the barn to where his caravan was parked. He'd never felt right about living in the house, not since the war, even though he kept it draught-free and in good repair. He'd even put in a bathroom for the old man, with an indoor lavatory, bought the toilet paper once a month from the cash and carry. He checked on him three times a day, got him his meals and sat with him of an evening, used the house to take a bath twice a week. But the old man couldn't hear a thing, so talk was hard, and what could they say to each other now, after all these years? Better he stayed in his caravan with his sunken memories and shattered dreams and the old man lived in the house with his.

He kicked off his wellington boots and stepped with stockinged feet into his van. He doubted it was roadworthy now, but then he wouldn't want to go anywhere. It was too large for the lanes of Jersey and had caused enough difficulty when he'd brought it down the road and manoeuvred it in place. He'd broken up the old Streamlite that he'd bought after the war with a sad heart, for it had stood him well. But thirty years was a good life for a caravan, and the Knowsley Juno that he had now was better for all-year living with its styrofoam insulation and double-glazed windows. He eased himself into the corner seat and picked up a copy of yesterday's *Evening Post.*

He turned back to the letter. There was a PTO at the bottom and an arrow. He flicked the paper over.

> *PS My mother had some connection with Jersey and has various mementos from that time, including some newspaper reports. Were you also known as the 'pugilist priest', Father Joe O'Cleary, boxing champion in 1943? It would be too much of a coincidence to have a Joseph and a Joe O'Cleary on that tiny island!*

Well. He might have something to say about that.

CHAPTER THREE

DORA

Jersey: February 1942 – January 1943

The phone call came through late that afternoon and there was no one but Dora to take it. Duty midwife. She'd have to brave it and venture out. It had been nearly two years since the Germans had occupied the place, but she'd never got used to them. It got worse, if anything. *Borrowed time.* She should have listened to Uncle Otto. 'Don't go. You're safe in London.' He had been right on that. 'Why don't you settle down? Charles has a soft spot for you.' He'd winked. 'He'll go far.'

'I'm young, Uncle Otto,' she'd said. 'I want to enjoy myself.'

He'd huffed and puffed, but he'd never married, so why force her? Jersey was far more inviting. Dancing and singing, sun and sea while London hunkered down with its ARP wardens and Anderson shelters. Where was the danger in Jersey?

What if the Germans were here to stay, like they said? The 'Thousand-year Reich'.

The wind was dancing like a dervish, thrashing the sea up against the promenade. Dora headed out across the island with her medical bag, head down low over the handlebars, against the storm. It was a farmhouse, she was told, La Ferme de l'Anse. This was not a part of the island she knew well, but the caller had insisted this was an emergency. The phone went dead before she could find out more.

Clouds banked grey and heavy behind the hills. A fork of lightning cleaved them apart and thunder thumped the ground. The clouds rolled closer and rain began to fall in large, thick gobs. Dora could barely see. Some of the road signs were now in German but the caller had used local names and Dora wasn't always sure. She had no idea what the emergency was about. Hoped it was just the usual panic of the father, 'come quick, my wife's in labour', as if his wife was the first woman to have a child.

Dora wished she had a torch. The rain was thick, the dusk inky. Hedges were gashed apart, trees bent double. And over. A sycamore with a broken back and jagged roots filled the road in front of her and she came to a stop. She would have to turn, approach the farm from another direction, but it was too murky and wet to read the map and it would be easy to make a mistake in the labyrinth of lanes. An *emergency.* Behind her she heard the scream of a branch, its slow agony as it ripped from its trunk, its roar as it plummeted and fell with a thud onto the road.

She left her bike by the side of the road, grabbed her bag, pushed her way through the tree ahead, twigs and branches snagging at her legs and cape. The wind lifted and propelled her forward, faster than she could run, so she stumbled, caught herself before the gale laid her flat. She had memorised this last part, straight on and right, left and right again. The evening was made darker by thick ebony clouds. There'd be no light in the farmhouse, not with the blackout, and Dora wasn't sure she'd find it on a night like this.

Her cape and skirt hung in sodden swags, stuck to her body, wrapped round her legs, making walking hard. Head down deep and shoulder to the wind, she saw the bobbing light of a torch and then there was a woman's hand on her elbow.

'Thank God, nurse, thank God.'

She followed the woman into the farmhouse, through the kitchen, up the stairs. The house was cold and unlit, save for an oil lamp in the bedroom.

A man sat on the edge of the bed, rocking a woman in his arms. He was lowing, like a wounded beast. Dora went over, lifted the woman's swollen hand. There was no pulse.

She freed the body from his embrace, laid it on the bed, fished the torch from her pocket, lifted a puffy eyelid and stared into the glassy vacuum. Delved into her bag for her Pinard horn, even though she already knew the baby would be dead.

'She was having fits.' His voice quivered, his face haggard in the glow from the lamp. 'Stomach pains.'

'We rang as soon as we could,' the other woman said. 'But the lines were down. We had to go into St Martin.'

'Put the kettle on,' Dora said. 'Bring me some warm water and make some tea.' She turned to the man. 'Do you have more lights?'

'The electricity's gone,' he said. 'The storm–'

'Do you have more lights?'

'In the shed,' he said. 'With the cows.'

'Fetch them.'

Dora took the lamp and placed it closer to the woman, touched the chalky skin and felt the chill of death. Rigor mortis had not yet set in. Her limbs and face were bloated, stomach bulbous with her unborn child, her hip bones sharp and angular against her flesh. Fits. Pains. Oedema. Pre-eclampsia. There was little she could have done even if she had arrived earlier, and the baby, that little frog of a child, dead within her. She was, Dora noted, young.

The man returned with two storm lanterns, and the woman came in with a pot of tea.

'Give it to him,' Dora said. 'Sweeten it, if you can.' She took one of the lamps, laid it by the bed. 'What was your wife's name?'

'She–' he broke off, swallowed. 'Margaret,' he said. 'Margaret.'

'And yours?'

'Geoffrey.' His voice was flat. 'Geoffrey Laurent.'

'I am so sorry, Mr Laurent,' Dora said.

'A doctor came this morning,' Geoffrey went on. 'Said the baby wasn't due for a couple of months and there was nothing to worry about.' He stood, a lantern in one hand, and began to sob, clasping his free hand across his eyes. 'She had a headache. He told her to take an aspirin.'

He was a big man, farmer's muscles, labourer's hands. Dora walked round the bed and took the lantern from him. Shudders of grief convulsed his body. She wanted to put her arms round him and pull him close and let him weep it free against her shoulder.

There was nothing to do except clean and wash the body and lay it out ready for the undertaker. She'd start the formalities tomorrow. The man was not in a condition to understand any of that now. He slumped in the chair by the bed, elbows on knees, fists balled tight, staring with glassy eyes at the young woman.

'Nurse,' the woman said. 'I have to go. Get back to my husband. He's not well, you know.'

'That's fine,' Dora said. 'I'll stay with him awhile.'

The woman tiptoed out of the room, as if Margaret was sleeping.

'Mr Laurent.' Dora kept her voice low. 'You'd be more comfortable downstairs. I'll light the fire.'

He shook his head again. 'The cows,' he said. 'Milking.'

He pushed back in the chair, stood up and left the room. Dora heard his steps on the wooden stairs, the thrash of the outside door as the storm slammed it shut.

Dora washed the woman, changed her into a clean nightdress, combed the hair and laid her arms across her stomach. She drew the sheet up and over.

It was nine o'clock by the time she went downstairs, lighting her way with the lantern. The man was sitting on a chair by the kitchen range, his hands on the armrests, still as death. The gale was screeling round the chimney, blasting draughts through the gaps in the windows and under the door. She wouldn't make it back by curfew. She'd have to stay the night, push the chairs together for a bed. At least the kitchen was warm, the stove giving off a deep, steady heat.

'Mr Laurent,' she said. 'Perhaps you should go to bed. Get some sleep.'

His breathing was slow and ponderous, as if the gale had blown away the oxygen in the house. His eyes were heavy and his cheeks lined with pain.

'She was going to christen the baby William, if it was a boy,' he said. 'Billy, for short.'

'That's a nice name,' Dora said. There was a grandfather clock in the hall filling the silence of the house, *tock, tock.*

'And if it was a girl,' she said. 'What were you going to call her?'

'Dorothy,' he said. 'Dotty, for short.'

'My name is Dorothy.' Dorothea, but she didn't say that. 'My father always called me Dora.'

'Dora,' he said. 'I like that.'

Tock, tock.

There were some logs in a basket. She fed the Aga. The hospital had heavy iron radiators that pumped heat and warmth throughout, like the old apartment in Charlottenburg. This stove just warmed one room.

'Can I make you some more tea?' she said. He nodded. There was a large brown pot on the dresser nearby and the tea jar was on the shelf. She opened the lid, smelled it. Real tea. She scooped some into the pot, poured on the water, turned the teapot three times. They stirred it in England, but she preferred this gentler German method.

'Milk's in the larder,' Geoffrey said. 'And some cake.'

She was glad of that. She'd missed tea, and supper, and her stomach felt hollow and empty. She wondered if Geoffrey had eaten. She poured the tea, added the milk, handed a cup to Geoffrey. Dollops of cream floated on the top. She wondered if she'd ever get used to drinking tea with milk, but people thought it odd to drink it black and she didn't want to draw attention to herself more than was necessary.

Dora settled into the chair on the other side of the fire. She would have pulled her cape around her, but it was still damp.

Geoffrey dozed off after a while. She watched him opposite her, *putt-putting* in his sleep, she a soft companion to his softer silence.

Dora slipped away in an amethyst dawn. The storm had blown itself out, left the sky opaque and tender and the earth with a trail of branches and scattered leaves. By day, Dora could see how the house was set in a dip on the cliff, in the face of the wind, overlooking the escarpment and its spinney of gnarled trees and, through it, the beach fenced off with the deadly bracken of barbed wire. The sea still moiled from the tempest, the waves breaking on the shore with a rhythmic roar, but beyond, the ocean and its cupola of sky melted into one and soared to eternity.

Dora stood for a moment and breathed in the briny air. She wrapped her cape round her arms and set off, sidestepping the puddles and debris of the storm. The back roads were tricky, but after St Martin the route was clearer.

She passed some children on their way to school. They were thin, knees red with cold, knobbly and undernourished. Lots of the schools had been commandeered by the Germans, Dora knew, and the children had to walk farther to their new classrooms. She wondered how many had had breakfast that morning, how many mothers had gone without.

'You must eat too,' Dora would say. 'If anything happened to you, what would the children do?'

'It's all right, Nurse.' She'd heard this so many times. 'I've already eaten.'

But everyone felt the bite of hunger now, were thinner and shabbier than they would like, mended and made do. Dora wondered whether she would taste a torte again, lick the chocolate and cream off her fingers, stick her fork into soft plums and crumbling pastry, or savour the sweet custard of baked cheese.

There was the drag of death about the island. That's what her father would have called it. The drag of death. *Der Sog des Todes.*

§

Midwives and sisters were allowed to live out, in approved digs. Dora and five others lived with Miss Gladys Besson who supplemented her income by taking in lodgers in the small terraced house she had inherited from her parents.

'Paying guests,' she said. 'I prefer to call you my paying guests.'

She let her lodgers use the parlour, a dingy room with velvet curtains and chintz chairs, plaster cats and dogs lined up on the windowsill. She had made patchwork covers for the cushions and crocheted antimacassars which draped in virginal swathes. There was a screen in front of the fire, embroidered with an image of a country cottage and garden. Horse brasses hung on leather straps either side of the mantelpiece. Her harmonium, an ugly beast, stood against one wall and would wheeze and heave on Sunday evenings as she thumped out 'Onward Christian Soldiers', looking at Dora to make sure she was singing too. Miss Besson grew potatoes in her back garden and stored them in sacks in the hallway and kitchen. She insisted that they all take turns to peel and grate the tubers, soak and drain the pulp and lay it out to dry, 'now that we can't get flour'.

The potatoes stained Dora's fingers, so she had to scrub them clean with a pumice stone. Miss Besson made tea out of carrot and coffee out of parsnip, boiled sugar beet for sweetener and sea moss for gelatine. She watered down the jam and eked out the meagre supplies so they stretched four days instead of three. Rationing and shortages were her *métier*, Dora thought. She was a naturally mean woman.

The kitchen was out of bounds.

'Private,' Miss Besson said. She always locked it, kept the key above the door jamb. She and her brother, Pierre, used the kitchen.

He was younger than Miss Besson, a short man, with Brylcreemed hair and foul breath, a chain-smoker who lit one cigarette from the embers of the last. Dora wondered where he got them, or how he could afford them.

Miss Besson did the cooking, and ate with the nurses most days in the dining room at the back of the house. They were expected to take it in turns to sit next to her and make conversation. Dora dreaded those days. Miss Besson had little talk beyond the good works of the Ebenezer chapel and the sins of others, never conversed, rarely asked a question of her neighbour, and Dora learned fast to nod and smile, although she always felt under scrutiny, without knowing why.

Miss Besson pulled on a pair of wire-rimmed glasses, hooked them behind her ears, put her hands together at the table.

'When thou hast eaten and art full, then thou shalt bless the Lord thy God for the good land which he hath given thee. Amen.'

Dora peered into her soup, a light-brown liquid in which chunks of turnip and carrot floated.

'I hear you were up at La Ferme de l'Anse the other day, Nurse Simon,' she said.

'Yes,' Dora said. 'But I arrived too late. The woman was dead. I don't think I could have saved her anyway.'

Miss Besson pinched her mouth and closed her nostrils. 'For the best,' she said.

'That's a shocking thing to say.'

Miss Besson raised an eyebrow. 'He knows what He is doing,' she said. 'Visiting the iniquity of the fathers upon the children, and upon the children's children, unto the third and to the fourth generation.'

'What are you saying?' Dora asked.

'Just that,' Miss Besson said. 'Just that.' She dipped her spoon in the soup and sucked its contents with a noisy slurp. 'Have nothing to do with that man, if you know what's best.' She paused, her spoon halfway to her mouth, her lips pinched into an oval.

'He's considered a pariah in these parts.' She put down her spoon, stirred the soup, scooped up a lump of turnip. 'But how would you know that? You being a foreigner.'

Miss Besson scraped the dregs of the liquid from the bowl and laid her spoon down with a clatter.

'I went to an auction today,' she said, taking Dora's bowl and stacking it on her own. 'The last of the Jew-boys' shops.' She gave a stiff smile, added, 'I bought you all a present.' She took the bowls to the sideboard, opened a drawer and pulled out a small package. 'Soap,' she said. 'Lux. He was hoarding it, can you imagine? But that's the sort of thing they do. Not a care about anyone else. Wouldn't you say?'

Dora looked down at the tablecloth, turned her knife over, and back. Dared not look up, sure her face would give her away. *Say nothing.* She hoped one of the others would answer, but they sat in silence.

'I'll divide it up after dinner,' Miss Besson went on. 'So you all have a piece. Our *Christian* duty is to share.'

Dora pressed her fingers against the prongs of her fork. She could sense Miss Besson leaning over the table, a pot of stew steaming on the mat.

'By the way, Miss Simon,' she said, pushing the pot towards Dora. 'A letter came for you this morning.'

Dora looked up. Perhaps Uncle Otto had managed to get something through. Perhaps the Red Cross had opened a link with the internment camp. Dora couldn't think who else would send her a letter.

'Unpalatable though it is,' Miss Besson went on, 'we need to work with the authorities.' She picked up the serving spoon, handed it to Dora. 'The letter is from the Chief Aliens Officer. I wonder what he wants?'

Dora gripped the spoon hard so her hand wouldn't shake. 'I wonder,' she said.

Miss Besson shifted in her chair and studied Dora over the rims of her glasses. 'I say you can always tell a Jew,' she said. 'They're very dark and shifty-looking. Don't you agree?' She delved into her pocket, pulled out the letter and handed it to Dora. 'Before I forget.'

Dora tucked it under her plate. She was not going to give Miss Besson the satisfaction of opening it in front of her. She probably knew the contents anyway. Steamed it open. Or island gossip. Dora wondered how many bars of Lux she'd kept for herself. She stuck her fork into a potato, blew on it to cool it down.

'May I ask a personal question, Nurse Simon?' Miss Besson said. She didn't wait for Dora's answer. 'Do you dye your hair, or is it naturally that colour?'

'Where would I get hair dye from?' Dora said.

'Just wondering,' Miss Besson said. Dora had seen that look before. *Refugees. Can't be trusted.*

§

It was a clear day but cold, with the hoar frost hanging like lace and a lemon sun hovering low. Dora pulled her bicycle free of its ramp, set off with a thermos of tea and a round of sandwiches. She longed to suck the bluster of the sea wind into her lungs, feel its dance pirouette through her hair. The coastal road was closed and guarded now so she headed north, for Rozel Bay. Perhaps there she could clamber down to the beach and climb among the rocks.

She arrived at St Martin's village, spotted the little church. Apart from Mr Laurent, there had been no one else at Margaret's funeral. Even the neighbour had not attended. Dora had been puzzled at the time, but if he was, as Miss Besson said, a pariah, that would explain it, though it was harsh not to pay respects to the dead, whatever their sins in life. The priest was young, she'd thought, barely into long trousers. Mr Laurent had shuddered in the front pew and the priest came over, put his eulogy away and his hand on Mr Laurent's shoulder.

She should see how he was. Whatever Mr Laurent had done to incur Miss Besson's vitriol, he was still a man who had suffered. Besides, it took little to disturb Miss Besson for her to spit out poison. Dora had learned to brush off her venom. It was nearly three months since Margaret had died. La Ferme de l'Anse was not so far away.

The farmhouse was long and low, with three gable windows in the roof and an ancient wisteria trained along the front. There were rose bushes in the beds. The door faced the lane, but there were barns at right angles on either side of the house. With the buildings and the hill, it formed a courtyard of sorts. There were cobbles on the ground with a skin of winter mud, white with frost where the sun had not visited.

Dora propped her bike against the wall of the house and knocked on the door. There was no answer. She wished she had a paper and pencil, could leave him a note. *I was passing and called to see how you were.*

She turned. He was coming down the hill across the field, leading a Jersey cow with a dun hide and gentle face. He opened the gate and led the cow through.

'Nurse Dora.' He wiped his spare hand against his trousers, held it out. She took it, rough skin and dry, but for all its strength, a generous hand. It was hard to tell how old he was. The outdoor life weathered faces. Forty. Perhaps fifty. Older than she remembered. His black hair was flecked with grey at the temples. He had dark eyes and a crooked nose with the remnants of a scar across the bridge. Nasal fracture, Dora noted, badly set.

'I was passing,' Dora said. 'Came to see how you were.'

'That's very kind,' he said. 'Let's go into the house.' He slapped the cow on her rump and she skipped, then ambled towards the barn.

Sitting in Mr Laurent's kitchen, her hands round a blue striped mug of tea, Dora noted the order of the place, with its plates and cups, the Aga in the chimney breast, the scrubbed pine table and the polished tiled floor. It had a very different feel from the kitchen in Charlottenburg, for the kitchen here was for living, not just cooking, and Dora guessed that at night, when his work was done, Mr Laurent pulled up the Windsor chair close to the range, the same chair he'd sat in the night Margaret died, opened a book or turned on the wireless and wound the day down before bed.

Mr Laurent was a practical man. He cooked for himself, he told her, washed his clothes, cleaned the house and swept the yard.

'Can't dwell on grief. Life goes on. But it's hard, Nurse Dora.'

'I understand that,' Dora said. 'Can you not get a housekeeper?'

'Why would I do that?'

'Without a wife to keep house–'

'Wife?' His forehead creased in deep puzzle lines.

She wanted to haul that word back in, *wife.* It had tripped out, was too soon to remind him. 'Margaret.'

'Margaret was my daughter,' he said.

'I'm sorry,' Dora said. 'I assumed she was your wife.'

He shook his head. 'She was my only child.' He paused. Dora could hear his hesitation, the sharp breaths before he spoke again. 'Her mother died long ago.'

'I'm sorry,' Dora said.

He shrugged. 'It happened. I brought Margaret up by myself.' His voice began to crack.

'And Margaret's husband?'

He stared out of the window. It was a while before he answered.

'Margaret could be a little headstrong at times,' he said. His body tensed and he clasped his hands tight. *Don't ask more.* It was a moment before he turned and faced her.

'She wasn't married. You may as well know. You'll hear it sooner or later from the gossips round here. The baby's father was a German.'

His voice was flat, and Dora couldn't make out whether it was resignation or sadness.

'Plenty abandon those children,' he said. 'Pack them off to the Westaway Creche. I wouldn't let her.'

He wanted to talk, Dora could sense.

'Why punish the child? It didn't ask to be born.' He turned to Dora, a smile on his lips. 'My own flesh and blood.'

His eyes were almost black, the lashes thick and dark, like the kohl-lined eyes of a film star. That would explain why so few people came to her funeral. Who'd mourn a woman who went with Germans? Was carrying a bastard child of one of them? That also explained Miss Besson's venom.

'My father brought me up too,' she said, trying to change the subject.

'Then he must be proud of you.' *And did Margaret let you down?*

'He wanted me to be a doctor,' she said. She was talking too much, added, 'But I was a woman. They wouldn't accept me. So I became a midwife, instead.' That was a truth, if not the full truth.

'That's a fine profession.'

'It is,' Dora said.

'And your father?'

'He died. A few years ago.' She hadn't uttered those words for a while and the pain kicked out fresh as yesterday. 'Out of the blue.'

'I'm sorry to hear that, Nurse Simon,' he said. 'Truly. We've much in common.'

Smiling, his face, with its crooked nose, was a kind face, for sure.

'Come and see me again,' he said as Dora lifted her bike free of the wall and pedalled off down the lane. She wanted to say, *I'd like that, very much,* but thought it might be fast. There was something compelling about Mr Laurent that she couldn't define, a gentle, alluring pull.

§

Jurat Clifford Orange, the Chief Aliens Officer, had a round face with grey hair and moustache and thick black eyebrows.

He coughed, a polite *ahem.* It didn't fool Dora.

'Distasteful business, this,' he said, pulling out a handkerchief and wiping his mouth. He looked behind him, nodded to the man sitting there, a notepad on his lap. Dora wondered if he was a secretary or a reporter. 'For me as well as you.'

'Oh?' She wasn't going to make it easy for him.

'The German authorities,' he paused.

Authorities? What *authority* did they have? They were occupiers. She resented the way this Jurat and Miss Besson, the Bailiff and the States, all of them, conferred legitimacy on the invaders.

'The authorities,' he repeated, as if that absolved him of culpability, 'need to be sure of,' he searched for a word, 'the *background* of all alien residents on the islands.' He sniffed. 'I have been tasked with the responsibility of finding out.'

He shook his head, studied her for sympathy with large doe eyes.

'Distasteful, as I said. But what can we do?' He smiled, as if *this* acquitted him too.

You can resist, she thought. *Resign. You don't have to do their dirty business.*

'Under the rules of the Hague Convention, we are obliged to obey' – *everything*? she wanted to ask – 'all reasonable demands.' The Chief Aliens Officer stared at her, eyebrows raised. 'We consider this a reasonable demand,' he said. 'A chap needs to know who he's dealing with, after all.'

The man behind him leaned forward. 'Who knows,' he said, 'what they would do if we refused to comply with their requests?'

Dora moved her gaze from the Jurat to the man.

'Sir Leonard de la Moye,' the man said, standing up and extending his hand. 'I'm just sitting in on this. Ignore me.'

Dora was uneasy. The Jurat alone was bad enough. Two of them made it an interrogation. *Keep calm*, she told herself. *Say nothing.* Background. That was the Jurat's euphemism. Couldn't bring himself to say, *Jewish.*

'You are, as I understand it, a German. Am I right?'

She took a deep breath. She hadn't been brought up to lie, wasn't sure how well she could do it. Sir Leonard sat without moving, his eyes fixed on her.

'No,' she said. She heard the Jurat start, elbows sliding forward on the shiny surface of his desktop. There would be no evidence to the contrary, she knew, at least, not in Jersey and they couldn't turn to London for proof. Besides, Hitler had declared her a non-German.

'I was born in Sweden,' she said.

That had been Matron's idea. 'I've destroyed your papers,' she'd said. 'Put down you're Swedish.'

The Jurat raised one eyebrow.

'Sweden,' she added, 'is neutral.'

He leaned back in his chair, stroked his chin. 'But you came from Germany, I understand. What were you doing there?'

'My father worked there.'

'Why did you leave?'

'My father died,' she said. That *was* true.

'Why didn't you return to Sweden? Why come to England?'

'My uncle took me in,' she said. 'I was a minor. I didn't have much choice.'

'And he was in England?'

'Yes.'

'Why?'

'I don't know.' She thought fast. 'His work, I think.'

The Jurat leaned forward and began to count on his fingers. 'Sweden, Germany, England. Quite the cosmopolitan family, wouldn't you say?'

She was trembling inside, nerves hot and tingling, sweat under her arms.

'Wanderers. Like Jews,' the Jurat said. 'Do you have loyalties, Miss Simon?' He stared at her, grey eyes narrowing from beneath his black eyebrows. Took a deep breath. 'Are you Jewish?'

'Jewish?' *Stay calm.*

'Don't make this difficult,' he said. 'It won't do you any favours.'

He looked at her and she looked back at him. Behind him, Sir Leonard nodded. She hoped her face did not betray her, that it stayed serious even though her heart played havoc within.

'Are your parents Jewish?'

'No,' she said.

'You're quite sure?'

'Of course.'

'Are any of your grandparents Jewish?'

'No,' she said. Her voice came out loud, too loud. She could see Grandfather now, sitting with his black kippah pinned to his hair and his gnarled old-man's hands together. *Hear, O Israel.*

'You're quite sure?'

'Yes.'

He sniffed. 'Simon is a Jewish name.'

'It's a common English name too.'

'Your first name is Dorothea,' he said. 'Not Dorothy. Your second name is Susannah. That sounds a Jewish name.'

'Swedish. English, too,' she said. 'French. Italian.' She spoke too fast, *nervous,* smiled, with a lopsided anxious turn of her lips. 'We Europeans have many names in common.'

The Chief Aliens Officer leaned forward and twisted a pencil on the desk, lead, lead, end, *tap-tip, tap-tip.* 'Are you Christian?'

She shook her head. Perhaps she should say she was a Quaker. She knew they weren't *quite* Christian, not enough for the likes of this Jurat. But she had lied enough as it was.

'Then what are you?'

'I was brought up agnostic.' Secular, but agnostic was less of a confrontation.

'Communist?' the Jurat said.

'I didn't say that.'

He thumped his fist on the desk. One side of his face twitched, lip, eye, an angry synchronised tic.

'At least you don't *look* Jewish,' he said, staring at her hard. Dora stared back, until he averted his eyes. 'Get out.' He stood up, Sir Leonard behind him.

She nodded, pushed her chair back and walked out of the room, gripping the door handle hard. She couldn't let it slip from her sweaty grasp, for that would give her nerves away.

Tante Lilli, Uncle Otto said, had seen the Gestapo at her door, knew why they'd come. *One moment, please, while I fetch my coat.* Went into the bedroom and threw herself off the balcony.

Dora was halfway down the corridor when she heard the Jurat's door open.

'Miss Simon.' Dora stopped. Sir Leonard stood in the corridor. 'One more thing.'

Dora turned, her heart thundering.

'I gather you paid a visit to La Ferme de l'Anse a while back.'

'I attended,' Dora said.

'Laurent is a most unsavoury character.' Then his voice softened, became sugary. 'But you're here alone, without family. Somebody needs to look out for you, help you find your way.' He smiled and turned on his heel. 'Take a little friendly advice. Steer clear of him. Good afternoon.' He tossed the words over his shoulder.

This was not a man to cross, Dora could sense that. Neither him nor the Jurat. Or trust. There was no explanation for why Moye was casting himself as protector.

'I can look after myself,' she said, but he'd already shut the door to the office.

§

It would be forward to visit Mr Laurent again, although she thought about him all the time. Odd, really, she'd only seen him three times. *An unsavoury character?* All the more intriguing, like one of those stories in *Titbits* that she'd read at the dentist. There she was, hoping she'd bump into him again, seeing his reflection in a window and turning to find it a fraud, spotting his head in a crowd only to have it evaporate. Did she dare take him at his word, cycle over on her day off, *Hello, is it convenient?* It was ridiculous, really. An infatuation. What was the other word the English used? A crush. Did she have a *crush* on him? A *pash?* He could be twice her age. Old enough to be her father. Was she looking for a surrogate? If so, he couldn't be more different. He was bigger than her father, taller, beefier, with hands – she'd noticed those hands – big enough to grab a whole octave as if the spread of the notes was no larger than a paperclip. Did he play the piano? She hadn't noticed one in his house. Nor many books, either. Her father was a dapper man, tall and slender, cultured, not muscular and rough like Geoffrey. But his eyes were kind, and his smile joyous, and each night Dora lay in bed imagining him, how they'd meet again, and again. If he really liked her, he'd make the first move, wouldn't he?

But the hospital dance, now, that was another thing. A charity event. She slipped the invitation in an envelope, cut the stamp on the diagonal, posted it. She waited for the mail next day, but nothing came, nor by second post either. Nor the next day. He wasn't coming. He didn't mean it when he'd said, come again. *Well. Forget him. That's it.* She'd go alone. Besides, it wasn't professional to go out with a man whose daughter had been a patient. The last thing she wanted was to be struck off. Trapped. No work. Who'd protect her then?

She heard the band before she even rounded the corner. Band?

Just a trumpet and a bass from the sound of it, but enough for her to sway and tap with the life of the rhythm. Nurses weren't obliged to be there, Matron had said, but it would be a gesture of goodwill to attend, *for our benefactors, once the war is over.*

Dora had put on a yellow summer dress, let her hair down so it fell in coils around her face, best foot forward in an elegant patent pump that she'd had from before the war. She drew a seam up the back of her bare leg. Managed to scratch out a dab of colour from the empty lipstick and squeeze the last of the perfume from her bottle of Chanel, a present from Uncle Otto.

The dance was in the dining room, the tables stacked at one end, the orchestra on a raised dais opposite. Charles Janvrin and his All Star Band. They used to play at the Pomme d'Or before the Germans came, and then there had been seven of them. Now they were two. The nurses stood along one side of the hall. The men hung around on the other wall. One or two were even smoking, a sliver of smoke unfurling from their cupped palms.

Dora smiled at her colleagues, walked closer to the podium. A woman had appeared on stage now, nodded to the trumpeter. Dora recognised her from the Pomme d'Or. Her voice was mellow and she swayed with the rhythm. *Rita.* Dora wrapped her arms around herself and swung her hips left, right, left. Rita Fitzroy, that was her name. Dora turned to smile at the others and came face to face with Mr Laurent.

'I didn't see you,' she said, a livid heat reddening her cheeks.

'May I have the pleasure?'

He took her by the hand into the centre of the floor, placed an arm round her waist and led her, gentle, light on his feet. She'd only ever seen him in heavy work boots and muddy trousers, never imagined him dancing, like this, urbane and sophisticated. She fell into his step, one arm on his, the sway and swell of his body beneath her fingertips. A heartbeat together, a rhythmic pulse. The floor had filled, couples together, forward, back.

'I hoped you'd be here,' he said.

'Well,' she said. 'I am.'

The lights in the dining room were bright.

Mr Laurent took her hand and led her to an adjacent room where the refreshments were being sold. They bought some tea and sat at a small table at the back, side by side, facing the wall.

'I sent you an invitation, Mr Laurent,' Dora said. 'I wasn't sure you received it.'

'Mr Laurent makes me think of my father,' he said, smiling, a dimple in one cheek. 'Why don't you call me Geoffrey?'

'Geoffrey,' Dora said, trying it on for size, making sure it fitted. 'You didn't reply.'

'Forgive me. I was busy. I wanted to see you again,' he said. 'But I'm an old man, widowed. Not great company.'

'I will decide that,' Dora said. He would think her fast, but she added, anyway, 'I thought you didn't want to see me, as you didn't reply.'

He laughed. 'Well, aren't we a pair?'

Her face relaxed, gave in, smiled from eyes to chin.

He reached over and placed his hand over hers, squeezed it. 'When is your next free weekend?'

'Next week,' Dora said.

He leaned forward, pushed a tress of hair behind her ear and breezed a kiss on her cheek, the touch of a butterfly wing.

'Perhaps,' he said, 'you might like to come to the farm? There's not much to do in town. The cinema only shows German rubbish these days.'

He placed his hands over hers. They were warm, his skin rough and calloused, dark hairs whispering on his knuckles, sneaking out under his cuff. A yearning for him tumbled inside her, turbulence in a storm, a wave crashing against rocks.

§

It was early May, hot and clear with an unexpected heatwave. She'd lost count of how many times she'd been here now. Once a week, since the dance. Was that six weeks? Or seven? Sometimes, just being close to him was unbearable with the ache of desire, the need to reach and touch. Did he feel the same? Did he have the same scorch if their hands brushed, the same flare at the thought of her? She'd never felt a force like this.

Geoffrey picked up the hamper and led her out of the door, through the gate and into the field. The grass was tufted. The wooden soles of Dora's clogs slid on the grass, and her feet twisted inside the canvas uppers. The field was on the slope and Dora struggled, tempted to walk barefoot, but she knew the dangers of tetanus. Just a little scratch from a sharp stone or a piece of rusty wire, that's all it took. From the top of the hill they could see the sea and the spinney in one direction, the fields in another. They went down into a small dell.

'Do you know,' Geoffrey said, 'we can't be seen from the house, though we can see it. I used to hide here, as a child.' He flicked a blanket out, laid it on the ground.

'You were brought up here?' Dora said.

'I was born here,' he said. 'As was my father. Grandfather, too.' He shook his head. 'Where are you from, Nurse Dora? I've never asked.'

He was sympathetic, this man, but Dora hesitated, even so.

'Let me guess,' he went on. 'Strawberry-blonde hair.'

Rotblond.

'Blue eyes.' He studied her, smiling, lines around his eyes white against the sun-beaten skin. 'Somewhere north.'

'There you have it,' Dora said.

'Norway? Sweden?' he went on. 'I thought Swedes were white-blonde.'

'Viking blood,' Dora said. 'Some were redheads. Horns. Curly hair.'

'Your English is good,' he said.

'I've lived here some time,' Dora said. 'And my father used to send me to England every summer before the war. Threw me in at the deep end. Insisted I must learn English. And French.' She smiled. 'It stood me in good stead.' Even so, she needed to watch what she said. She thought in her mother tongue. It would be so easy to slip.

'And your father?' Geoffrey said. 'What did he do?'

'He was a doctor,' Dora said. 'A surgeon.' Ran the field hospital in Verdun and came home with the Iron Cross and skills no surgeon wished they had, but she didn't tell him that.

Geoffrey took a chicken out of its greaseproof wrapping and laid it on a plate, finger to his lips. 'Fell off the back of the requisitions list,' he said. 'It's a seagull, if anyone asks.'

Dora laughed.

'I forgot the carving knife.'

'Oh, well,' she said. 'We can manage. What are fingers for?'

He reached into the basket, pulled out two glasses and a bottle.

'Elderberry,' he said. 'From before the war. Ripe and fruity, and rather sweet.' He poured into the glasses, passed one to Dora. 'Happy birthday.' He raised a glass. 'To you.'

'How did you know it was my birthday?' Dora said.

'I sneaked a look at your identity card,' he said. 'It's not just the Germans who find it useful.'

'So you saw my place of birth too?'

'Of course. That's how I guessed.' He laughed. 'And I know how old you are. Today.'

'Oh?'

'Twenty-seven.' He moved closer. 'I thought you might be younger.'

'Would that have disturbed you?'

'Yes,' he said.

Young enough to be his daughter? Was he thinking of Margaret?

'Dora.' He put his finger to her chin, lifted it up and towards him. She felt the brush of his skin, hot as cinders. 'Would you make love with me? I promise I'll be careful not to make you pregnant.' And kissed her.

She had no hesitation.

§

Love was amber. It trapped her in its honey resin, warm and glowing as they lay curled, melted into one, heart and soul. Love was a deep hunger that pined in its greed, an anarchy of desire that blew reason afar. Love needed no words.

'When will I see you again?' His breath was soft on her cheek, his whiskers rough on her skin, arms tight and close, dark flesh against her freckled fairness. She pressed tight to him, as if he could absorb her whole.

'Don't come to the house,' she said. 'Miss Besson doesn't like us to have gentleman callers.'

It was bad enough that Dora had to tolerate Miss Besson's insinuations, there was no need for Geoffrey to have to put up with them too, whatever he had done to incur her disapproval. She had asked Miss Besson once about Geoffrey. Miss Besson had curled her lips and walked out of the room.

Dora met Geoffrey on the parade ground, or near the market where there was a teashop. Sometimes they went for a ride, sitting on the box seat in the front of the cart, watching Ernest move his head left, right, as he pulled them along. Dora had never had much to do with horses, but she loved the solid smell of his hide and the ancient leather harness.

That day, driving down Elizabeth Place, a man in a homburg hat stepped into the street. Ernest shied, swung to avoid him as the cart tilted and Dora slid along the seat, banging her hip on the side rail.

'Watch out,' Geoffrey called. The man turned. It was the man who'd been present with the Jurat. Sir Leonard somebody or other. Dora swallowed, saw Geoffrey clench his jaw so that his bone stood proud beneath the skin. Sir Leonard raised his fist and shook it hard.

'*You* watch out,' he said.

Geoffrey raised his fist in response and spat in the road. Dora went cold. It was a side of him she'd not seen. It made her uneasy. Was he a crude man? A bitter man? Like those old German soldiers who followed Hitler and his false promises? Was this what Miss Besson had meant? And Sir Leonard? *Unsavoury*, he'd said.

The cart lurched to a halt.

'I said, are you all right? You're quiet. Are you hurt?' Geoffrey's face had relaxed back into the familiar folds.

Dora said nothing. She wanted to get down, go back home.

'I apologise,' he said. 'Did I shock you?'

'Yes,' Dora said. She didn't like the Jurat's sidekick, but everyone can make a mistake, step out into traffic, their mind on other things.

'I'm sorry,' Geoffrey said. He turned and looked at her, poised to talk. He was chewing the words, contemplating whether to say them. 'I've had altercations with that man,' he said at last. He pointed to his broken nose and smiled. 'He's a two-faced bastard, if you'll forgive the expression.'

'You were angry.' Dora's voice was soft, shaken.

'Did I frighten you?'

Dora nodded. She had no time for other people's anger, not now. Keeping alive took all her energy.

He reached over and folded his hand over hers.

'It's a side of you I've never seen,' Dora said. 'A temper.'

'I don't have a temper,' Geoffrey said. 'I have a rage.'

A rage goes deep, Dora thought, *like love*. Rage was passion, not a veneer that could be scraped away.

Ernest moved forward, his head down, his rump swaying with the rhythm of his walk, his hooves *click-clicking* on the road.

'I've met him,' Dora said after a while. 'He was there at the Chief Aliens Office. I was interviewed by them.'

'That's the kind of work he'd do.' Geoffrey shut his mouth tight so the skin grew taut once more. 'Be careful.'

Dora laughed. For all her foreboding of a moment ago, she'd trust Geoffrey over Sir Leonard.

'Friends?' he said.

'Friends.'

§

She visited him on Wednesdays. She always wore her midwife's uniform, threadbare and patched. She carried her bag with its instruments in her basket. It didn't prevent her being stopped at the road checks, but it was a kind of *laissez-passer*, a permission to travel. Legitimate business.

Geoffrey had returned to his old, calm self and the memory of the incident faded. She longed for those days when they were together, could barely sleep for the imagining of them, the *dreaming* of them, the caress of their love as they lay in his soft down bed. She wanted to bury herself into the tissue of him, feel the weight and thrust of him, the smack of their skin, sweat on sweat. She smelled of him, of happiness and vitality and the promise of earth. *Love*, she thought, *hurtles*, a helter-skelter of tenderness and desire. In all the scourge and mess and pain around her, she was wildly, deliriously happy.

On sunny days they'd go for a ride, she sitting on the crossbar of his bicycle, he pedalling, his arms embracing her as he gripped the handlebars, nibbling her ear or kissing the back of her neck. She yearned for his touch, his company. He was her nectar, she its thirsty drinker.

Today, as the sea licked the shoreline in large crescent dribbles, she thought she could live here forever, make a home with

Geoffrey in the farmhouse, a family. She thought how small her world had become, reduced to this tiny promontory on this tiny island, she who had only ever known the grand cities of Europe. And how huge her world had become, with just she and Geoffrey. It was always in the detail that you saw the bigger picture. That was what her father used to say. Geoffrey was her haven, a refuge from the turmoil of war and her jagged fears and emotions. One day they would leave the island, break free. Once the war was over. Surely, it couldn't last forever. Not a hundred years. She tried to think ahead, but the concrete defences around the island shut off her dreams, along with her escape. Geoffrey was in the here and now, the today of her life, her happiness and release. Climbing the hill from Anse la Coupe, freewheeling down to Geoffrey's farm, the Germans and the island, her worries and her troubles were cast into the breeze. Who knew what kind of future would turn a corner, come from nowhere, tucked inside a wheelbarrow or falling from the sky?

CHAPTER FOUR

JOE

Jersey: January 1942 – January 1943

Joe missed the boxing. He may have been small and light, but his arms were strong and his feet nimble. Every morning he did his press-ups, *eleven...nineteen...thirty-one...forty-two...forty-nine, fifty,* until he lay sprawled and panting on the floor. The boxing had bulked him up as a boy, so his body had taken on the definition of muscle, the markings of a man, even though he was tiny enough to be a jockey.

Boxing was an art, a clever sport, with the finesse of a dance and the manners of gentlemen, not the bare knuckles and brute strength of ruffians. Jab and cross, slip and parry, bob and weave. In another world, he'd have chosen the boxing. In another world, he would have been brave enough. But it was a hard choice, the finger of God wagging in his face and his *daidí* firing rage. He didn't have the daring.

Of course. He should start a boxing club on the island. A boys' club, give them something to do in the evenings, especially now that the schools were closed half the time. Next to birds, boxing had been his passion. Boxing didn't take too much equipment. Gloves. Hand-wraps? Bandages would do. Shoes? Plimsoles would be fine. Gumshields? Improvise, cotton and tape, a bit rough and ready, but he doubted that the lads would pack too hard a punch, not at first. Skipping ropes. Punching bag. Canvas, sand, rope, a strong beam to hold it. Easy enough.

§

'Boxing gloves?'

Pierre raised his eyebrows, pulled out a cigarette.

Joe wasn't sure what to make of Pierre Besson, or his sister Gladys. He knew his type from the wide boys in Cork. A wheeler-dealer. Mr Fixer. A survivor. Charming with it. He wasn't much older than Joe, but he emitted a worldly wisdom beyond his years. Joe thought he may as well hitch his star to Pierre's wagon as anyone else's.

'I'll see what I can do.' Pierre knew who had the key to the Boy Scouts' hut in Minden Place. 'It's going begging.' He touched the side of his nose, *an old favour*. 'They can't use it now the Boche have banned the Scouts. I know a sign writer, too.'

Two days later, Joe put up a spanking new notice, maroon with black lettering:

Boys' Amateur Boxing, ages 12-15
With Fr Joe O'Cleary, Bantamweight Champion of
Ireland 1931
Tuesday and Friday evenings 6-8.

Pierre had mustered three pairs of second-hand gloves. The leather was cracked in places and the fist too big for most of the boys who were likely to come, but they were better than nothing. Together, he and Pierre rigged up two punching bags, painted a ring on the floor and mocked up the sides with old rope and four used newel posts. Pierre put a notice in the *Evening Post* and Joe sat and waited.

Nobody came, not that first night. Joe rolled up his trouser legs and stripped to his vest and punched and sparred. After all these years it felt good, the churn of the adrenalin, the sweat on his face, the jar of his muscles against the bag. 'Boxing's not a sport for angry men,' he had heard Doyle, his old trainer, remark. Joe had taken it up in cold blood, knew what he wanted to do with it.

They began to drift in, the boys. Three, five. Eight. Hungry lads. Joe wished he had food to give them, oranges to suck, oatcakes to munch, Lucozade even. Build them up.

The boys took it in turns with the gloves.

Twice a week, he held his boxing club. Pierre came along at the end of each session, lounged on a metal fold-up chair, waiting for Joe to finish and send the boys home.

'Nippy in here,' Pierre said one evening in February. 'I admire you, you know. What you do for the boys. Some of the other Irish hobnob with the Boche. But not you, Father O'Cleary. Not you.' He pulled out a packet of cigarettes, took out two, lit them both and handed one to Joe. 'I like to think a bit of your goodness will rub off onto me.' He flicked the ash into his hand. 'Bit of your angel dust.'

'I wouldn't be so sure of that,' Joe said. 'I'm a sinner like any man.' He took a drag on his cigarette. 'Is that why you're happy to oblige me?'

Pierre shrugged. 'I like you, Father,' he said. 'There's parts of you that go deep. I respect that. Don't often get a good man.' He paused and laughed. 'At least, not in my line of business. Hang in there, Pierre, I said to myself. Hang in there.' He flicked the ash again, then blew it onto the floor. 'You still interested in birds, then? You need new field-glasses?'

'Thank you, Pierre, but I have a pair.'

'I could get you a pair of Zeiss, if you're interested,' Pierre said. He ran his fingers through his hair, tossed his head, casual.

The finest opticals in the world, so it was said.

'Zeiss?' Joe said. 'They're German.'

Pierre sniffed. 'So?' he said. 'How do you think we all survive, without a little trade here and there?' He began to laugh. 'Always happens, trade. In the centre, at the margins. Trade makes the world go round. You know the way to stop wars?' He walked towards the empty stove, holding out his hands. 'Trade. Do you know the Russians and the Norwegians carried on a trade for centuries? Grain and fish. Never a cross word.'

'If I remember,' Joe struggled to recall his history lessons, 'trade causes wars.'

'Nah,' Pierre said. 'That's land. Name me a war that hasn't been about land. Resources.' He felt the stove. 'You've got no heating here. No wonder it's so bloody cold, pardon my French, Father.' He wrapped his scarf tighter round his neck. 'Land grabs. But if we all *traded*, it'd stop tomorrow. Trade's the glue, see. You get stuck together, in trade.'

Joe wasn't sure, but it was late. He was tired, didn't want to argue.

'Why do you do this, Father?' Pierre said.

'Do what?'

Pierre shrugged. 'Be a priest.'

'I had a calling,' Joe said. He didn't expect Pierre to understand that, him being a chapel goer.

'Joseph Mary has the mark of the miracle,' his mother used to say. 'I promised Father Murphy. If he lives, Father, I said, I'll give him to the Lord.'

Kneeling at the eight o'clock mass, back to the congregation, *Confiteor Deo omnipotenti*, Joe'd fancied he'd seen the blood drip from the precious wounds of the Christ hanging above the altar at St Brendan's. Father Murphy smiled when Joe told him in the sacristy afterwards, said he was blessed now and gave him a scapular to wear at all times. Maybe, Joe thought, he had a calling, though in his heart, if he was honest, he thought the church a morbid place with as much blood and gore as his father's butcher's shop or his mother's undertaking business.

'Must be lonely,' Pierre went on, 'no wife, no kiddies.'

'Are you married, Pierre?' Joe said.

'No.'

'Are you lonely?'

'I'm busy.'

'That's not the same,' Joe said.

'Is that why you do this, then?'

'What?'

'With the boys. Boxing,' Pierre said.

Joe hesitated. The boys gave him company, that was right enough.

'I like boxing,' he said. 'Birds, too.'

Pierre laughed, wheezed, coughed, stubbed out his cigarette on the top of the stove.

'I mean,' he said. 'Birds and boxing. Not things you usually put together. And not in a priest.'

Joe hadn't put them together, not till Pierre said it. But they'd walked either side of him, he realised now, and had done for the longest time. They'd been his crutches. He took them for granted, like his guardian angels.

'Maybe not,' Joe said, added. 'But they saved my soul, believe me.'

Pierre raised an eyebrow and Joe wished he'd never opened his mouth. The words had slipped out, away from him, just like that. He thought they were wedged more tightly.

'Saved your soul?' Pierre emphasised the words. 'That's a bit dramatic, isn't it? How so?'

'Well, now,' Joe said, 'that's my secret.' *Between me and my confessor*, he wanted to say, though he'd never confessed, not to a priest, not to anyone. He couldn't tell Pierre. No. This was not a thing you told to any man. Joe wasn't sure he had the words anyhow. It was never talked about.

'Whoa,' Pierre said. 'A priest with a secret. Now, there's one for the books.'

Joe wanted to yank back those words too. It made it all worse. He wanted Pierre to forget it, let the subject drop. He'd spoken too much and he didn't know why.

'Enough,' Joe said. He spoke with force, so Pierre looked startled and hurt. Joe picked up a glove from the floor, paired it with another. 'I didn't mean to shout. I don't know why I did.' He breathed hard. 'I'm just tired, Pierre. Tired of this war.'

'We all are, Father,' Pierre said, his voice subdued. 'Amen to that.'

'You may be right,' Joe said, as he ushered Pierre out of the door, and delved in his pocket for the keys. 'Perhaps I am lonely.'

Joe walked back to the convent, let himself in, footsteps clicking on the flagstone floor. His shoes had metal caps, tapped as he walked. The nuns now, their shoes were silent. You knew they were close by the click of the rosary beads and the smell of their laundered habits.

'Good evening, Father.'

'Good evening, Sister.'

Joe didn't know them all by name for the nuns never stopped to spend the time of day with him. Sometimes, he thought, a little common or garden friendliness wouldn't go amiss. Just for one day, take him off his pedestal and ask, *Father, do you have a family at all?* Or, *how are the boys at the club? The birds that you watch so keenly?* He might be nearer to God than them, but he was still a man, and lonely. Pierre understood that, had stepped forward to be his friend and Joe was grateful, willing to overlook Pierre's misdemeanours.

He walked into his cell, a small room in the basement, with a single bed and a table and chair. He wanted to talk to his mother, to his *daidí* even, to Pat Junior, little Bridey. All of them. He didn't think his last letter had got through. He'd never had a reply, that was for sure. He sank to his knees by the side of the bed. *Please God, help me through this.* Tried to think of Jesus wandering in the desert, knowing the fate that was to befall Him. At least, Joe thought, I don't have that to contend with. Still, he wondered again if he was cut out for a solitary life. He took off his clothes, pulled on his pyjamas and lay on his bed.

When Father Murphy had come round for tea after benediction on the Sunday of his fourteenth birthday and peered over his half-moon glasses and asked his mother Bridey for an ashtray and a tot, Joe knew he had come for a purpose. Joe'd thought about souls as if they were a trade, like any other. Souls went on forever and ever. You never ran out of souls. The church wasn't poor, had never gone out of business, and though the priests and nuns banished their worldly wealth, so Father Murphy said, he looked plump and well on the housekeeper's cooking, smoked sixty a day and O'Sullivan stood him the cost of a Guinness and chaser in the pub. What else would a man want? A priest couldn't take a wife, but Father Murphy lived with his housekeeper, and that seemed much the same.

'Have you prayed to your guardian angel?' Father Murphy said.

Joe nodded.

'And you're choosing this of your own free will?'

Joe looked at his mother, and behind her the picture of the Sacred Heart. He nodded.

He'd spotted a plover on the dunes that morning, lying there with a broken wing. It flew away as Joe got close. 'Fibber,' Joe had called after it. 'You'll do that once too often.'

'Well, if you're really sure,' Father Murphy said, handing his glass to his father, Pat, and pointing two fingers to indicate the level, 'I'll ask at St Xavier's to see if they can take you on. Just to get your Latin up to scratch and give you a decent education, ready for the seminary.'

What nobody told him was that the souls of the faithful departed weren't ones for company, that a priest was second only to God, and that was the loneliest place in the world. Living like a stylite. No one thought a priest was flesh and blood, had needs like any other man.

§

'Who knows what the deceased might have been, had she lived longer?' Joe paused. This borrowed surplice was too big for him and the sleeves snagged on the pulpit. His voice echoed round the empty church, sounded on the sole mourner in the front pew. 'Or what her unborn child might have become?'

The deceased woman's father leant forward, his frame shuddering. *Geoffrey*, Joe reminded himself, his name was Geoffrey. The deceased was called Margaret. He'd never met her and had only just met Geoffrey. 'It's short notice,' the parish priest had said, 'but can you do the funeral?' Curate to the convent, locum to the island, Joe sometimes didn't know whether he was coming or going.

'But God has a design for us all,' he went on.

Geoffrey howled, an anguished, animal cry of pain.

'And He tests our faith from time to time.' Joe was about to say, *in this vale of tears*, but stopped himself. He'd picked up the words from a book of eulogies, empty phrases that had no link with the living. Why go on? The man was in agony, and this made it worse.

There were times Joe thought his priesthood was a coat to grow into, like one of Pat Junior's hand-me-downs. Deep inside, he knew he wasn't up to the job, that despite his mother's private intentions read out at Sunday mass, he didn't have a real vocation. But what could he do? He couldn't back out now. People looked to him for help. He was a fraud, if truth be told. A mountebank for wounded souls. A pardoner who peddled hope. What succour could he offer a sinner?

The church door swung open and a nurse walked in. The door slammed behind her and Geoffrey started in his pew, looked over his shoulder. Joe beckoned her to come forward, but she shook her head, sat at the back. Perhaps she was seeking sanctuary, Joe thought, had stumbled into the funeral by chance.

What kind of a funeral was this that no one else came to, not even the parish priest? Joe was not going to judge either Geoffrey or his daughter, though plenty did. He'd heard rumours about them both. Perhaps he should be railing about sin and purgatory. But who was he to cast the first stone? The man was suffering now and was alone in the world. Joe knew how that felt.

He put his notes back into the copy of the New Testament, stepped out of the pulpit and up to Geoffrey, in the front pew. Arm round his shoulders, man to man. He needed a friend now, not priestly platitudes, sympathy not insincerity.

'I'm sorry,' he said. 'I'm so very sorry.'

Geoffrey swallowed, tears on his cheek, nodded. Joe put his hand on Geoffrey's, squeezed it. Better than any words.

Joe stood up, returned to the altar, heard the click of the door as the nurse let herself out. A protestant, for sure.

'Come back to the house,' Geoffrey said. 'When you're done.'

Joe couldn't say no. He disrobed, folded away the vestments, pulled on his jacket and coat and picked up his binoculars.

It was a while before Joe found the farm. La Ferme de l'Anse. Strange for such a small island that there were still hidden nooks and crannies. He leaned his bike against the gate and looked around. A distinctive call. *Ptar-crrrp.* Like little Bridey when she had the croup. *Listen.* He pulled out his binoculars and trained them overhead. *Look. A textbook case*, he thought, flying loose and disorderly. They needed a sergeant major to drill them, *Mark time, forward! Silence in the ranks, about turn*! Brent geese. He hadn't seen them since he'd left Cloghane, and even there they were few and far between. He pulled out his notebook from the inside pocket of his jacket, disentangled the pencil that he had threaded down its spine and secured with a string and wrote in careful script, *branta bernicla. La Ferme de l'Anse. 8th February 1942.*

He put his binoculars back into their case, snug against the cushioned velvet innards. 'Dolland & Co' was etched on the lid. The leather still smelled the same as when Colonel Waring had stood in the passageway of their house in Cloghane fifteen years ago, with his puckered eye and an empty sleeve pinned to the chest of his jacket.

'I don't have use for these,' he'd said, handing the case to Joe. 'Not now.'

'You should be careful, Father.'

Joe jumped. He hadn't heard Geoffrey approach.

'Jerry wouldn't take it kindly if they thought you were spying on them.'

'It's the birds I follow,' Joe said.

'Even so,' Geoffrey said. 'Be careful.' He framed his arm around Joe's back and led him towards the kitchen door. 'But it's a good place to spot them, so come anytime,' he said, nodding towards the field. 'No need to ask permission.'

§

The boxing was taking off and another five boys had joined, which made thirteen in all. Joe's skills came back, *nimble feet, on your toes,* hammering the punching bag. He ran through the matches of his youth, those he'd fought and those he'd watched.

Pierre conjured three more pairs of boxing gloves and six gumshields, tapped his nose, *no questions asked.* It wouldn't be long before Joe could spar against one or two of the bigger boys. Some of the lads now were learning how to throw a punch and he didn't want broken teeth on his conscience, let alone a broken jaw. They were learning fast, and word spread, kept Joe busy all through the spring and then the long summer evenings. Now the wirelesses had been taken by the Germans, there was little else to do. Joe was happy to teach the boys every night, they were that keen. The days stretched into the autumn, September, October, November.

It was Pierre who suggested the boxing match. He had a pal, he said, who could set it up. Joe remembered the Troubles in the twenties. Brother against brother. Bitterness as sharp as a sword. Would they have battled so hard if they had played a bit more? Fought it out on the hurling pitch, then gone for a jar in the pub? What harm would a boxing match do? Ireland was not at war, so he wouldn't be a traitor. Nor a collaborator. *A friendly match.* There was good and bad on either side, after all. The more Joe thought about it, the better the idea sounded. This could smooth over hostilities, be a bridge to the enemy. Like the Christmas truce.

Christmas. Let it happen at Christmas. Peace on earth to all men. He'd have time to train.

§

The match was scheduled for Wednesday 9 December 1942 in the assembly hall of the Maison St Louis Observatory. It was advertised on the front page of the *Deutsche Inselzeitung* and at the bottom of the classified ads on the back page in the *Evening Post.*

Joe was to fight Wilhelm Weber, the bantamweight champion of Silesia, 1937, and the *Wehrmacht*, 1939. Weber was younger than Joe. Joe couldn't think why he had agreed to do this. It was over ten years since he'd fought and though he was fit, and practised every day in the club, he wasn't at his prime, not against a younger man. He'd had no one to spar against, not at his level, not even one of the bigger boys. Smashing a punching bag was no substitute for ring practice.

Nor was he as well fed as the German. He ate enough vegetables, and drank plenty of water, but he lacked protein, for the rationing hit hard. Joe knew those things made a difference. He'd make a fool of himself, but he couldn't back out now.

They weighed in, like professionals. Weber met Joe's eyes, a steady stare.

You can't spook me, Wilhelm.

Strapped up, gloves on. Weber was left-handed. A southpaw. Get the measure of that. *Don't trade blows*, he told himself. *Don't let him wrong-foot you.* Tactics came flooding back. *Counter that left hand.*

Joe heard the audience as they settled down, loud, rowdy. The door opened. More squaddies, by the look of them. The room was full of cigarette smoke, and Joe could smell beer. German soldiers in their grey army uniforms. There were no civilians that Joe could see.

Weber threaded his way through the crowd as they roared their support. Joe followed in his dressing gown. No Jersey men present to cheer him on. This was how the Christians must have felt, he thought, going to the lions. You needed nerves for the fight. Good nerves that fired muscles into steel and tendons into springs. The crowd were chanting, 'Weber, Weber'. He'd need some support, otherwise they'd bay only for Wilhelm. It was human nature, after all, to stick to your own.

Ignore them. Don't get distracted.

There'd be three rounds. Point winners, unless one was knocked out. Joe was glad. He wasn't sure he'd have the strength or the stamina for a full bout.

Pierre was in his corner for him with a towel and water bottle. Joe clambered into the ring, could feel the adrenalin rise and pump through his body, taste its metal in his mouth. Weber was taller than Joe, with spidery legs and a haunted, bitter face. He's not hungry, Joe thought. He's angry. Boxing's not a sport for angry men.

The referee, a German sergeant, called them over to the centre of the ring. Held their hands up, glove to glove.

'*Sauber kämpfen, Jungs*,' he said. 'Play clean, boys.'

Joe took off his dressing gown. The bell went.

Watch his left ran through Joe's brain like a mantra. *Get your foot on the outside.* Dancing, jabbing, left cross, right hook, Weber slammed into Joe's chest between the ribs so Joe lost his breath and staggered to the ropes gasping for air, arms close to his body as Weber rained down the punches on Joe's head and shoulders. Joe threw his right and left hand at Weber's body as many ways as he could until he hit him in the liver and then between the ribs. Joe watched as the spindly man bent double and fell.

A hefty jeer went up from the crowd and they began to chant, 'Weber, Weber!'

Joe went back to the corner, spitting and washing. His eye had been cut and was swelling fast. Pierre wet the towel with the water, dabbed at the cut. Joe winced.

'Weber! Weber!'

'Get the referee to shut them up,' Joe said. 'It's not fair.'

Joe'd been pushed against the ropes, made to look a fool, a bumbling novice. But Joe had learned too that Wilhelm Weber had no technique, only the advantage of his left hand. He was a low fellow with an easy fist. Joe had met his type in Dublin. He had to wear him out. Rattle him. Go in for the slam.

The bell rang.

Joe had his foot on the outside now, *keep it there,* jabbed and punched with both of his hands, crosses, hooks, before Weber slipped around and they danced, sparring, jabbing. *Footwork. Position.* Joe backed him onto the ropes with a forearm crush, covered his head to soften Weber's overarm, right hook to Weber's head, square on the nose which exploded in blood, ducking and weaving round his left while Joe hammered him with his right until the referee pulled them apart and they began to dance again in the centre.

Blood was running from Joe's nose too and his left eye was beginning to close, but Weber's face was swelling, eyes bloody and blackening, a livid red mark on his cheekbone, and the look of fury. Joe was hot, slippery with sweat, but not tired, too fired for that. Joe had to win. He lunged with a fast one-two, pulled back his head to slip Weber's cross counter, then slammed into him again with his right hand. Weber staggered back as the bell went and the crowd stopped baying.

'If I were you,' Pierre said, mopping Joe's bloodied face with the towel, 'I'd let the bastard win.'

'Never,' Joe said, spitting blood into the bucket at Pierre's feet. 'Not now.'

Gumshield in, Joe danced to the centre. He looked round as the bell rang again, and Weber charged towards him. Joe made sure of his foot position, used both hands to lay into Weber, who was throwing his left cross, his right hand in front of his head. *Go for the temple.* Joe aimed a right hook, slammed into the side of Weber's head, watched him crumple and fall while the referee counted out the seconds.

The crowd fell silent. Joe panted in the centre of the ring, raised his arm above his head. A nurse was standing to the side with a man in a white coat. Then the jeers began, the whistles. Weber struggled to his feet and the audience cheered, stamped their feet, hammered on the chairs.

The nurse and doctor climbed into the ring, went over to Weber, helped him into a chair in his corner.

'I hope the fuck he's all right,' Pierre said. 'Because God help you otherwise.'

'I don't understand,' Joe said. 'I won it fair and square.'

It was the *Feldkommandant* himself, Colonel Knackfuss, who held out his hand to Joe. 'My congratulations,' he said. 'To the winner.' He paused. 'A man to watch.' He beckoned to the nurse. 'Perhaps this man needs some medical care too.' He smiled, a stiff stretch of his lips, without warmth or conviction. 'We treat all opponents fairly.'

'A clean-up,' she said. 'At the least.' She leaned over Joe, so the crisp of her uniform brushed his chest, and he smelled its starch. 'Congratulations to the winner,' she said, her voice cold and formal as she dabbed at his cut with disinfectant.

Knackfuss nodded, walked away.

The nurse smiled. 'Well done,' she whispered.

Joe felt as large as a giant. For wasn't he Jack Dempsey himself? Or Jimmy Slattery?

§

When he went to the clubhouse on Minden Street the next evening, there was a swastika daubed across the notice and a large V had been painted on the door. *British Victory is Certain* had been chalked beneath it.

No boys turned up that Friday. It would be the run-up to Christmas, Joe thought. Carol singing. Nativity plays. Advent services.

None turned up the following Tuesday. Joe waited until eight o'clock, penned a notice, *Boxing Club closed for the season. Will re-open in January.* Pinned it to the door as Pierre arrived.

'Word is, they don't see it as a friendly. They see it as fraternisation. What's worse,' he added, 'nor do the Germans. They see it as humiliation.' Pierre lit a cigarette, handed it to Joe. 'Your face is a treat,' he said. 'Every colour in the rainbow.' He slapped Joe on the back.

Joe opened the club again in the new year but still no one turned up. He'd enjoyed the club, the company of the boys, at least. He handed the keys of the hut back to Pierre, took the gloves and skipping ropes and a punching bag back with him to his room, rigged up a hook on the door frame and hung the bag from it. At least he could keep in training. He rammed his right fist into the belly of the bag. It was such a paltry thing to have done, for the best of motives. Pounded with his left. It wasn't even his war. *Right, left.* Who here stood up to Jerry? Who'd been counted? *Left, left, right.*

Pierre openly consorted with the Germans. He paused, steadied the bag. People grumbled at Pierre's prices, but they bought from him, even so. No one was so high and mighty that they didn't do what they could to survive. Filled in the registration cards like lambs. *Right, right.* Penalised the Jews without a second thought. Shed a tear for the British when they'd been deported. *Left.* Well, Joe thought, steadying the bag again, and lifting it off its hook, the Irish have lived with centuries of occupation. As many connived with the British as resisted. That's the way an occupation worked. So why pick on him? Let he who is without sin.

CHAPTER FIVE

DORA

London: April 1985

Dora firmed up the soil round the white-currant bush. It'd take a year or so before it matured and she could gorge herself on its fruity pearls. Their housekeeper, Anni, used to sugar the currants into a rich, sweet compote. Along with afternoon coffee and bitter chocolate, that compote had been the taste of home that Dora missed most. You couldn't get white currants in England, any more than you could get Bramleys in Germany.

It had been years since she'd thought of Anni, squat and square with her short grey hair and floral apron. Anni had lived across the courtyard, in the back building in Charlottenburg. Dora could see it now. The long windows of the art nouveau apartments that lined the inner square, dressed with venetian blinds and demi-nets. She could smell the meatballs and sausages cooking in the kitchens, hear the clatter of the families as they ate. The courtyard was in the shade and Anni's apartment was always cool. Anni had packed her bags the day she and *Vati* had to tell her they weren't Aryans.

'How could you do this to me?' Anni had said. 'After all this time? You never told me.' Anni never spoke to them again.

This was the first time in all the forty years Dora had been gardening that she'd seen white-currant bushes for sale in the garden centre. She'd bought one straightaway, planting it in a sunny corner in the vegetable patch. A sycamore had self-seeded nearby. She'd need to dig that up before it grew into a monster and strangled the bush. Dora reached for her fork.

Anni's cousin lived in the countryside near Ravensbrück and gave Anni currants. Dora could remember her coming home with punnets filled to the brim. It was over fifty years since Dora had left Berlin, or thought about that. She'd been in mourning for her father, her late mother's jewellery sewn into the hem of her coat.

Did that happen in old age? Thinking more and more about the past? She'd have to ask at the bridge club. *Do you all reminisce too?* She was doing a lot of it these days. But apart from Charles, who else could she remember with? And even then, what could she say? *Do you remember sleeping in a bed with white sheets again?* He wouldn't know what she was talking about.

She straightened up, studied the bush, looked towards the house as if expecting Uncle Otto to be waving at her from the window. He never asked her what happened in the war.

'You'll tell me,' he'd said. 'In your own time.'

Dora had never told him. She hadn't the words. She hadn't a story, and couldn't borrow one either. There was nothing in the Bible, or Dante, nothing in Dostoevsky, or Goethe that she could point to, *it was like this.* Who wrote about what happened to *women* in war, apart from Berthold Brecht? She was no Mother Courage, and what had happened to Dora was not part of *that* version of war either.

She hadn't slept in those early days when she'd first come back. She startled at every sound. Lay rigid in fear until she thought her head would crack with the weight and pain of it. Every creak and groan of the house was a footstep closing in, a soldier-in-waiting. *To sleep, perchance to dream.* She daren't dream. She put off the moment of sleeping, made sure she had everything around her, counted her books each night, her shoes and stockings. She made sure her underwear was in order, felt in the drawer that nothing was missing, that the soap in its wrapping paper was still tucked in her box at the bottom of her wardrobe. That was her talisman. She had to lock the front door, and check it twice before she went to bed, make sure the windows were shut and fastened, even though the summer air was hot and stifling. Uncle Otto put a bolt on her bedroom door.

'No one can get in now, Doralein. You can sleep securely.'

He prescribed her barbiturates.

Night terrors. She wanted to build a wall between day and night, between what happened before 1943 and what happened after, to keep the barbarians at the gate. She tried to put that baby out of her mind, too, but it crowded in sometimes, the soft smell of it, the touch of the slippery skin. It hadn't even cried.

Dora had sat listless and silent in the chair in her bedroom while Uncle Otto saw to his patients in the room below. Once her hair had grown, Uncle Otto organised a stylist from John Barnes in the Finchley Road to come to the house. He used his clothing rations and bought her some frocks and a pair of shoes. He bought her powder and lipstick, Yardley's Natural Rose. Even then, she didn't feel she had a woman's face, not yet.

'You should get out, Doralein. It's not good to brood like this.'

She'd forgotten how to go to a shop, buy cigarettes, soap.

They sat in the sitting room in the evenings, she, curled like a baby, while he held her hand and stroked her fingers and they listened to a play or a concert on the wireless.

'A funny thing happened today,' he'd say. He couldn't tell a story, but he loved a joke. 'You'd have laughed, if you'd been there.'

You have to laugh. But inside. You laugh *inside.*

He'd tell her how he came to London and had to live off charity, renting the basement flat and taking his medical exams again even though he had been a practising doctor for fifteen years.

'People were generous.' His voice had a catch in it. 'But British bureaucracy was icy. Unforgiving. They made life hard for us.

Refugees? You'd think we were criminals. Beggars and idlers. Here to live off public assistance...'

She'd heard his story many times. Uncle Otto needed to talk, to get it off his chest. Now, Dora wondered whether he wasn't trying to get her to do the same. Would it have made a difference?

'I was the lucky one. The Board of Deputies guaranteed me. Did you know you needed a sponsor? Who had that kind of money?'

And now look at me.

He'd tell her how he bought the house in Fitzjohn's Avenue, only he called it 'Fitz*Jews* Avenue'. 'The *whole* house, with a sitting tenant on every floor.'

He'd been too old to fight when they released him from the internment camp, and doctors were needed in London. Some other poor refugee was now living in the basement with the curling linoleum and mouldy bathroom.

'Enough of this,' he'd say. 'We are alive. *Gott sei dank.*'

Dora listened, absorbing his story so it became her own too. She was a refugee. Dispossessed and disconnected. What more need she say? The things that had happened, *those* things, were best not spoken about. *Last heard of in 1943.* That's what that Hummel woman said. She positioned the fork and pressed it into the soil, levering out the roots of the sycamore. *Gott sei dank.*

How long had it taken her to leave the house when she'd come back from the war? Several months, for sure.

He told her he had a friend called Anna who'd invited them for coffee.

'What could I say, Dora? Of course we must go.'

She lived round the corner, in Maresfield Gardens. He'd shown Dora a map.

'One hundred metres, that's all,' he said. 'Give or take.'

Dora had slipped her hand under Uncle Otto's arm and he'd gripped it tight, patting it as they'd walked from their home to hers, *you are safe, Doralein. I won't let go.* Dora, with her strawberry-blonde curls, Utility courts and Natural Rose lipstick, and he in his tweed jacket and Royal College tie, *more English than the English.* She was sure people were looking at her, would recognise her. She kept her eyes to the ground, but their gaze seemed to bore into her, *There she goes. That's her.*

It was a warm day and she hadn't needed a coat, but the leaves on the plane trees were turning orange. Was it September? October, perhaps?

Anna took her out into her garden and Dora was too scared to resist. She gave her a pair of secateurs and taught her how to deadhead the roses.

'So the plant thinks it must flower again.' She spoke English with a stronger accent than Dora. 'To compensate. To renew. The body does that too.' She added, 'And the mind. Compensates. Genius is a form of renewal, did you know that? It often comes from suffering.'

They snipped the dead roses and the dahlias and asters and the red-hot pokers and the Japanese anemones.

'It's a defence,' Anna said. 'A way of coping with trauma.'

She wasn't sure what Anna was talking about but found the rhythm of the flowers and the precision of their cuts soothing.

'I'm a city girl,' Anna went on. 'Like you. But when I come out here at the end of the day, I am restored. Look.' She pointed to a moss-drenched birdbath that stood in the middle of the lawn. A great tit was splashing in the water. 'The bird knows no stress. Has no memories, no anxieties. Only instincts. Lucky him.'

They went indoors and sat on sofas in the sitting room which overlooked the garden. The maid brought the coffee in a silver pot and placed it on the table with a plate of thin wafer biscuits.

Sometimes, Dora thought, those events were far away, as if they were disconnected from her. They languished in hazy forms on the flats of her mind. At those times, she wondered if they had even happened. Then they would return, like the tail of a storm and whip her to the ground.

That December, Uncle Otto bought a garden fork and a spade and gave them to her as a present. 'To take your mind off things.'

After the visit to Anna she'd ventured into the garden, stood at the end with her back to the wall and looked at the house with its blackened bricks and shabby green paint. She picked up the fork, and Uncle Otto nodded.

'Go on, go on. I'm watching. You're safe.'

The grass was wet and left streaks of damp on her shoes. She stuck the fork in the soil and a robin sat on the handle. Dora laughed. *Laughed.* She'd heard herself laughing. She looked up at Uncle Otto and waved. No, she'd ignore those *after* events. Let them run amok behind her back. *The bird knows no stress. Has no memories, no anxieties. Lucky him.* She was laughing out loud, not inside.

She'd dug the vegetable patch and in the spring planted potatoes and radishes, beans and lettuces. She'd walked over to Maresfield Gardens with the surplus and left them at Anna's door. Uncle Otto told her that Anna was Sigmund Freud's daughter. Of course she hadn't invited them for tea. Uncle Otto had engineered it, tricked Dora, to get her to leave the flat. Doctor to doctor. She knew that now.

Dora brushed the soil from her hands, kicked off her wellington boots and padded through the flat in stockinged feet. The second post had come and she picked the letters off the mat. Gas Board, Electricity Board. She stuck the bills on the mantelpiece. She'd deal with them on Saturday morning, sitting at her desk with her paperknife to one hand, her chequebook in the other. The house gave her an income, tenants in the basement, tenants on the top floor. Supplemented her modest pension. Even so, she had to watch her pennies, dreaded the bills. The house was a constant drain, 'a bottomless pit', Uncle Otto used to say, with the damp and the roof, the decorating and modernising. Tenants demanding central heating and the like, were careless with her carpets and the paintwork. Sometimes Dora thought it would be easier to sell up and go and live in a bungalow. But she'd be alone then.

She flicked through the other letters. There was a postcard from a neighbour in Rome, and another letter with a Crawley postmark. Dora recognised the writing. She went to tear it up, thought better, and ripped open the envelope.

> *Dear Miss or Mrs Simon,*

Dora wished she'd get it right. There was much to be said for the new 'Ms'. It might grate on the ear, but at least it was neutral.

> *I was very pleased to receive your letter which caught me just before I left London today (I am posting this at Gatwick airport). I will be away for a week or so but would like to make contact with you again on my return.*

What could this woman want? Dora had been careful not to include her telephone number. She'd have to write first, and that would give Dora time.

> *I believe my mother had some connection with Jersey which I am anxious to explore further and hope to meet with Mr Joseph O'Cleary to see if he can shed further light on this.*

Well, that explained nothing. Lots of people passed through Jersey. Though she'd like to know who this Joseph O'Cleary was.

Dora fingered the letter. Sometimes, flashes from the past caught her unawares, slammed into focus with exacting detail. Those *after* events weren't entirely dormant, they could still ambush her from within. Was that him? Had it been an Irishman who'd saved her? It'd happened so fast. He hadn't said police. He'd said, 'Call the gardaí.' Curled his 'r's. *Garrdaí.* Like the Irish did. Had he told this

Hummel woman how he knew her? *I rescued her. Thought they'd kill her.* She'd told no one. Not a soul. Not even Uncle Otto. Had this O'Cleary chap blabbered her business out loud, where it had no right to be?

She wandered into the sitting room. Uncle Otto's photo was framed on the piano. It had been taken at the palace when he received his MBE. The pair of them. She in a borrowed panama with a big brim, he with his top hat and tails. He was grinning. Proud. 'Chuffed,' he'd said. He'd never lost his accent, made two syllables of the word. *Chuff-tt.* It was just before he died. A heart attack, like her father. Far too young. Dora always thought that's how she'd die, but she was already older than either of them, and her heart was as fit as a fiddle, the doctor said. Blood pressure too. She'd go on forever.

She picked the photo up, dusted it with her sleeve. He'd collected her from Southampton. Didn't recognise her at first. Thin as a rake, and covered in bruises. She'd wrapped a scarf round her head, tied it into a turban so no one could see her. He'd pulled her close, without a word, arms folding round her. He'd smelled like her father, of tobacco and sweat, his tweed jacket scratching her cheek. He was the same size as *Vati*, the same build, and she didn't cry until he whispered, *Doralein. Mein Doralein*, the way her father used to say it.

§

Only the Hummel woman didn't write. She was standing on the doorstep one morning, unannounced, expecting to be let in.

'No,' Dora said. 'You can't just turn up without warning.'

The woman reminded Dora of someone, but she couldn't think who. She was slim, well-dressed, her face carried a mature beauty, like the models in *Woman's Own*, older women for the most part, with worn-in faces. Perhaps that's where she'd seen her. She might be a model. Her skin was fair, but her hair dark. Sometimes Scottish people had complexions like that, or Irish. She'd heard once it was because of the Spanish. It was said they'd peopled Hibernia in the early days, before proper history, but she didn't know how true that was.

'Is it not convenient?'

'No,' Dora said. That was a fib, but she didn't want to give the woman encouragement. Perhaps she had been one of her tenants? Rented out the basement to her? Or a student? She'd had so many pass through her hands, it was difficult to remember them all. It wasn't as if she had taught them. She'd see them once at the start of term pleading with her to find them accommodation, as if she could conjure rooms out of nowhere.

'When would be a good time?'

Dora wanted to say, *Never*. 'What's this about?' she said instead.

'I just have a few questions,' the woman said.

Barbara Hummel. The name meant nothing. Besides, a tenant or a student wouldn't have had the wartime connection. It could still be a hoax. A con-woman.

'They are very important to me.'

'What about?'

'Please,' Barbara said. Her face puckered and Dora thought she was about to cry. She didn't have time to cope with that. Dora was tempted to say, *Pull yourself together*.

'It's difficult to explain, in a few words, on the doorstep. When would be a more convenient time?'

Her English was very good, but Dora could spot a German accent a mile away. She could even tell which part of Germany the speaker came from. This woman came from the north. Bremen or Hamburg. Hannover, perhaps. Wouldn't be Rostock or Lübeck, because that was in the Communist East, and they had a different accent anyway, as different as a Scouser from a Geordie.

'I don't know this Mr O'Cleary,' Dora said. 'If that's what you think. He must have the wrong person. Dora Simon is a common name.'

'You were in Jersey,' Barbara said. She smiled, a touch of irony drifting about her lips, as if she knew more than she was letting on. 'I doubt there would be two Dora Simons there at the same time.'

'You are very sure of yourself, young woman,' Dora said. She could hear her voice, crisp and bitter. *Forbidding.*

'Yes,' Barbara said. She was looking Dora in the eye, standing up to her, tears gone. 'Yes, I am.' She shifted her weight. 'I don't want to upset you,' she went on. 'It wouldn't take long. Why don't we meet for tea? There's a little café in Bury Place, opposite the British Museum. It will be my treat. Perhaps tomorrow?'

Dora calculated. She was planning to go to the new exhibition on Aztec treasures after lunch anyway. She wasn't sure this woman would take no for an answer. She'd have to meet her sooner or later and Dora didn't want to spend any more time fretting. Quick cup of tea together. Get it over and done with.

'I know the café,' Dora said. 'This afternoon. At four. Goodbye.' Shut the door before Barbara could answer.

She went into the sitting room, watched through the window as Barbara walked down the path and headed up the hill. She waited until she was out of sight, then turned to go into the kitchen, catching sight of the silver coffee set that sat on the console table to the right of the door. Her colleagues had clubbed together and bought it for her from John Lewis when she retired. It was plate, but they'd had it engraved. *To Dora Simon, Housing Administration Officer, University of London 1949 to 1975.*

The design, they told her, was a copy of a Bauscher Weiden coffee-pot. Her father had had the same. How were they to know? They also gave her a travel poster, a rare and elegant 1930s original, framed, simple art deco lines of sea and sand and sky. *Jersey. The sunny Channel Island.*

'Now you have all the time in the world,' they said.

She'd cried when they gave it to her.

§

Dora walked to the window of the café and stood with her back to Barbara, studying the photo. It was a mugshot. The sides had curled and the image was specked with mildew. Her hair had been fair then, her eyes, even in the grainy picture, were light. Her lip was swollen and there was a graze on her chin, though you had to look carefully. The dress had been red, rayon, a cocktail dress before the war. It was backless. From the front, it looked demure with a high halterneck. In the photo, it looked grey. Lifeless.

She returned to the table, her shoulders rising and falling with her breath.

'I'm afraid I can't help you,' Dora said, handing back the photograph. She wanted to say, *Where did you get this?* But that would unleash too much and she wasn't ready. She could hear those demons already howling to be let out.

'Joseph O'Cleary said it was you.'

'I've told you,' Dora said, hoping the quiver in her voice wasn't telling, 'I don't know who he is. If I don't know him, how can he know me? He is mistaken.'

Barbara picked up her teacup and leaned back. 'The photo was with my mother's things, when she died.'

'So?'

She wished she had never agreed to meet Barbara. She'd had a strange feeling all along. Something was amiss. Barbara Hummel was a good actress, fraudsters had to be. What did she want? Money?

Barbara took the photo from Dora, turned it over.

'It says *aus Jersey* on the back.'

'So?'

Whatever she wanted, this was a shabby, sordid trick. Dora signalled to the waitress for the bill. She dabbed at the crumbs on her plate with her finger, aware that Barbara was studying her.

'Before you go,' Barbara said. She delved into her bag and pulled out another photo. A fraudster would have given up, surely, but this woman persevered.

'Do you know this man?'

An *SS* officer. Grey tunic. Three silver pips on the left-hand collar. Cap with a black band, leather belt with a revolver. He wore the Iron Cross. Breeches. Boots. High-ranking. *Hauptsturmführer.* Captain. A studio portrait.

Dora's hands were trembling and her heart pounding. She could feel the blood rushing to her face. She knew the physiology. Uncle Otto explained it to her in those early days when she couldn't sleep. Your mind perceives a threat, so your body responds. Blood diverts itself away from the stomach and into your muscles. Your heart pumps harder to inject sugar and fats into the system for energy. Fight or flight, *mein Liebling.* But if there is no threat, if it's just in your imagination, in your memory…

Who *was* this woman?

'No,' Dora said. 'Never seen him before.'

She was tempted to say, *Who are you? How did your mother have these photos?* But that would give away the lie. Dora'd had to live on a lie. She didn't want to do it again, thought those days were over. But here she was. Lying. *Lies have short legs*, her father used to say. Lies corrupted, built fear. Lies caught up with you. She could feel the bitter taste of fury swell inside her, the choking resentment at this woman churning up so much, without explanation, without a care. She was aware that Barbara was still studying her, weighing up Dora's expressions, the way her body moved, her eyes flickered. She picked up her teaspoon, polished it with her napkin, returned Barbara's gaze. Barbara looked away and Dora saw a brittleness there, a fragility she'd not spotted before.

'Do you have children?' Barbara said.

'I never married.' That was easier than the truth. She couldn't have children. Not after what they did.

'You don't need to be married to have children.'

'You did in my day.' Dora pushed her chair back and pulled the jacket up on her shoulders.

'Could I explain?' Barbara said.

'Explain what?'

'Why these photographs are important to me. Why I have to know why my mother had them.'

'I am not interested,' Dora said. She put her hands in the pocket of her jacket so Barbara could not see her shaking. 'Nor can I help you. Goodbye.'

'May we meet again?'

Dora walked out of the door, into the street. She couldn't – wouldn't – contemplate how Hummel had come by those photographs.

Jersey: January – May 1943

'We live a topsy-turvy life,' Geoffrey said. 'We farmers. Dawn to dusk, dusk to dawn. Always on duty.'

Back to front, upside down. Dora had never felt like this. It wasn't just that the days were turned inside out. *She* was turned inside out, looping the loop, tangled vapour trails across the sky. She understood now what it meant, being head over heels in love, for love somersaulted, bounced. Love was reckless. Breathless.

She wished she could have someone to ask, *Is this what it's always like?* It would have to be a special friend who could keep a secret and Dora had no one like that. Certainly not her landlady, Miss Besson, nor the other nurses she lived with. Dora had never felt so alone, or so exhilarated. She saw herself as a rocket blasting into the sky with blazing engines. Excited. Terrified.

Geoffrey had a gramophone. He kept it in the sitting room, but if they left the door open they could still hear the music in the kitchen, the only room he could keep warm now there was no coal. He polished the records before he placed them on the turntable, winding the handle, balancing the needle.

Sang in her ear as he waltzed her round the kitchen table that winter day. The record finished in the room next door.

'I'll put another one on,' Dora said, added, 'don't worry. I'll be careful. I know how to do it. Wind the gramophone first and all that.'

His collection was small and modern. American music. Dance. Nothing like her father's collection of operas and symphonies. Dora riffled through the records, picked 'Moonlight Serenade', pulled it from its cover and picked up the duster to clean it. The fabric was soft, perfect for removing the static and dust, but there was no mistaking. This was one of Geoffrey's underpants, and Dora blundering into something so intimate. She wanted to laugh, clapped a hand over her mouth in case he heard, guffawed into her fingers. And there he was behind her, taking the garment away and wiping it round the black shellac. He held the record by the edges and lowered it gently onto the turntable.

'Now you know one of my secrets,' he said, taking her hand and leading her back into the kitchen.

'One?' Dora said. *The sins of the fathers.* Could she draw him out? 'You have others?'

'Who doesn't? I bet you have a few, Nurse Simon.'

She shook her head but a blush was working its way up her neck, burning as it went. He brushed the back of his fingers against her cheek and pulled her close so her head rested on his shoulder. She wanted him to kiss her then, but he didn't make a move. Perhaps he didn't care for her, not deep down. Perhaps her breath smelled, her diet was not a healthy one. Perhaps he had another girlfriend who visited at the weekends. What was it Sir Leonard had said? *A most unsavoury character.* Or perhaps he was still in love with Margaret's mother, even though he never talked about her. It was silly to be so unsure, but she didn't know if he loved *her*, too. He'd never said.

'Tell me about your wife.'

'What do you want to know?'

'What was she like?'

He paused. She felt his chest rise and fall as he breathed, heard him swallow, a hard gulp shoving past his Adam's apple and down his gullet.

'I'm sorry,' Dora said. She felt a rip of panic, a premonition. Perhaps he'd abandoned her. Or something dreadful had happened. An accident. Worse. 'I shouldn't have asked.'

'You have every right to ask,' he said. 'I'm not sure how to answer. Bea died, in childbirth. I'd met her nine months earlier. She'd been here on holiday.'

'Oh,' Dora said. 'How terrible. How did she die exactly?' It was such a risky business, childbirth.

'Eclampsia.' He rested his chin on her head and she listened as he breathed in the kitchen air with its steam and wood smoke.

'Like her daughter,' Dora said.

He nodded. 'I was powerless to help her. I thought her the most beautiful creature that walked the earth,' he went on. 'If that doesn't sound too corny.' He pushed Dora away, held her shoulders at arm's length, added, 'Before I met you, that is.' He smiled and pulled her close again. 'I thought my grief was fathomless, that I could no sooner see my life without her than live on the moon. I wandered the beaches longing for a rip tide or a freak wave to suck me away and into oblivion.'

Dora pressed her hand against his waist. *I know about sorrow.* She shouldn't have raised the question, but she was glad she had. He had loved his wife very much. She thought she'd be jealous, but Geoffrey was sharing this part of himself with her, this intimacy, and she felt included, part of him, one with him. She knew now that he was capable of great love. Passion. Rage?

'My parents were still alive then. My mother was looking after Margaret.'

'And?' Dora said.

'She placed her in my arms and said "This baby needs its father," and I looked at her and saw not Bea, but myself, this little daughter who looked like me.' He laughed. 'I was like Narcissus. I fell in love with her. Bea had died for her, my child. Does that make sense?'

Dora nodded. She'd known grief, could smell and taste its maw, had watched helpless as it gobbled down her past, and future too. She knew Geoffrey's anguish, its weighty pain.

'And you, Dora,' he went on. 'Do you have sorrows like that?'

'My father died too.' Dora couldn't say what other sorrows went with that death, the grim crumble of her being.

'You told me.'

Her life sundered, shattered by the Nazis. And all the while Geoffrey was living his private tragedy here, in this farm. *Life was strange, that way*, she thought, the way a war roiled and churned the world so she and Geoffrey had washed up together, like flotsam and jetsam.

'I was told I looked like my mother,' Dora went on. 'She died when I was tiny.'

She felt his fingers through her hair.

'Your mother's hair?'

'My mother's colouring,' Dora said. 'My father's curls. A bit of both.'

A bit of comfort, too.

She moved her hand around his back, pulling him closer. He'd said, 'you have every right to ask.'

§

It was spring. Geoffrey had invited her for lunch. She bought a hat, in de Gruchy's. A ridiculous hat, old-fashioned, expensive, but there was no choice, a cloche of forget-me-not straw, finished with airy blue feathers. She wore the blue spotted dress that she'd bought before the Germans came. It matched the hat and highlighted her blue eyes and hair. She remembered Miss Besson's question, 'Do you dye your hair, or is it naturally that colour?' As if you could get dye these days. Not even on the black market. What had she been insinuating? Dora couldn't bear to think about that. It was a sunny day, the kind of day she remembered from the posters on the underground for holidays in Jersey. *The sunny Channel Island.* Weary troops would find a welcome home. There were pictures of children playing on the sand, striped beach umbrellas, a woman in a swimsuit. Lapis skies and yellow suns.

Where once every lane led to the ocean, now they turned back, devoured themselves. The beaches had become forbidden zones, *verboten.* Military property, flanked with anti-aircraft guns with their long steel barrels. She missed the cries of children as they jumped in the waves or built sandcastles, she missed the joy of being alive that they promised. There were few spaces left for them to play now, few parents happy to let them out into the streets. Silence. That's what Dora hated most about the island now. The Germans had suffocated sound, joy, desire.

Dora had to cut across country these days, avoid the main routes where the soldiers milled and marched. Her bicycle was second-hand, a heavy machine, and it was hard going up the hills. Scabius and cornflower flickered in the hedgerows and Dora stopped to pick them, threading them through the band of her hat. She looked around. The last of the bluebells hovered in a wood across a nearby field. Dora pushed her bike through the gate, propped it against the hedge out of view in case a passer-by took a fancy to it. That happened now, people stealing bikes, and replacements were like gold dust and as expensive. Thirty pounds. *Thirty.* She set out towards the wood. A posy, for the table. A small gift for Geoffrey.

The least I could do. She entered the wood, bent down to pick the flowers, snap the stems without pulling the bulb.

'*Fräulein. Bitte.*'

Dora froze.

'*Was–*' She stopped herself in time. *Was wollen Sie?* Caught off guard, so easy to slip into German. She looked around, could see no one.

'*Bitte.*'

There was a hawthorn bush, its blossoms spent and brown, its leaves in full furl. A shape moved behind it and a man crept out. His hair was matted and unkempt, his face grubby and unshaven. A German soldier, his uniform soiled and crumpled. He looked like a tramp, a rough sleeper. He held his cap in his hand, fingered and wrung it as the dying might clutch and twist their bedclothes.

'*Gibt's was zu essen?*' He pointed to his mouth with one hand.

Dora dropped the flowers and ran. As she neared the road, she saw the search party, two jeeps, the *Kübelwagen.* Eight *Geheime Feldpolizisten*, secret policemen, jumped down, pistols in their holsters, rifles in their hands. They pushed open the gate and ran towards the wood. One spotted her, stopped, came towards her, cupped his hand round her chin and shoved her against the hedgerow.

'*Was tun Sie hier?*' He sneered, as if Dora was a child, or a dog. Dora shook her head. He had smoked a cigarette, his breath stale and fusty. 'What are you doing here?' His English faltered. 'Vat are you doing? Who have you been with?'

He twisted her head, left, right, fingers pressing hard, the skin coarse.

'No one. I was picking flowers.'

'Let me see.'

'I dropped them,' she said. What if they took her in? Questioned her? The soldier was a fugitive, she realised now, a deserter. He'd be shot. If they thought she'd helped him, they'd shoot her too. People had been killed for much less.

'I heard a noise,' she added. 'It gave me a fright.'

The *Feldpolizist's* grip on her chin tightened and she cried out. He pressed harder. He could break her jaw. One twist, a struggle, the hinge would snap, like a wishbone. She saw, over his shoulder, that the search party had flushed out the deserter, had tied his arms behind his back and were shoving and dragging him towards the waiting jeeps. Dora was choking, eyes and nose watering.

'Please.' Her voice was thin, the words unclear. 'Let go.'

The party came towards her.

'What have we here?' It was a sergeant. He nodded to the *Feldpolizist,* who released his grip. Dora shuddered, stepped back, her hand soothing the hinges of her jaw.

'Your girlfriend?' The sergeant jerked the prisoner forward and back. Dora saw him wince, his arms pulled so far behind him she thought his shoulder could be dislocated.

He looked at Dora, shook his head. '*Nein.*'

The sergeant shoved him so he stumbled. 'In the jeep.' Turned to Dora. 'You should choose your boyfriends more carefully.'

'I've never seen him,' Dora said. 'Look,' she pointed to the flowers in her hat. 'I was picking flowers. Bluebells.'

'Papers,' the sergeant snapped. *Papiere!*

'In my basket.' Dora pointed to her bicycle. The sergeant pulled his revolver, aimed at Dora, watched as she walked to her bicycle and took the card from her bag. She sensed his jumpiness. One false move, turn too fast, rummage too deep, *bam.* She passed him the paper, studied his face, *what can he see?*

Holder...Simon, Dora. *Residing at*...14 Gloucester Place. *Born on the*...17th May 1915

At...

Dora held her breath, waited, ready.

'Stockholm?' the sergeant said. 'Sweden?'

Dora nodded.

The sergeant peered at her. 'You prove it?'

She shrugged, rolled her hands. 'My papers are in London.' *Be polite, courteous and obedient at all times. If we do not provoke them, they will not provoke us.* 'I didn't think I would need them.'

'London?' the sergeant said. 'Why London?' He was a young man, perhaps nineteen years old, blond hair and flushed cheeks, the scratch of manhood just visible on his face.

'I had moved there.'

'We need your papers.'

'I can't get them,' Dora said. 'You've cut us off from England.'

His face was blank, hard as a pavement. 'But not from Sweden, *Fräulein.* There will be records there.'

Dora swallowed. 'Of course,' she said. Of course they would demand that. *Lügen haben kurze Beine. Lies have short legs*, her father would have said.

He was looking at her, the veins on his forehead pulsing, as if memorising every tuck and blemish in her face, every wave and ripple of her hair.

'I know you now,' he said, placing the revolver back in its holster. 'I will look out for you.' Walked away, called over his shoulder. 'I never forget a face.'

She pulled out her bicycle, wobbled away. She'd tell Geoffrey she'd been stopped. Nothing more.

CHAPTER SIX

JOE

Jersey: May 1985

Joe had been thinking more and more about home of late, of that house above the butcher's shop in Cloghane, of the mist coming up the estuary from the sea, of his brothers and sisters, uncles and aunts. He'd been happy enough here with Geoffrey, but he hadn't been *home* for forty years. He still called it that. Home. Could see the heavy horsehair chair that his father used to sit in, the dark mahogany chiffonier that his mother polished every Saturday, the kitchen range with its blackened pots and the privy outside with its horseshoe nailed to the door. He hadn't seen any of the family for forty years either. The time had passed quick enough, but he should make amends before he died. Perhaps it had something to do with the letter from the Hummel woman, setting his mind on a train towards the past.

He pulled out his pad of Basildon Bond, his old Burnham fountain pen and bottle of Quink and sat at the table in his caravan. He hadn't used the pen for years, and the ink-sac had corroded. He had to dip the nib in the ink, be careful it didn't drip because he couldn't find the blotting paper and he doubted you could buy it now. Everybody used biros these days, but he couldn't use one of those, not for something important like this.

Dear Pat, he wrote. *It seems to me that enough water has passed under the bridge and it is about time that we forgot and forgave. I trust you and your family are doing well.*

He was about to write, *and how is our mam?* but thought better of it. She'd be well over a hundred by now, if she was alive. She'd probably been dead for years and no one had thought to find Joe and tell him. Was he so hard to track down? Hadn't he sent them his address? They must have guessed he wouldn't go far, would settle somewhere with the birds and the sea. Oh, that hurt, that they hadn't sought to bring him back. Put a SOS notice out on the BBC. *Will Joseph O'Cleary, late of Cloghane and St Helier, please contact his mother who is seriously ill…* Pat Junior always had a spiteful streak about him, took after their father like that. Joe put down his pen, tore up the paper.

On the other hand, perhaps they *had* tried and he never knew. *No,* he told himself, placing the lined paper under another sheet. Give them the benefit of the doubt. Write.

There must be all sorts of nephews and nieces now who maybe don't know their Uncle Joe. For all I know, there could be grand-nieces and nephews.

I am doing fine these days, with a farm. Now, this is why I am writing. I'm not getting any younger and could do with some help and I wondered whether there was anyone in the family who'd like a new start in life? As you see, I live in Jersey, have done since the funeral. That's a long story, for another day.

Because you didn't want to know about it, even back then. Yes, there was a lot of hurt, a lot of bitterness to swallow, bile, even now. He paused a moment, read over the letter. *No, let bygones be bygones, make the peace.* He had an uncle, their mam's brother, who'd emigrated to America in the 1920s and wrote back from Boston, *your loving brother.* It had made his mam cry, so he thought he'd try it now.

Your loving brother, Joseph O'Cleary.

He put it in the envelope, wrote O'Cleary & Sons, Family Butchers, Main Street, Cloghane. He had no idea if Pat still lived above the shop, but he reckoned that Cloghane wouldn't have changed so much that the postie wouldn't know where they'd moved to. It was about time he put out feelers, like, to see if they couldn't make it up now.

It was forty years ago, after all. The war had been over for two months. Joe had got off the Tralee bus and walked down the main street in Cloghane. He could imagine his mam's face, and his *daidí*'s, as he walked through the door. *Will you let me take a look at you.* Kettle on for tea in the big brown pot and his *daidí* bringing out the Jameson. Oh, there'd be a grand party. Cissie Mooney's soda bread lathered with butter, cold beef and black pudding from the O'Connors, beer and whiskey and the Waring cook's *poitín.* The kitchen thick with tobacco smoke, stubs in brimming ashtrays, smouldering pipes. *Good to have you back, Father.* The whole of Cloghane squeezed into the tiny front parlour which doubled as the dining room at Christmas. Singing and dancing. His mother and little Bridey and his Uncle Gerald's wife, pushing through with cups of tea, while his brothers and his *daidí* and uncles and the other men stood to the side with bottles of beer and picked tobacco from their lips.

But his father's butcher's shop was shut, a black ribbon hung on the front.

'Well, our prayers have been answered,' his mother Bridey said as Joe walked through the door, as if he'd only been round the corner for five minutes and not lost in the war for five years.

His brother, Pat Junior, clapped his hand on Joe's shoulder. 'Sad times, eh?' He pulled out his cigarettes and offered one to Joe. 'How was your war?'

Joe wanted to say, *Terrible, since you've asked,* but he knew Pat didn't want an answer, most likely blamed him for the war, him being on British soil and all.

It rained all through the days of the wake and was still falling when Uncle Gerald came with the hearse to collect the body from the house. The rain drummed on the slate roof of St Brendan's. It rained as they left the church and walked towards the burial ground, his *daidí* in his pine coffin with the flowers dripping and the wilting wreath in the shape of a chopper. The rain turned to hail, glacial to the touch, icy water skidding to the earth and soaking into the soil, falling in grey rivers over the tombstones and monuments, eddying in the dips in the paths and the space around the graves. It splattered off the umbrellas and the hats of the mourners and soaked the trouser legs below the raincoats. It seeped into the leather of the shoes. The mourners walked to where the pit was dug, six feet deep, in a plot big enough for Bridey too when her time came, and stomped their sodden feet in the soggy earth at the side of the grave. Father Murphy in his white surplice and purple stole, Joe in his, sopping cassock heavy with water, clinging round his legs so it was difficult to walk. The coffin was lowered into the grave and the ropes relaxed and Father Murphy nodded to Joe who stepped forward with his rain-soaked missal.

'May his soul,' his foot began to slip in the quagmire round the rim of the hole, 'and the souls of all the faithful departed,' Joe put his other foot behind him to keep his balance but the waterlogged ground couldn't hold the pressure and with a slurp, 'through the mercy of God,' sucked him down so that he slid over the side of the grave as if it were an open scree. He flung out his arms and let go of the missal, 'Rest in peace,' and landed with a thud on the foot end of the coffin, which tipped in the sludge and settled with a slap, spitting gobs of black mud over the crisp white lace of the surplice he'd borrowed from Father Murphy.

Joe stared at the layers of earth in the mud wall in front of him: the thin, black topsoil and the red clay beneath marbled with severed roots, washed white like a slab of best porterhouse veined with fat, and beneath the clay the cracked tips of grey stone. The hole smelled like a winter night, dank and decayed, and as he tried to push himself up, the sides began to crumble with the weight of water and there was a roar as they caved in around him, pushing him back, covering his feet and legs and waterlogged cassock and splattered chasuble in a thick flow of ooze.

'Hold on there.'

The gravediggers lowered a ladder and Joe heaved himself up and stepped out and onto the boggy ground, little Bridey standing there wiping an eye with her grubby handkerchief.

'Only Jesus himself climbs out of a grave,' Father Murphy said afterwards in the sacristy, handing him a glass of Jameson. 'Drink up. It'll do you the power of good.'

Only Joe didn't go back to the house, not after that. O'Sullivan's was open, half a dozen men with crumpled tweed jackets and black ties staring into their glasses.

The publican looked up. 'What'll it be, Father?'

'A whiskey,' Joe said. 'A large one.' He waited while the publican poured.

'I'm sorry for your loss,' he said, handing it to Joe. 'On the house.'

Joe stood as waves of hot and cold rolled up and down his body, corrugating his flesh, spinning his head. He finished the whiskey in one easy gulp.

Sitting on his father's coffin, eye to eye with marbled roots and raw-red worms, earwigs and beetles, as the rain washed down from above and the sludge pushed up from below, he had seen, as clear as daylight, that there was no difference between man and animal. No immortal soul. No life hereafter. When you died, that was it. Buried deep and feasted on by maggots who were gobbled up by pheasants who were shot down by hunters and served up as game in his father's butcher's shop.

His teeth chattered and the hairs at the back of his neck stood proud. He nodded to the publican who filled his glass again. Joe walked over to a small table in the corner, lifted the chair, turned it so he faced the wall and sat, the liquid forming rainbows in the glass as it swirled and settled. He stared into the amber void, conjuring again the cadavers of his war, the skeletal frames he'd called his friends, the wanton, casual cruelty of it all. God had turned a blind eye to all of that. And no one here gave a damn.

He swallowed the whiskey, waved to O'Sullivan for a refill. Nothing scared him now. Not the Church, and all its holy fathers. Mortal sin and venial sin, guardian angels and purgatory. Lies. All of it.

'There, Father,' O'Sullivan said, placing the bottle on the table. 'Take it easy.'

Joe thought of the hard man who'd once been his *daidí*, lying in his coffin, fist coiled like a mace and knuckles sharp as rocks. *I will not hear this filth. Do you hear? He's a man of God, so help me.* Joe had cowered on his knees, head in his hands, elbows to the fore, a wounded crow, while his father, shoulders hunched, hovered over Joe, breathing fire like a bull. 'It takes a lot for a man to punch his own son,' he'd said. 'But I will not hear a word against Holy Mother Church.'

If his own father didn't believe him, who would?

Pat Junior was hammering into his ear. 'And our poor *máthair* worrying herself sick. Get up, man.'

'I've lost my faith,' Joe said, the whiskey giving him strength. He pulled himself to his feet. 'I'm leaving the priesthood.'

'That's the drink talking,' Pat said.

'No,' Joe said. 'It's not the drink.'

'How could you?' Pat Junior loomed over Joe, so Joe cowered against the chair. 'And with our poor *daidí* not cold in his grave.'

Joe reeled back.

'Have you broken your vows?' Pat said.

Pat stared at him, and Joe stared back.

'You can clear off out of here if you have. You're a fecking disgrace.'

'So is the church,' said Joe. 'I'll have nothing more to do with it.'

Pat punched him in the mouth, and what more could Joe do but slam Pat one so he was out cold for ten seconds? Pat made him sign the Pledge when he came to, gave him twenty pounds to leave and never return. Said he'd poured shame on the family, broken their *máthair*'s heart and they'd have no more to do with him.

Now it was time to make amends.

He picked up the letter. It was a good letter, with a fine sign-off. An olive branch, for sure, with the offer of work and all. He was sorry he'd floored Pat Junior, for it had been the drink that made him handy with his fists that day, but even so, to force him to leave town without saying goodbye to his own mother was harsh, Joe thought.

Perhaps he'd wait a bit before he went to the post office and bought a stamp.

He fingered it again. *No.* Tore it in two, and two again. Letters like that churned up too much. *Best let sleeping dogs lie.*

The old man would be wanting his tea. Joe slipped on his shoes and stepped outside. The car was still there, but no sign of the woman. No sign of Pierre either. If Pierre didn't come soon, and that wretched woman didn't leave, it would be too late for Betsy. He still had to do the milking.

He crossed the farmyard, walked into the kitchen. The old man sat at the table with the copy of the *Evening Post* open before him. He was staring at the photograph and the request attached. *If anyone knows this person, or knows anything about her, would they please contact PO Box 39, St Helier.* He looked up when Joe entered, adjusted his hearing aids. 'Well?'

'Someone answering to her name may have been found,' Joe said. 'But it's a long shot.'

The old man nodded, eyes fixed again on the photograph. He needed a shave and a haircut. The collar on his shirt was frayed and the stitching on his elbow patches had come undone. Joe'd fix him up tomorrow, make sure he had a bath, change his clothes. When had he started calling him the old man?

It had been six months after the war, and not long after his *daidí*'s funeral in Cloghane and the incident with Pat, when Joe had drifted back to Jersey and into the farmyard at Anse la Coupe. He couldn't think where else to go. Geoffrey had limped out of the barn on that day, a shell of a man with his clothes too loose. His hair had turned white, although his eyebrows were still black. Joe thought he'd died in the war. Seeing him there in the farmyard caught Joe on the hop and he'd stood, mouth open, staring.

It had taken Geoffrey a while to recognise Joe, too. They eyed each other before they shook hands, palms locked while they searched for clues in each other's faces.

'Father O'Cleary,' Geoffrey said, and smiled, open and friendly. If Geoffrey knew anything about that day in 1943, he didn't show it.

'Not *Father*,' Joe said, 'an ordinary *mister*, now.' Joe tried to sound casual, as if nothing had happened. That's what they all did these days. *Forget the war. Look to the future.*

Geoffrey had scythed the grass round the house, cut the roses back to their roots. Joe couldn't say he'd tried to keep the place in order while Geoffrey was away, though it was hard without fuel or light, and he couldn't leave traces in case some busybody told the Germans he was living there. He'd had to leave the plants unpruned, the grass uncut, the yard in rack and ruin. But Pierre had been right. The Germans wouldn't suspect so long as Joe kept his head down.

'Oh?'

Joe nodded.

'How come?'

What could he say to Geoffrey? He'd violated his vows? He'd witnessed too much to believe in a munificent God?

'The church now,' Joe said. 'A pack of lies.'

Joe was a pack of lies too. He should be a man, own up, but he couldn't bring himself to say it was his fault.

'I tried to help after you were arrested,' he said. 'I did. But' his voice trailed away. He couldn't say what he did, for that would give away too much.

Geoffrey nodded. Neither of them spoke for a long moment.

'You'll need help to get the place shipshape,' Joe said instead. 'I'd be happy to do it.' He should have said *atone*, but he was a coward, no two ways about it.

'I've no money to pay a man,' Geoffrey said. 'Or put the farm in working order. I've been told there may be compensation, but who knows how much? Or when? I'm going to have to sell up.'

Joe turned his gaze to the field behind the house. Couldn't look Geoffrey in the eye, not right now.

'Where did they send you?' Joe said.

'Germany,' Geoffrey said. 'Neuengamme.'

Joe turned to face him as Geoffrey pointed to his left leg, rigid in its boot.

'That's where I got this.' He cupped his hands to his ears. 'And this.' Added, 'Munitions. They deafened me.' He shook his head. 'What use am I now? I can't farm, not like this, not with a gammy leg and no money.'

Joe hadn't a clue what he would do with his life now he was kicked out of the priesthood. He was too old to box. He could teach, but children could be cruel, especially to someone like himself, a feeble little man. He knew a bit about animals, and his *daidi* had taught them all how to slaughter and butcher. He couldn't live among cadavers, not now. Laid out on the marble, with the heads removed, the stiffened, skinned corpses of cows or pigs looked like the bodies his mother had prepared for their coffins or the empty husks of his friends.

But a farmer's life, that could be grand, to wander with the cows in the fields, to listen for chiffchaffs in the hedges, to watch for white-tailed eagles in the skies. Joe wasn't afraid of work. He could be up at dawn and bed down late at night, haggle over prices in the market and complain about the cost of hay.

'I have money, Geoffrey,' Joe said, thinking of the twenty pounds Pat Junior had given him. 'I could help you get back on your feet.'

'You're a young man, Joe,' Geoffrey said. 'I'm an old man now. You don't want to be tied down here.'

'Well, old man,' Joe had said. 'That's just what I'll be wanting to do. At least, for the time being.'

As Geoffrey got older, Joe cared for him more and more. Two old bachelors. That's what this Barbara Hummel woman would see. Two old men sitting on their Windsor chairs either side of the ancient Aga, the quarry tiles on the kitchen floor none too clean, dust on the skirting boards. Geoffrey had always been meticulous, and Joe tried to keep the place in order, but he couldn't do everything and he wasn't getting any younger. Still, he and Geoffrey had proved to be a good pair, if an odd couple.

It was only when Geoffrey'd seen the photograph of Dora in the paper the other week and told Joe who she was and what she'd meant to him that Joe had made the connection between Dora and the nurse, had remembered he'd had the woman's address all these years. He'd got it off the Red Cross that day but had never written to her, what with one thing and another. He'd meant to, mind, see how she was. It was a terrible thing they did to that woman. They did it to Maureen Davy in the field outside Cloghane and all she'd done was serve a British soldier a pint of stout. Joe was only little but he'd wondered if that was so bad when his own *daidí* sold the British his meat at the dead of night.

He didn't tell Geoffrey how he'd met Dora that day. Best not to bring those sorts of things up.

Joe lifted the pan and put it to heat on the Aga. He sat in the other chair, closest to the cooker, fished in his pocket and pulled out his pipe. Felt in the other pocket for his tobacco. He always had a pipe before tea, and one after. They'd never spoken about the war, he and Geoffrey, not since that first encounter. Joe had never told him how he'd lived in the farm once before, during the final year of the war, or how he'd betrayed him that day in 1943. Buried and forgotten. What would this Hummel woman want to know, apart from the boxing?

There was a knock. Joe pushed himself off his seat. He could see through the kitchen window that it was her. He walked through the lobby and opened the door.

'My name is Barbara Hummel,' she said, smiling. 'Are you Joseph O'Cleary?'

Close up, the woman was older than Joe had imagined, with dark-brown eyes and hair. Her skin was fair and freckled with fine creases on her forehead and round her mouth. *An attractive woman*, Joe thought, as she stood with her hand outstretched ready to shake his.

'I am that,' he said, taking her hand and not sure what to say.

'It's a nice place you have here,' she said. 'You were out earlier, so I took the chance to have a long walk by the sea.'

She had an accent that Joe couldn't place. 'You need to be careful,' he said. 'When the tide comes in, it can cut you off.'

'You are expecting me? May I come in?'

Joe looked behind him. Geoffrey sat oblivious to what was going on. He couldn't hear a word.

'It's not convenient, right now,' Joe said. 'I'll walk you to your car.'

He stepped out, shut the door behind him.

'That's a shame,' Barbara said. 'I go back to London tomorrow. I came here especially. Were you the boxer?'

'That I was,' Joe said. 'That I was. Yes.'

German. Her accent was German, though her English was good, colloquial. Her mother must have come from Jersey, for how else would she have a connection here and know of him? That would explain her English. Perhaps her mother had had an affair with a German, gone back with him at the end of the war.

'This is such a beautiful place,' Barbara was saying. 'How did you find it?'

'I'm the caretaker,' Joe said. It wasn't true, but it would do. 'It's Geoffrey's place.'

'Geoffrey?' Barbara said.

'The old man. You saw him. As a matter of fact, it was he who recognised the photograph.'

'Oh,' she said. 'May I talk with him?'

'Presently,' he said. 'Presently.'

They had reached the car, and Joe opened the door for her. In the distance, he heard the unmistakable bray of Pierre's engine as he changed gears for the steep hill down to the farm.

'I am expecting a visitor,' Joe said. 'I can't talk now.' Or never. Why did she want to churn up the past?

'Some other time,' Barbara said as she lowered herself in her seat and put the key in the ignition. 'I'll be back, later this summer. Goodbye then. It's good to put a face to a name. Perhaps I could talk to Geoffrey, too?'

She started the vehicle, put it into reverse, then forward. *Turns on a sixpence*, Joe thought. But that's a modern motor for you. She stopped, wound the window down again.

'I almost forgot,' she said. 'I bought you a small present, from Germany.' She held out a small package. '*Butterkäse.* Cheese. Delicious on potatoes. I hope you like it.'

What was she doing bringing presents? Joe took it, because he couldn't think what else to do, but he wouldn't be bought.

Jersey: January – April 1943

Joe travelled everywhere on the bicycle Pierre had given him. It was too big, so his feet tiptoed the pedals. He had to stand on them to pick up any speed. It had a broken spoke and a rusty chain, went *clickety-clickety* as he cycled. People knew when he was coming and waved. It reminded him of home, where no one went unnoticed, even if the attention wasn't always welcome. Sometimes he'd look out to sea and fancy that he was back there, and know that across the grey expanse he could touch America. Not that he wanted to go to America, like his Uncle Gerald, but the sound of the place rolled off the tongue and the idea of the vastness of the ocean, its infinity, thrilled him.

Like the birds, those fragile specks floating in the firmaments from pole to pole. Did they understand infinity? Emptiness?

Once a week, more often if he could, Joe pedalled to the farm. Geoffrey had pointed out the best place to watch them, hidden in a dell on the upper field. There were birds in the town, but the special ones, those that hopped off by mistake on the coast, they wouldn't be found there. They were on the shore, feeding and prancing and circling and screeling. He saw other birds too on his travels, ones he'd never seen before: the short-toed treecreeper with its little white breast and long curved beak, hopping up the tree trunks, hunting for grubs, and all manner of noisy little warblers foraging in the foliage.

If he was to be a saint, Joe thought, let it be St Francis, with birds on his shoulder and a community for friendship. St Francis had never had to eat alone. Joe wasn't cut out for godliness. Try as he might to offer up his loneliness as proof of his suffering, he couldn't get used to solitude. He'd never lived on his own before now. He'd always had family, or the boys at St Xavier's, or his fellow seminarians at St Benignus' for company.

It was time, Joe decided, to take the matter of the boxing club into his own hands. At least twice a week – more in the summer – he'd had the companionship of the boys and he missed it more than he could say. He knew the lads by name, and where they lived. If he spoke to them, or their parents, explained things, he was sure he'd be able to win them round into coming back. Time was always a good healer, and it was water under the bridge now, surely? If one returned, the others would follow. Tommy Dauvin was a case in point. The lad had shown promise, and interest.

Sometimes stayed behind to help Joe tidy up, ask questions, 'And is it true you beat Jacky Quinn himself?' Joe knew his address, near the Parade Gardens.

The February day was overcast, the sea and the sky fused fawn across the island. He turned the corner, faced the quay. A small group of people stood with suitcases and shabby coats, forlorn, middle-aged. Joe back-pedalled his bike and put a foot down to steady it. There'd been some deportations a few months ago and people hoped that would be the end of it. Nobody could get a ticket to leave, so where were they going? There was a member of the *Feldgendarmerie* standing on the corner of the pavement, and another four with rifles at the ready, standing guard.

'Well now.' Joe didn't make a habit of talking to the Germans, not after the boxing match. But the policeman was young, clean-shaven and bore a resemblance to his cousin Michael. 'Where are they going?'

The *Feldgendarm* looked down at Joe, taking in his clerical suit and dog collar.

'*Juden*,' he said. 'Jews.'

'Are they now?' Joe'd never met a Jew, though he'd prayed for them all his life. As far as Joe could see, they did no harm, not now. And hadn't the Jewish lands been occupied by the Romans? Bit like Ireland, in its day, or Jersey, now. To have your homeland occupied was a terrible thing and people didn't always do right.

'So where are they going?'

'Away,' the *Feldgendarm* said.

'Why?'

'Why? Because they are corrupt, a danger.'

'This lot wouldn't hurt a fly,' Joe said. He knew the Jewish businesses had been taken over, but hadn't thought much about it. 'What have they ever done to you?'

'Move,' the policeman said.

'I only asked,' Joe said. 'What are you going to do with them?'

'Move.' The policeman butted the stock of his rifle in Joe's chest.

'Don't push me like that,' Joe said.

The harbour clock struck five. No time to stay. It was already getting dark. Joe pressed on one pedal, teetered, caught his balance and cycled off.

'Mind you take care of them now,' Joe said over his shoulder, nodding towards the group. He cycled along the esplanade. Tommy Dauvin lived somewhere in the streets behind. He stopped, twisted round and looked, but the group was out of sight.

A shove was all it had taken and he'd crossed the road to the other side. What kind of a Samaritan was he? A coward, that's what, didn't have the stuff of charity, or of martyrs. One arrow in his leg, one turn of the rack. Couldn't even stand up to a young policeman. If the police treated Joe like that, what chance did that lot have? How could he be seen as a saviour of souls, when he'd rather save his own skin?

He turned into Castle Street, past the town hall, swastika flags unfurling in the breeze. Tommy lived in a tall, thin terraced house, with chipped stucco and flaking woodwork. Joe leaned his bike against the wall, knocked at the door and waited. There was a workshop opposite, a carriage works by the look of it. Joe made a mental note, in case the bike needed repairs. He knocked again. There was a pub further up the road. It looked a rough-and-ready sort of place, but didn't they all, these days? He heard footsteps and a voice. Joe turned to face the door as the bolts shot back and a woman in an apron and slippers stood, arms akimbo.

'It's you,' she said. 'What do you want?'

Joe had hoped for a friendlier greeting.

'Yes.' He felt his words slide away. 'Father O'Cleary. It is.' He ran his finger around the inside of his dog collar. 'I was wondering if young Tommy is about?'

'And what d'you want with him?'

Joe shifted his weight. 'Well, you see,' he said. He couldn't admit he was lonely, though he felt a lump of grief rise in his craw. He swallowed hard. 'Would it be possible to talk to him about the boxing at all? He has promise and it's a shame to let that slide.'

'Is it now?' Mrs Dauvin said. She took a step forward so her face was level with Joe's. He felt the puff of her breath, smelled the fusty must of her hair. Her eyes were ringed with worry, sunk with hunger and her mouth cast in rigid lines. She poked a finger at Joe. 'My husband isn't risking his all for the British so you can hobnob with the Germans,' she said.

'No,' Joe said. 'No, no. Not at all. Can I explain?'

'No you bleeding can't. Now clear off.' The hallway was dark behind her, but Joe fancied he saw Tommy peering round the door at the end.

'Tommy, now,' Joe said, mustering his courage. 'He loved the boxing, that he did. There's not so much for the lads to do of an evening, and it keeps them out of trouble. Teaches them discipline. Teaches them–'

'I said, clear off.' Mrs Dauvin stepped back inside the hall, went to close the door, then paused, looking past Joe. 'You can clear off, and all. Bloody scavenger.'

Joe turned to follow her gaze as the door slammed shut behind him.

There was a young boy ten yards or so behind Joe. Even in the gloom, Joe could see he was filthy and barefoot, his clothes in tatters and a look on his face that Joe knew well, the way fear haunts, the loneliness of suffering. He was one of the labourers the Germans had brought in.

'*Organisation Todt*,' Pierre'd said when they had first arrived a year or so earlier. 'After some Nazi or other. They build roads and things. Riff-raff, for the most part. Criminals.'

No, Joe thought, stretching the word. What could that lad have done? He was no delinquent, Joe would put money on that. The boy was short, young, and Joe saw himself in Cloghane standing on the flats as his *daidí* wound back his fist. *I will not hear another word.* The lad's face was pinched, his eyes white against the grime and he was gesturing to his mouth, *food, food.* Joe delved in his pockets. He had a tobacco pouch and his pipe, a handkerchief and a box of matches. He knew there was no food, but he turned his pockets inside out and shook his head.

'I'm sorry,' he said, pulling his bike free of the wall and pushing down hard on the pedals so the wheels squeaked and scraped the ground with their threadbare tyres, *scratch-scratch* on the broken tarmac.

He took to looking out for the lad, searching him out in every gang he passed, breathing in the sickly cloy of the men, the sour of festering bodies. No flesh or muscle, sallow skin on bone, covered in dust and sand, as ramparts thirty feet high grew along the strand at St Ouen, cut off the sea with thick concrete walls, shrinking the island, shrivelling it to wrinkles in the landscape, to sulphurous craters, the vistas brown and small. It was like being buried alive in a vast, open mausoleum, watching as the masons sealed the vault, the air and the light diminishing day by day.

Joe didn't have the heart to try to open the boxing club again, couldn't face another angry mother. He thought of going to the pub, but he didn't have the money for a beer and though no one back home would have let Father Murphy pay for his Guinness, he knew they did things differently here. He wasn't sure he'd be welcome, either. Now they had no wirelesses it was difficult to know what to do in the evenings.

Pierre had taken to coming round to the convent in the spring, once the boxing club had closed.

'There's only so much of my sister I can take,' he said one Friday. He pulled out his cigarettes and a small flask of brandy. 'She doesn't drink. Doesn't smoke. And her lodgers, those nurses.'

He paused. 'They've got as much sense of fun as a cuttlefish with a budgerigar.'

Joe wasn't sure what that meant, nor was he sure why Pierre had taken such a liking to him. Perhaps Pierre was lonely too. Perhaps he was being honest when he thought some of Joe's grace could rub off on him. *No matter.* Pierre broke the monotony of the evenings. His cigarettes and brandy were welcome and Joe didn't ask how he got them. He knew he had one of the trading concessions, but even so. They played rummy in the little parlour of the convent, or swapped stories. Pierre had a fine repertoire and was a good raconteur even though he embroidered the truth and played with the words as if he'd kissed the Blarney Stone itself.

One evening, Pierre put a missal on the table, opened it up. An oblong had been cut in the centre and inside was a small tin of Fisherman's Friend cough sweets. Joe wondered for a moment whether he had a sore throat, though why he should keep it in a missal was both a mystery and a blasphemy.

Pierre lifted out the tin and prised open the lid. 'Ever seen one of these before?'

Joe was expecting to see the familiar beige lozenges, but instead he was staring at coils of wire and tiny cylinders. He shook his head.

'Magic. Here.' Pierre pulled out a small wire and threaded it out of the window, adjusted a miniscule dial and a faint voice could be made out through the static. *This is the BBC Home Service. The nine o'clock news…*

'A crystal set,' Pierre said, finger to his lips. 'Present from that Jesuit, Father Rey.' He spoke with emphasis. 'So you know what's going on. Now the Bosch have taken our wirelesses.' He took the tin from Joe, recoiled the antenna and closed the lid. 'Father Rey said people need *hope*, and what better way to deliver it than through a priest.'

Joe pulled a face. 'I beg your pardon?'

Pierre opened his brandy flask, offered it to Joe. 'He said you'd know what he meant.' He shrugged. 'Pass on news, through the confessional. Or on your travels. Tunisia fallen. Ruhr bombed. Short and sweet. That sort of thing.'

Planes took off and landed all the time. The rattle of a *Focke-Wulf*, the howl of a *Messerschmitt*. Joe was sure the war wasn't going well for the Germans. He looked at the tiny wireless.

'He said stack it on the shelf between the Bible and your breviary. No one would guess. He said they wouldn't search a convent.'

Pierre placed the tin back inside the missal. Pulled out a packet of Gauloises. 'Father Rey thought you might be able to open your boxing club in a month or so,' he said, taking a long drag on his cigarette and blowing the smoke out in rings. 'The Lord moves in wondrous ways, don't you think?' He put the cigarette in his mouth and pulled his coat on. 'I told you things would calm down.' He turned his collar up. 'I'll see myself out.'

Joe waited until he'd left, picked up the missal, sat down hard on the straight-backed chair, fished out the tin of Fisherman's Friend and pulled out the antenna.

§

The boys came back. Even Tommy Dauvin.

'And is it true, Father, that you beat the *Wehrmacht* champion, Wilhelm Weber?'

The boys were thin, undersized, and they were cherished sons, looked after. How had that young *OT* lad ended up here? If Pierre was right, what had he done to merit this punishment? It was a hard price to pay.

'Watch the footwork, Tommy.'

These lads, Joe thought, could be rounded up for no reason, set to labouring work. It wouldn't take long before they, too, were scrawny as the devil and would thieve for a living.

Joe thought about it. The nuns grew vegetables for their own use. He couldn't take anything that would be noticed, but no one would miss half a dozen carrots or leftover taters from tea, an apple or two. It only went to the pig. Now the evenings were getting light, there were nearly three hours after the Angelus and before the curfew and the bedtime prayer. He knew the prisoners roamed at night, scavenging, as dynamite thundered in the tunnels of St Lawrence and the ground vibrated, that great bed of war tossed and ruptured.

He put the vegetables in an enamel bowl, placed it in his basket and cycled off. He wished he had some cheese. That made a good meal, cheese and potatoes. But who had cheese in these times? The penalties for feeding the labourers were severe, but, Joe reasoned, if no one saw him, who could denounce him? Send an anonymous letter to the *Feldkommandantur* at Victoria College House? If he hid the food in a ditch, or a hedgerow, close to one of the camps, there was a chance a man would find it, before a feral dog or fox. And with a bit of luck, it would still be warm.

He was caught up in this war, like it or not.

CHAPTER SEVEN

DORA

London: May 1985

Dora had held Charles's hand at Sal's funeral, feet heavy as lead, black ribbons in the breeze while he sobbed through the *Kaddish* and threw the first clods of earth on her grave. He proposed to Dora a year after Sal had died.

'I'm no good on my own, Dora,' he said.

'I'm an old maid,' she said.

'Wine and women,' Charles said. 'Best matured.'

She said she'd think about his proposal.

She hadn't, of course. What would she do marrying Charles? He was more like a brother than a friend. Never a lover. He and Uncle Otto had met on the train out of Berlin in 1933. Half Otto's age, and two years older than Dora, Charles was a short man, smiley and tubby, with a round face and crinkly hair. He'd wasted no time in anglicising his name – no longer Karl Rosenberg but Charles Ross – and himself, and didn't so much *speak* English, she'd say to him, as *articulate* it with a careful, exaggerated accent.

Marriage was out of the question, to Charles, or anyone.

Would she have told a sister, if she'd had one, about the war? Sworn her to secrecy? She used to think so, but not now. She was used to her burden, carried it around wherever she went. Her memories were all she had in the world. Sometimes she thought of them crammed into a Gladstone, or a carpet bag, something soft and shapeless that expanded, with secret pockets and compartments.

But she liked Charles. He was fun, and funny. They spent hours these days talking about the old times. She'd open her bag then, rummage through the top layers, leave the false bottom untouched. She'd forgotten sometimes what she'd hidden there.

Charles had had a good war. Had volunteered to fight with the British when he was released from internment. A friendly enemy alien, they called him. Pioneer Corps. Then RAF. He became a pilot. Uncle Otto had told her this.

'The only German-Jewish pilot, apart from Heinie Adam. Imagine, Doralein. That we should know him.'

'Just as well I never had to jump,' Charles said once. 'I'd have pulled the wrong bloody cord on the parachute.'

Never mind what would have happened if he'd had to bail out. Shot on the spot. They knew that now. He'd been awarded the Distinguished Flying Medal. Sergeant Charles Ross. DFM. He'd shrugged.

'Nothing to it. Those Tiffys flew themselves. Clever machines.'

But he was being modest, Dora knew. He'd flown more times than fate permitted. He never talked about the war, but he never missed the Cenotaph on Remembrance Day. How had he felt as he climbed into the cockpit and pulled his goggles over his eyes? She could taste the fear, the adrenalin, the metal tang of bravery. He'd fought, and survived and killed at a distance and, yes, he'd had a good war.

'Your war?' he asked.

'My war? A woman's war.' Make do and mend.

'You're lucky your hair was fair,' Charles said. 'And you could pass for a goy.'

Charles and Sal had upped and moved to an oast house in Kent when he retired a few years ago, and left her high and dry.

'Nonsense,' he'd said. 'You'll come and visit.'

But she hadn't, not yet, though he came up to London once a week and they always had dinner, one way or another.

He'd rung a couple of years ago. 'It's Sal,' he said. His voice had the dull thud of sadness. 'Cancer. It's gone to her liver.' She heard him swallow back tears. 'She has three months.'

In the event, it was six weeks.

§

She had other friends that she'd met through work, university administrators like herself. Janet, Beryl, Roger. Jackie, Val, Derek. They met up every couple of months for dinner at the Koh-i-Noor in Warren Street. It was cheap, and crowded, a favourite with students. It served curries in dim light and dark decor.

'So you can't see what you're eating,' Roger said. They washed down the food with a pint of Kingfisher. These friends had other lives, busy social lives. She envied their hinterland of friendship. Their chums from school, their mates from university. English, she thought, was good that way, it had more words than other languages, even German, could distinguish between a chum and a mate and a pal, a companion, a comrade, a crony. Apart from Charles, Dora didn't have old friends from her youth like that. No one to reminisce with.

She had acquaintances. That was another word, another level of sociability, not intimates, not kindred spirits, not people you hobnobbed with on a regular basis. People she knew that she could chat to, but not share a secret with. Her bridge partners. People she met at exhibitions, or on courses at the City Lit. Or through music, in her choir once a week, or through a festival.

'There's a new Italian,' Derek said. 'Round the corner in Store Street. We're going to try it.'

Their table was at the back of the restaurant, tucked away so the waiters didn't see them. Service was slow, and they were drinking too much. Dora saw her face in the mirror opposite, flushed with wine. *I look old*, she thought.

Derek had just come back from America.

'The papers were full of it,' he said. 'The trial. Scheduled for later, sometime in the summer.'

'Trial?'

'Don Nichols. Don't you remember? He kidnapped that athlete, Kari Swenson, to use as a wife. Weird case.'

Dora remembered. It had happened last year.

'Not for himself,' Janet said. 'For his son.'

She'd been rescued, Dora recalled, in the nick of time, though her rescuer was killed and she'd been chained to a tree. What would have happened to her if she hadn't been found? Would she have grown to love this man's son? Dora opened her bag, fished around for her cigarettes. *Damn.* She'd left them at home. She stood up, pushed back her chair and squeezed past her friends. She'd spotted a machine as they'd come in. Gold Leaf or Rothmans. No Benson and Hedges. She'd have to make do. She fed in the coins, pressed the button, delved for the cigarettes and walked back to the table, unwrapping the cellophane as she went. The conversation had moved on to Patty Hearst.

Dora hadn't taken much notice of the Hearst case at first, but as the trial had gone on, she'd grown more interested. Had the young woman been brainwashed? Or had she committed the robbery of her own volition? Had she been raped by her kidnapper, or were they lovers?

'A real conundrum,' Derek was saying. 'A lawyer's paradise.'

'POW survivor syndrome,' Roger said. He worked in the student welfare department. 'She showed all the symptoms, lowered IQ, raised pulse rate, cold sweats. Couldn't talk. Depressed.'

'Says who?' Val asked. She leaned forward, reached for a bread stick and snapped it in two, offering one half to Dora.

'Says one of the psychiatrists who spoke to her,' Roger said. 'But they wouldn't admit that evidence.'

'Could she have been brainwashed?' Janet said. 'I mean, people are.'

'*The Manchurian Candidate*,' Derek said. 'Now *that* was a good film.'

'They were communists too, weren't they?' Jackie said. 'The Symbionese Liberation Army, or whatever they're called. Brainwashing. The Reds do that sort of thing.'

'Not all of them,' Dora butted in. Uncle Otto was a communist, and many of his friends. They'd fought against fascism. All this Cold War stuff made people paranoid, dupes to propaganda, only Dora didn't say that. She stubbed out her cigarette, nibbled on the bread stick, wished the food would hurry up.

'But the brainwashing, now,' Janet said, ignoring Dora. 'Stockholm syndrome and all that.'

'Stockholm syndrome's when the victim sympathises with the captor,' Derek said.

'And sometimes vice versa,' Beryl said.

'Rarer.'

'But why would you want to sympathise with someone who terrorises you?' Beryl said. She'd spilled some red wine on her jumper and was dipping the corner of her napkin in her water glass. She began to rub at the stain.

'Salt,' Dora said. 'Put salt on it.'

Beryl mouthed *Thanks*. Dora was older than them, and she knew they treated her like a mother, not a peer, not someone with whom to share a confidence. She'd bumped into Beryl once, in Heal's, shopping with her husband.

'Ted,' Beryl had said, turning to the man beside her. 'This is Dora, my colleague.'

Would she have done the same? Dora had wondered at the time. Introduced Beryl as her colleague? Or as her friend? Her friend from work?

'Survival,' Val was saying. They all turned to her.

'*Survival?*' Beryl said.

'I read in *New Scientist* ages ago that the victim identifies with the captor, takes on their values. All to do with Freud. Defence mechanisms, and all that.'

'That makes no sense,' Beryl said.

'Aha,' Val wagged her finger. 'If you think that what your captor's doing is right, then it stops being frightening. You accept it.' She sipped at her wine. 'Makes sense to me.'

'No,' Beryl said. 'It's just potty.'

'They bond,' Derek said. 'Look at the case in Stockholm, that bank robbery. The women there even *defended* their kidnappers.'

'Women are especially prone,' Val went on. 'They have less control. Think of all those women in history. The Sabines. Battered wives.'

'They're not the same,' Jackie said.

'Who knows?'

Dora wasn't sure about any of this. She reached into her handbag and pulled out her cigarettes again.

'Swap places, Roger,' she said. 'So we smokers can sit at the same end.' She waved the Rothmans at Val.

'Hearst kept some trinket her captor gave her,' Derek went on. 'I rest my case.'

'That's odd,' Jackie said. 'If she'd been raped, why would she do that?'

Dora took a deep drag at her cigarette, watching the smoke curl towards the ceiling.

'Are you all right, Dora?' Val said. 'You've gone awfully quiet.'

'I'm fine.'

Humans, Dora had read once, were the only animals that showed kindness. And went to war. You had to believe that, otherwise what hope was there?

'Anyway,' Roger said. 'She got twenty-five years. That's a hell of a sentence.'

'I wouldn't survive a day behind bars,' Janet said. 'Poor girl.'

'Excuse me.' Dora stubbed out her cigarette, pushed back her chair, left a five-pound note on the table and left.

She stood for a moment outside the restaurant, one hand against the plate-glass front, steadying herself.

'Are you sure you're all right?' Val had followed her out. 'Are your nerves bad today?'

'Something I ate,' Dora said. *A bitter pill I swallowed.* 'I'll be fine.'

She pulled herself up straight, walked as steadily as she could. She'd drunk too much, on an empty stomach.

'I'll ring you,' Val said. 'See how you are.'

Fixated. That's what she'd been. She saw that now. That wasn't love. Never had been. Never could be. Her world had become topsy-turvy, and she'd tried to make sense of it, to grope for something to hold onto, like a child in a funhouse with tipping floors and moving walls. She hadn't played into his dreams. He had played into hers.

How long had it taken her to understand? Forty years. Forty *bloody* years. And all this time she'd held onto – what? Hope? That he'd find her? What kind of stupidity was that? She was an intelligent woman, yet she had fawned at the memory, licked the boots of a worthless fantasy, just as she had battened onto him in the flesh all those years ago.

Pathetic bloody woman.

She caught the bus home. Didn't trust herself on the underground. It would be so easy to slip between the platform and the tracks as the train approached. She sat on the top, at the back, smoking. She should give up. That's what the doctors all said. But it calmed her. Nerves. That was a very old-fashioned thing, these days.

She let herself in. She always left a light on when she went out. She told herself it was to fool a burglar, but it was for her. She couldn't bear to come into a dark house. She walked towards her bedroom, snapping on more lights.

She kept it now in an old shoebox at the bottom of her wardrobe, with some other mementos, her old midwife's badge, her nurse's watch. She hadn't thought about it for years. The wrapping paper was still stiff and the pencil lines unfaded, but the waxed paper beneath had softened. The soap was now almost odourless, so only the smallest hint of sweetness wafted in the air.

Savon de Violette.

Dora rushed through the house, out of the door, down the steps. She threw the soap into the dustbin, where it landed with a thud, tore up the wrapping paper into shreds and chucked them in after. She went back in, scrubbed her hands until the skin glowed pink, nausea churning and curdling her stomach.

If Val rang tomorrow, she'd say she had a bug, one of those twenty-four-hour things.

Jersey: May 1943

A week after the incident with the soldier, Dora cycled into the farmyard, propped the bike against the wall and knocked. Geoffrey didn't come. She tried the handle, but it was locked. Something must be wrong. Had she missed a message? He said he'd send word to the hospital if he had to go out, cycle into St Martin and use the telephone box. She knocked again. If he didn't answer, she'd check the cowshed, or the fields. You never knew, there could be an emergency. Then she heard footsteps, the grind of metal as the bolts were drawn free. He opened the door a crack and beckoned her inside.

'Dora.' His voice was hushed and urgent. 'Thank God.'

She was unbuttoning her cape, pulling off her hat. 'What's the matter?'

'I have to trust you.' He looked at her, studied her face. 'Can I?'

'Of course,' she said. 'Of course you can trust me.'

'Regardless?' He was looking over her shoulder as if someone was expected. She saw desperation, pleading.

'What's happened?' Panic began to scratch and claw at her. 'What's wrong?'

'Come,' he said. 'Give me your bag.' He took it from her before she could answer, went upstairs and stopped by the door that led to the attic. 'Follow me.'

They climbed the narrow stairs to the garret. The room had a small window at one end and three dormer windows, but even so it was dark and dingy. It was barely high enough for them to walk upright, and the eaves were full of old furniture. Dora saw an iron bedpost, picture frames stacked against the wall, a table, a chair with its stuffing hanging out. Things that were too precious to throw away, too old to be of use. The dust made her cough.

'Watch your step,' he said, pointing to a broken floorboard through which the joists were visible.

She followed Geoffrey across the room, to a carved wooden screen. Behind it, an old mattress had been lain on the floor and on it an untidy pile of blankets. Breathing.

'Geoffrey.' She was unsure what else to say.

'Can you help him?'

'Who is he?' She crouched on the floor, peeled back the blanket, saw a skull with tufts of hair and skin drawn tight across the bone, mouth open, breath sweet and fruity. The veins on his temple stood out, throbbing blue.

'*Bitte*,' the man said. '*Bitte. Helfen Sie mir*.'

Geoffrey was crouching on the floor beside her.

This was no deserter from the *Wehrmacht*. He was one of the labourers who were building ramparts, hollowing tunnels, whom she'd seen on the road in dusty, weary gangs. This man was too weak to work, too ill. Dora leaned close to him.

'Do you speak English?' He looked at her with vacant eyes. Dora didn't think, just said it. '*Sprechen Sie Deutsch*?'

'*Ja*,' the man said. '*Ich bin Deutscher*.' He coughed, a thin rasp of pain. '*Ich bin ein Gefangener*. Prisoner.'

He stopped, his face twisted with pain. It hurt to talk, but Dora could see he wanted to.

'*Wir sind Sklaven*,' he went on. 'Slaves. *Nicht genug zu essen. Hungernd*.' He began to cry, sobs rattling his bones like mallets on a xylophone, high and low.

'*Wie heissen Sie*?' Dora said.

'Alfred,' the man said.

'*Mein Vater heisst Alfred*,' she said. '*Es ist ein guter Name*.' Without looking away from him, she said to Geoffrey, 'Bring me some water. Towels. Sheets. I need to wash him.'

'He's wounded,' Geoffrey said.

'Where?' She could feel his eyes on her, curious.

'His thigh.'

Dora lifted the blanket from Alfred's feet, rolled it up against his body. His trousers were torn below the knee, gaped at the fly from where the buttons had long since gone. His shins were bare, the skin smeared with dust and grease. Geoffrey had cut away the fabric from the wound, wrapped it in a bandage, but blood was soaking through, wet and crimson. The gash was deep, several inches long.

She heard steps echoing on the wooden floor of the attic.

'How did you do it?' she spoke in German.

'I fell,' he said. 'On the edge of a shovel.'

'When?' she said.

'Yesterday.'

The injury was old, but still weeping. He must have broken the scab. She'd have to clean it as best she could. Alfred would have to stay here. She'd instruct Geoffrey on how to keep the wound dry and clean.

'Where?' she said. 'Where were you?'

His voice was dry, his throat rasping air. 'On the beach.'

Sand. Dora was almost relieved. Geoffrey would have to watch for signs of lockjaw, but there wasn't too much swelling, and the sand would be clean, washed by the sea.

Geoffrey appeared with the water and a flannel, and a storm light which he held as Dora cleaned the wound.

'*Sachte, sachte!*' *Gently, gently.*

The man screamed as she delved into the depths of the cut. She could hear her father, *How many layers does skin have, Doralein?* Could see him, *Look here.* Probing. He'd done this, in his war, all the time. *Deep wounds? Leave them. Let the air do the curing.*

It would take time to heal. And then what? *For* what? He couldn't be returned. He needed food, care. A place to hide. Here? For the duration of the war?

'Has he had any food?' Dora asked.

'A little soup,' Geoffrey said. 'That's all.'

'Are you hungry?' Dora said.

Alfred nodded.

'Fetch him some more soup,' she said to Geoffrey. 'Little and often.'

Geoffrey had brought up a sheet and they lifted Alfred, one side, the other, laid the sheet taut and white on the bed, arranged the blanket around him, so the bad leg was exposed. She'd see if Geoffrey could make a cage to support the bedding. The attic was cold and dirty. He needed warmth, a bed, clean surroundings.

'He should be in a hospital,' Dora said, as she spooned the soup Geoffrey brought into his mouth, blowing on it to cool it down.

'*Danke*,' the man was saying between mouthfuls. '*Danke*.'

'Why are you a prisoner?' Dora said. He looked at her with watery eyes, their irises faded and purple, like an old man's.

'*Kommunist*.'

He was weeping.

The kitchen was warm. Geoffrey had found some fuel and fed the stove. Dora burned the soiled dressings, aware that Geoffrey was watching her, following her movements.

'I didn't know you spoke German,' he said finally. She heard betrayal there, fear. She leaned forward on the range, her back to him, its heat seeping into her body.

'Yes.' She had no choice now, she had to tell him. 'You trusted me, just now,' she said. 'Can I trust you?'

He looked at her, eyes level and suspicious. She took a breath, *wait a moment.*

'I'm German,' she said. 'And Jewish.'

She heard him breathe in, a sharp *huhhhh*. He had not been expecting to hear that, she could tell.

'I thought you were Swedish,' he said. He was frowning, his lips tight in a snarl.

'Does that make a difference?' she said.

She'd met them, in London, two-faced liberals who hated Jews.

It was a beat before he spoke. What did that tell her?

'No,' he said.

'You hesitated.'

'Because I was thinking,' he said. 'If I were German. Or Jewish, would I tell a lie too?'

Are you sure? That's why?

'It's not brave,' Dora said. 'Or honourable. But I don't want to be rounded up. Sent away. Treated like a slave. Like these poor men. Or worse. Who knows what they're doing, the Nazis?'

She could feel the anger grow inside her, bitterness, too.

'But you wouldn't know. You wouldn't know what went on in Germany, before the war. Not to Jews. That was never talked about here. It was never in the papers.' Except the Jewish ones, and the Communist ones, but who listened to Bolsheviks? *Jewish* Bolsheviks?

'No,' he said. 'So tell me.'

'They humiliated us,' she went on. 'Isolated us. Took our businesses. Our livelihoods. Like they did with the Jews here, in Jersey.'

He was sitting at the table, listening. He looked chastened, confused. She couldn't stop, not now. It had been bottled up for too long.

'They threw me out of school. I had no right, they said, to education. I wanted to be a doctor, like my father, but they threw me out of school with nothing. I was top of my class. Said I wasn't worth it. They wouldn't spend money on Jews.' She paused. 'There were rumours about camps. They locked the troublemakers in camps.' She paused, blew through her lips. 'And Jews. Such camps. The stories. People dying.'

He pushed himself up from the table, walked over and pulled her close.

'I would never betray you,' he said.

Did she believe him? He had hesitated, one beat.

'Nor me you,' she said. Easy words, easy words. How strong would *she* be?

He squeezed her close, took her hand, led her back to the table.

'If you've kept a secret from me, then I've kept this one from you,' he said. 'A few of us do what we can against the Germans. We don't do much, we can't do much. We have no weapons, no support. Nowhere to hide.'

'We?'

'It's best you don't know names. Safer. There's nothing you can tell, if you were caught.'

Whoever they were, this had been thought through.

'If workers escape, we help them, if we can. Hide them. Feed them. Forge papers.'

'But that's dangerous,' Dora said. 'If you were caught–'

'If we were caught, we'd be sent away, perhaps killed. Yes. It is dangerous. But who can stand by and watch…' He searched for a word. 'This *criminality*. That's what these camps are. Criminal.'

'Plenty do,' Dora said. 'Turn a blind eye.'

'No one wants to play the hero.' His voice softened, and he added, 'I have no family, not now.' He swallowed, as if the memory of Margaret had been there all along, stuck in his craw. 'I have nothing to lose, no one to put in danger.'

You have me. Dora bit her lip instead.

He leaned over, brushed his fingers against her cheek, squeezed her hand. She smelled his sweat, the pungent onion of it. Nerves, it had to be nerves, for the room wasn't hot, despite the range, not hot enough for natural sweat. 'Now I've put you in danger. I am sorry.'

'When would you have told me?'

'Perhaps never,' he said. 'When would you have told me?'

'Perhaps never,' she said, smiled.

'Have there been others, before Alfred?'

He nodded.

'Hiding in the attic? How many? Who were they?'

'I can't say how many,' he said. 'Mainly Russians. But not all. They come from all over Europe. He is the first German.'

'How do they find you?'

Geoffrey shrugged. He wouldn't say.

'Do you run this?' She wasn't sure what to call it. Resistance?

He shrugged again. *Not a word.*

'You arrived on the wrong day.'

'Or the right day,' she said. 'That wound is serious. He could have died. I'll need to come back, in a few days, to check on it.'

'You shouldn't be involved. It's too dangerous.'

'I am involved now, Geoffrey,' she said. 'I'm glad to be. I *want* to be.'

He smiled, tipped his head to one side. 'You can be our nurse,' he said. 'Our trusted nurse.'

'What happens to them?'

'We have safe houses.'

'And if they die?' Dora said. 'What do you do then?'

'We bury them, with dignity.'

'Where?'

'In the four-acre field,' Geoffrey said, as if it was obvious, matter-of-fact. 'And if we find a corpse that the Germans haven't thrown in the sea or sunk in the cement, we bury that too.'

Dora looked at their hands, entwined, her skin pale against his. The grandfather clock in the hallway whirred and began to strike the hour. She counted out. One. Two. Three. Four. She had to go, be back in time for tea.

He took her elbow, led her out to her bike, held the handlebars while she mounted it.

'Thank you, Dora,' he said. 'Thank you.'

Not a word.

CHAPTER EIGHT

JOE

Jersey: May 1985

As Joe went back indoors he had the feeling that he'd seen the Hummel woman before. She seemed familiar. He couldn't think how. He never went anywhere these days, not to socialise, like, and she didn't look to be the sort of woman he'd have met taking Geoffrey for his appointments, or going to the Co-op, or stocking up on animal supplies at Brouard's. He couldn't place her.

The saucepan was bubbling on the hob, the steam pushing the lid so it rose and fell. James Watt had invented the steam engine from watching his mother's kettle boil. He could see the picture now in his schoolbook, a little boy in old-fashioned knickerbockers staring at the stove. It took a particular kind of man, that, to go from seeing one thing, to discovering something else entirely. What did they call it these days? *Lateral* thinking. The fear and excitement. The anxiety. *Would it work?* Joe moved the pan to one side and the lid calmed down. Irish stew. He was good at that. He made it almost the way his mother did, neck of lamb boiled up with taters and carrots and onions. His mother made the stock from scratch, but Joe didn't have time for that. He used Oxo cubes, crushed them up as he brought the meat to the boil, then let it simmer. He foraged like her, though, for wild garlic and other herbs, mushrooms in season, threw them into the pot. He made up a large pan at the start of each week and it did them for three days. Tasted better the longer it was left.

Joe wasn't a fancy cook, but Geoffrey never complained. Fish on Fridays. Corned beef or sausages or hamburgers on the other days, though why they were called hamburgers he never knew. You could swear they hadn't been near a pig in their life. More like the rissoles his *daidí* made in his shop, full of gristle and fat. Sometimes, on Sundays, he cooked a joint, a shoulder of lamb or a leg of pork with crackling. Chicken, too. That did them a meal for several days. He made desserts. Bird's Instant Whip in the winter, or a rice pudding with milk baked in the Aga. He made sure they had fruit. An apple a day and all that, strawberries in the summer, or a tin of peaches with evaporated milk or Wall's ice cream. He'd buy that in the Co-op, two slabs, Neapolitan for Geoffrey, vanilla for himself. It was a grand life. Joe wanted for nothing. He even owned half-shares in the farm.

'Only fair,' Geoffrey had said. 'You invested your money and your time. And who else would I leave it to?'

Joe wondered much the same. Who would he leave his share to? Damned if any of those O'Clearys were going to put their thieving paws on it, not after the way they'd treated him, with their *daidí* not cold in his grave. For sure, he'd had a few whiskeys after the funeral, and who wouldn't after what he'd been through? They'd all had a drop, and that was the truth. But to hound him out, that was harsh.

Pierre drove into the yard, yanking the handbrake before the car had stopped so it screamed in protest. Joe heard him crash the gears, put the thing into neutral. Pierre'd never learned to drive properly and was rich enough not to worry if he wore out the innards of a car long before the rust got to its bodywork. He'd be wanting his tea, too. Joe reached for three bowls and put them on the table as Pierre came into the kitchen. He didn't bother knocking, not after all these years.

Pierre placed the Jameson on the table. 'Duty-free,' he said. He turned to Geoffrey, raised his voice, made a drinking gesture with his hands. 'Shall I pour you one now?'

Geoffrey smiled, nodded. He didn't have many pleasures in life, since his hearing was blown and now his eyesight was fading. Taste, touch and smell. Jameson did the lot. Pierre poured the glass and Geoffrey closed his arthritic fingers round it. He didn't complain, but Joe knew they pained him. He could barely turn the page of a newspaper, let alone write, these days.

They didn't have a big herd, no more than seventy milking cows at any one time, but Joe had hand-picked them all, and bred them. Betsy was their first cow, bought at the market in December 1945. When she'd calved in the spring, they'd called her daughter Betsy, and in turn, *her* daughter. Joe'd lost count of the generations now. They gave up naming the other cows, except the Betsys.

It was a trick he'd introduced to Geoffrey, putting them out to grass for a few years once their milking days were over, resting and fattening them on nothing but clover and grass. You couldn't do the whole herd like that, for that would be a waste of the grazing, but one at a time. It took the three of them to slaughter her. There was a lot of meat on an old milker and a whole cow was too much for two, even with the chest freezer that Joe had bought second-hand. But Pierre knew a restaurant that would buy what they couldn't use, charged a fortune for *mature Galician beef.* Paid Joe and Geoffrey in cash and kind, what with the drop of Jameson and a helping hand and a quiet word with the Food Safety boys.

Joe checked on Betsy as he walked over to the milking shed. She was lying down, chewing her cud. He'd get her up in due course, put her in the head gate. The poleaxe was ready and he'd never missed yet. Swing it behind him, aim between the eyes, pierce the skull, kill the brain. She wouldn't know a thing. The knife was nearby, and the bucket. Slit the throat, catch the blood. Cut the

Achilles tendon, then hang her by the hind legs with the block and tackle slung over the beam. Split her down the middle from throat to groin so the guts spread thick as a delta, peel back the skin, sever the head and slice the animal down the backbone with his chopper. The skin pulled back easy when the animal was still warm. He'd never used anything other than a boning knife, like his *daidí* before him. Quartered and hung. The room where Joe kept the freezer was spick and span, and they'd carry the quarters there and hang them from the hooks.

They worked well as a team, but Joe wasn't sure how long Geoffrey could carry on. He'd been born at the turn of the century, as the century turned. A minute past midnight on the first of January, 1900.

'Nowadays,' Joe said, 'you'd most likely be in the papers.'

Joe did the slaughtering, and the other two did the hoisting and lifting. Geoffrey still had his marbles at eighty-five, but he wasn't as strong as he used to be, and his hands meant he sometimes let slip the pulley. This might be the last Betsy they'd be able to slaughter. He'd have to send *her* daughter with the rest of the old milkers to be minced up for pet food.

He cleaned and disinfected the machines, readied the churns for the morning pickup, poured a jug of fresh milk, went back into the kitchen. Geoffrey had put the bowls in the sink and spread out the copy of the *Evening Post* on the table. He was standing over it, staring at the photograph.

'I didn't know her that well,' Pierre was saying. 'She lodged with my sister. They all seemed a bit strict in that house.'

Geoffrey was nodding, not hearing a word.

'So who was the woman who had her photo?' Pierre said.

'Her name,' Joe said, putting the milk on the table, 'is Barbara Hummel.'

Geoffrey looked up. He was straining to follow the conversation, looked at Pierre, then at Joe.

'Margaret,' Geoffrey said. 'What was Margaret doing here?'

'Margaret?' Joe looked at Geoffrey, then Pierre.

'Margaret. The young woman.' Geoffrey went on. 'Earlier.'

He must be losing his marbles, Joe thought. *Dementia.* Joe'd need to keep an eye on him. Still, you had to be straight.

'That wasn't Margaret,' Joe said. 'We buried her, if you remember.' He didn't say, *When I was a priest.* Didn't say, *I wasn't up to the job, not at Margaret's funeral.* How could he have given comfort to Geoffrey at that time?

'Her name was Barbara Hummel,' Joe said, raising his voice and enunciating the syllables. He turned to Pierre, spoke softly. 'I sent her away. You probably passed her on the road.'

Pierre looked across at Geoffrey, who was still struggling to hear over the feedback from his hearing aid. 'Why?' Pierre said. 'Why send her away?' Added, softly, so Geoffrey couldn't hear, 'You know he loved that woman Dora?'

'I won't rush into having the Hummel woman in my kitchen without–' Joe paused, reached for the word. 'Without *provenance.* I want to know who she is and how she got the photo of Dora.'

'You can ask her,' Pierre said.

'She looked nice,' Geoffrey was saying. 'Reminds me of someone. Will she come again?'

'She'll be back.'

'You're sure?' Pierre said.

'She said as much. See,' Joe said, lowering his voice again so Geoffrey couldn't hear. 'She could be up to mischief. One of those journalists who stir up dirt on the war.'

'Did she say why she wanted to find out who Dora was?' Pierre said.

'No. But she did say she thought she might have traced Dora. I want to be sure. Why upset him unless we know for certain?'

'We could have done Betsy some other time,' Pierre said. 'You could have pressed her.'

Joe shook his head. 'It's Betsy's time now. And the woman will be back. Are you ready?'

Pierre stood up. Geoffrey folded the newspaper and put it back on the dresser.

It had taken a dram or two to steel them up before, and a few more drams to soften them down after, for none of them, Joe thought, were natural slaughter men. It was past midnight by the time they'd cleaned up and Pierre had salted the hide ready to take to Docherty's haulage, *no questions asked*, and they'd polished off the last of the whiskey. Joe took Geoffrey up to bed, helped him undress and put on his pyjamas, made sure he'd been to the lavatory and his pot was under the bed. The old man needed to get up in the night and Joe didn't like him going down the stairs by himself, not with his dodgy leg and his poor eyesight.

'We'll be going to town tomorrow,' Joe said. 'You need new underpants, and a couple of shirts wouldn't go amiss.'

Geoffrey climbed into bed and pulled the blankets up to his chin. He was an easy man and never complained. Some men got difficult in their dotage, but not Geoffrey. Joe had looked after him for decades now and wasn't sure what he would do were Geoffrey to die tomorrow. He was fond of him, loved him even, though that could be misconstrued, he knew, and there were gossips in Gorey who eyed the pair of them with disgust.

'I'd like to see Dora again,' Geoffrey said. 'Before I die.' He reached for his hearing aid. He seemed far from sleepy and the drink had made him talkative. Joe had no idea that he'd really loved the nurse, and that made the matter a whole lot worse.

'Don't get your hopes up, old man,' Joe said. 'It may not be her.'

'And people change,' Geoffrey said.

'They do change, that's for sure.'

'I've thought about nothing else but her.'

'Sure you have,' Joe said. But Geoffrey had never shared this with Joe, until now. Joe had wondered, all those years ago in the war, whether the nurse had been his proper sweetheart but had put it out of his mind once the war was over. Joe reasoned that if they'd been sweethearts, Geoffrey would have said something. *It could all be part of his own imagining*, Joe told himself, and imagining had got him into no end of difficulty.

'So why did you never look for her?' Joe said.

Geoffrey squinted. 'What's that?'

He adjusted his hearing aid as Joe leaned forward and repeated himself loudly.

Geoffrey shook his head. 'I thought she was dead,' he said. 'I grieved for her. I *died* for her every day for forty years.' He pulled out his handkerchief and wiped his eyes. 'I didn't know where to begin then. The world was such a muddle in 1945 and I was broken.'

And all along Joe had had her details, without realising it.

'You see, Joe,' Geoffrey said, looking up at him with rheumy eyes. 'She was Jewish.'

Joe took a moment to absorb the news. He'd never imagined *that*. No wonder the old man was so excited by the prospect of Dora, for wasn't it a resurrection?

What could Joe tell Geoffrey now? It would have broken his heart.

Jersey: April – May 1943

'By the way,' Pierre said, not long after Joe had re-opened the boxing club. 'Do you want company on your birdwatching?'

'You?'

'No. A friend of mine would like to meet you. Bit lonely. Could do with getting out a bit.'

The one time Joe loved solitude was in the birdwatching, the stealth and silence of his footstep, the communion with the creatures, at one with them, in that moment. He'd focus his field glasses on the birds on the shoreline, his favourite. The red bills and legs of oyster catchers, listen, *squee, squee.* Or the laugh, soft at first, slow, working its way into a cackle, like two old biddies joking at some other's expense, then he'd spot the speckled plumage of the dunlins, and after, dancing into view, his favourite, the sandpipers, skittering across the sand, too fast to count, for all the world like a class of colleens doing a jig. If the boxing took the edge off his loneliness, the birds took the edge off his doubts. That was his cross. Doubts. In the shadow of the birds, he would weep, and feel better.

Company would shatter that. But he owed Pierre a favour, and he should be charitable. Besides, birds weren't to everyone's taste. Sitting, still as a stone, hours on end, for what? A rare glimpse, at the most. A chough, perhaps, *Pyrrhocorax*, red bill, red feet. Pierre's friend would soon get bored. *I'll give it a miss this week. Thank you all the same...*

'All right,' Joe said. 'But I'm busy, what with the boxing and all.'

'No rush,' Pierre said.

§

Pierre was already at the junction, with his friend.

A woman. Why had he assumed the friend would be a man? They had propped their bicycles against the wall, and stood gazing at the harbour, cigarette smoke unfurling from their cupped hands. Pierre had to charge Joe for cigarettes now, *supply and demand,* he'd said, *scarcity puts up the price.* He'd imported tobacco seeds from France, promised that, come the end of the summer, he'd have a home-grown crop, free of charge, for him.

'I can even get you a machine, if you want,' Pierre had said. 'So you can roll them, neat, like.'

Joe was tempted to turn back, but Pierre had seen him, was walking towards him. Joe ran his finger inside his dog collar.

There's no reason, he thought, on the face of it, why he shouldn't take a young lady birdwatching.

'Father O'Cleary,' Pierre held the handlebars steady while Joe scrambled off his bicycle. 'I want you to meet my friend, Gertrude.'

She stood beaming, brown hair in a short bob, plump, plain face and a round, buxom body. Joe recognised her. The nurse, from the boxing match. She held out her hand.

'Call me Trude,' she said. 'Like your Trudy, only spelt with an "e".'

She was German. Pierre hadn't told him *that* either.

'Thank you for taking me with you,' she went on. Her English was very good. 'I love nature. Birds. Wildlife.'

'Do you now,' Joe said. It wasn't a question. He'd never wanted company on his birdwatching trips, let alone from a woman, let alone a *German.*

'Well,' he said. 'I hope you can keep quiet.'

They ended up in the Vallée de St Pierre.

'Listen.' *Kweek-kweek-kweek, burru-burru-burru.* He handed her the binoculars. 'Ruddy breast, flash of white. Look, there he goes.'

Chaffinch.

'You see, Miss.' Joe wasn't about to be familiar and call her by her Christian name. Nor was he going to use *Fräulein.* 'Listen. That's why you can't make a sound. You need to *hear* before you look. Listen, look, the ornithologist's motto.'

'Am I making a noise?' she said.

'No.'

He pushed his way through some hawthorn. An angry screech, a flash of white and blue. Trude breathed in sharply.

'Beautiful,' she whispered.

'Don't be fooled,' Joe said. 'It's a jay. A crow in fancy dress.' He added, 'Do you not have these in Germany?'

She smiled. *She hasn't a clue,* Joe thought.

Trude was harmless enough. She didn't chatter, so when she asked to come again, Joe said yes. *She needn't come every week*, he reasoned. He could be selective with the invitations. Besides, he enjoyed sharing his knowledge with her. It was the one thing he was sure about.

Trude had the makings of a fine ornithologist, Joe finally had to admit, watching her as she squatted motionless, field glasses trailing a distant fluttering form. Hours together, with scarcely a word between them except to identify a bird call or a sighting, jotting down in their notebooks the ordinary birds, *Phasianus colchicus*, and the rare, *Pernis apivorus*. It was companionable, in its way. Perhaps, Joe thought, this was what friendship with a woman was about.

'You must know the island well,' she said.

'I get around,' Joe said.

'And where's the best place for birds?'

'Well, now.' Joe hesitated. 'That depends on the time of year. And what kind of birds you're interested in.'

'Let's say seabirds?'

'Well, seabirds,' Joe said. He stared into the distance. 'The north is good in spring. The east in autumn. The south and west, all year.'

'Ah,' she said. 'Perhaps this autumn we should go east. What kind of birds would we see?'

'Gulls,' Joe said. 'Auks. Divers.' He could head for St Catherine's.

'Listen. Look,' she said. 'Is that what you do with people too?'

'Sometimes,' he said.

'You must know a lot, then.' She laughed, sweet as a song thrush.

'And you,' she said to him one day as they cycled back. 'A boxing champion.'

'Well,' Joe said. 'It was a long time ago now.'

'Why did you stop?'

'I had to choose,' Joe said. 'Boxing or the priesthood.'

'Why a priest?' Trude went on.

Joe slowed down, back-pedalled, toes on the ground. 'I had a calling,' he said.

Trude looked puzzled.

'This was God's plan for me and I felt it keenly.'

'Don't you want to marry?' she said.

'Why should I marry?'

'You're a man.'

'The Church is my bride,' Joe said. He'd never thought of himself in *that* way. 'That's more than enough for one man.'

'You've never made love with a woman, have you, Father?'

He could feel the heat rise, his neck and face sting with embarrassment. That she should even *say* such a thing. He looked at her, at her round face and round eyes. Not a trace of guile.

'Unmarried,' Joe swallowed. 'Unmarried, I can love everyone. I don't suppose you could understand.'

She shrugged, pedalled away. He followed her. They parted at the parade ground.

§

Joe hadn't taken Trude to La Ferme de l'Anse. That was his special spot, his private hide. He came there once a week, on a Wednesday, and he hadn't thought of sharing it. But that week he'd had to miss a Wednesday so decided to take Trude there on their Monday excursion. An exception.

'A rare treat,' he said as they let themselves in to Geoffrey's field. It had been sown with winter oats, and now the shoots were growing thick and lush.

'Walk between the rows,' he said. He led her through the field into the small dell that gave them the best view of the shoreline and the wooded hills that surrounded it. Sea, shore and spinney.

'This place has it all,' Joe said. 'It's very special.'

'All year?'

'All year.'

'I like it,' Trude said. When Trude smiled, her face melted into a sunbeam. She held her binoculars, trained them on the wood, edged her feet round, one by one, until she faced the sea. 'I agree. It is very special.'

Listen and look. Note well. *Whoohohoho*, the ghostly haunting call of an Arctic loon, *Gavia arctica,* the flat, dead chatter of the fulmar.

'*Fulmarus glacialis*,' Joe said. 'They mate for life.'

She wore woollen fingerless gloves but her hands looked cold. Joe had an urge to hold them, rub them tight to warm them through.

'I like that,' Trude said. 'Being faithful.'

'Yes,' Joe said. 'Yes. To be faithful. It's a great virtue.'

She turned towards him, her eyes golden in the daylight, and he had a vision of her turning those eyes to other men. The sharp, sudden pain of that took him by surprise.

'Do you have a sweetheart, Trude?' He couldn't stop himself. He had to know. It was the first time he'd called her Trude and he could feel the red-hot burn of a blush.

'No,' she said.

'You're an attractive woman,' Joe pressed.

She shook her head. 'There are women who go with any man,' she said. 'But not me. If I have a sweetheart, it will be forever. Why do you ask?'

'I know very little about you,' Joe said. 'Who you are. Where you come from.'

'There is little to know.' She trained her eyes on his and pouted her lips. Joe had an urge to kiss her but knew it wasn't priestly. 'I am a simple girl from the country. One day I would like to marry.'

He could feel the suspense building within him. 'And have you met the man yet?'

'Perhaps,' she said.

Was she teasing him? She said she didn't have a sweetheart.

'And could you share that with me now?'

She smiled, tapped his nose with her forefinger. 'Perhaps,' she said. 'One day.'

Trude turned and trained her glasses on the spinney by the house. 'Are there woodpeckers, do you think?'

'I would think so,' Joe said. 'The great spotted. But you won't see them from here. We'd need to get into the trees for that.'

'Oh,' she said. 'And do they mate for life?'

'Well, now,' Joe said, 'I believe they do. But the male does the hard work of digging out the nest.'

'Like us.' Trude laughed. 'Tell me, Father. Do men and women come to you for help?'

'I suppose,' Joe said. 'It's all part of the job.'

'But if they want advice, say, on their marriage, how could you give it to them? Without knowing it yourself?'

'Well,' Joe said. 'You don't need to touch fire, to know it's hot.'

'But do they tell you things?' Trude said. 'In the confession.'

'Oh yes,' Joe said. 'They tell me all sorts.'

'Like what?'

'Now I can't tell you that.'

'But aren't you ever curious?' Trude went on.

'About what?'

Trude looked at him with clear brown eyes. 'About love.'

'Oh no,' he said quickly. 'We know what the sacrament of marriage entails.'

Trude raised her eyebrow. 'Really?'

This was not a suitable conversation, not for a priest. Too close to the bone, too familiar. Trude was straightforward, in a modern, German way. Why ask him at all?

'What about other things?' she said.

'Such as?'

'I don't know. About the war. Us Germans.'

Joe wasn't sure how to answer that. Another forthright question. He thought for a moment.

'People grumble,' he said. 'Of course they do. It's not easy, for anyone.' Apart from his friend Pierre, but Pierre was a law unto himself.

'But if there's anything *in particular*,' she said. 'Let me know. I'll see what I can do to help.'

'Well,' Joe said. 'You can't say fairer than that.'

He levelled his field glasses towards the spinney. Nobody had ever been curious about him, asked him what *he* thought. Trude was the first. Question after question. No one had ever really gone out of their way to be his friend before. Intimate. He didn't bare his soul to Pierre, not in the way it seemed he could do with Trude. He liked that. It broke his isolation. There was nothing wrong with that. Maybe she understood him.

It was difficult to tell how old she was. She had a face that would look the same at twenty as at fifty. Plain as a pavement. Round as a muffin. But her skin was unlined and her hands were young. Clean hands, unchafed. Most of the women he knew from home had raw, chapped hands, coarsened by the soil or the washtub. Hers were smooth and small. She had fine bones, vulnerable in their film of skin and dimpled flesh. 'Stout' was the word his mother would have used. Joe preferred chubby, *a little chubby*.

'Actually,' he said. 'There is something you can do.' One of the nuns was a diabetic but they were running out of insulin. 'You're a nurse, aren't you?'

'Yes,' she said. 'You know I am. Why?'

Nothing ventured, nothing gained. His mouth was dry, so he licked his lip, swallowed. 'Could you see your way round to letting me have a phial or two of insulin?'

Trude frowned. 'You know I can't do that,' she said. She was wearing slacks, the colour of acorns. She ran her hands down the creases, smiled. 'But I'll see what I can do. On one condition. Will you bring me here again?'

Joe hadn't thought about sharing this, but Trude was so enchanted by it.

'Perhaps,' he said.

'This will be our special place, for the birds,' she said. 'And no one else. Do you ever come at night?'

'Well, no.' Joe was surprised she had asked. 'We're bound by the curfew.'

'I forgot,' she said. 'Silly me. But I'm not. I could come. Look for nightjars.'

Joe laughed. 'You'd be lucky to see one of those.'

'I could try. Tell you all about it. Would you mind?'

Well, Joe thought, put like that, it would be churlish to say no.

§

Every time they met it was like the first day. A smile dancing on her lips as if she was pleased to see him. Joe could just make it out. He wanted to place his finger under her chin, lift up her face, *look at me.* He was pleased to see her too, though that surprised him. Shocked him. He thought about her when she wasn't there, talked to her in his head. She was a devilment that had entered into his soul and he should cast her behind him. But he was weak, he knew that now. And was it so sinful, to have a friend?

'Where shall we go?' he said.

'I don't mind. No. I do. Our special place.'

'What shall we look for?'

'I don't mind.'

Joe felt himself blush, a sticky pink heat churning through his cheeks. It was all too much, as if he was walking into the sea, with cross-currents and rip tides tugging and pulling. He was out of his depth. But he couldn't pull back to shore, not now.

'I can't stay long,' she said that day.

'Then we won't go far.'

He pushed away on his too-big bike. Perhaps they'd see some swallows. Or swifts. Migrate in the winter, return in the summer. Perhaps Trude was like a migratory bird, going home to nest.

'A swift,' he said. 'Listen.'

Soft, high trill, like a chorus, all together. Black against the sky.

'I thought it was a swallow,' Trude said.

Joe shook his head. 'A swallow, now. They *natter*, like a couple of biddies, with their pale breasts and red throats. You can't mistake them.'

He watched as she trained her ear, head on the side, then lifted the glasses and focused on the flock.

'Remarkable birds,' he went on. 'They eat and drink and sleep on the wing.'

He followed her gaze. For all the world, they looked like a squadron of fighter planes in formation.

And for all the world, he should not be feeling like this, because now he wondered if he wasn't falling for her. Or she him. No *girl* had ever fallen for him.

He should stop seeing her. But what could he tell her? *It's best we don't see each other again.* He couldn't tell her the truth. *I am falling in love.* And what was wrong with a priest in love? He wasn't being unfaithful, not to his calling. Infidelity meant carnal knowledge, that's what they taught in the seminary. He wondered whether Trude wasn't right: what would a priest know about love, what could they advise? Wondered too, whether, in a roundabout way, she was testing him, do you have a sweetheart, Father?

§

Birch and hawthorn were floating green, and the earth shimmered with the sapphire of bluebells and forget-me-nots. Joe spent his regular Monday afternoons with Trude and his solitary Wednesdays cycling over to Anse la Coupe.

The weather was warm at the very end of May, the ground dry enough to sit on. Trude said she couldn't meet him anymore on Mondays.

'Then Wednesdays,' he said. 'We'll go to the dell.'

'Our special place.'

'Oh, that it is,' Joe said.

They pedalled to the bay, he on his bike with the *clickety* spoke, she on her lady's bicycle with the basket on the front, rubber tyres and a pump clamped to the down tube. It was a miracle it hadn't been stolen.

He nodded to the red-headed nurse they passed as they free-wheeled down the hill.

'Who was that?' Trude said.

'I don't know her name,' Joe said. 'But I see her here every Wednesday.'

'Why does she come here?'

They had reached level ground and rode side by side. Geoffrey was the only one who lived at the end of that lane.

'How would I know? Perhaps she has a sweetheart at the farm.'

Just like old Aiden Docherty at home. Not even the match-maker could find *him* a wife, until the nurse came visiting. She was young, too. And a redhead, if he wasn't mistaken.

He looked over at Trude and smiled, but she didn't see him glance. She was focused on the road ahead, as pretty as a posy in her soft poppy-print dress.

Joe opened the gate to the field and they filed in, propping the bikes against the hedge. They walked along the rows of waist-high oats, swathes of soft, dark-green fronds, through which the tips of pale golden heads could be glimpsed. But Geoffrey had not sown the dell with oats and it was neglected. Cowbane and ragwort were pushing up through the rough grass and a small oak had self-seeded. It took years to build a pasture, Joe knew. It must have broken Geoffrey's heart to plough it up for oats. German orders. Geoffrey would have his time cut out returning this to grazing land. He felt a spit of anger at the waste of a good meadow, as he observed Trude shaking a blanket free of its folds. *She has nothing to do with this*, he told himself. The blanket billowed to the ground, grey regulation-issue, borrowed from the German hospital. Had she asked permission? He liked the thought that she had smuggled it out.

She sat down, pulling her skirt over her knees, and patted the space next to her.

'If we sit,' Joe said, 'we won't be able to see.'

'Perhaps we can look at the voles and mouses.'

'Mice,' Joe said. He crossed his legs, pivoted and sat in a single movement.

'That's clever,' she said. She lay back, stretched out with her left arm above her head. Her skirt had risen up her leg and fell in folds over her knees, and through the opening in her sleeve Joe could see a faint tangle of brown hair under her arm. He looked away.

'Lie beside me,' she said.

Joe blushed, coughed. 'I'm not sure that would be right,' he said.

'What harm does it do?'

What harm indeed? Was it wrong to lie down next to a woman? Father Ciarán had railed against the temptations of Eve. But what right did Father Ciarán have to say such things?

Joe stretched out alongside her, one arm supporting his head. He was aware of her next to him, of her short, plump body rising and falling as she breathed. He had an urge to reach over, stroke her, tell her it was all right, tell *himself* it was all right. He walked his fingers towards her and met her fingers as they crept towards him, and they lay, hand in hand. He had never been so happy.

'I like you,' she said. She had stopped calling him Father.

'I like you too, well enough,' he said. He wanted to say, *I love you,* thought that wouldn't be right, him a priest, and maybe a sinner now, too.

'Have you ever touched a woman?'

'No,' Joe said, added, 'apart from my sisters and my mother.'

'They don't count,' she said. 'Has a woman ever touched you?'

'No.'

He wanted her to touch him. He was on a helter-skelter, hurtling round and round.

'Are you frightened?'

'Yes,' he said. That was an easy answer.

'What is there to be frightened of?'

The jangle of his feelings, his tingling flesh. A woman.

'You're a good-looking man.' She laughed. 'Almost pretty.'

Joe shut his eyes. He'd never told a soul, never breathed a word of it, only to his *daidí*, that once, and never again. *You're a pretty boy, Joe.*

'Did I say something wrong?' Trude said.

Joe shook his head. Dared not open his eyes. He was weeping, the moisture trickling down his cheek, his lips puckering like a little boy's.

She was leaning over him. He could feel her warmth, the brush of her blouse. 'Tell me,' she said. 'What's troubling you?'

Not even in confession had he said a word, *bless me, Father, for I have sinned.* A grievous sin, but he couldn't *name* it, could only touch its carnal agony. He could feel a gathering force, as if Trude's soft words had lanced the boil and the pus would erupt in an unstoppable flow. He should get up, leave, have nothing more to do with her, but the pain was too abrupt, too deep.

'You can trust me,' she said. 'What's the matter?'

He wasn't sure he had the words, nor could face the disgrace. The mortification of it. Not to Trude, not to anyone. He'd done a wicked thing.

'I don't think I can tell you.' It sat on his conscience, an abyss of misery, his personal hell. He had no right to burden Trude with the truth.

'You can try,' she said.

For her sake, he had to bear it. She was not a worldly woman, he could tell by the angelic purity of her face. It would destroy her. And wasn't it his duty to protect her from such things?

'What do the English say? A problem shared is a problem halved.'

Could he make a clean breast of it? Would she even comprehend what he was telling her? What did she know of such obscenities?

Yet he wanted to spill it out, lighten the load. Perhaps she wouldn't blame him. Perhaps a woman would understand, in ways that his own *daidí* couldn't. Could he tell her without sullying her beauty, destroying her innocence? Without ruining this tender union they had? What would she make of him?

'You'll think the worst of me,' he said.

'Why would I do that?'

Because of the nature of sin, Joe thought.

He leant up on his elbow. Her face was close to his. She smiled.

'I will never think the worst of you.' She ran her finger across her throat. 'I promise,' she said. '*Ich schwöre bei meinem Leben.* On my life.'

The sunlight brought out the colour of her eyes, flecks of green and gold, the light down on her skin.

'Will you lie back the way you were,' Joe said. He didn't want her to see his face, couldn't bear her to see his shame. He didn't know how to start. Or where. With the gates of St Xavier's? The loneliness of the dormitory?

'I was only young,' he began. Searching for the words. 'And small. For my age. And there was this priest, Father Ciarán–' A clumsy man, with an over-ripe face and a dirty cassock. 'He asked me to pray with him in his cell, after the others had gone to sleep.'

Joe could feel the tap on his shoulder as he lay under the blankets, the soft, *Follow me, Joe.*

'Then, one night–' Joe's breath came and went in short, shallow puffs. 'He took off his clothes.' His voice was cracking and he swallowed hard to make it whole again. 'He made me take off mine.'

Trude lay beside him. She didn't move, though he could hear her silent breaths.

'I was a child.' Tears had welled up, were rolling down his cheeks. 'What did I know?'

He paused, sniffed. Trude on her back, eyes gazing at the clear blue sky. 'Go on,' she said. Her voice soft and gentle. 'Did you think it strange?'

'I thought people would laugh at me if I said anything.'

He wiped his eye. Trude wasn't laughing. She was listening, giving him strength to go on.

'One night, he grabbed my wrist and clamped my palm over his–' he swallowed, put a hand to his face, thumb and finger pressing into his eyes. He couldn't say the word, not to Trude. He whispered, hoped she couldn't hear. 'Down there.'

Goosebumps rippled over his skin. 'Father Ciarán called it his special–' He stopped. Sobbed. 'His special grace.'

'You were very innocent,' Trude said.

Joe wasn't sure if she was smiling. 'I was,' he said. 'That's the truth.' He reached out for Trude's hand once more, as if holding it could earth him, deflect the pain, drive it into the ground.

'And was that the end?' Trude said.

'No,' Joe said. 'No, it wasn't.'

He began to cry, man-size sobs that wracked his slender body. He *couldn't* say what happened. What words to use? What order did the pain come in? The shame?

'I understand,' she said. She leaned over, stroked her fingers across his face. 'You poor thing.'

'I was a child.'

I am a child. Frightened and confused. Fresh and raw, as if it happened yesterday. Lying in bed with the corner of the pillow stuffed in his mouth so no one would hear his screams. Alone.

'Homosexuals.' She spat the word out.

Joe had never known Trude angry, and he didn't want to hear it now. He wanted to curl up and be held, rocked to sleep, an innocent, *there, there.* Fourteen years old. Small for his age.

He hated himself, for what Father Ciarán had done to him. He'd wanted to punish himself, slam his fist against a treetrunk, his head against a wall. A *hard* pain that helped drive away the other, the soft, agonising ulcer inside him.

He took up boxing. He didn't say why.

'You'll have your nose broke,' his mother wrote at the time. 'Cauliflower ears.' It would be a fitting punishment. He had sinned, had made himself unworthy of all grace. His sin, his *secret,* had cut him off from love and trust.

He thought the other boys went through this and it hadn't worried them. He thought he'd have to grow up, get over it, like they had. He wanted to hit Father Ciarán so hard his teeth would clatter across the floor like dice. *Fight with your brains*, the first rule of boxing. Joe had raised his fists at the priest, had glowered at him, saw the beads of sweat breaking out on his nose, the broken veins in his cheeks.

'We lock them up,' Trude was saying. 'Degenerates.'

He was just a man. A pitiful coward.

'What happened to that priest?'

Boxing filled his mind and dulled the pain.

'Was he punished?'

Joe looked up at Trude. She was smiling, tender, and he was here, with her. A pitiful boy.

'What's that you said?'

'What happened to him?'

'Nothing,' Joe said.

'And you never told a soul?'

'Who would believe me?' Joe said. His own *daidí* didn't, had floored Joe instead. 'He was a priest. Like God himself.' He lay still on the blanket, blinking at the sun in his eyes, listening to Trude's gentle breath and the rustle of the breeze in the fronds. 'Boxing saved me,' he said, though his voice was low. 'And the birds. Deadened the pain. Lifted me above it.'

Trude reached over again and trailed her fingers on his lips. 'Do you like me to touch you?'

Light and soft. Enough to break Joe from his thoughts. He should push her fingers away, get up and leave. This could cost him his immortal soul. But Trude understood him, shared his secret now, carried his pain too. She must love him, and wasn't that what it was all about? Could a priest not love?

She leaned close. Sitting in the dell, smothered by the emptiness of the sky, Joe didn't know how it happened, but there was her tongue, and his. She was on top of him now, her cotton dress up around her waist as she opened the buttons on his trousers with clumsy hands and sticky fingers.

He was shaking, soft as jelly. Had never experienced such a grand sensation before. Had they made love? It didn't seem like such a sin. It had all happened so fast. She lay on him, and he coupled his arms around her, held her close. Grafted together.

'Are you happy, Joe?' She had never called him Joe before. It was a new step, a new era.

'Troubled.' His vows lay in tatters. 'This can't go on.' He wanted to say, *Will you marry me, Trude?* Were they not as one now, in holy union? Forever.

'Troubled?'

He'd have to leave the priesthood. Muster the courage. Get a job. Give her a home.

'I have made you whole again,' she said. 'A proper man.' She rolled away, lay on her side, one arm over his waist. 'That must be good.'

A proper man? Was that a dreadful thing? Was that what he needed, to drive it all out?

'What if you are pregnant?' Joe hadn't thought of that, not when it was happening.

'Don't worry.'

'No?' Joe said.

'Oh Father O'Cleary,' she was laughing. 'You know nothing.'

She pushed herself away from him, stood and held out her hands to pull him up. 'I have to go. Thank you, Joe.'

She kissed him on the lips. Bent down, picked up the blanket, shook it free of earth and grass and folded it with the deft movements of a practised nurse.

'Can't you stay?' She was the only person he had ever told his secret to and he wanted her to be with him until it settled down and was back in its place. She was the only person he had ever truly loved, been close to. The only woman he had kissed, caressed, done *this* with, had intimacy with.

But she was shaking her head. 'I have to get back,' she said. 'It's best we aren't seen together.'

'Why?' he said. 'Why *now*?' They'd cycled freely together before.

Trude hesitated. 'I found a note, in my basket,' she said. 'It made fun of Hitler. It was signed "the soldier with no name".' She pulled a face. 'Don't you see?'

'No,' Joe said. 'I don't, I'm afraid.'

'If they see me with you, they may think it was you who put it there.'

Joe didn't understand the logic of that, but it was a reminder. They were at war.

'Stay here,' Trude said. 'Give me half an hour, to get away.'

He watched as she weaved her way through the oats, a small podgy figure in a poppy dress with short brown hair. He felt a surge of sadness, as if his skin had been peeled back, exposing him, defenceless, to the world. He started to run. He had to talk to her.

'Trude!'

She dropped out of view, and he heard the gate shut.

'Trude.' He sat down in the field, held his knees tight close to his chin, rocked from side to side. He shut his eyes, the poppies of her dress floating around him like petals on the feast of the Visitation. He knew he would have to choose. *Please God*, he found himself saying, *let me be wise and brave.*

CHAPTER NINE

DORA

London: June 1985

Half of her wanted nothing to do with Barbara Hummel again. The other half wanted to know who she was, how she'd come by the photos, what she wanted with Dora. The meeting in the café by the British Museum had churned up memories, even though she hadn't told Barbara a thing, and they hissed and squirmed like the serpent himself, tempting her to find out more, *your eyes shall be opened and ye shall be as gods, knowing good and evil.*

She didn't have the woman's address. Well, Dora reasoned, if she makes contact again, then she might agree to see her. If not, so be it. At least now she was aware, and if the woman *was* a con artist, she'd be on her guard. She couldn't sleep. She'd taken to double-checking the lock on the doors again before she went to bed, lay counting the hours, her head swimming and sweating. *Don't fight insomnia, Doralein.* She could hear Uncle Otto's voice as he soothed her each night in those early days. *It fights back.* She'd had to go to the doctor. They didn't give out barbiturates anymore. There was this new stuff, Valium. The demons only came at night, she said, and she needed to be in a deep, dreamless sleep when they visited.

A letter came two weeks later.

I am so sorry if my questions disturbed you and I won't bother you again. If, however, you change your mind, and wish to get in touch with me I am staying with friends in Richmond and can be contacted at the above address and telephone number. I will be in the United Kingdom for the summer, on and off, travelling mainly between London and Jersey.

Dora rang the number after breakfast.

§

Barbara Hummel was standing on the doorstep holding a large bunch of lilies in one hand and a carrier bag in the other. It was a hot June day and the sun was high in a cloudless sky. Dora felt better disposed towards her, now she was meeting her on her own terms. She was good-looking, Dora could see that. Tall and dark-haired with a smooth, freckled skin, elegant in a simple white dress with a mandarin collar, and blue sandals, nails painted a deep, dark red. Dora envied her that. Gardening put paid to any notions of a manicure. Or a pedicure, come to think of it.

'Thank you,' Dora said, taking the flowers, beckoning Barbara in and closing the door behind her.

'I thought you would also like this.' Barbara handed her the bag.

Dora peered inside. White asparagus. She breathed in, a sharp, excited *hah.* She hadn't tasted white asparagus since before the war. 'Thank you,' Dora said. 'Let me take it to the kitchen. Come, follow me.'

She had knocked through the front and rear rooms after Uncle Otto died, made a new kitchen at the back overlooking her garden. She placed the asparagus on the draining board and reached for a vase, putting it in the sink and turning on the water.

'May I ask you a personal question?' Barbara Hummel said. 'Are you German, by any chance?'

Dora pulled the lower leaves off the lilies. 'Why do you think that?' she said. 'Is it relevant?'

They were getting off to a bad start again, as if those memory demons were sitting on her shoulder egging her on. *Be nasty, make her unwelcome.* Dora took a breath. No need to answer the question.

'I heard your accent–' said Barbara.

'I didn't think I had an accent anymore,' Dora said.

'It takes a German to know a German. When was the last time you spoke your own language?'

'English is my own language now.' She lived in English, thought and dreamed in it. 'I haven't spoken German for many years.' Not since before the war, apart from the odd endearment with Uncle Otto and the occasional phrase with Charles. 'Maybe I have forgotten I used to be German.' She tried to smile.

'Then we'll speak in English. I'm a translator. Pretty much bilingual.'

Dora nodded. She didn't care what this Barbara woman did for a living but understood she was trying to make Dora relaxed. *Start again.*

'Thank you for the asparagus,' she said. '*Der Spargel.* I haven't had that since I was a child. I shall look forward to it.' She placed the lilies in the vase and held it to her. 'My father and I would make a meal of asparagus when it was in season. With melted butter and salt and pepper. New potatoes.'

'Nice food memories,' Barbara said. 'Like Proust.'

'My father used to say it was the food of angels.' Stick with food, Dora thought, it's neutral, safe.

'My mother said something similar,' Barbara said.

'Was she nice, your mother?'

Barbara's smile faded and it was a while before she spoke again. *Says it all,* Dora thought. She had touched a nerve.

'To be honest,' Barbara said, 'I didn't get on with her. I couldn't wait to leave home. Perhaps that's why I studied languages, to be sure of getting away. What about your mother?'

'I never knew her,' Dora said. 'She died when I was born. My father mothered me, and I adored him.'

'You're lucky,' Barbara said.

'I think so,' Dora said. How had they moved to sharing such intimacies? She nodded towards the asparagus. 'You can't buy this in England. Only the insipid green varieties that the English prefer. Where did you find it?'

'My friend teaches at the German School in Richmond,' Barbara said. She said it in German, *Deutsche Schule*. 'Her mother lives in Hanover and brought some over.'

Dora entered the sitting room and put the vase on the coffee table. She indicated the sofa, *Please make yourself comfortable,* and sat in the chair opposite, the one she used every evening to read or watch television. The sun showed up the motes of dust in the air. The armrests, Dora noted, were grubby.

'And you?' Dora said. 'Where were you brought up?'

'In Hamburg,' Barbara said.

'That was bombed, was it not? Like London.'

Barbara nodded. There was a stiffening in the atmosphere. Uncle Otto had a friend, a German like himself, Jewish, a businessman, who'd returned to Germany after the war, working for the British, taking stock of the industry that had survived. They'd listened to his stories, the flattening of Hamburg.

'What was it like?' Dora said. 'Growing up there after the war?'

Barbara laughed. 'I didn't know any different,' she said. 'We played in the bombsites, can you believe? We were told not to pick up anything metal. I was a sickly baby, my mother said. She said she couldn't feed me properly, I didn't thrive. She sold a silver bangle to pay for photos of me, in case I didn't make it, so she could remember me.' Her face grew serious and she paused, running her finger in the seam of the piping of the armrest. Dora was about to ask her to stop doing that, when Barbara looked up and began again.

'We didn't always have enough to eat,' she went on. 'So I was often hungry. I shared my mother's bed for years, and we shared an apartment with another family. I was about seven when we got our own place. That's when I started school. The afternoon shift. It fitted with my mother's work. My mother talked about the bombing, but of course, I don't remember that. I wasn't born. Why do you ask?' She paused. 'You never went back to Germany after the war?'

There was no guile in Barbara's face. Of course. She assumed Dora had been in Jersey with the occupiers, that she was German. She could lie again. *Actually, I'm Swedish.* She didn't have the energy. And why? She wouldn't fool Barbara.

'No,' Dora said. She would give nothing away. 'I chose to stay.' She pulled the cushion from behind her, pummelled the feather stuffing into shape, tucked it into the small of her back.

'This is a nice room,' Barbara said.

'It has memories.'

Uncle Otto's old medical books were still on the bookshelves, his Kienzle clock on the mantelpiece. He'd only brought what he could carry with him when he left Germany and although the clock no longer worked, it was a reminder of his house in Dresden, along with the Bauhaus rug which he'd rolled up and carried under his arm. Of course, Barbara would be noting all of it.

'Tell me,' Dora said. 'Why were you so anxious to meet me? You've gone to a lot of trouble.'

'After my mother died,' Barbara said, 'I found the photographs. I didn't know why she had never shown me them. She never talked about the war.'

'Perhaps that's why,' Dora said. 'It was difficult, for that generation.'

'Perhaps,' Barbara said. 'But it set me thinking. I knew my mother had been a nurse in the war. She told me she never left Germany. Seeing those photographs, taken in Jersey, made me curious. Then suspicious.' She paused, added, 'I think she lied.'

Dora wished she'd listened to her cautious half, *have nothing to do with this woman again.* Barbara was rubbing memories, stirring their genie, and they were rushing out too fast.

'So I went there, to try and find out,' Barbara was saying. 'Silly, I know. But it mattered to me in a way I can't explain. I'm sorry.' She sniffed, delved into her handbag for a tissue. She is persistent, Dora thought, consistent too. But she was warming to this younger woman, less inclined to think ill of her.

'It would be provocative to have put the photo of the *SS* officer in the paper,' Barbara went on. 'But the photograph I showed you was of a woman not in uniform. It wasn't obvious that she was German. Of course, she could have been someone's wife or mistress, but I thought I'd risk it. When I heard you were a nurse too, I wondered if perhaps you knew my mother, or recognised the woman, or the officer. Especially after I heard your accent.'

Dora smiled, tempted to say, *I was on the British side, not the Germans. No,* she told herself, *keep your counsel, for the time being.*

'I believe my mother was in Jersey during the war,' Barbara went on. 'I just don't understand why she lied to me.'

She wasn't the first German to lie after the war, Dora thought.

'May I show you one more photograph, please?' She produced an envelope from her bag and passed it to Dora.

'I need my glasses,' Dora said. She could feel the blood draining from her face. Fight or flight. She knew she didn't want to see this new photograph. 'And light.' She took the picture to the kitchen window and stood with her back to Barbara.

Nurse Hoffmann, in the uniform of the *Deutsches Rotes Kreuz*, the German Red Cross, arm in arm with Maximilian List. Dora put her hands to her mouth, stifled a cry. Had she given herself away?

Dora didn't hear Barbara walk up behind her and jumped as Barbara placed her hand on Dora's arm.

'I am sorry,' she said. 'I didn't mean to startle you. Do you know her?'

Dora stared at the photo again. *Compose yourself.* 'No,' she said.

'Are you sure?'

Dora shrugged. 'I *may* have seen her. In a general way. You know, out and about. We'd often see German nurses in their uniforms. But I didn't *know* her.'

Barbara took the photograph from Dora and studied it. 'You see, this woman was my mother.'

'Your *mother*?' Dora had no idea what to say. She thought she'd heard the last of Hoffmann long ago, and now her *daughter* was standing in front of her. Barbara didn't look anything like her mother, that was for sure. A relief, too.

'I believe the man is Maximilian List,' Barbara said.

Dora swallowed. 'And why did you think I may know him?'

'Just because your photo and his, the studio shot of him, were together, in that box. You know,' Barbara said. She leaned forward, narrowed her eyes. 'I'm not really interested in you. I should have made that clear. But I am interested in him.'

'Why?' Dora said. She didn't want to know or be reminded of that man, but she needed time to think. She walked back into the sitting room and Barbara followed, sitting on the sofa with her, sideways on. Her face looked different from this angle, oblique, *like an Auerbach painting*, Dora thought.

'He was in the *SS*,' Barbara was saying. 'He was the commandant of Lager Sylt, on Alderney, the concentration camp.' She paused. Dora knew she was studying her closely. 'Sylt was a subsidiary of Neuengamme, and he'd been a captain there.'

'But if you know who he is, what more do you want to know from me?'

Barbara paused, shifted on the sofa, tucking down her skirt as she did so. 'I think he may be my father.'

Dora looked away, stood up. 'Let me make some coffee.' She walked into the kitchen. 'How could I help you answer that?' she said, over her shoulder, filling the kettle, hands shaking as she rummaged for the coffee in the cupboard to the left of the sink. 'Wouldn't your mother know?'

'I can't ask her now,' Barbara said. Her mother was dead, of course. That was a tactless thing to say. Still, Dora thought, good riddance.

'My mother said my father had been killed in the war,' Barbara said. 'She said he was in the *Wehrmacht*, a foot soldier, caught up in it all. Never a Nazi.' She paused, and Dora saw her smile. 'There were never any Nazis in Germany, not after the war.'

Barbara took a deep breath, got up from the sofa and followed Dora into the kitchen.

'My father's name was Detlef Hummel,' she said.' I never questioned her. It had been a whirlwind romance, my mother said. That sort of thing happened in the war. She was widowed before I was even born.'

'But you saw photographs of him?' Dora said. 'Surely?'

'She had no photos. She said they were lost in the turmoil.'

'Does he not have family?'

'They live behind the Iron Curtain. We couldn't visit, couldn't write. Still can't. I accepted that.'

'That all sounds very possible,' Dora said. 'Why do you doubt it?'

'Woman's intuition.' Barbara leaned on the sink, looked out of the window. 'You have a beautiful garden,' she said. 'Do you do it all yourself?'

'Yes,' Dora said. 'It's hard work.'

'I'd love a garden. But I live in an apartment. I can only admire from afar, sow seeds in my head.'

'You could have a window box.'

'I do. And houseplants. But it's not the same.' She turned round and smiled. 'I envy you.'

'Why do you think this man was your father?' Dora pointed to the photograph.

'I think List and my mother were lovers,' Barbara said. 'She looks happy here. But she was never a happy woman, as I knew her. She kept his picture, despite the war, but did not keep my father's. And there is a date, here.' She turned the photograph over. 'Christmas, 1943. She must have been pregnant.'

'Perhaps she was already a widow.'

Barbara shook her head. 'There is no marriage certificate.'

'Perhaps there was no wedding. You said yourself you didn't need to be married to have a child.'

Barbara leaned forward, hunched her shoulders. 'It's crazy, I know. I just have this feeling. I never felt at home with my mother. We didn't get on.'

'What happened to this Maximilian List?' Dora said, hoping Barbara did not hear the quiver in her voice.

'He's still alive,' Barbara said.

Dora felt dizzy and clutched the side of the sink for balance.

'He lives in Hamburg,' Barbara went on. 'That's the irony. I could have met him at any time. Perhaps I did, and never knew it. As a matter of fact, I have to go back to Hamburg next week, on business.' She smiled. 'So much for my holiday, but I work freelance, and you can't turn down work.'

'Will you visit him?' Dora said. Willed Barbara to say, *No, I'll leave it at that.*

'Perhaps.'

'You're good at turning up unannounced,' Dora said, and smiled though her heart was beating as fast as a baby's and she could feel the blood flooding to her hands and feet. 'Springing surprises. Like your mother.'

'Like my mother?'

'Yes.' Dora thought fast. 'With her box of memories. What else did she have in there?'

'Not much,' Barbara said. 'A newspaper clipping of a boxing match between a priest called Father Joseph O'Cleary and the *Wehrmacht* champion.'

'This Joseph O'Cleary who told you about me? Who lives at the farm?'

'I think so. I shall ask him if he knows my mother.'

'Anything else there?'

'A beer mat. A pressed flower. A bird's feather. Bits and bobs. Nothing of interest. Why did you ask?'

'Just in case,' Dora said. 'Just in case.'

Jersey: May – June 1943

The trees fizzed with green and dog roses coated the woodlands. Dora cycled down the hill to Geoffrey's farm, feet off the pedals and her legs splayed out, with the breeze in her hair and the soft kiss of the day's warmth. She looked over the cliff to the sea beyond, at the white tufts and crests of the waves that churned beige and grey on a cloudy day, to the sapphire and emerald and turquoise that shimmered when the skies were cobalt, the sun high and the breezes becalmed. She pretended not to see the rolls of razor wire on the beach.

Some days, when Dora thought she wouldn't get pregnant, they made love in the afternoon, his eyes as soft and creamy as the surf below. Lying spooned in the late sun, his arms holding her tight, she felt his breath mingle with her own, his muscles tighten against hers, his skin and hers, smooth together. Those days, she forgot.

Other times, she'd crouch beside a gaunt and wasted figure and lance an abscess, or wash a wound, hand on a brow, *there, there,* as the planes droned overhead, or dynamite thundered in the tunnels and the ground vibrated.

It was Wednesday in late June. It was a long haul up the Grande Route de Rozel, feet pressing hard on the pedals and the makeshift rubber hose tyres sticking to the road. Dora was hot and thirsty when she arrived. The iron shoe-scraper was to the left of the front door, their signal that someone else was inside, and the front door was locked. Dora made sure no one had followed her, walked to the back of the house, fished the key from under the flowerpot, opened the scullery door, locked it behind her and went through, into the kitchen. She dreaded the days when there were people there, never knew what she would find, never knew whether she, too, like her father in Verdun, would feel the drag of death.

The kitchen was empty. She walked through the hall, the grandfather clock with its steady, homely *tock-tock*, so *normal*, up the stairs, along the landing, steep steps to the attic.

'Who's there?' Geoffrey lurched from behind the screen.

'Me,' Dora said. She walked towards him. There were two escapees this time. One was a young man. Her age, perhaps, wizened with hunger, his face lined and wrinkled. The other was a boy, with emaciated legs and a face no more than a skull. They sat on the mattress, elbows on knees, dying hawks with jagged broken wings. 'Are they injured?' Dora said.

Geoffrey shook his head. 'Only their spirits.' Smiled.

But she smelled it. 'You've been drinking,' she said.

She saw him swallow, his Adam's apple move as it pushed down the spit, like a guilty schoolboy. He put his hands to his temples.

'Yes,' he said. 'Yes. I've had a glass of brandy.'

Brandy? Where did he get brandy from?

'I thought these two poor sods could do with it.'

'You gave it to them?' Dora said, unable to conceal her shock. 'Are you mad? That could kill them.'

He just looked at her. 'Why shouldn't they have a drop?'

Sometimes, Doralein, we gave them brandy in Verdun. There was nothing more to be done.

'Come,' she said. 'Let's go downstairs. I'll make something hot for us all.'

She smiled at the men, signalled with her fingers that she was going away. '*Ich werde zurückkommen*,' she said. 'I'll be back.' She held her hands together and placed her head on them at an angle. 'Rest. *Ausruhen.*'

They nodded, smiled, parchment skin cracking.

Geoffrey shut the attic door behind them, locked it. He put the key in his pocket.

They sat in the kitchen, elbows on the table, hands clasping their mugs.

'You seem anxious,' Dora said. 'Why?' Perhaps it was the brandy, made him jumpy.

He shook his head. 'You never really know, do you?' he said. 'They could be Germans. Dressed up, to catch us out. They do that, you know? Pretend they're *OT* workers, trick us.'

'Those men are starving,' she said. 'They're not Germans.'

'Spies, then.'

She leaned over, placed her hand over his. 'No, Geoffrey,' she said. 'They're not spies.'

'But if I was caught,' he went on. Dark fears surfacing as the brandy took hold. 'I don't think I could survive. Locked away. The walls pressing in. I'd suffocate.'

'You won't be caught,' she said. 'And you'd be fine. How's the farm? Your potatoes. Oats.'

He lifted his cup, drained it noisily. 'You're changing the subject.'

'Yes,' she said. 'At least things look healthy here.'

Geoffrey shook his head. 'Colorado potato beetle,' he said. 'They tell us it's on the island. Nonsense. We've never had the beetle here.' He reached over and poured himself some more tea. 'They just want us to spray everything. God knows why. Poison us all, I suppose.' He lifted his cup, put it down.

Dora shook her head. *Surely not.* But she was thinking about what he had said earlier, about imprisonment, locked in a cell where the walls marched forward and squeezed, tighter and tighter.

'Have you ever been in prison?' she said.

He looked at her for a long time before he nodded.

Dora shivered. 'What for?'

'Drunk and disorderly.'

'Drunk and disorderly?' She laughed, the *relief.* 'Was that all? Was that how you broke your nose?'

'I didn't break my nose,' Geoffrey said. 'It was broken for me.'

'In a brawl?'

'In a manner of speaking.'

She wanted to know, wanted him to be honest, not evasive, like he had been in the past. After all, a brawl was not so serious, and she'd seen him with a temper.

She leaned forward. 'So what happened?'

'I'm not proud of this,' he said.

'Is that why you've never told me?'

'You'd have to know, sooner or later. Perhaps you've heard rumours already.' He smiled. 'You know what this place is like.'

'Nothing specific,' she said. 'Though I was warned off you.'

'Really? By whom?'

'That would be telling.' Two could play at secrets.

He shrugged, took a breath. 'When I was nineteen,' he said, 'I was engaged. It seemed a good idea, the next step. It's what you did. Leave school. Get a job. Get married. It's a small island. Families know each other. Parents have ideas. You go along with it.'

Dora understood that pressure, she'd witnessed it time enough in Berlin. Her cousin Naomi, for instance, just had to look at a boy and her aunts were arranging the wedding. *Vati* disapproved. *A waste*, he'd say. *What's the hurry? Get the girl educated.*

'So who was she?'

'Her name was Vanessa.' He paused and looked at her, a smile teasing his mouth. 'You had dealings with her father. Sir Leonard de la Moye.'

Do you understand now?

'Ah,' Dora said. 'Go on.'

'It was announced in the *Evening Post.* And *The Times.* There was a big engagement party. A rather grand affair.'

Apart from the hospital dance, Dora had never seen Geoffrey dressed up, couldn't imagine him mingling with the good and the great of Jersey, although he must have been a catch at one stage with his farm and land, and he was handsome enough.

'That doesn't seem like you,' she said.

He smiled. 'It was a world away.'

'So what happened?'

'About two months before the wedding, I met Bea. She was on holiday with her parents. She was a very *modern* woman. A stenographer. Vanessa didn't work. All she was expected to do was marry, settle down. I'd never met anyone like Bea. A working woman, with her short frocks and bobbed hair. I was bowled over by her. Attraction of opposites, I suppose. Perhaps it was infatuation, but at the time it seemed real.'

He was holding his cup, flicking his thumb on the handle so it sung.

'One thing led to another. I didn't think. Nor did she. We were young, impulsive. Frankly, I was an idiot. Infatuated. Never gave a single thought to Vanessa, or the consequences. After the holiday, Bea returned to Manchester.' He paused. 'I'd told her at the start I was already spoken for. That our affair had no future. She agreed. She said she had a job to return to anyway.'

He gazed past Dora, stared at the Aga.

'I thought about her after she left. Of course I did. But I was caught up in the plans for the nuptials. Vanessa and me. Where we'd live. Practical things.'

He turned back to look at Dora.

'Then a week before the wedding, Bea turned up, with her father. She was pregnant. He was a policeman. He threatened to break every bone in my body if I didn't do the decent thing and marry Bea.'

His eyes focused once more on his cup, his finger scratching at a small chip on its rim.

'I was prepared to marry Bea, even though I hardly knew her. So I had to break it to Vanessa.' He twisted the cup so the tea made brown waves inside. 'I was a complete cad, and I knew it. Goodness knows, Vanessa didn't deserve it. Nor did Bea. I should have taken precautions. Who wants a shotgun marriage? Just didn't think.' He shrugged. 'I drank a brandy, to give myself courage. And another. Maybe two. Maybe more. Went round to Vanessa's house, hammered on the door and blurted it out.'

His hand was shaking. He put the cup down on the edge of its saucer. Dora reached over to steady it.

'And?'

'*Her* father threatened to break every bone in my body if I didn't do the decent thing and marry *his* daughter.'

'I hope you were ashamed,' Dora said.

Geoffrey nodded, but he didn't look up. Dora wasn't sure she wanted to hear the rest, wasn't sure that she could trust a man who'd behaved so badly. She'd told him her secret, had given him her love, put her faith in – in whom? A reprobate? A scoundrel who was quivering at the prospect of prison when he'd trapped one woman and humiliated another, and could yet betray her?

'What happened?'

'I was in a mess. I was nineteen. I was drunk.'

'You're making excuses,' Dora said.

'Yes,' Geoffrey said. 'I said I was ashamed of myself. But it gets worse. I told Sir Leonard he was a two-faced bastard, balled my fist and went to smash it into his face, only he moved and I missed and fell flat on the floor.'

'That was shocking,' Dora said. That a young man should swear like that and resort to violence was bad enough, but to the father of your fiancée? Had he no respect? She pushed herself away from the table. 'I don't want to hear any more.'

'Please. Listen.' Geoffrey was watching her. Dora hesitated. 'He had me arrested by the States Police,' he went on. 'I was still a minor. I should have been Parish-Halled, but he put me up before the *Juge d'Instruction.* Common assault. Drunk and disorderly. Breach of promise. He threw the book at me. Made sure I had a custodial sentence, criminal record.' He looked up at her. 'You don't shake a record off lightly. And for good measure, he made sure I was roughed up in the cell with no medical attention.'

He pointed to his nose.

'How long were you in prison?'

'One year,' he said. 'I couldn't marry Bea, though I planned to when I was released.'

'And then she died,' Dora said, her voice soft.

'Yes,' he said. He flicked the cup, so it rang again. 'Bea's parents had thrown her out. They were Roman Catholic, so was Bea. So she stayed with my mother, who looked after Margaret until I came out of prison and came to my senses. I've told you that bit already.'

Dora nodded.

'Margaret was illegitimate,' Geoffrey went on. 'Sir Leonard made sure of that. She had to live with that stigma and I've been pretty much ostracised ever since.' He chewed his lip, a worried expression on his face. 'I think that's why maybe she went with that German.'

Dora had all but forgotten that.

'What I did was shocking. A real scandal at the time. But this is what really *enrages* me.' He looked up and Dora saw once more the fury in his face, his jawbone set firm and hard. 'What really gets under my skin is that the very same man fathered at least one child out of wedlock, possibly two. Common knowledge, but he never acknowledged them. Hypocritical bastard.'

'And Vanessa?'

'She married a couple of years later, moved to England. I never heard from her again.'

He pushed himself up from the table so the chair juddered on the floor. 'What was that?'

'Your chair,' she said.

'No. *That.*'

Dora listened. 'I can't hear anything.'

'Listen.'

Dora strained her ears. In the distance, the unmistakable *clug* of a *Kübelwagen.* The noise was coming closer.

'It's at the top of the hill,' Geoffrey said, pushing himself away from the table. 'Coming this way. More than one.' He stood up, pointing to the ceiling. 'Tell them to keep still. Lie low. Hide. Under the blankets. Not a movement.' He grabbed Dora's arm, pulled her to her feet, handed her the key. 'Hurry.'

Dora ran out of the room, up the stairs, two at a time, her heart beating fast. Into the attic, *Soldaten, Soldaten.* Finger to her lips, as she signalled to them to scrunch up under a blanket. She folded another blanket, and another, half and half again, laid it on the top, so it looked like a pile. *Pathetic.* Tiptoed back across the floor, locked the door, down to the landing. She could hear the hammering. Why wasn't he answering it? Had he escaped? Left her? She dared not go down in case they saw her through the window. Perhaps he was hoping they'd think the house was empty, unoccupied. Would leave. But her bike was outside. They'd know someone was in.

Hammering at the back door too. Dora could taste the metal of adrenalin, could feel her muscles and tendons quiver, *on your marks, get steady...*

Go. A crash as the wood splintered. Dora could hear the soldiers, butting the panels with their guns, opening up.

'What do you want?' Geoffrey's voice, calm in the storm. 'How dare you.'

She heard him cry out, a man's scream. Her father would have heard that scream too on his battlefields. A war cry. She shut her eyes, crouched on the landing, one hand on the baluster. She should go down, feign surprise. Innocence. They mustn't come upstairs.

She pulled herself up.

'Geoffrey? What's happening?' One step, another, slowly down the staircase. Saw the soldiers in the hallway below, rifles aimed. Only they weren't the *Wehrmacht.* They were from the *Geheime Feldpolizei*, the secret police. 'What are you doing here?' she said. Voice steady, though she could hear the chip of fear, nearly said, because it came first, now. *Was machen Sie hier? Was wollen Sie?* No German. No German.

A *Feldpolizist* came towards her, three steps at a time, grabbed her arm, yanked her forward so she almost tripped, marched her into the kitchen. Geoffrey's hands had been tied, arms pulled back, head down, eyes to the floor. Another *Feldpolizist* stood close, Mauser at the ready. Geoffrey stayed motionless as Dora came in, didn't look up, no eye to catch, no sign, no hope, no *we'll be all right.*

Three *Feldpolizisten* now climbed the stairs to the attic. She heard their heavy boots overhead, kicking each door on the floor above, their shouts, *Nichts! Nichts!* The door to the attic stairs. The clomp of toecaps on the wooden steps, the rattle of the handle as they tried the lock, the splintering crash as they kicked it open. Silence.

And a scream, the broken gargle of the young lad. The *Feldpolizisten* were shouting. *Raus! Schnell!* The roll of their boots and the shuffle as the prisoners tripped and fell down the steps, across the landing, down the stairs, heads banging on the walls as they tried to keep their balance. She shut her eyes. Felt her arms pulled behind her, the cold metal of the handcuffs, the pinch as they clamped tight.

'I know you,' one of the *Feldpolizisten*, a sergeant, said. She gulped, *don't look him in the eye.* 'I told you I never forget a face.'

They pushed her forward. Behind her she heard Geoffrey, his

breath heavy, growling. The front door was open. Dora stepped outside. A glint of sun on glass from the hillside hit her eye and she squinted. It was gone. There were two *Kübelwagen.* They had meant business. Shoved her towards the first. The *Feldpolizisten* paused and Dora watched as they manhandled the prisoners out of the door. The sergeant, the one she'd met that last time, picked up his Mauser, held it against the young lad's temple.

Head open like a starburst.

Dora smelled the soot. Vomited. The *Feldpolizist* shot again and again and laughed, came towards her, pistol steaming, pushed it against her arm so she felt its burn.

'*Steigen Sie ins Auto.*'

She tripped on the running board, was yanked up, thrown forward. She scrabbled into the seat, turned round. Geoffrey was being thrust into the second *Kübelwagen.* Behind him, one *Feldpolizist* was tying the other prisoner to the back of the car while another pistol-whipped his feet so he jumped and danced like a performing bear.

Geoffrey looked up, caught Dora's eye. *I'm sorry.* He'd guessed this was coming. Or had he known all along? She looked at him, *courage.* The *Feldpolizist* shoved Geoffrey's head down, pushed him into the car. Dora heard the engines turn, the mechanical chug as the pistons and cylinders ground into motion and the vehicles moved forward, dragging the screaming prisoner behind them.

§

The cell had no window. Dora had no idea how long she had been there sitting in the pitch-black. She ran her finger along the cold, tiled walls, feeling the condensation. There was a wooden platform for sleeping and a galvanised bucket in the corner, smelling of urine. A small grille was set into the door, and the guard used it to run his baton across, *clink-clank, clink-clank, clink-clank.*

'*Mögen Sie meine Musik?*'

She wanted to cry out, '*Nein*, leave me alone.' But her jaw was too tender from where the *Feldpolizist* had punched it, her throat too sore to talk.

'Who were you working with?'

'What are their names?'

'How many prisoners have you helped?'

'Who are your accomplices?'

'Who gives you the money?'

I don't know, I don't know, I don't know.

The grille had been opened once and a chipped enamel cup passed through. In the dim light from the opening, she saw it was filled with a thin, grey liquid in which bits of cabbage floated.

It was tasteless. She sat on her bed, back up against the corner, hugging her knees. Where was Geoffrey? What had happened to him? What had he been thinking when he caught her eye in the *Kübelwagen*? *It will be all right.* Or more? *I love you.* Did he love her? Or was she just *convenient* for him? With her nursing skills and German? Had he even betrayed her? Was he saying, *forgive me*, searching for absolution? He'd betrayed a woman before. Her shoulder sockets ached from where the *Feldpolizist* had wrenched her arms behind her back, and her lip throbbed from the blow she had received from one of the *Feldkommandant*'s henchmen.

He had stood there, Colonel Knackfuss himself. Polite at first.

'I am the *Feldkommandant*, *Fräulein* Simon. Permit me to introduce *Oberleutnant* Zepernick.' He'd smiled, bowed, a click of his heels. 'Head of the *Geheime Feldpolizei*.'

Zepernick had bowed his head, too. Civilised. *Just like us.*

'We have a few questions to ask you. It won't take long.'

They didn't ask about Geoffrey. Not a single question. Didn't ask her why she went to his house, how often she went. What did they know?

Knackfuss had stepped forward, face close to hers so she saw the bristles in his nose and his crooked teeth. She smelled his sour breath. What did Geoffrey know?

'*Sind Sie eine Jüdin?*'

Are you a Jew? She'd looked up, caught off her guard. He'd said it in German, and she'd responded. And he'd come straight out with it. She'd given herself away. It didn't take much. One look.

'*Antworten Sie mir auf Deutsch.*' *Answer me in German.*

'You see,' Zepernick said. 'We know you are a Jew.'

Who had told them? The Jurat? He had no proof.

'And you speak German.'

'No,' Dora said, shaking her head. 'No.'

Nein, nein, nein.

Geoffrey was the only one who knew. Had he told them? Turned her in to save his skin?

'*Warum geben Sie es nicht zu?*'

'I don't understand,' Dora said.

Zepernick slammed his fist into her jaw, and her head jolted to one side. 'Why don't you admit it?'

Her hands were still tied behind her. She could do nothing to soothe her jaw. *They're bluffing*, she told herself. *They have no evidence.* Did they need evidence? These weren't rational, civilised people.

'What do you know?' Knackfuss said.

'Nothing.' Her voice was hoarse. 'I know nothing.'

'Put her away,' Zepernick said. One of the *Feldpolizisten* yanked her by the arm. It was numb, dead, tied too tight. She cried out, her shoulders wrenched and sore. He pulled her towards the door.

'Oh, Miss Simon,' Colonel Knackfuss said. 'One more thing before you go.' He walked towards her. 'I am a fair man, you will find. A reasonable man.' He signalled to the *Feldpolizist* to release her handcuffs. The blood came rushing back, the nerve ends in her shoulders and elbows stinging, her fingertips a mass of vicious pins and needles. 'Allow me to share a few ideas with you.'

There was a table in the room and he sauntered over to it, perched himself on the edge, swung his leg. 'You are guilty of a very serious crime,' he said. 'Aiding escaped prisoners. Consorting with the resistance, with the enemy. I could shoot you. I *should* shoot you.' He drummed his fingers against his chin. 'At Charing Cross, perhaps, or the parade ground. Somewhere public, as an example. You are a respected woman, after all. A respectable woman. Do you speak French, Miss Simon?'

Dora stared at the brown and black floor tiles, at the dust that had gathered in balls by the skirting.

'I asked you a question,' Knackfuss said, slapping his hand on the tabletop. 'Answer me. Do you speak French?'

'A little,' Dora said. 'I speak a little.'

'Then you will understand my thinking here,' he said. '*Pour encourager les autres.* Or–'

He paused and Dora could feel the pressure of his gaze. She dared not look up, meet him in the eye.

'I could send you to *Ravensbrück.* That is a camp, for women like you. We have already sent a number of women from Jersey there. You won't be alone.' She heard him push himself off the table. 'They will determine whether you are Jewish and will deal with you accordingly.'

He began to drum his fingers on the table, then stopped, walked towards her, his boots a steady *clop, clop* on the hard floor.

'Or.' He put a finger under her chin, tilted her face so she was forced to look into his. He pushed her hair away from her cheek, tucked it behind her ear. Dora flinched. 'Bruising fades, wounds heal.' He brushed his fingers against the side of her face. 'We could use you here, in Jersey.' He threw back his head and laughed. '*Oberleutnant* Zepernick, what do you think?'

He flicked his wrist in dismissal and the *Feldpolizist* marched her from the room, his fingers digging into the tender muscle of her arm.

§

A cramp began in Dora's stomach, a slow squeeze along her bowel. She felt for the bucket in the dark, squatted over its rim. There was no paper, not even torn-up scraps of newspaper. She felt sick and soiled.

Who knew she was here? She could just vanish. Plenty of people in Germany disappeared when Hitler came to power. Or ended up in labour camps like the ones in Jersey. What had happened to the Jews they'd sent away? Or the British? Or the men and women who'd stood up to them? Kept a wireless, helped a prisoner? Gone. Not a word since.

And Geoffrey? What had they done with Geoffrey? She closed her eyes, seeing his bowed frame as they led him away. Had they broken him?

The baton rattled across the grille. She jumped. The keys were in the door and a *Feldgendarm* in an ill-fitting uniform and cap grabbed her arm, slapped on handcuffs and pulled her towards the door. He walked fast and she had difficulty keeping up with him, tripping on her wooden shoes, which slipped from her heel and twisted under her foot. Upstairs, down again, along one corridor, then another, green below the rail, cream above, brown and black tiles on the floor.

They had entered the main entrance hall. Two more *Feldgendarmen* were there. The scruffy one yanked her back so she stopped. She saw the man nod. A movement behind her, and a sack tugged down over her head, the strings tied round her neck. *No.* She tried to scream, *no,* to breathe. *They were going to kill her, string her from a lamppost.* They covered heads first, didn't they, when they did that? *Shoot her through the temple.* Her breath came in shallow gulps. The hessian stuck to her mouth and nose. Her head spun, her knees buckled. Her stomach cramped again. *No, please no.* The soldier pushed her forward, clumsy palsied steps. She was crying, her nose running, the hessian rubbing. *I don't want to die.*

And Geoffrey? Would they kill him too, the pair of them, together? Lined up and shot, a single bullet to the head. Who first? Would they make her watch him die, as they had when they killed the prisoner? Or would it be the *rat-a-tat* of the machine gun, and falling together, like skittles, limbs tangled in death? She didn't want to die. *Please.*

She was propelled down the stairs, tumbling, dragged. Shoved into a car. She could sense the two *Feldgendarmen* following, sitting either side of her. She was aware of their arms, the hard metal badge on their chests, aware of them making gestures.

The car was driving fast, tyres squealing as they rounded corners, hitting the kerbstones as they went, throwing Dora against the *Feldgendarmen.* The car came to a halt, the door opened.

'*Raus.*'

They pulled her out. She could smell the sea, hear the breath of waves as they lapped against stone. Gulls screeched above. She was still in town. Perhaps by the harbour, in the square in front of the Pomme d'Or. A *Feldgendarm* grabbed her arm, marched her up steps. The Pomme d'Or had no stairs. She caught the scent of jasmine through the mouldy hessian of her hood. *Jasmine.*

She knew where she was. Not in town at all. She knew the place where jasmine climbed the walls and filled the gardens with its fragrance. She was pushed through the doors, into a hall, shoes clattering on the marble floor. She had no idea why they had brought her *here.* She could picture it, black and white chequered floor, the sweep of the stairs with their polished balustrades, the heavy Victorian furniture, to the left the saloon bar with its gracious chairs, to the right the dining room. She'd known this place too, before the Germans came. A door opened, laughter, the refrains of a song drifting through, Dora knew the words. *Lili Marleen.* The door shut. These weren't offices of the *Feldkommandantur.*

She was in the Hotel Maison Victor Hugo. La Greve d'Azette. The tide was in, the jasmine in bloom, 'Lili Marleen' was playing on a gramophone through the hallway and she was being led up the stairs.

'Walk forward.' A woman's voice, in English. The sack round her head smelled of earth and mushrooms, of Miss Besson's house. She sensed the woman coming close, heard her breathing, fiddling with the ties of the sack, forcing a cold blade between it and her neck, sawing. The sack loosened, was pulled off. Shafts of sunlight danced like a kaleidoscope on the floor. Dora breathed deep. Behind her she could feel the person tugging at her handcuffs, the sharp edges of the steel pinching Dora's palms.

'*Gottverdammt.*'

The woman went over to her desk. She was wearing a nurse's uniform, her black lace-up shoes squeaking as she walked. She rummaged in a drawer, produced a bunch of keys, returned to Dora. Her face was round and ruddy, her body force-ripe, the kind that would go to seed fast. Her hair was dull brown, cut short.

Dora waited, heard the lock on the handcuffs grind and click, felt the pressure on her wrists give. She shook them free, winced as the blood rushed back.

She looked around the room. A doctor's surgery. A set of scales stood next to the desk, and a measurement chart. There was a surgical bed at right angles against the wall and a set of powerful lights hanging from the ceiling. There was a medicine cabinet on another wall with a red cross painted on the door, and beneath it a large refrigerator. The contents of the room looked proficient.

'Undress.'

'Undress?' Dora said.

'Take your clothes off and go over to the bed.'

Dora unbuttoned her uniform, stepped out of it.

'Everything,' the nurse said. 'Underwear.'

Dora did as she was told, stepped over to the bed, sat on it.

'Lie down, open your legs.'

Dora had examined enough women to know what the nurse was about to do. Prodded, poked. The nurse ticked items off her list as she went.

'To the scales.'

She was weighed and measured. The nurse brought out a small steel contraption, placed it on Dora's head, adjusting dials, wrote down the results. Shone a light into Dora's eyes, cut a lock of her hair and held it against a chart.

'Is your hair dyed?'

'No.'

Dora stood in the centre of the room. She folded her arms over her breasts, naked, vulnerable. The nurse had returned to her desk and was transferring the data into a ledger. Dora reached over for her clothes.

'*Nein*,' the nurse shouted. 'You wait for the doctor.'

Dora waited as the sun sank low. She watched the sky turn deep as the devil's lapis and the jagged kaleidoscope on the floor retreated into shadow. Finally the door opened and a man came in, white coat, stethoscope. He pointed to the bed.

'Lie down.'

He was rougher than the nurse.

'Sit up.' Clamped the stethoscope to her chest and back, pulled back her lips, studied her teeth, peered into her eyes. The nurse showed him the ledger and he studied it.

'Aryan,' he said. Nodded, left the room. '*Sicherlich nicht jüdisch*.' *Certainly not Jewish*. 'Proceed.'

'Come,' the nurse said. Dora followed her into a small room that led off the surgery. Dresses hung on rails, meticulously ordered by length, colour and, Dora guessed, size. The nurse pulled out a red one, a cocktail dress with flimsy straps and a fishtail skirt. She pointed to a sink underneath the window. 'Wash. Then put this on.'

The dress was tight, and Dora had to step into it and pull it up. There was a row of buttons on the side, covered in the same slippery fabric as the dress. Dora's fingers fumbled as she did them up.

'They say strawberry blondes shouldn't wear red,' the nurse said. 'I disagree.' She spoke without a smile or warmth, although, Dora thought, it was such a womanly detail to share. Intimate, almost, after the cold intricacies of the medical examination.

'Shoes.' She pulled out a pair of high heels. 'They should fit.'

They returned to the surgery. 'A photograph.' The nurse pulled down a screen, turned on the lights. 'Stand.' She fished in her drawer, pulled out a small box camera. An Agfa, Dora knew. Her father'd had the same.

'Face me.' She took her time adjusting the lens. *Click.* 'To the side.' *Click.* 'The other side.' *Click.* 'Follow me.'

'I have no underwear,' Dora said.

The nurse sniffed.

She led her into a room at the end of the corridor, with thick flock wallpaper, a large bed, and velvet curtains that hung in swags. There was a rug on the floor, a console table with bottles of schnapps and scotch and brandy, a large mahogany wardrobe and a tallboy. The fireplace was marble and in front of it was an embroidered fire screen, like the one that sat in Miss Besson's parlour, a picture of a country cottage out of place in the high-class opulence of this room. An ornate sofa upholstered in red brocade faced the fire and Dora knew, in that moment, what kind of use Knackfuss had in mind for her.

The nurse left, locking the door. Dora ran to the window. The room was on the second floor, faced the sea. It must be ten metres to the ground. High enough to kill her, if she jumped. Dora pulled at the sash, but it would not move. The panes were too small to crawl through. She swallowed. Rushed to the chimney. She'd heard they used to build them with steps for cleaning. She could climb up, wait on the roof, shimmy down when it was dark.

The door unlocked, opened, and a man came in. He wore a greyish uniform, not one Dora had seen before. He took off his cap, placed it on the console table.

'Pour me a scotch,' he said, sitting on the sofa, crossing his legs. Dora was shaking. Perhaps he hadn't locked the door. She could make a run for it.

'Now.' The German turned round. 'I am watching you.'

Dora walked towards the table. His cap had a skull on it, an eagle too, the visor shiny. She eyed him on the sofa, staring at her. He was in his thirties, she guessed, blond hair shorn at the temples. Handsome, in a Germanic way. She'd seen his type in Berlin, bankers, lawyers. Educated men with manicured nails. She pulled out the stopper, poured the scotch. *Vati* drank scotch, poured it halfway up the glass, *No ice, no water. Like a Scot.*

'Half and half,' the German said. 'Remember that.' There was a carafe of water, and Dora filled the glass, walked over to him, hand shaking.

'That is a lot of scotch,' he said. 'Do you want to kill me?'

Dora said nothing. She saw the runes of the *SS* insignia on his collar and was back in Berlin as Brownshirts poked her father in the chest, pushing him so he toppled. *Who are you? Some kind of Bolshevik? A Jewish traitor?*

SS Totenkopf. A skull, Dora thought, *the death's head.* She hadn't seen them in Jersey before. Not the *SS.*

'I am a busy man,' he said. 'Have you washed?'

CHAPTER TEN

JOE

Jersey: June 1985

Two weeks after Barbara Hummel's visit, Joe wrote three letters, scribbled *please forward* on the envelopes. He sent one to the PO box number, one to the Hotel de France and one to the editor of the *Evening Post*, who, he thought, may have her contact details. He'd heard nothing more and regretted sending her away now. Geoffrey looked hurt and puzzled.

'I don't have much time left,' he said.

'That's not fighting talk,' Joe said. 'You've got thirty more good years.'

That had always made Geoffrey laugh, but he didn't smile now. It would mean the world to him to see Dora one more time. What would they say to each other? Where would they *begin*?

Geoffrey's brown eyes had clouded with time, become rheumy and lavender. He pulled out a handkerchief, and wiped them. 'Will you write again?' he said.

Joe pulled out the pad of writing paper, *Dear Mrs Hummel…*

§

Finally there was a reply. The postman brought it up on Friday morning and handed it to Joe. He'd just finished the milking, was about to clean himself up in the caravan. He took the letter, turned it over. The postmark was English, from Richmond. *Well,* Joe thought, *she gets around.* He opened the letter.

I must apologise, but I was called away on business. She had no idea of the turmoil she'd caused, otherwise she wouldn't be so casual. *I would still like to talk to you, if possible, and will be returning to Jersey in the near future, although at this stage am unable to give you precise dates. In the meantime, I have another photo relating to this time and wondered whether you may be able to throw some light on this also?*

Joe felt it with his fingertips, clipped to the back of the letter.

> *I do appreciate that the subject of the German occupation is still very sensitive in Jersey and the Channel Islands, so forgive me if I tread on toes. The photograph is that of a German nurse. I can find no trace of her in the records in Germany, though they are incomplete for the Channel Islands. I need to know, however, if she was in Jersey during those years and wondered whether you may have seen her round and about? I quite understand if you cannot remember that far back, or if I am stirring up unwelcome memories of that time, which, I understand, were painful for so many islanders. I am already asking perhaps too much of you. Thank you for your time.*

Joe pulled the picture free and Trude's plain, round face stared back at him across the years.

Jersey: May – June 1943

Joe watched the boys file out, their faces hot and sweaty.

'Now, mind you do those sit-ups,' he called after one. 'Work on them. Fitness is the key.' Nodding at another. 'Mind the footwork.'

Pierre was waiting behind the ring, stepped forward as the last of the boys went out.

'Are you all right, Father?' he said.

'And why wouldn't I be all right?' Joe looked around the room, making sure the boys had left nothing. Some of them would leave their heads behind if they weren't screwed on.

'Only you're working those boys too hard.'

'Nonsense,' Joe said, picking up a boxing glove from the floor. He took off his jacket and slipped the glove over his right hand, clenched his fist and lunged at the punching bag hanging from the beam. The force jarred his wrist. Joe swung his left arm, bare knuckles into the bag so the canvas scraped the skin. *Right, left. Right, left.* Dancing back, light on the toes, pummelling hard, hard, *hard.* He could feel the sweat building up, the adrenalin surging. He knew the damage it could do, a boxer's fracture or a sprained thumb, twisted joints or tissue damage. Boxing had helped him before. Why shouldn't it help him now? The agony would kick in later as he lay in bed at night, releasing the hurt within, as if the tortures of his flesh could soothe the lash of his conscience.

'And Sister Benigna said you broke down at mass this morning,' Pierre went on.

Joe saw Trude's face in every woman he passed, heard her song-thrush laughter in every breeze and felt her gentle hands stroke his own. He had begun to smell her in the convent chapel, the clean, starched apron scent of her as he said mass and took the chalice and wiped it clean with the veil.

The bag went still as Pierre grabbed the sides and steadied it. 'She says you're not yourself. You're moody. Silent.'

Joe knelt down by one of the benches, sweeping his hand underneath. All manner of stuff found its home there. Gumshields. Socks. Shoelaces.

'What's going on?'

Joe wasn't sure himself what was going on, except that at night when he was alone he thought of Trude and felt his flesh ripple and his mouth go dry.

But he'd taken his vows and he couldn't see how to cast them off, even though they'd never fitted properly. He needed Trude, needed to talk to her. She would understand. She had precipitated this. Yes, that was the right word. *Precipitate*, as if he was standing on the edge of an abyss. She said she'd make him whole but instead she'd opened up a chasm inside him, a pit so deep he could see neither the bottom nor the way out, could feel only the vertigo of confusion, the demon that said, *jump, jump.*

But she had gone. No word sent, even though he waited for her day after day. For sure, something terrible had happened.

'Nothing,' Joe said. 'Nothing's going on.'

It seemed he had been forsaken by her, though it was a blasphemy to use those words.

§

Joe waited again at their junction for half an hour the following Wednesday. Checked his watch over and over, looking down the road to see if she was coming. He didn't want to be spotted loitering. It didn't do to draw attention to himself, or the bird-watching glasses, in case they thought he was a spy. He'd been lucky, so far. Never stopped nor searched. He guessed his clerical collar gave him a licence to pass unmolested.

Trude didn't come. He wanted to write to her, but he didn't know where to send the letter and didn't want anyone to read it by mistake. But what could he say? What could a *priest* say? He loitered for as long as he could at the junction where they used to meet on Monday afternoons, then set off for La Ferme de l'Anse, just in case she'd gone there instead. He would have given anything to have Trude here with him. He had never been obsessed with another person before, but he recognised that's what it was. *Obsession.* He should confess, seek guidance, but he couldn't bare his soul, not for this. It ran too deep within. Too fast. Too twisted.

The leaves were fresh and verdant, and the sun cast a dappled shadow on the narrow lanes. The hedgerows either side were tall and thick, the frail limbs of new growth grafted onto old dark twigs. He stopped, *listen, look.* He could hear life scurrying in the undergrowth, see a robin with a worm in its beak plunging into the interior. He'd need to keep an eye out for fledglings in due course.

He pushed off again, turned right at the mill, wove his way up and down the by-lanes, until he reached Geoffrey's field. Bike tucked safely behind the gate, binoculars hanging round his neck, he began to thread his way to the dell. He heard a soft, insistent *twi-twi-twi-twi-twi* and turned to see the yellowhammer squatting on the gatepost, head to one side, its saffron head and breast glinting in the sun. He smiled at it, *hello little friend,* wanted to wave, *have you seen her?* The oats were taller, swayed in the breeze like waves in the sea, and the grass had grown in the dell into clumpy hillocks.

Joe lifted his field glasses. He'd train them onto the woody hillside first, start there before he'd focus on the shoreline. He caught Geoffrey's farmhouse in his sights. Quiet and peaceful in the June sunshine, a bicycle against the wall next to the front door, an old iron shoe-scraper to its side. *Listen.* The *chug-chug* of a *Kübelwagen* broke the silence. He trained his glasses. The top road could be glimpsed through the copse and he saw a jeep driving along, followed by a second. They turned the corner, came into view along the lane. Joe watched as they drew up in front of the farmhouse and four men in the distinctive grey uniform of the *Geheime Feldpolizei,* two from each vehicle, spilled out. The secret police. Joe had heard of them. Everybody had. The first two hammered on the front door, the last two ran into the yard behind the house.

No one opened the door, and the *Feldpolizei* at the front joined the others at the back of the building. Joe heard their shouts echo round the farmyard, the sharp splinter of wood. He stood, his glasses trained on the house, tasting the adrenalin from his stomach, feeling his heart race and his hands grow cold and clammy. Something terrible was amiss. They were taking their time inside the house. Why had they come? The farm was such an insignificant little holding.

In time, the front door opened and Geoffrey stumbled out, his hands tied behind his back. Behind him came the nurse. She had lost her cap. Her hands were tied behind her, too. Two *Feldpolizisten* pushed them forward with their rifles. One grabbed the nurse and threw her towards the first *Kübelwagen*, another pushed Geoffrey towards the second.

Two more men, arms pulled behind their backs, staggered from the house, prodded by the other *Feldpolizisten*.

'*Abschaum*!' Shoving them forward. '*Russen*!'

The men wore tattered, grey rags. Labourers, from the *OT* gangs. Joe saw them squint in the sunlight, as if they were coming out of a cave. A *Feldpolizist* grabbed one, the shorter of the two, pulled out his pistol, placed it against his temple.

The crack echoed round the farm and the man slumped to the ground, blood pumping from his head. The soldier aimed again at the body, and shot again. And again.

The glasses slipped from Joe's grasp and he stifled a cry. Picked them up and trained them once more. The body lay still now, blood blackening the cobblestones. The *Feldpolizisten* were busy securing a rope to the other prisoner, one end tied round his feet, the other attached to the *Kübelwagen*, pistol-whipping him as they did so, forcing the prisoner to duck and jump. *No*, Joe opened his mouth, *no*, but the words dried. He moved forward, pushing his way through the field.

The *Feldpolizisten* clambered into the jeeps, started the engines, turned and drove away, dragging the second prisoner. He was jolted off his feet, head thumping the ground. He screamed. Once. They drove off through the farm gate.

All was silent except for the *chug-chug* of the *Kübelwagen* as they climbed the hill, and the *twi-twi-twi* of the yellowhammer on the gate.

Joe slumped in the middle of the field. Life snuffed in the puff of a gun, the jolt of a *Kübelwagen*, Geoffrey and his nurse, heads down, arms back, stiff as corpses.

He pushed himself up. The farm was deserted now. He thrashed his way through the oats which tangled and dragged at his shoes, clambered over the lower gate, ran towards the body. The top half of the head was a mass of broken bone and slimy brain. His chest an open cave, shattered ribs cream against the blood. Fibres and strings had tumbled out in the gore.

Joe leaned over and retched. The tangled corpse had been a man once. He looked again, at the frail, immature bones, the slender, scabbed hands strapped behind its back. Not a man. A boy. Perhaps no more than fifteen.

A child. Perhaps the same lad he'd looked for once.

Joe shut his eyes, spoke without thinking, 'Eternal rest grant unto him, O Lord.' He couldn't bear to look anymore. He had to do something. Tell someone. He'd heard talk of the Germans' brutality. The executions. The cruelty in the camps. He'd never seen it, apart from the starvation, and that was too obvious to miss. Had he chosen not to? *And may perpetual light shine upon him.* The nurse's bike was leaning against the farmhouse wall. He pulled it away, one foot on the pedal, pushed off. *May the souls of the faithful departed.* He had to find Trude. Tell her what they'd done. She'd be as shocked as him. Perhaps she could intercede for Geoffrey and the nurse, beg the *Feldkommandant* to show leniency. *Through the mercy of God, rest in peace.* Amen.

He was blind to the road in front of him, heedless to the quivering in his gut, the stretch of his tendons and muscles. He had to find Trude. He knew she didn't work at the general hospital because she'd told him that – couldn't think where to look for her, who was in charge of the German nurses and doctors.

Except the *Feldkommandantur.* They would know. They kept lists and records of everything. Everyone. Knackfuss. Colonel Knackfuss, the *Feldkommandant* himself. He would remember Joe, from the boxing match. He'd tell Joe where Trude was. He could talk to Knackfuss direct. He seemed a reasonable man. What had he said? *We treat all opponents fairly.* There's surely been a mistake, Joe'd say. *OT* workers roamed the island, they must have broken into Geoffrey's house. They were the guilty ones. They'd been punished. Killed, in cold blood. *You have to be lenient*, he'd say. *Give them a chance.* The penalties for helping runaways were too severe.

§

He propped the bicycle against the kerb, ran up the steps to the *Feldkommandantur* headquarters. A *Wehrmacht* soldier stepped in front of him.

'Business?'

Joe hesitated a moment. 'I need to find someone,' he said. 'One of your nurses.'

'Why?'

Joe thought. 'It's a personal matter,' he said. 'Her name is Trude.' He did not know her surname. He had abandoned everything for her, flung caution to the wind for her, and he did not know her name. He was going to have to throw himself on her mercy now, *and he did not even know her name.*

The soldier studied Joe under his brown tin helmet and narrowed his eyes. 'A moment,' he said. 'Wait here.'

Joe nodded, watched as the soldier went inside. He was shaky, knees trembling and weak. He felt dizzy. Sat on the steps. He would have given anything for a cigarette. He patted his pockets, although he knew they were empty. His binoculars were still round his neck, but he couldn't leave them in the bicycle. Anyone could steal them. He'd left the case in his own bike at Geoffrey's farm. If the soldier asked what he was doing with them, he'd be honest. I'm a *birdwatcher. It's my passion. That's all I ever watch.*

The soldier had returned. 'Come this way.'

Joe stood up and followed him into the building, with its tiled floors and half-panelled walls. A large portrait of Hitler hung above the stairs, draped by two Nazi flags. The soldier's heels clipped on the floor. He knocked at a large mahogany door.

'*Eintreten.*'

He opened the door, ushered Joe in. A plain man, in uniform, with spectacles and a small moustache, sat behind a large desk on which there were two telephones, a variety of rubber stamps and three trays filled with buff folders. Wooden filing cabinets lined the walls. The man looked up as Joe entered. He pointed to the corner.

'Wait there.'

He carried on reading from one of the folders, turning over each sheet of paper with studied order.

Joe put his hands in his pockets, ran his fingers round the balls of fluff that had gathered in the corners, fished them out again. Rubbed his fingers together. Shifted his weight from his left foot to his right. He had no idea who this man was, or whether he was the man to see. Perhaps he was the secretary. He had that kind of indifferent air. Joe coughed.

'Excuse me,' Joe said. 'Can you help?'

The man looked up, glowered, said nothing. There was a large, round clock on the wall, the hours marked in grand Roman letters. Two o'clock. German time. One o'clock, old time. Dinner time. Joe wasn't hungry, but he wanted the lavatory. Dared not ask the German at the desk, *excuse me, may I use your WC?*

The telephone rang, jarring in the silence. The man looked up. 'Go through.' He pointed to another door.

Joe nodded. He walked towards it, knocked quietly, went in.

Colonel Knackfuss himself was standing there in the centre of the room. Hands behind his back, rocking on his heels. He was taller than Joe remembered him, beefier, too. He waited until Joe had entered the room.

'You are enquiring about a nurse,' he said.

The timbre in his voice said it all.

§

Joe rubbed his neck, fingers on the welt left by the strap when Knackfuss had ripped his binoculars off him. Tough leather, cutting into his flesh, sharp as a whiplash. Snapped like string. Knackfuss was holding the glasses up to the window, adjusting the sights.

'Not bad,' he said, lowering them and turning to Joe. 'But not good, either.' Threw them onto the tiled floor.

Joe was about to say, *Please*, but Knackfuss was grinding his heel on the tube, pressing down with all his weight. Joe heard the lens pop free and shatter into tiny shards which spilled across the floor. He stared at the debris. The only possession he really cared about, had ever cared about. *I don't have use for these. Not now.* Colonel Waring had taken his life a week later. He was still a young man.

'I will ask you again, what business do you have with this nurse?' Knackfuss said.

Joe didn't know what to do. He never thought he'd be interrogated, treated as if he was a criminal.

'A friend,' Joe said. 'She was just a friend. I thought she could help.'

'Help?'

'With Geoffrey and the nurse,' Joe said. Knackfuss raised an eyebrow, ran his tongue over his teeth, *not interested*.

'You arrested them,' Joe went on. 'But they haven't done a thing. You have to let them go.'

'Your friend,' Knackfuss said, ignoring Joe. 'What did you do with your German *friend*?' He emphasised the word, made it something dirty. 'And those.' He pointed at the broken binoculars.

'Birds,' Joe said. 'We watched birds.'

'Birds?' Knackfuss kicked the broken glasses across the floor. He walked close to Joe, loomed over him. 'You have to do better,' he said. 'Why would a woman be interested in birds?'

Joe thought of Geoffrey's words, *Jerry wouldn't take it kindly if they thought you were spying on them.*

'I wasn't spying,' Joe said. 'If that's what you think.'

Or Trude. Did they think Trude was a spy? A traitor? She had that note in her basket making fun of Hitler. She'd been protecting Joe when she left him that last time. She knew she was being watched.

'Where is Trude?' Joe said. 'What have you done with her?'

'Trude,' he said. 'Trude. We have a name.'

'What have you done with her?' Joe was too small to throw his voice and he could hear it break as he shouted. 'Where is she?'

He knew how ruthless the Germans were now. Had seen it for himself.

Knackfuss walked to his desk, picked up the telephone. He spoke in German, put the receiver down as the door opened and two *Feldpolizisten* entered. Knackfuss nodded. One of them came up to Joe, two large strides, clamped handcuffs round Joe's wrist, tugged him away.

'We will go somewhere more comfortable,' Knackfuss said. He picked up a folder from his desk. 'Lead on,' he said to the *Feldpolizisten.* 'I will follow.'

Joe's trousers chafed as he walked. He had to skip to keep up with the *Feldpolizisten*, along a corridor, through a door, down two flights of stairs, into the basement. Thick pipes ran along the ceiling and the walls had not been painted for years. Joe smelled the acrid stench of a furnace, glimpsed it as they passed a room, a big, ugly beast devouring the coal that surrounded it, even in the summer heat.

They stopped at a door, *Verhörraum.* Went inside. The only light hung from a dim bulb in the centre. There was a table and four chairs arranged around it, and to the left, another door. Joe was pushed towards one of the chairs.

'Sit.'

The *Feldpolizisten* stood behind him. Knackfuss sat on a chair opposite him, laying the folder on the table and opening it.

The walls were dirty and stained, and the floor cracked and broken. Joe's wrist was red from where the handcuffs pinched. He wanted to ask, *Why I am being held like this?* He'd done nothing wrong. He was an Irish citizen and didn't that count for something? He opened his mouth, shut it.

He didn't dare.

Joe wasn't sure how much time had passed before the door opened and another man came in. Joe could tell from his uniform that he held high rank. He wore shoulder straps, with *GFP* embossed in metalled letters. *Geheime Feldpolizei.*

'*Oberleutnant* Zepernick,' Knackfuss said, standing up, holding out his hand. 'Busy day, eh?'

The man pushed out his lips, said nothing until he had sat down. 'What have we here?'

He looked at Joe as he might a worm.

'He's enquiring about a nurse,' Knackfuss said. 'Called Trude.'

'Trude?' Zepernick pulled a never-heard-of-her face.

'They go,' Knackfuss paused, smiled, '*bird*watching.' He made it sound like an absurd activity. 'With high-powered binoculars.' He turned to Joe. 'I expect you can see France through those lenses?'

Not anymore, Joe wanted to say. 'Why would I want to look

at France?' he said. 'That's of no interest. It's the birds. Puffins. Gannets. Sanderlings.'

'Tweet-tweet things?' Zepernick roared with laughter.

'With one of our German nurses,' Knackfuss said. 'In whose basket we found malicious notes about the *Führer* from "the soldier with no name".'

Joe shut his eyes for a moment. Trude was under suspicion, had been arrested. He couldn't bear it. He had to protect her. He might be small, but he could be mighty.

'Did you put them there?' Zepernick said. 'Or did she write them herself?'

'No,' Joe said, shaking his head. 'No. Not at all, at all. Why would she write such a thing?' He felt breathless, on a train hurtling in the wrong direction with no way of stopping it.

'Did you write them?'

'Of course not.' He added, 'Listen, I don't know what you're getting at, but it's not like that.'

'Like what?'

'What you're suggesting. We just watch birds. That's all.' They had to believe it. 'Ornithology,' Joe said. 'As old as the ancient Greeks. Older, even.'

Zepernick had opened the folder, was studying it, taking his time to read each page, before turning it over with a slow, steadied hand. Knackfuss was staring at Joe. Joe knew the tactic from his boxing days. *You don't scare me, Colonel Knackfuss, you can't wrong-foot me. I fight on nerves alone. I can win this.*

Zepernick delved into his pocket, pulled out a small packet and slapped it on the table in front of Joe.

Fisherman's Friend. Joe felt the blood drain from his head. They'd searched his room. The game was up. But this was no *game.* This was life and death.

'Have you seen this before?'

Joe couldn't lie. He nodded.

'What is it?'

He swallowed, and his voice came out thin as a reed. 'A crystal set.'

'A crystal *wireless* set,' Knackfuss said. '*Verboten*. Against the law.'

Zepernick closed the folder, pulled the tin towards him and opened the lid. 'Did you make this yourself?'

Joe thought fast. He didn't want to give Father Rey away. 'Yes.'

'Clever. What did you listen to?' Zepernick said. 'The BBC?'

Joe nodded.

'And then you broadcasted it? Who did you tell? Did you tell Trude?'

'No,' Joe said. 'Of course not.'

'Why not? You put lies in her basket, why not whisper in her ear?'

'It wasn't like that,' Joe said. 'You have it all wrong.'

'Who did you tell?'

'I don't know.' Joe stumbled. He knew no one by name, could barely see their faces through the dark mesh of the confession box.

'Spreading enemy propaganda.'

Joe stared at his shiny black trousers, his scuffed shoes. He hadn't thought he'd ever be caught, hadn't prepared himself. Now most likely he'd be shot, or sent to prison, if he was lucky. There was nothing he could do but hold his nerve.

'Tell me about your German sweetheart,' Zepernick was saying. 'Your *Trude*.'

'She's not my sweetheart,' Joe said. *But she was, and he loved her.* What kind of a Judas was he? 'I'm a priest. A Catholic priest.'

'Catholic priests are not supposed to have girlfriends, are they?' Knackfuss said. 'You'll burn in hell, won't you? Isn't that what you believe?'

Joe shut his eyes, *Lord have mercy.* There was nothing he could say. Zepernick drummed his fingers on the table, *dum-diddle-dum, dum-diddle-dum.*

'Are you aware,' he said after a while, 'that it is forbidden to have sexual relations with any personnel from the German occupying force?'

'No,' Joe said. 'And I'm not.' Words were jumbling. He didn't know what to say, which way to point a sentence. 'I wasn't.'

'Defiling the best of our womanhood.' Knackfuss ignored him. 'With your sordid desires.'

Joe shook his head, looked at Knackfuss, at Zepernick. 'I'm Irish,' he said. Would that make a difference?

'Irish.'

'Ireland's not part of this war,' Joe was stumbling. 'It's neutral.'

'Neutral?' Zepernick shouted, the veins on his temple pulsing. 'Spying on us? Spreading British lies? Corrupting our women? That is not the behaviour of a neutral agent.' He slammed his fist hard on the desk. 'Those are the actions of a partisan.'

'No,' Joe said. 'That's not how I see myself.' He wasn't a criminal, wasn't even a rebel, but war made monsters of everyone.

Zepernick stood up, resting on his fists on the tabletop, the knuckles white. 'You disgust me,' he said. 'With your lies, your self-delusion.' He walked round the table, stood over Joe. He was a tall man, well-built. Joe had never been easy with big men.

'What disgusts me most,' he said, 'is your perversion.'

'I don't understand.'

Zepernick leaned forward and slapped Joe's face with the back of his hand. 'Sodomite.'

Joe reeled back. 'What are you talking about?'

'Pederast.'

'No,' Joe said.

'No?' Zepernick said.

He had only ever told Trude. She wouldn't betray him. They must have forced it out of her.

'Did you enjoy it?' Zepernick said. 'Encourage him, with your pretty boy looks?'

No, no. What tortures had Trude endured? 'What did you do to her?' Joe said.

'Degenerate.' Zepernick spat out the word, small vapours of spit dissolving into the air. 'Diseased. Polluting our women.'

'Where's Trude?' Joe shouted, caution to the wind. He could only think of Trude, the torments they had put her through. Thinking she was a spy, a traitor. Now this. His mind was reeling. He could do nothing. *Powerless. Not a proper man.*

Zepernick nodded at Knackfuss, held his arm in a salute, *Heil Hitler*, left the room through the door at the side. Knackfuss waited until he had left.

'So.' He leaned forward on the desk, hands together. 'The charge list is long, Father O'Cleary.' He unclenched his hands, tapped his fingers. 'You are guilty of spying. You are a partisan. A propagandist for the enemy. You have broken the law on possession of a wireless set and on relationships with German personnel. You are a homosexual.'

Terror and rage burned inside Joe. He had to know. 'Where is Trude?'

'A moment,' Knackfuss said, nodding to one of the *Feldpolizisten* behind Joe. The *Feldpolizist* came into view, knocked on the door, returned to Joe's side.

Knackfuss tapped and twisted the pencil on the table, looking at Joe all the while, a sneer playing on his mouth. He turned.

Zepernick was leading Trude in, accompanied by another man, tall, well-built, in a dark-grey uniform that Joe hadn't seen before, two jagged lines on the collar. She was wearing her poppy frock, her hands wrenched behind her. She looked at the ground, broken and dejected.

'Trude,' Joe shouted, mustered the power from the depths of his body. 'Trude.' Turned to Zepernick. 'What have you done to her?'

Zepernick looked at one of the *Feldpolizisten.* 'Release his handcuffs.'

The blood rushed back to Joe's hands and he pushed himself off the chair.

'It's all right, Trude.' He moved towards her. 'Trude, I'm so sorry.' The *Feldpolizisten* grabbed his arms, one either side, yanked him back. 'I'm so terribly sorry,' he shouted, his voice breaking like a little boy's.

He tried to reach out. Zepernick nodded to the man in the grey uniform.

'*Hauptsturmführer* List,' he said. 'Proceed.'

List pulled out his Mauser and held it to Trude's temple.

'This is what we do to those who break the law on sexual fraternisation. She knew the penalty.' He smirked. 'You must have had quite a hold over her. What was your secret?'

'No. You can't do that.'

'Come here,' List said. 'Shoot her.'

'No.' Joe was shaking his head. 'No.'

'She would rather die by the hand of her lover,' he said. 'Quick and simple. Will you put her out of her misery?'

'No,' Joe said. 'No I will not. I will have nothing to do with this.'

The *Feldpolizist* pushed him forward.

'No,' Joe was shouting. He was wiry, strong, stood his ground, but he could feel them lifting him. 'No.'

Zepernick nodded to them. *Let him stand.*

'What a coward,' he said. 'You'd put down a bird with a broken wing, but you can't put your lover out of her misery.'

'Trude. Look at me,' Joe said. 'Trude.'

Her head stayed bent down, her eyes cast to the floor. She stood motionless next to List, the pistol at her head. He loved her then more than ever. Her strength. Fortitude. Bravery. He would never pull that trigger, even if it cost him his life.

'Take him,' Zepernick said.

The *Feldpolizisten* spun Joe round, marched him out of the door.

Joe heard the shot and the thump of her body on the floor.

'No.' He tried to twist free but the *Feldpolizisten* held him firm, dragging him down the corridor, the thud echoing in his mind. Urine was seeping round his fly and trickling down his leg.

§

Just the crack of the bow and the drum of the waves as they slammed the side. Joe saw only darkness, heard the pistol smack and the dull thump of her body as it hit the ground, over and over, while the sea moiled and tossed him against the oily ropes and the sharp edges of the cargo crates. He had killed her, as surely as if he had pulled the trigger. He'd led her into danger, because she made him feel grand. A flimsy, fleeting pleasure that had cost her life. Why should he live now? By what right? He clenched his fist and drummed it into the side of the hold.

Sick as dogs and not a drop of water. Forced through the hatch last night, they had slept as best they could before the ship began to move. There must have been at least thirty other men on board, and none spoke English. Joe thought they could be Russian. No knowing where they were going and Joe couldn't ask.

The engines droned, a steady *chug-chug,* the fumes from the kerosene clogging the foetid air of the hold. Joe gagged, fought for breath. Maybe they were going to kill them all here, suffocate them, fill the space with noxious gases. It would be right and fitting, Joe thought, an end to his despair.

The men slid in their vomit, its stench clinging to their beards and clothes. The rhythm of the engines changed, softened, and Joe knew they must be coming close to land. The boat bumped as they drew up alongside a harbour, the motors humming and idling.

A blast of light illuminated the hold as the hatch was pulled up. Joe could hear German voices, boots on the deck above, orders bellowed down.

'*Raus*! *Schnell*!'

The men shuffled towards the ladder. Unkempt, unshaven, their baggy striped clothing stiff with filth, they pulled themselves onto the deck. They were surrounded by soldiers who pushed them forward, rifles at the ready. These soldiers wore a different uniform from the ones in Jersey. The prisoners stepped onto the quayside.

Silence. No screeling gulls, no piping guillemots. No gannets or shags. No raptors. No waders. Joe had never been on a coast without life, a land without birds. Never been close to the sea when all that could be heard was the wind, a breathless whine that hummed above the *clack-clack* percussion of the soldiers' boots on the stones and the shrill trumpet of orders. *Schnell.*

There were ships in the harbour. Gangs of men in rough, torn clothing were unloading cargo. At the far corner, there was another gang working on what looked like breakwaters. In front of them was a row of workshops, with anchors hanging against the wall and fishing nets strung with glass floats. *Welcome to Alderney* was visible on the faded signage. They hadn't travelled far at all.

'*Schnell!*' The men were butted into line, two abreast.

'Water,' Joe said. 'I need water.' He wanted to add, *Food, too?* There'd been nothing for almost two days. The soldier ignored him and Joe could see from the set of the soldiers' faces that they would give no quarter. The other men were resigned, as if they were used to starvation and thirst. Used to orders. They formed a crocodile.

'*Abmarsch! Links. Links,*' the guard yelled. '*Zwei. Drei. Vier. Singen!*'

The men either side of him began to sing. The men behind sang, as did those in front. Male voices filled his ears, tenors, a baritone. He felt the hairs on his arm rise. What twisted logic did those Nazis have that forced these men to sing? Like this? What went through the hearts of the guards? Joe heard that the slaves in America had sung as they worked, spirituals of loss and longing. Of hope and redemption.

Kalinka, Malinka.

The way his shadow fell, Joe knew they were moving east. *Links*! *Links*! In the distance, Joe could make out the silhouette of fortifications with their thick, high concrete walls and square, solid bunkers. Joe saw the labourers, some in the blue striped uniforms like the men he'd travelled with, some in ragged shirts and trousers with a white stripe painted down the leg, others dressed in old cement sacks. All of them were covered in grey dust, their hair thick and matted, their feet clothed in rags or clumsy wooden clogs. Soldiers stood by, rifles and whips at the ready, while the labourers fed the vast mixing machines with sand and cement, pouring in water, pushing wheelbarrows of wet concrete. Thin as skeletons. They looked even more emaciated than the Russian prisoners in Jersey.

The guards stopped the men by a section of land marked out in a rectangle with pegs and rope. They divided the prisoners into four gangs, each with their own guard. Joe was pushed towards the third gang and marched to a pile of rubble and stones. To the side of the mound, Joe could see the sea and a long, sandy shore curling round. It should be full of waders prancing and dancing. He longed to see their jigs, hear their calls, to sit still as a millpond and wait for them to hop and frisk. That would calm his soul, as it always had. It was the silence that Joe couldn't fathom, a land without the chatter of birds. You could talk back to them, mimic their cry, wait for their answer.

A blast in the distance shook the ground. It lingered in his ears.

He heard first that raucous, grating cry, saw the large white wings as it flew up and away. A gannet. Long grey beak and eyes kohled up like one of those American film stars with loose morals. *On its own.* Gannets weren't solitary birds.

'*Anfangen*,' the guard was pointing to sledgehammers that lay on the ground. '*Kleine Stücke*.'

The hammers were all the same size, with a hefty head on them and a handle a yard long. It would take some strength to wield that. Some of the men were already crushing the stones, scattering them into small pieces. Joe took off his clerical jacket and laid it on the ground, lifted the hammer, swung it behind him and smashed it down. The force of the blow, the weight of the head, took Joe off balance and pulled him over.

The boot caught him in the ribs.

'*Aufstehen!*'

Joe didn't understand the words, but he got the meaning. Pushed himself up and lifted the tool and swung it again. And again. Dared not pause, dared not look towards the shoreline, to search for the lonely gannet, for meandering, carefree birds. The aggregate piled up and one of the other gangs shovelled it into a wheelbarrow. Joe could hear the sound of pickaxes in the distance.

Joe kept an eye on the sun as it drew lower in the sky. His arms and shoulders ached, his muscles were tender and torn. A whistle blew as the sun grew low and the men downed their tools, formed into a line. Joe looked for his jacket, but it had gone. The men began to march and Joe saw that it was a trench they were digging, footings, he guessed, for more fortifications. Other labourers joined them as they left the building area, started along the road.

The land was bleak, barren save for the clumps of coarse coastal grass that covered the earth and a few stunted hawthorn and elder which had curled their roots on the rocky land and grew twisted with the wind. Every ten yards or so there were signs, *Achtung! Minen!* Joe's hands were swollen, gave him pins and needles, sharp as an alligator's teeth.

'Even the *SS* call it the arsehole of the world,' a man said. Joe turned. His neighbour wore a striped uniform, with a red triangle sewn onto his breast.

'*SS?*'

'*Schutzstaffel.* The worst of them all. Makes the *OT* look like kindergarten teachers.'

He smiled. 'Ernst. Your name?'

'Joe,' Joe said. This was the first time he'd spoken to anyone that day and he was grateful. 'Where are we going?'

The man tilted his head at a watchtower in the distance.

They marched on in silence. Joe saw a tough chain-link fence with razor wire coiled along the top, interspersed with round concrete towers. They approached a pair of large iron gates, above which were the words, Lager Sylt. Ernst hawked and spat when he saw the sign, turned to Joe. 'Welcome.'

They filed through the gates, across a yard. The men lined up and Joe followed their lead.

'*Nein*!' He was yanked out of the ranks by one of the guards, pushed with the others who had arrived that day, filed into an office where a guard handed them a metal bowl.

'*Ein. Drei. Vier. Sieben.*' He wrote the number on Joe's hand. 1347. They joined the others in the yard as the roll call continued.

Joe could barely think, or stand. No one spoke. Fatigue made mutes of them all. When it was over, the men filed into a narrow wooden building, stood in line with the bowls as another prisoner, a cook, Joe guessed, a large man with curly hair and a swarthy complexion, a green triangle sewn crudely on the breast of his jacket, tipped a ladle of grey, watery cabbage soup, and a slice of hard black bread into each bowl. Joe stood, shuffling forward. Sometimes the ladle, Joe noted, was full to the brim, other times, it was half empty. The cook didn't care whether it all went into the bowl or dribbled down the side. He breathed like a raging bull. He has a temper, Joe thought. Vicious. His bowl was half filled. Joe said nothing. The men crammed the bread into their mouths and slurped the soup and Joe did the same, dust from his hands forming a film over the surface. It was lukewarm, tasteless, but he could feel it dribbling into his belly, making him sleepy.

The prisoners walked out, towards a row of huts. It was dusk now, the purple light turning the world into shadows and silhouettes. It took a while for Joe's eyes to adjust inside, but he saw the rows of bunk beds and the huddled forms of the labourers in their striped clothing. He pulled off his clothes and knelt down, made the sign of the cross, hands together. *Forgive me, Lord, for I have sinned.*

It was the first time he'd thought of Trude since they had arrived.

§

The guard pushed Joe with his baton.

'*Sie, hier.*' Pushed Ernst too. '*Bringen Sie diese Stücke weg.*'

Ernst said nothing, turned away from the gang, grabbed Joe's arm, *follow me*, walked back to the huts. A truck started up, crawled behind them. Joe could feel the heat from its bonnet. Ernst stopped at the first hut. Three bodies lay on the ground. The truck stopped, engine running. Ernst opened the tailgate.

'You take the legs,' he said. 'I'll take the arms.'

Joe stared. *What?* These bodies. Tossed and tangled.

Joe'd never lifted a dead body before, only ever touched them when they were laid out, clean and calm, ready to meet their makers. Joe placed a hand on one of the shins. The bone was hard, the skin soft, cold, the flesh spongy.

'Now,' Ernst said. 'Now.'

Joe shut his eyes, gripped the ankles, swayed as Ernst swung the body and threw it into the back of the truck.

'Forgive me,' he said. And again. Each hut. Bodies. Knotted. Naked. One was a woman's body.

'Get up,' Ernst said, climbing into the back of the truck and holding out a hand for Joe. He pulled up the tailgate, stepped over the bodies to the side, held onto the railing. Joe followed him as the truck began to lurch forward. Joe grabbed the rail. Dared not lose his balance and fall.

Ernst stood in silence as the truck picked up speed. Joe couldn't look down at the corpses by his feet, or those that lay behind him.

He looked ahead, at the barren grasses and the shore beyond. He could see the coastline wherever he turned.

The truck pulled to a halt and backed close to a cliff, next to another pile of bodies, the flesh bloated and mottled.

'Executions,' Ernst said, releasing the tailgate. 'Garrotted. That's the way the bastards do it here. Or beaten to death.' He flailed his wrist, as if it held a truncheon. 'Crucified, sometimes.'

It was a sheer drop to the sea. Joe could see its shades of violet and sapphire, hear the waves lick against the edge. No birds. No birds. If he jumped now, he'd smash his head against the rocks. It would be over.

'Come,' Ernst said, pulling at a body, holding it by the arms.

Joe hesitated. *Jump. Do it. Now.*

'Throw them over.'

Joe stared at Ernst. This wasn't true. He couldn't mean it.

'For fuck's sake,' Ernst said. Yanked at a body, rolled it over. Joe heard the splash as it entered the water.

'No,' Joe said. 'I can't do this. I can't.'

'Do it,' Ernst said. 'They're dead.'

Joe raised his right hand, *in nomine patris.*

'Shut up,' Ernst said, eyeing the guard who leaned against the door of the truck, smoking. 'Work.' He pulled at another corpse. 'Faster.'

Joe spoke the rest of the prayer quietly, so Ernst couldn't hear. Swinging the bodies over the cliffs like mailbags from a train. Eyes stinging with the salt from his tears. 'Rest in peace. Amen.'

Tailgate up, the truck moved off. Joe heaved, wept. Dry tears. Shock as deep as a crater, black, fathomless, infinite. Neither Ernst nor Joe spoke. The sentences couldn't come. The words weren't there.

In the back of the truck with the sun bright as a spotlight, Joe could see that Ernst was a young man, no more than a year or two older than himself.

'Pieces,' Ernst said. 'Bits. That's what the bastards call us. *Stücke*.'

The truck bumped over an unmade road towards the building site. Joe held on tight.

'You steel yourself,' Ernst said. 'But you never get used to it.'

§

There was a small table in the middle of the barrack and four men were playing poker with a deck of cards that they had filched from a German. They were betting high, Joe could hear, fantasy money, stakes in their dreams.

Ernst stood by watching them.

'How long have you been here?' Joe asked.

'On Alderney? About six months. But I've been a prisoner for ten years.' He smiled. 'And I'm still here. The bastards won't kill me.'

'Ten years,' Joe said. 'That's a long time.' He wasn't sure he'd last ten days.

'I was arrested in 1933,' Ernst went on. 'Clamped in Sachsenhausen.'

'Why?'

'I didn't agree with them.' He smiled. 'We're all commies here. Or crooks. What happened to you?'

Joe wasn't sure what to say. He saw her frail body, the dark sweat under her arms. Had they thrown her off a cliff? Fed her to the fishes and the monsters of the sea? He felt the tears run down his cheeks, his lips quiver. *Don't cry.*

'No matter,' Ernst said. He put his hand on Joe's arm. Joe swallowed. *Be a man.* The poker players roared, slapped the cards on the table. The dealer began to shuffle.

'Your English is good,' Joe said, for want of something to say.

'I need to practise,' Ernst said. 'So stay strong, little man.'

Little man. He hadn't been called that since he left Cloghane for the seminary, felt a rush of homesickness as sudden as a squall.

CHAPTER ELEVEN

DORA

London: June 1985

The asparagus. Dora cooked it all that evening, testing it as if it was a precious spice, *just right.* She'd been to Waitrose and bought unsalted French butter, melted it in the little pan and poured it over, sprinkled ground sea salt and pepper. New potatoes. Jersey potatoes, but no matter. Parsley. Treated herself to a bottle of Riesling, chilled down. *Asparagus. The shortest season. Enjoy, Doralein. Enjoy.* Tasting the lush, tender spears, savouring their sweetness, she was transported back to *Vati* at the table in Charlottenburg, *this Hitler man. It will blow over. He won't hurt us.* Uncle Otto had already left by then.

She'd try and grow it. She could ask at the garden centre whether it would be possible to buy the crowns. If not, perhaps Barbara could bring her some seeds, next time she went to Germany? Or send them to her? Asparagus took years to mature, Dora knew that, but there was room enough in the garden, and Dora had all the time in the world.

There was nothing to worry about. Barbara's interest was in List. Dora had been a means to the end. There would be no reason to show List *her* photograph. And if she did? Would he try and find her now?

And if he did?

No, Dora thought. *No.* That could not happen.

Barbara had accepted her word that she didn't know who the woman in the photograph was. If she asked her again, she'd deny she knew, over and over. This O'Cleary man who claimed to recognise her. What did he know? Dora was puzzled as to how he had her address. If Barbara suspected anything, Dora would suggest that the woman was a friend of her mother's. Why shouldn't her mother have a photograph of her friend?

In an odd way, Dora understood Barbara. She was probably lonely. Was reaching out for truth, for family. She would want to indulge her curiosity, if she thought there was a story. Dora couldn't help her solve her quest, but she understood loneliness. She had done something similar when Uncle Otto died. Tracked down some cousins in New York who had escaped the war. Spread feelers, *tentacles*, to the world. *Let me touch you. You tell me I came from somewhere.* Was that the cry of a refugee? The howl of the exiled?

She'd opened her heart to Charles then, too. *I don't want to be alone.*

'I want you as a friend,' she'd said. She knew it was lame.

'And a husband is not a friend?' He'd winked. 'We could just live together. In sin.'

He had to be more than a friend, and she wasn't ready. The scars were too deep.

§

Barbara returned from Hamburg ten days later. They sat outside, on the green wrought-iron chairs that Dora had bought in the Homebase sale, a pot of coffee and some cherry torte that Dora had made placed on the garden table.

Dora had never been back to Germany. The country had made strides in the last forty years, she knew that, the cities rebuilt, the past confronted. But she had no one there now, although her *soul* was with *Vati*, in the Jüdische Friedhof in Weissensee. She could see it now, the branches of the beech and birch trees linked into a canopy that shed a dappled light over the ground, amber in the autumn when the fading sun filtered through a filigree of red and yellow, luminous in the spring when the world was fresh and the leaves were green. He lay next to *Mutti*, beneath a matching granite slab. She'd chosen the inscription. *Hier ruht mein geliebter Vater. Dr Alfred Simon. 1880–1933.* He'd died too soon, in a rush. She should have written, *always in a hurry*, as his epitaph, but that would have been frowned upon. It was her last memory of him. But the Weissensee cemetery was on the eastern side of the Wall. It would be difficult to visit it, even if she went to Berlin.

'He's an architect,' Barbara was saying, 'Maximilian List. Still designing. His name was there, in the telephone book, in plain view.'

Dora didn't want to hear this. She slumped her head forward, put her hands to her forehead. 'Still designing?'

'Yes.'

'What kind of things? Offices? Houses?'

'I've no idea,' Barbara said. 'Are you all right?'

'Yes, yes,' Dora said. *Ja, ja.* Added, 'I don't know this man, and I don't understand why you want to tell me about him.' Couldn't say, *Don't you understand how this kills me all over again? Brings out demons that I must confront?*

'If you prefer,' Barbara shrugged. 'I didn't meet him, as it happens. He's old, and ill, and his wife guards him like a Rottweiler.'

She broke off a piece of torte with her fork, took a sip of coffee.

'But I want to tell you this, if I may. I did speak with his wife. They've been married now for sixty years, she told me. Apparently, my mother turned up in Hamburg one day in 1944 with a baby and claimed List was the father. She said that my mother had been infatuated with her husband during the war, followed him to the Channel Islands when he was sent to Alderney. Made a real nuisance of herself.'

'Well there you are,' Dora said. 'He wasn't the only one who was unfaithful in the war.' And I know that, she thought, more than most. 'So that must be the end of the question.' She sat straight up, *imagine a string*, her physiotherapist had told her once after she'd had some back pain, *pulling your spine*... 'Out of curiosity,' she said, trying to sound casual. 'What was his house like?'

'His *house*?' Barbara said.

'Yes,' Dora said. 'I've always wondered how architects live, since their buildings are often so brutal.' She smiled, added, 'It's a little beef I have, you see.'

Barbara picked up her coffee, sipped. 'Well, I must disappoint you,' she said. 'It was a square box.' She threw her head back and laughed when the telephone rang, loud and shrill, and Barbara jumped, splashing her coffee into the saucer. Dora pushed herself up from her chair, glad of the interruption and padded into the house.

Jersey: June – December 1943

Dora sat on the edge of the bed, breathless. She tried not to think about what had just happened, but the memory was too large, too overpowering. She could still feel his weight, smell his sweat, his semen. Her heart was racing, her muscles quivering, out of control. She'd never felt so tired, a weariness that drilled to her core. And numb. *Numb.* She couldn't think where she was, what she should do. Wash, *wash*. Rub the filth away. She was contaminated, used. *Entered.* She heard the lock turn. She jumped.

'Follow me.'

The nurse led her along the corridor, down two flights of narrow stairs. She opened a door, pushed Dora inside. Slammed it shut, pulled the bolts. It was night outside, and the room was dark save for a shaft of moonlight that filtered through a light well. A cellar. Dora stood while her eyes adjusted. She could smell the unwashed bodies and hear the slow breathing of sleepers. She could make out platforms, stacked in tiers, and on each a huddled form or two. Bunk beds. She walked along the rows but they were all occupied, except for one on the top in the far corner. Dora took off her shoes, heaved herself up and lay down on rough sacking. She was exhausted, but too scared to sleep.

She must have dozed off, for she woke with a start. Someone was hammering on the door. It was twilight outside and the room was shadowy, but Dora saw the bodies stir in the gloom and shuffle in a line.

'*Venez!*' A woman pulled Dora's ankle. '*Appell!*'

Dora pushed herself down from the bunk and joined the queue. They were all women, dressed in identical, shapeless cotton dresses.

'What is this?' Dora said.

'Do you speak French?'

'A little,' she said.

'The roll call. They count us every morning.'

Dora wanted to say, *At this time?* But the door had been opened and the women were filing out, along the corridor and out through the back door into a small courtyard behind the kitchens. Three soldiers guarded the space, rifles at the ready. The women lined up in rows, about ten in a row. Stood. Dora shifted her weight from left to right, right to left. The dawn air was cool and her flimsy evening frock gave no warmth.

The sun rose and illuminated the sky and Dora could hear, in the distance, a clock chiming the hour. Five. Five o'clock. A man came out in the grey uniform of the *Wehrmacht.* Next to him was a woman wearing the same shapeless frock as the others, except she wore a green armband on her left arm. They walked along the rows.

'*Nummer*?' the *Wehrmacht* officer said. He ticked a form, stopped at Dora. '*Nummer*?'

'I don't know,' Dora said. *What for?*

'*Name*?'

'Dora Simon.'

'Your clothes?'

'This is all I have,' Dora said. The officer threw his head back and studied Dora through slits of eyes. He curled his lip, nodded to the woman with the green armband.

'*Kommen*,' the woman said, adding in French as they left the parade ground. 'I'm Agnes Moreau. I'm the *Kapo* here.'

'*Kapo*?' Dora said.

'The boss. I run the place.' She tossed her head towards the officer. 'They haven't a clue.'

She led Dora into a small room stacked with folded dresses. Took one from the shelf, handed it to Dora, lifted a pair of shoes from another shelf and threw them down on the floor. 'Change.' She pointed to Dora's dress. 'That is for the evening.'

'I have no underwear,' Dora said.

Agnes blew through her lips, shrugged.

'You don't understand,' Dora said. 'I need knickers.' *I want underwear.* It was privacy, security. Comfort. She was bruised.

'Puh,' Agnes said. 'Dress.' She spoke in French. Dora slipped out of her red frock, threaded her arms through the cotton garment and tugged it down. It was rough and coarse, cheap cotton, shapeless. Agnes handed Dora a metal bowl and spoon.

'Keep hold of this,' she said. 'Your number is two hundred and seventy-one.'

'What's the number for?'

'*For?* To keep count. You're the two hundredth and seventy-first woman to pass through. The Germans like their records.' She laughed, and Dora caught her breath, foul as a bat's cave. '*Alors, sors!*'

Dora followed her out. The other women were still standing in line and Dora took her place. The soldier began the roll call again, from the beginning.

'*Nummer? Nummer?*'

The women were subdued, and Dora caught their mood. They were counted three times. There was no order to the numbers, and there couldn't have been more than seventy here. No wonder the Germans were muddled. They had been standing for two hours. She was tired, too, with a headache. She hadn't eaten for twenty-four hours.

§

They carried the meal from the kitchen to the dormitory. A slice of black bread. Dora swallowed hers, swilled it down with foul brown liquid.

'What is this place?' she said to the woman sitting next to her, an emaciated creature, her face lined. Gaps in her teeth. Her name, Dora learned, was Collette.

Collette coughed, a deep phlegmy *caagh.*

She could have TB, Dora thought, she's thin enough.

'You haven't guessed?' Collette said, adding, 'It's a brothel. For the soldiers. A *Soldatenbordell.*'

Dora swallowed. This was what Knackfuss had in mind. To be forced. Over and over.

'Who are you all?'

'*Nous sommes prostitués,*' Collette said, added, 'from France, mainly. What you English call "tarts".'

Dora didn't let on she wasn't English.

Collette's eyes grew round and she smiled, a grin wide enough to crack her fragile skin. She must once have been beautiful, Dora could see, with her clear cheekbones and high forehead. Two soldiers were standing in the doorway.

'Uh-oh,' Collette said. 'Nearly time.' She was still smiling, gums raw and bleeding. 'How come you're here?'

'I was caught,' Dora said. 'Nursing a sick man.' She added, 'A runaway. From the *OT*.'

'Nursing?' Collette said. 'Are you a nurse?'

Dora nodded. 'Midwife. *Une sage-femme*.'

'That will be handy,' Collette said. 'I'd rather you fix us up than the cow in the *Revier*.'

It took Dora a moment to register what Collette was saying.

'You get pregnant?' Dora said. Her period had been due when she was arrested, but it hadn't come yet. It was being here, the shock and stress of it all. She knew the biology, the hypothalamus gland couldn't cope, closed down, ceased producing the hormones.

'Of course,' Collette said. 'You've never done this before, have you?'

Dora shook her head. Collette placed her hand on Dora's arm.

'Courage,' she said. 'Don't think about it when they're going at you. Be someone else, some*where* else, in your head, when it happens. And laugh, inside. Oh,' she added, 'and listen. They think you can't hear, but if you keep your ears open, you can learn a lot. That way you'll survive.'

Dora's legs grew weak. 'I can't,' she said.

'You can,' Collette snapped. 'If you want to live.'

The soldiers were banging their batons on the door frame and the women began to push themselves up from their bunks or the floor where they had been sitting.

'Why are you here?' Dora said. 'What did you do?'

'Do?' Collette winked. 'A brothel is a good place to hide a man. Listen,' she lowered her voice and added, 'Agnes Moreau. Thick with the Nazis. *Kapos* do their dirty business for them. Be careful.'

Dora nodded.

'But she likes her smokes,' Collette went on. 'Give her all the dog-ends you find. That'll keep her sweet.' They began to file out, shuffling in ill-fitting shoes. 'We're called asocial. But we're necessary for *their* war effort, to keep their men virile.' She laughed again. 'Work that out.'

'Were you all prostitutes?' Dora said.

'We are now,' Collette said. 'Right in the belly of the beast.'

Dora had been assigned to the officers' mess, Agnes told her. '*Hand-picked.* For the top brass. Being pure Aryan, and that. Don't want the *hoi polloi* fucking you up.'

Dora moved her head, but the smell of Agnes's teeth curled up her nose anyway.

§

The same *SS* officer reserved Dora for himself. He was, she learned from Agnes, on leave for two weeks. Dora braced herself. Shut her eyes, clenched her teeth. What had Collette said? Be someone else, be somewhere else. He forced her legs wide and she lay stiff and passive, hating him. On the third night, he rolled back, naked, one arm behind his head.

'Do you know who I am?' he said.

'No.'

'*Hauptsturmführer* Maximilian List, *Kommandant von Baubrigade I*,' he said, 'Neuengamme. *Im* Alderney.'

He said it to impress, but Dora pretended not to understand and showed no recognition. There was something absurd, she thought, about this man boasting his importance with his member lying small and limp on his groin.

'I was an architect before the war,' he said. 'In Berlin. Beautiful buildings.'

Then why are you building hell now? Dora thought.

'Great plans,' he went on. 'When this war is finished, we will rebuild the city. Have you been there?'

He leaned on one elbow, looked at her. Dora couldn't work out why he was talking to her. This was not what she expected, not what he'd done on the other nights. His eyes were pale and grey, flecked with gold, his features even. He was a youngish man, a few years older than herself. A captain already. *Kommandant*, no less. He must have made an impression on the bigwigs in Berlin.

'No,' he said, not waiting for her to answer. 'Of course not. How could you have been there?' He smiled, reached over her for a cigarette, and lit it. 'An avenue of splendours. A people's hall. The *Führer*'s palace. Such magnificence to come.'

The smoke blew towards her. Dora crinkled her nose.

'You are a beautiful woman,' he said. 'Don't pull a face. There, look.' He stubbed it out hard so it snapped in two, and the tobacco spilled out across the ashtray. 'I have finished it. It won't bother you anymore.'

He picked up his clothes from the floor and walked towards the bathroom. Dora listened as he splashed the water, heard as he sang the opening lines of *Liebchen, ade*. Darling, goodbye. It had been one of her favourite songs, a big hit just after her father died, the year she left Berlin, so it had a special memory for her. He had a good singing voice, a powerful baritone. She hated him singing this song, as if he was wrenching it from her, gouging it out of her memory. But he was giving it back to her too, reminding her that beyond this room with its flock wallpaper and Persian rug, there could be a man who sang a love song to his sweetheart.

He arrived promptly at six the next night.

'You know how I like my scotch,' he said. 'You know my tastes.'

Routines, too, Dora thought. *This is not a man who likes surprises.* She poured the scotch.

'Take off your clothes.'

Dora breathed hard, clenched her teeth, yanked the dress down over her thighs. She was already raw and chapped from the ersatz soap they had to use and the rayon dress caught on her rough skin as it fell, a thousand needles pricking. She winced, glanced up. He was looking at her, studying her. He put down the glass and walked towards the bed.

They lay together after. Dora tried to think of the word. After he had *expended* himself, as they had the night before and the night before that.

'And you?' he said. 'What did you do before the war?'

Why should she converse with him? She was his prisoner, his plaything. He wasn't interested in her. Talking would give him the wrong impression. She was under duress. He had to know that.

'I asked you a question,' he said. 'I expect to be answered.'

Let him wait for an answer. She wasn't one of his subordinates.

'We can do this two ways,' he said. 'I can tell you're not a professional prostitute.'

Dora watched him from the corner of her eye, his mouth stern. The muscles in his jaw twitched once, twice.

'But make no mistake. I can treat you like one if you choose.'

She heard the threat behind his words. Collette had told hair-raising stories of men with quirky, brutal needs. List had been straightforward in his desires. Now she saw his menace, the lust for power and pain.

'Or we stay civilised,' he went on. 'Whichever you prefer.'

Dora felt a lump in her throat, and her eyes stung. His voice was cold, contemptuous. He'd been well-mannered so far. Why rouse his anger? Why make things worse?

'I was a nurse,' she said. 'A midwife.'

'A noble calling.' He spoke quietly. 'I know your number. Two hundred and seventy-one.' She felt his fingers walk towards hers across the sheet and he brushed the back of her hand with his thumb. 'But not your name. What are you called?'

Dora swallowed. He sounded soft, conciliatory, stroking her hand as if they were romancing, as if no threat had just passed between them.

'Dora.'

'That's pretty,' he said. 'Like you.'

He turned to lie on his side as the mattress bounced up, down. She could feel his breath close to her face.

'I hear you're Swedish.'

She was waiting for this moment, for someone to question her, find her out. *Lies have short legs.* Well, let them do with her what they will. Anywhere would be better than this.

'Born in Stockholm, I'm told,' he went on. 'It's a beautiful city, is it not?'

'I wouldn't know,' she said.

'Oh? Why not?'

She could own up, admit who she was. Get it over and done with, packed off to Germany. But the thought terrified her. She remembered her geography classes from school, Swedish cities close to the Arctic Circle, Luleå, Kiruna. Would he know those? Take the risk. She braced herself. One more lie.

'I wasn't raised there.'

'But you weren't raised in Jersey, either. So where were you brought up?'

'Luleå.' She hoped she sounded Swedish. She had no idea how it was pronounced.

'Luleå? Where's that?'

'In the very north,' she said. 'In Lapland.'

'In the Arctic Circle? Land of the midnight sun?'

'Yes,' she said. 'Almost.'

He rolled onto his back, reached for a cigarette from the bedside table and lit it. 'I always think that climate and landscape build character, don't you?'

'Perhaps,' Dora said.

'So how would you consider the land of the midnight sun influences the Swedish character?'

Dora couldn't imagine, said the first thing that came into her head. 'It makes us pessimistic in summer,' she said. 'When it's light all day and night.'

'How come? I would have thought you would be happy for that.'

'We know it will come to an end.' Dora thought fast. 'And in the winter, we are optimistic, because we know it cannot last.'

He laughed, from the belly, so the bed shook, his mouth wide open. He had a gold tooth, lower premolar, left side.

'I like you, Dora,' he said. 'I will look out for you.'

I never forget a face.

He stubbed out his cigarette, stood up and dressed. She lay still, stared at the window, couldn't bear to watch as he pulled on his trousers and tucked in his shirt, ordinary things that suggested he, too, was a man. He stood by the door, his cap under one arm. He raised his other, '*Heil* Hitler.'

Heil Shitler. Schmittler. Dora picked up the cigarette butt. A useful currency.

§

He reserved her for his exclusive use when he was there, and demanded that she was, as Agnes put it, 'clean' for three days beforehand.

'List's special whore,' Agnes Moreau said. 'The *SS* get all the privileges.'

Dora was glad. He was not like the others with their cut and thrust and cold indifference.

Some were lonely men who wanted companionship. Family men, from the *GFP* or the *Wehrmacht*, who missed their wives, *SS* on leave from France, or the Low Countries. They'd try to kiss Dora, touch her breasts, hit her when she stiffened and curled her toes, pushing their hands and faces away. *Put a bit of life into it.* Why should she? She cared nothing for these men, their needs, their isolation, their infidelities. They could do with her what they wanted, but she would not give them the intimacy of a kiss, the satisfaction of a caress. There were others, perverts who despised her, debased her, brutalising her with foul language and unnatural needs and who left her bruised and sore, and in despair.

Once or twice they introduced an *Obergruppenführer* or some other big shot from Germany or France, offering Dora like a delicacy.

'Don't resist,' Collette said. 'Just gets them madder. It's not worth it.'

In the belly of the beast. She and Collette and the other women, even Agnes, they were the true face of war, they paid the real costs. The Trojan War, Dora thought, would have had a very different hue if Briseis or Chryseis had told the story, revealed the *impotency* of Agamemnon, his need for women to satisfy his manhood.

Agnes made sure Dora had no rough trade before List's arrival. She knew which men to divert elsewhere, so Dora read the clues, knew when he was due a visit. List was not like the others. He behaved well, mannerly. He must be from a good family, Dora thought. He was familiar now, his body known. He called her Dora. *Doralein.*

He didn't dismiss her as soon as he had ejaculated. Didn't shout, *get out,* as if she was the unclean sinner. He talked about his wife and young sons, laid his head next to hers on the pillow. He was a long way from home, lonely. She could smell his shaven skin. He was a fastidious man, clean, careful. She supposed that came from his training. Architects had to be precise, saw beauty and form in three dimensions.

'Do you like music, Dora?'

'Yes,' she said.

'I would like to be able to render music in my buildings,' he said. 'To make a sound wave into a structure. Don't you think that would be sublime?'

He was talking to her, one to one. He did that now. She'd lost count of the number of times he'd come to her. It was autumn already, and she had been here for months. Sometimes she wondered whether he came to Jersey just to visit her, and he came often. He was an intelligent man, engaging. She had to admit his idea was novel.

'It would be wavy,' she said, adding, 'I thought architects liked straight, classical lines.'

He lay back, and shut his eyes for a moment. 'You're right. A sound wave oscillates. Perhaps it's the energy I'm thinking of. To capture that in a building. Oh, Dora,' he rolled over, placed his head on her stomach. 'I have such dreams, such plans.'

One evening, she ran her fingers through his hair without thinking. Fine and straight, different from her own coarse, curly hair, or Geoffrey's thick black crop. She had known men like him in Berlin, urbane, sophisticated, professional men. She saw them at the opera or the theatre when she went with her father, in those halcyon days before Hitler came to power. What *Vati* would have called suitable men, eligible men. She could have fallen for a man like this, if they'd met under different circumstances. Maximilian was an oasis in a rough, stone-strewn desert, compared to the other men she had to endure in this prison. She tried to think of Geoffrey, but their last conversation, about the way he had behaved towards Vanessa, had made her doubt him, his integrity, his loyalty. The memory of him was fading. Time and place, she thought, shrink. List would call it perspective, the way trees in the distance looked smaller than those close up, the way life's experiences became dots on the horizons of memory. Geoffrey was *there*, gone, and List was *here*, now, in this room, in this bed. Could they have even met in Berlin? In the foyer of the opera, perhaps?

'We can mould wood or steel, curve and bend it, for our ships, submarines,' List was saying. 'Our aeroplanes. We have the science, and the skills. So why not build concert halls like that? Great opera houses? Wrap ourselves in a womb of sound? Or let it dance like a living organism? Do you see, Dora?'

He pushed himself onto his elbow and reached across for his jacket, pulling out a pencil and a small notepad.

'Look.' He sat up, crossed his legs. 'I have this with me always.' He tapped the notepad and balanced it on his knee. 'I jot down ideas, inspirations. Let me show you.' He slapped the space next to him. 'Sit here.'

Dora leaned into him as he turned the pages. There were sketches of trees and plants, clouds and waves. There were designs that followed the shape of a branch or leaf, mimicked the fluidity of form and movement.

'Sit still,' he said and shifted his position. He lifted the pencil, looking at her with an intensity that was both detached and passionate. 'Don't move.'

'I have to breathe,' she said.

He sketched her for a few minutes, then smiled, stopped, turned the page so she could see it. 'There.'

A few simple lines but he had captured something in her face, an openness, a happiness perhaps. He had made her beautiful. Is that what he saw?

'Pull your hair back, on top of your head.'

Dora piled it up, twisting the curls and knotting them. It would hold for a moment.

'And lie on your side.'

She slid down on her elbow and stretched herself along the bed. She could hear the scratch of his pencil as he drew her naked body.

'I should design you a house,' he said. 'Perfectly poised. Like you. In repose.'

'How could that be?'

He waved his hand, soft undulations in the air. 'I'll ponder it,' he said. 'Give me time.'

'I'd like to see that,' she said. She was content to give him something of herself, if only inspiration.

'I'll call it after you. *Das Dora Haus.* Would you like that?'

He pushed himself up and dressed. This time, he leant over and kissed her forehead.

'I have so many ideas,' he said. 'You see, I will become the most important architect this century has seen. I will stretch the boundaries of what's possible, design living organic buildings. And you, my dear, have given me something special. You are my muse. My beautiful, beautiful muse.'

He walked towards the door, and turned. 'I will be back in a week or two. I will look forward to that with huge pleasure.'

Dora smiled and nodded. *Me too*, she found herself thinking.

§

Agnes kept a close eye on them all, tipped off Nurse Hoffmann at their monthly check-ups, who needed a scrape, who didn't. Dora didn't require Agnes or Nurse Hoffmann to confirm what Dora knew herself. The *SS* didn't use protection.

'One of the perks,' Agnes said. 'With *certain* women. *Chosen* women.'

It must have happened early on, that first night even.

'No wire for you,' she said. 'They've got other plans.'

'What do you mean?'

Agnes laughed. 'Just wait.'

A worm within, an invasion. Dora eyed Nurse Hoffmann's curette, but wasn't sure she could use it on herself, even though she felt dead to the child. Perhaps that would be enough to kill it. Willpower alone.

Nurse Hoffmann made sure Dora had extra milk.

Jewish. If only they knew, Dora thought, with their spurious science. *You have to laugh.* Only that would be too dangerous. *Laugh inside.* She could tell no one, not even Collette. Every evening she sweated, nerves tight as a drum. It would be so easy to let something slip.

Yet her guard was down so often with List now. He took his time, had become easy with her, and Dora wondered whether he'd grown to like her, even to love her a little, despite himself. He talked with her, took to staying the night, curled by her side, hand on her belly. Dora was comforted in those times, when she could lie in a soft bed with clean sheets, listening as his breath grew slow and deep, feeling his limbs grow heavy and relaxed. He made life bearable.

Then he kissed her once again. A soft pucker on her sleeping eyelids, the tip of her nose, his lips resting on hers, as if to say, *May I enter?* A kiss was intimate. A kiss touched her inner fibre, joined her body to its spirit. She had little left of herself to give or withhold. A kiss was private, was freely offered. *Don't let them kiss you*, Collette once said. *They think they own you then.*

He didn't force her, no bulbous muscle rummaging in her mouth, just a tender touch, lip to lip, and despite herself, Dora opened her mouth and there was the tip of his tongue and that was all.

He had vision, schemes. What young man didn't? Perhaps, after the war, if the Germans won, he'd realise them. What would she be doing? Would he come for her, make a case to free her, *let this one go*? Did he wonder if they would be together when this was all over? In the house he designed for her? Dora's house.

He was a professional, a perfectionist, and she admired that in him. Everyone was caught up in this war. He was only doing his job. You couldn't blame him for that. *He* didn't send her to the brothel. He was, after all, a man. Not a monster, not like Knackfuss or Zepernick. She began to think about his visits, almost to look forward to them. He wasn't a bad man, she knew. Something had turned him. Ambition. Signed up with the Nazis to get the better commissions. Who could blame him? She couldn't believe he shared their attitudes to the Jews, turned a blind eye to the Nazis' worst excesses. If he discovered she was a Jew, he'd protect her.

Plenty of Germans disagreed with the Nazis, after all. Why would an *SS* officer be different?

She began to like his smile, the fine lines round his pale grey eyes, along the contours of his mouth.

She ran her finger along his cheeks, traced the form of his nose and lips.

He took her hand and rubbed it against his chin. 'Perhaps you could shave me?'

'I don't know how. I'd be scared I'd cut you.'

He leaned over, his mouth close to hers. 'Shave me. My razor is in the bathroom.'

Dora had watched *Vati* shave from when she was a little girl, standing by the basin in the bathroom as he pulled his face this way and that. 'It's not hard, Doralein,' he'd said. 'Thirty-degree angle, down, up.'

It had been one of the most private moments of the day, just she and *Vati*. They had their best talks then, shared their deepest secrets.

'Go on,' List said. 'There's plenty of hot water. Soap.' He smiled.

Dora picked up the facecloth and ran it under the hot tap so it steamed. She returned, laid it on his face. Fetched the soap, and the blade, tying the strap to the bedpost as she prepared to strop it.

'You've done this before,' List said, his voice muffled by the steaming flannel.

'I used to watch my father,' Dora said. 'But I've never shaved anyone.'

He pulled her close. 'It is one of the most intimate things you can do for a man,' he said. 'Despite my better judgement, this is what I want from you.'

She rubbed the soap onto his face, lathering it with her fingers. The soap the women had to use was made from lye and scoured the skin. But this was soft and fragrant, tender as foam in her hand.

She felt its balm anoint her own skin, its goodness seep through as she massaged it into his cheek with gentle circular movements.

She took the knife and laid it flat against his skin, pulling it back at an angle, stretching the skin as she remembered her father doing and running the blade down his cheek. Her hand was shaking, so she held the shaft tight. *Keep steady.*

'You could kill me,' he said.

'Then I'd die too,' Dora said. They'd execute her, for sure.

'But would you die *inside*?' He took her hand and pushed it against her chest. 'What do you feel there, in your heart? Do you see a monster, or a dutiful man?'

'Not a monster,' she said, after a moment.

'Don't you want to kill me?'

She shook her head. 'No.' Her voice was soft. 'No. I want you to live.' This man who shielded her from the other men when he visited. And frightened her. Could danger be enchanting? Did she thrill to that? Did that make his love elusive, enticing? Exotic, even?

He smiled. 'Carry on.' He shut his eyes as Dora scraped, lifting his face, left, right, up, down, before patting it dry. He rubbed his hand around his chin. 'You have just been promoted,' he said. 'Barber to the *Kommandant*.'

He took her hand and led her to the bed. 'Make love to me,' he said. 'As if you care.'

Dora smelled the scent of the soap, the delicate, freshness of violets.

Afterwards, they lay together in bed. He watched her, stroking her skin with his fingertips.

'Why don't you sing me a Swedish song?' he said.

She felt the blood drain from her body, rush to her head. *This was it.* He had been tricking her, waiting to catch her off guard.

'I don't know any,' she said.

'No? I heard the Swedes were great singers.'

'Not me,' Dora said, adding, 'I'm afraid.' Adding, again, 'You sang a song once. Something like '*Liebchen, ade*.' Will you teach it to me?'

He smiled at her. 'You heard me sing that?'

'In the bathroom,' she said. 'I thought it sounded pretty. Far prettier than any song I know. Please sing it to me. You have a good voice.' She meant it too, she realised.

'If I teach you the song, will you teach me Swedish?'

Dora swallowed hard. Now she would be caught out. Why did he want to learn Swedish? Nobody spoke Swedish.

'But you are German,' she said. 'The most powerful country in Europe. We must all learn German.' She warmed to her theme. 'Swedish will be forgotten.'

Vati had gone to a medical conference in Stockholm once. He learned how to say hello, thank you, goodbye, and Dora practised the words. She was five years old. It was their private code, their special way of saying goodnight, just she and *Vati*. *Hej då, Sverige*. Arms round his neck and his moustache tickling her chin. *Hej då, Tyskland*. Here *Vati* was, protecting her now, even from the grave. And here she was, sharing those words with a German.

'*Hej då, Sverige*,' she said, raising her arm in the air. 'Swedish,' she added.

'How do I know you're not insulting me?' he said. 'Or *Herr* Hitler?'

'Because,' she had become cunning, 'you like me, so why would I insult you?'

'So what did those words mean?'

'Goodbye, Sweden. I believe you would say, *auf wiedersehen*.'

He laughed. 'You learn well,' he said. 'Do you like me, Dora*chen*?'

'Yes,' she said. She couldn't imagine anything else now. 'Do you like me?' *Love me, even?*

He pushed himself off the bed and walked to the bathroom. She heard him wash, watched as he came out and strode towards her. He grabbed her arm and with his free hand smacked her across the cheek. She breathed hard, feeling the smart as the blood rushed to the blow.

'What am I doing here? With you?'

He yanked her onto her stomach and forced himself into her from the rear, a sharp thrust that made her scream in pain. She lay silent on the bed, quivering, fearful. She felt his hands grip her shoulders and he flipped her on her back.

His eyes were glacier-pale in the half-light. 'You made me do this,' he said. He snatched his clothes from the chair, pulled up his underpants, shook the trousers before he threaded his legs through them. 'Help me dress.'

She felt faint, feeble, her skin clammy. *Shock*. She knew the symptoms.

'Now.'

She crawled to the edge of the bed, stretched her feet onto the floor. Her legs buckled and she fell back on the bed, her breath in short, anxious starts. A log fell in the grate and the sparks snapped too loud. She had been unprepared for this, lulled by his manner.

She heard his steps on the floor, felt his presence before her, his finger on her chin as he lifted her face.

'Did I hurt you?' he said, his voice quiet and calm once more.

Dora nodded. It wasn't the physical pain, though that was bad enough. It was her own stupidity, her naivety, to think he cared.

'I'm not a brute,' he said. 'But I like order. Things in their place.'

He turned, pulled on his shirt, grabbed his jacket and cap, his gloves and boots, and left.

§

She was summoned the next morning. Agnes pulled her out of the workshop.

'Hoffmann wants to see you.' She'd made a toothpick from a feather stub, was digging at her gums. 'Now.'

Dora laid the webbing flat, walked up to the *Revier*, knocked on the door of Hoffmann's office. Maximilian List was sitting at the desk, his cap on the table, his gloves, flattened and smoothed, next to it. Hoffmann stood beside him. Dora shut the door behind her, leant back for support. *This was it.* He was ordering her to leave, would send her to Germany.

'Why didn't you tell me?' he said.

'Tell you what?'

'That you're pregnant.'

Dora looked at the nurse, but Hoffmann's face was hard and impassive. 'I wasn't sure if you should know,' Dora said.

'Of course I should know.' He smiled. 'This is wonderful news.' He stood up, walked towards her, flattened his hand over her belly and the coarse linen shift that draped it.

'I can feel the baby move. You should be proud,' he said. 'Are you? Are you happy?'

I am a prisoner, she wanted to say. *You brutalised me. Rejected me. How can that make me happy?*

'Remove her from the brothel. Forthwith.' He was addressing Hoffmann, a rebuke. Dora understood that tone.

§

Collette died two days before Christmas.

'*Du und du*.' The soldier pointed to two women, his breath unfurling, frosty and cloudy against the night sky. '*Holen Sie das Stück*.' *Get the piece.* Collette wasn't even a body, had no dignity, even in death. She was a piece, a *bit*. Dora's eyes welled up and the tears overflowed down her cheeks.

There was a Christmas tree in the centre of the hallway, a lanky pine that reached to the ceiling and shed needles that worked their way into the women's feet. They always had a tree, she and her father, in that comfortable flat in Charlottenburg. The housekeeper,

Anni, insisted on buying it each year, decorating it with candles. *So what, Doralein,* he'd say. *Let her have it. We're Germans, after all.* Now, it was mocking home with its remembrance, its scents.

She'd only known Collette a few months, but she felt her death as keenly as she had her father's. It was ten years since he had died. December, 1933. Six months since her capture. It felt like time had reversed, that her father was alive yesterday, that this prison had enclosed her for a decade.

That evening, Maximilian List called for her. There was a bottle of champagne in an ice bucket. He poured her a glass.

'I have been thinking,' he said, handing her the glass. 'I was too hard on you.'

Was this a trick? Would the nurse burst into the room, see her with the drink, charge her with impertinence, or theft?

'At another time,' he went on, 'you would be my mistress.'

Was he lulling her again, or wooing her?

'Drink,' he said. 'It's good. Moët and Chandon. A vintage year.' He lifted his glass. 'To victory,' he said and linked his arm through hers as they sipped and the bubbles burst on their open mouths, sharp and close to.

'Victory,' she repeated. *But for the Allies, not for you.* Was she being disloyal? What would happen if the Allies won? Would she try and save him?

'I've been thinking too,' he went on, taking her hand and leading her to the sofa. There was a fire burning in the grate, homely logs that cast a warm, flickering light across his face. He placed his hand on her stomach, laid his head against her breasts. 'Perhaps I should take you to Alderney.'

'Alderney? Away from here?'

He nodded. 'Have you for myself. Would you like that?' He cupped her chin in his hand, searching her eyes for an answer.

'Yes,' she said. To be free of here, of its stench and pain, of the daily toil.

'I designed the residence myself.'

Was he planning on making her his housekeeper? *Das Dora Haus.* Why else would he tell her that? She'd learn to trust him again. She'd like that. Sitting together in the evening light. And when the baby was born, the three of them, together. She'd learn to love this baby.

'I forget the war when I am with you,' he was saying. 'You give me strength. If you were by my side every night, I could achieve so much. Are you enjoying this?' He nodded towards the champagne, reaching for a small package from the table. He gave it to her. 'Open it.'

She undid the ribbon, spread the wrapping paper. He had used the portrait he had drawn of her. Inside was a smaller packet, covered in waxed paper.

'Please use it when I visit,' he said. 'Sweet violet. Soft on your skin. We can imagine we are lovers and you will remember me by the scent.'

Savon de Violette. She pressed it against her nose, breathed in the flowery aroma, fingered the soft wax, the powdery crumbs.

'*Frohe Weihnachten*,' he said. 'Happy Christmas.'

She cried. *Soft on your skin.* He had noticed. Cared.

CHAPTER TWELVE

JOE

Jersey: June 1985

Joe couldn't get the image of Trude out of his mind. It was a solemn likeness, an official mugshot, the sort you have for a passport. Unsmiling, face-on, stiff-necked. Joe sat in his caravan all afternoon, tried to distract himself. He made the bed, cleaned the kettle, repaired the faulty window catch. But the photograph sat like a magnet, drawing him back. Trude. Did he feel for her *now*? Well, for sure, but not the way Geoffrey still had feelings for Dora.

At teatime, he went over to the house to make dinner. There was bacon, eggs, tomatoes in the pantry, a tin of mini frankfurters left over from Christmas, some Co-op baked beans and a bit of black pudding. Cold potatoes from yesterday. He lifted the old cast-iron frying pan onto the Aga, melted the lard, flicked the sausages and bacon over as they hissed and spat.

Ate in silence, dipping bread and butter into the yolk of the egg, knife squeaking on the plate as he sliced into the bacon, wiping the tomato juice from his mouth with the back of his hand.

He looked up: Geoffrey was studying him.

'Would you mind telling me what's going on,' he said. 'Have you bankrupted us?'

'No.' Joe looked up. 'Why do you say that?'

'Because,' Geoffrey was smiling, 'I've never seen you so distracted. Have you seen a ghost?'

Joe stood up and filled the kettle for their tea. 'Perhaps,' he said.

'And would it have anything to do with the letter you received today?'

'How did you know I had a letter?'

Geoffrey laughed. 'The postman told me. Said it was from England. Said the sender had a German name and he wondered what you were doing, *corresponding*.'

Joe poured the water into the teapot. 'It's none of his business.'

'He's curious. You've lived like a hermit for forty years and suddenly have a penfriend. That's how he sees it. Thinks you have a fancy woman.'

'Why does he think it's a German?'

'Hummel. He said that's a German name.'

'Does he now,' Joe said.

Was it a coincidence that the same woman had images of both Dora and Trude? *My mother had some connection with Jersey.* Perhaps her mother wasn't English. Perhaps she was German. Joe had taken Barbara Hummel in good faith. But now she'd shown him Trude's photo too, he wasn't sure who she was, or what she was after. How could he break that to Geoffrey after all he'd been through?

Geoffrey had poured out his heart to Joe. Joe should come clean with him. He owed it to him, after all these years, to confess his part, hard though it was. He poured the tea, sat with his elbows on the table, spooning in the sugar and stirring his mug.

'I have something to tell you,' he began. 'About the day the *Feldpolizei* arrested you, in the war.'

He stared at the tea eddying in the mug, brown rings and froth.

'You see,' Joe took a deep breath and went on. 'It was me who led them to you.'

Joe paused, watched as Geoffrey raised his head and looked at him. 'You?'

'I didn't mean to,' Joe said. 'But there was this German nurse, you see.'

He lifted out the spoon and it fell with a clatter on the plate.

'Sorry,' he said, picking it up and laying it down silently. 'I don't know how to say this, but I had an intimate relationship with her. Yes.' *Say it how it was*, that's what they called it in the papers. No time now for euphemisms. 'And in the course of that I led her to the field with the dell, where I watch the birds.'

'You?' Geoffrey said again.

'It was me who led her to the farm.'

Geoffrey sat there shaking his head.

'I've never had the courage to tell you, see,' Joe said. 'I was a coward. I thought if I stay here I can make amends. Atone. It was a terrible sin, what I did. And there's no excusing.' Joe stood up, pushed back his chair so the legs grated on the flagstone floor. 'I can pack my bags now, if that's what you're wanting. I quite understand.'

He picked up his mug and walked towards the door.

'I'll be in the van.'

Joe stepped out into the evening, with a light head. He should have confessed forty years ago. He was a weak man, that was for sure. *Feeble.* Faint-hearted, a moral slouch. *A charlatan.* Oh, he had guilt, by the shedload. But what was guilt, without true remorse? Without penance? An indulgence, that was all. An affectation. All breast-beating and *mea culpas.* Empty, selfish gestures.

He let himself into the caravan, turned on the lamp, kicked off his shoes. He'd be out of a home now, of course, but he could throw himself at the mercy of the Little Sisters, if needs be. He sat on the window seat that doubled as his bed and looked across the yard at the kitchen. The light was on and he hadn't cleared away the tea things. He watched as Geoffrey pushed himself up, held the table for support, lifted a plate and took it to the sink. No, he couldn't just walk out, like that, after all these years. Geoffrey needed help.

Joe put his shoes back on, crossed the yard and opened the door.

'I can leave in the morning,' he said. 'We–' He corrected himself, 'You can hire a nurse.'

'Stop being so daft,' Geoffrey said, sitting down, indicating to Joe that he sat too, his arthritic hands trembling on the back of the chair. 'And that's the end of it.'

Joe wasn't sure he should sit, but he also knew that he could no sooner leave Geoffrey now than run a four-minute mile.

§

'I've been thinking about what you said.'

It was a few evenings later, after supper. Geoffrey was sitting by the stove, on his usual chair. The varnish on its arms had long worn off, and the bare wood was polished with age. The kitchen faced north and was always cool, but the Aga gave out a gentle warmth which they were always grateful for, even in the summer.

Joe looked up.

'It made no sense. You're too hard on yourself.'

'For what?'

Joe heard Geoffrey take a breath, pause before he spoke. 'For what happened to Dora and me.'

Joe folded the newspaper he had been reading. They had talked more about the war of late. It had something to do with that Hummel woman, churning up old memories. Something also, Joe thought, to do with a reckoning, now their span was nearly up.

'Why do you think that?' Joe played for time. He hadn't meant to betray them, but that was little consolation. His *sin* had had consequences.

'Because the light reflected off your field glasses,' Geoffrey said. 'In the top field. And I thought to myself, he's there, watching. He's seen everything.'

Joe opened his mouth, lost for words. He had no idea he'd been spotted, *could* be spotted. Geoffrey had known all along that it was Joe. Had never said a word, for these past years. His voice was gentle. Had he forgiven Joe? How could he? Joe wasn't sure how to answer him. This was such an intimate thing to say.

'I couldn't bring myself to say anything to you,' Joe said. *Be frank*, after all this time. 'I was too full of shame. Guilt.'

A coward, two and three times over.

'Why?' Geoffrey said. 'You had nothing to do with it. You couldn't have stopped it.'

Well no, Joe thought, maybe not from the field, not as he watched it all unfold. But *before*, there was plenty of time. If he'd never fallen in love, if he'd never broken his vows, none of it would have happened.

'But don't you see?' Joe said. 'I had–' he hesitated. *Tell the truth. Get it off your chest.* 'Trude. I shouldn't have, I know. I was a priest.' He looked at Geoffrey, but Geoffrey sat, impassive. 'She was a German,' Joe went on. 'Don't you understand? With the German army. Not like your nurse, with the British. I took her with me, birdwatching. In your field. I'm sorry. Had I realised–' he paused, swallowed. 'She knew.'

Geoffrey laughed. 'But how would she know, unless she had been spying on me for months?'

'Well, you see,' Joe said, 'I think now that's just what she did. I think she went there at night, spied on you. She'd hoodwinked me. Tempted me. She was a Jezebel, for sure. And I gave her Naboth.'

Why blame someone else? He alone was responsible.

'I fell for her womanly wiles,' Joe said. 'I was as guilty and as gullible as Ahab. Or Adam.'

'No, Joe,' Geoffrey said. 'More likely one of the men we helped was caught, and talked. Or was a spy. They knew exactly where to come.'

Pierre had hinted, too, that anyone could have betrayed them. People with a grudge. And here was Geoffrey wiping away his sin, absolving him.

'And you tried to save us,' Geoffrey said. 'Even though it cost you dearly.'

Well, Joe thought, he had tried to undo it, after all, and had ended up a prisoner for his pains. Perhaps he *had* made too much of it. Why had he thought he was the only one to blame? Flagellated himself over it for all these years? Confessing made it easier, lighter, absolved him in some way.

'I hope I've made amends,' Joe said. 'Guilty or not.'

'You're a fine man,' Geoffrey said. 'A true friend.'

'I tried,' Joe said.

Geoffrey reached into his pocket and pulled out a handkerchief. He wiped his mouth. He'd been drooling of late, as if his muscles had lost their clinch. 'When I'm gone, will you promise me one thing?'

Joe hated when Geoffrey spoke like that. *When I'm gone.* The hints at his mortality. *This will see me out.*

'And what would that be?'

'That you move into this house,' Geoffrey said. 'And tuck yourself up at night in a warm bed. That leaky old caravan is no good for old bones.'

Joe laughed. 'Is that all?' he said. 'I'll gladly do that. That I will.'

He flicked open his newspaper. The light was fading and the print was hard to read. He heard Geoffrey's breath, rasping a little, as if his lungs had got rusty after all the years.

'Why didn't you ever say anything to me?' Geoffrey's features were in the shade, out of sight. Perhaps, Joe thought, it was easier like that.

'I wanted to,' Joe said. 'But could never find the words or the right moment. But it roiled me. It did that. All this while.'

The clock in the hall whirred and chimed. Joe had got it going again when he came back in 1945, and it had never stopped since. It ran a little slow, these days, but didn't they all?

'Nobody wanted to talk about the war,' Geoffrey said. 'It was a painful time. People wanted to forget. Nobody wanted to listen.'

Joe and Geoffrey never spoke, so why should they expect differently? Who wanted to hear, anyway? What would be the point? The history of the occupation was written. Why stir things up? People wanted the past to be forgotten.

'Our war was different,' Geoffrey said.

Joe supposed it was, come to think of it. At least, from the rest of Britain. France and Holland knew what it was like to live under the Germans.

'It's never been brought to book,' Geoffrey continued. '*Our* war.'

Why should it? Joe thought. What more could be said?

'Some people did well out of the war,' Geoffrey went on, his thoughts rolling free now. 'Our friend, Pierre, for a start. Got off scot-free.'

He's right, Joe thought, there was no accounting, not for what went on. Pierre had spent some time in Britain, after the war. Never said why. Had slunk back some years later, none the poorer.

'But they'll pick on some wretch of a woman fast enough,' Geoffrey was saying. 'Shame her for sleeping with the enemy. Shave her.'

Joe creased his forehead. Perhaps Geoffrey was thinking of Margaret. He was shaking his head, his eyes rheumy and watery. Hadn't she gone with a German? Now, it wasn't right to sell your body, Joe knew that, but what wouldn't a man – or woman, come to think of it – do to survive? Oh no, Joe wouldn't condemn a soul for that. He'd been there himself, right enough.

'Still,' Joe said. 'It was tough.' He'd admit that, though he wasn't sure where this conversation was leading.

'Tougher for some more than others,' Geoffrey said.

You and me. Joe stared through the open window at the darkening sky. This time of a June evening, it folded around them like an indigo scarf. The silence was broken by the *chirring* of a nightjar, his soft hum rising and falling. It was a difficult bird to spot. Bad enough by day, impossible by night unless you caught it flying. But you could hear it. *Listen and look.*

'Nobody wanted to hear about the war's victims,' Geoffrey continued. 'Only its heroes.'

Joe looked up. 'That's not true,' Joe said. 'There were trials in Germany.'

'It happened here,' Geoffrey persisted. 'There were victims here. But no trials.'

'Victims leave no trace,' Joe said.

'That's not so,' Geoffrey said. He twisted in his chair and Joe heard it creak as it adjusted to his weight. 'The traces are all around, in every bunker and gun placement, in every sea wall and tower.'

Joe hadn't considered it like that, in those words. People went to look at the bunkers, never gave a thought to the poor buggers who built them, suffered and died for them. Geoffrey put those thoughts into words so much better.

'I've banished it out of my mind,' Joe said.

'Some things can't be banished,' Geoffrey said. 'They come back and maul you later.' He wiped his mouth again, the white handkerchief glowing in the dusk. 'Would you care for a Jameson?'

'Aye,' Joe said. He'd never seen himself as a victim, not till now. Geoffrey was right. His war was not the war the British fought and won. His war was one of cruelty and loss. Guilt and betrayal. Savage as wolves that return to their prey, that it was.

He pushed himself up and padded over to the cupboard, lifting out the whiskey and taking two glasses from the shelf above. He walked over to the window, poured out the measures in the last of the light. He didn't want to turn on the lamp yet. There was something comforting about the dark, about this conversation. Geoffrey had spoken about Neuengamme, but that was the war *over there.* People talked about that war, but not this war, at home.

Joe sat back in the dark, charged by the fire from his whiskey, and began.

Lager Sylt, Alderney: February 1944

It wasn't long before Joe's hair was as clogged and tangled as the rest, his skin the colour of ash, his trousers stiff with concrete. They stood up by themselves when he took them off at night, rubbed his flesh when he put them on in the morning. The lice left painful bumps and rashes on his skin, had darkened it too. He'd been wearing his clerical shirt when he was arrested, but now it was as stiff and soiled as his trousers, frayed at the seams. His shoes were ripped and torn, but it was all he had. He'd hang on to them as long as possible. Cement bags, the only alternative, were no protection, he knew, and now the nights were short and the winter rains were cold and heavy, he'd need all the armour he could get. He hoped whoever had stolen his clerical jacket needed it as much as he did. Joe couldn't begrudge him that.

He could live with it all except the hunger. He barely thought of Trude now. Her suffering was over, at least. Starvation devoured him from the inside, as if the whale had not heeded Jonah's prayers and was digesting him, bit by bit. He could only think of food. He and Ernst, and the others. They took it in turns to sneak into the Germans' fields and pull a potato, sharing it between them, eating it raw, a mouthful each. They talked of nothing but baked ham and plum dumplings. They listed the ingredients, worked out the recipes, cooked them over the roaring ranges of home, roasted them in the oven. *Argued*, even, dried paprika or fresh hot peppers? Did you fry it first to release the aroma, or plunge it directly into the stew? They drank the best wines. *Riesling. Weissburgunder.*

Spätburgunder. Trollinger. Vodka. Brandy. Poteen, Joe said. *Poitín. Now, there's a drink to put hairs on your chest.*

Joe was digging foundations, trenches a yard deep and two yards wide, hewn and hacked from the rock with nothing more than a pickaxe and shovel. If they fed us more, Joe thought, we'd work harder, and men wouldn't drop like flies. Six months, Joe reckoned. That's how long it took to work someone to death. An extra slice of bread cost a cigarette, and sometimes that bastard cook, *forgive me Lord,* charged double. Cigarettes were in short supply, until the next Red Cross parcel. It wasn't right that a man had to barter for his food.

The men were fearful of the cook. He had a temper and pointed teeth that grew in crooked rows, and he used them when crossed, sunk them into his victim and spat out the flesh. He'd snarl as soon as look at you. Even the guards, Joe noticed, gave him a wide berth. A wild shark of a man, that was for sure.

There was a raw, urgent cry. Joe looked up. The man next to him had fallen in the trench. The mixing machine on the edge of the footings was spewing out the wet cement, filling the dug-out ditch, moving fast.

'No.' Joe threw down his pickaxe. 'Turn that thing off.' He dropped to his stomach, crawled alongside the top of the trench, reached with his hand. The trench was at least three-feet deep, but if he stretched down far enough, and his neighbour up, they could do it.

'Grab it,' he yelled. The concrete was running like a lava flow, splashing Joe's hand. He flexed his fingers. 'Now.' The man had no strength left, Joe could see that, not even a will, not in his eyes. He shook his head, let it fall forward into the cement. Joe saw a bubble, and that was all. He pushed himself up, stood face to face with an *SS* officer in a peaked cap. The officer said nothing, signalled. *Keep pouring.*

Arbitrary. That's what Joe couldn't take. You never knew when death would strike. A beating for nothing. Garrotting for less.

Drowned in cement. Thrown to the waves. *We walk in the valley of the shadow of death*, Joe thought. He wished they'd shot him with Trude.

§

It was an Irish rain. Light and steady, soaking to the bone in a quiet polite fashion. Belied its menace. There was heather here as well, long past its bloom, squatting with the gorse and the scars where the Germans had stripped the soil. Joe's cap kept the worst of the rain from his face, but his shirt was wet through, and his trousers too, his shoes brittle from the dirt, soles separating from the uppers so they flapped when he walked. Twelve hours a day, seven days a week. They got up in the dark, stood for *Appell* in the frost or the fog, worked till the winter day drew in. German hours, so the night was later, longer.

Joe had cut holes in a cement bag, head and arms, tucked the sack underneath what was left of his shirt so the Germans couldn't see. One extra layer against the biting wind. His hands were calloused, but his arms were strong, and swinging a pickaxe or raking cement or shovelling grit kept his boxing muscles firm, even if he didn't have the protein to build them up.

'Only fools give in,' Ernst said almost every night. 'And who here is a bigger fool than the goons who run this place?'

Ernst kept Joe going, buoyed him up. Buoyed them all up, Joe thought. They couldn't do much to resist, but they wouldn't give in. Even their *Kapo* had respect for Ernst. Ernst was a *gentleman*, polite, considerate, though his language was sometimes blue. But who could blame him? He protected Joe, befriended him, never asked why he no longer said his prayers, slipped him a cigarette if he had one spare.

They all had coughs, thick catarrh that clogged their sinuses and filled their lungs. Or airy coughs that spat blood. Shivered and sweated at night. Died. Or left to die. The bastard cook, *forgive me Lord*, refused to feed the sick.

'Orders,' he said, his sharp teeth a warning. 'Why waste food on the dying?'

Only that night as they queued for their meal, Joe stood next to an old man he hadn't seen before. He wore a yellow star. The Jews were French, so Ernst said, newly arrived. The old man must have been over seventy, watery eyes and hands with liver spots that shook as he held his bowl. Joe had seen him struggle with the rest, the sledgehammer too great a weight for his frail frame. He coughed. The cook looked at him.

'*Juif*,' he said.

Went to the next man, poured the soup half in the bowl, half on his hand. The man behind him, likewise.

Joe pointed to the old man's bowl.

'You missed him,' he said. The old man was shaking his head at Joe, *leave me be*. *No*, Joe thought. *Only fools give in*. Joe left the line, doubled back, came up behind the cook.

'*Feed him*.' Joe never shouted, but he did now, filled his lungs and bellowed. A band of fear and anger had snapped inside him, pumped his body with fury, his muscles with adrenalin. The kitchen went quiet, but the prisoners' eyes cheered loud.

The cook spun round and flew at Joe, his lips curled back like a dog, but Joe was fast and sharp. He darted, danced, sparred. *Fists up. On your toes*. Rage was in the cook's eyes, but he couldn't focus. Joe was moving too fast. Jump, left, right, right and left. Dainty as a sanderling. The cook was a big man, clumsy, all fury and brawn. *Boxing's not a sport for angry men*. Joe had never fought someone outside of his weight, but the cook was floundering, screaming, lunging at Joe as Joe ducked and weaved. Joe knew he couldn't keep this up for long, had to throw the knockout soon. He'd have one chance only. The cook was right-handed, baffled, maddened. This was not the way he was used to fighting. *Strike*. The cook was trying to scrap like Joe, like a boxer, closed fists, arms up, aim hard. He had no technique, no idea. He could be beaten even though he was twice as heavy as Joe, but if Joe got it wrong, the cook would sink his teeth into the back of Joe's neck. He could feel the brute tensing and grinding his jaws. He flailed out with his right and Joe saw his chance. *Now.* Head down. *Go.* Joe breathed hard, slammed an uppercut to the liver, hammered the kidneys with his last ounce of strength, a single, vital thrust of adrenalin mustered from the deep. Caught the beast unaware, watched as he twisted and sank to his knees, walloping the back of his head on the hard cement pillar and his temple on the floor as he fell. He lay crumpled, his neck bent. A trickle of blood oozed from his ear and a black trail of lice were leaving the body, crawling towards Joe.

Joe heard cheering, the banging of metal bowls, knuckles rapping the tables. The cook lay motionless on the floor. Joe had killed someone. *God forgive him.* He hadn't meant to. Lying twisted on the concrete, the cook was no longer a monster. He was a man. Like Joe. Like the others. Joe breathed in sharp. He had killed a person. Taken a life. A mortal sin. *The worst of all sins.* He was a murderer. He sank to his knees, making a small cross on the cook's clammy forehead.

'*Was ist los?*' A guard pushed himself through the crowd. 'Who did this?'

Joe nodded. *I did.* The cook was hand in glove with the *SS*. They'd kill *him*, retribution. A life for a life. Joe was ready. It was right. He hoped they'd shoot him. *Now.* They'd crucified a Russian not that long ago, and that was just for stealing a loaf. Joe'd stolen a life, and a *Kapo*'s at that.

The guard turned to Joe. 'Take it out.' He pointed to the body. '*Schnell.*'

Joe took the cook by his ankles, dragged him across the floor. Four or five guards had entered the kitchen. The cook was heavy and Joe stumbled as he stepped backwards. Kept his balance.

Pulled him over the doorstep. The cook wore a leather jacket, lined with sheep's wool, that one of the guards must have given him. Joe took it off, wrapped it round himself. It was far too big but, by God, it was warm. Shoes, too. What use were these to the dead?

§

Joe waited but no one came for him in the night, nor at the morning *Appell.*

Eins. Drei. Vier. Sieben.

'*Ja wohl.*'

He knew what duty he'd be assigned.

He started with the corpse of the cook, picked up the others along the way. He knew the routine by now. Grab the ankles, over the shoulder, toss them in the back of the truck like carcases in his father's slaughterhouse. Sometimes they buried the dead from the camp on the heath, if there weren't too many, one coffin, over and over again. You never knew.

The truck moved, jerked along the stony road, down to the beach. Joe had a shovel. He'd have to dig the grave in the sand this time, wait for the tide to wash the bodies out to the ocean. Two guards watched him, would shoot if he wandered into the sea or lay down in the shallow trench with the shifting sands and his murdered corpse. *Take me too.* Would that be so bad?

The waves broke along the shore, rollers from the North Sea. A bitter wind blasted from the Arctic. Joe was glad for the cook's jacket. He could stuff it with cement sacks. Never be cold again. He didn't hear the *Kommandant* coming, padding like a camel over the sand. Saw only the shiny black boots.

CHAPTER THIRTEEN

DORA

London: June 1985

'Since Mohammed won't go to the mountain.' Charles was at the other end of the telephone, his voice catching with humour. 'The mountain must come to Mohammed.'

She was happy to hear him, she always was, but she couldn't talk now, not after what she'd heard. She knew if she asked him to ring back, he'd say to her, *What are you doing that's so important? Why can't you talk to me now?* She couldn't lie to him, not directly, couldn't answer him either. She breathed in deep, tried to sound normal.

'So you're coming to London,' Dora said. 'That would be nice.'

'Not only coming,' he said. '*Moving.* I'm rattling round that house with no one for company. The neighbours are not my cup of tea. My children are too busy to visit. And you, Doralein, *never* set foot outside London unless there's neon lights.'

'I don't like the countryside,' Dora said. It wasn't true. She loved it in the abstract, the vistas and the skies, the silence and the dark. But the lowing of cows, the smell of their byre, the houses and hedgerows, they were rambling memories, with burs and thorns.

'So I gather,' Charles was saying. 'There's another reason. You've gone silent on me these last few weeks. Are you all right?'

'I'm fine,' Dora said. Charles, more than an acquaintance. Her friend. Her oldest friend, with a hinterland, a shared history. Why didn't she tell him about Barbara? Why didn't she tell *him* about her war, her real war? Not the ersatz war she fed him, mending and making do on Jersey until the British put a stop to it all. Because, she thought, her war didn't compare to his. She couldn't march to the Cenotaph every November with the other veterans, ribbons pinned to their lapels, heads bowed in homage to their dead comrades, brave, strong. He could do that, with pride. Sidling off afterwards to the Reform for lunch and reminiscence over claret and roast beef. A good war. That's what a good war gave you. Freedom. Freedom to choose your memories, to forget, to forge a fresh path. Dora knew plenty of war dead, but women didn't count in the same way.

'So when are you going to marry me?' Charles went on. 'I've proposed twice. I'm keeping count. If I propose a third time, will I be lucky?'

She twisted the telephone cord round her fingers. 'Let me think about it,' she said. Dora put the receiver down, shut her eyes. She needed a moment or two before she went back to Barbara.

Truth was, she'd lost her nerve. She was used to loneliness now, solitude. It was her condition. Her decision, that day when the war was over and the world had changed.

Jersey: February 1944 – May 1945

'I am told that you were a nurse,' Nurse Hoffmann said.

Dora touched the soap which she kept in her pocket. She held it like a lucky charm, the promise of good fortune, kindness, special treatment. The soap would be stolen if she left it in the dormitory. She lived among thieves. She didn't tell a soul that she had it. This was for her, the secret bond between her and Maximilian.

'Well,' Nurse Hoffmann said, *vell*. 'It seems you have a surprise.' She rarely spoke to Dora. 'Would you like to know what it is?' She made a snide, knowing grimace. Hoffmann was breaking the news. Alderney.

Dora raised her eyebrows, couldn't let on that she knew.

'So,' Hoffmann went on. 'He has made you a *Kapo*.' She twisted her face into a parody of a smile. '*Hauptsturmführer* List.'

Dora was not expecting this.

'Agnes.' She couldn't think what else to say. 'Agnes Moreau is the *Kapo*.'

'*Hauptsturmführer* List decides who is a *Kapo*,' Nurse Hoffmann said. 'Not Agnes Moreau.'

Dora took a deep breath. What was it Collette said? *Kapos* do their dirty business for them. *Thick with the Nazis.*

'I don't want to be one,' Dora said. It was worth a try, saying that. Dangerous, too. Nurse Hoffmann could turn like a snake. *You don't argue.*

'It is *Hauptsturmführer* List's expressed order,' Nurse Hoffmann said. 'Not many are so lucky.' She sneered and her voice tightened. 'Perhaps he is a little sweet on you, who knows?'

'There is a mistake.' Dora shook her head. He was taking her to Alderney, he'd said. Not this. Unless. Of course, it would take time to organise. There would be permissions to seek, paperwork. The Germans were meticulous about that kind of thing. Besides, there was no love lost between the *SS* and the *Wehrmacht*. Perhaps this was some kind of temporary compromise, he'd persuaded the *Wehrmacht* to make her a *Kapo* in order to expedite the move. He had done this for her, had already taken her out of the brothel, so she could join him. She wouldn't be a *Kapo* here. He had no jurisdiction here. *This* brothel was under *Wehrmacht* authority.

What sort of *Kapo* would she be on Alderney? Perhaps there were women prisoners there. Could she do the Nazis' dirty business? What if they made her carry out a beating? Or worse? Would she have the courage to say no? For his sake, she'd have to show her gratitude. No. *Kapo* was a ruse, to bring her over. They'd be together, in his home, she his affectionate housekeeper. She'd be sure this time to keep her distance, not to *presume*.

'There is no mistake. Here.' Nurse Hoffmann grabbed Dora's arm, pushed the green armband up it. The badge of office. Dora wanted to rip it off, knew she wasn't brave enough. 'You will work in the *Revier*. With me.'

'Here?'

'Where else did you think you'd work?'

This must be temporary. Maximilian had a plan. She should trust him.

§

The *Revier* had two wards. One, no more than a cupboard, at the rear of the building, had two bunk beds and was for women too weak or ill to work. Those with VD or TB or who were deemed too difficult were packed off to France. Dora hated signing that form, as if it was a death warrant. Replacements would arrive by the next ship. Dora's number was two hundred and seventy-one. They were up to three hundred and eighty-eight already.

The other, in the front, was the ward reserved for soldiers who had contracted venereal disease. Bright and airy, it could accommodate up to ten soldiers and one officer, staying for weeks at a time. Dora had to scrub the floors and walls, wash the men and change their beds. It was heavy work and hard, in her condition, lifting and bending. It could bring on a hernia, or worse. She had to treat the chancres and lesions, fearful lest she contract the disease too, reporting back to Nurse Hoffmann, who wrote the notes and made Dora copy them out in triplicate.

'You make no mistakes,' Nurse Hoffmann said. 'It's as if you knew German.'

'Anyone can copy,' Dora said.

Working with Nurse Hoffmann was hard. There was something about her that made Dora especially wary. She had a temper and was free with her fists if Dora's work was not up to scratch. That didn't worry Dora. It was her spite, as if she resented Dora, was in some absurd way, *jealous* of her. Dora lived on a knife-edge, one false step, *kaputt*. But for all that, it was better than the brothel, and even though Maximilian List had not yet brought her to Alderney, he had rescued her from the whorehouse.

'Do you miss your boyfriend?' Nurse Hoffmann was injecting one of the men with Salvarsan. It was a painful injection, Dora knew, deep into the gluteus muscle and sometimes the men howled like babies. It was February. It had rained all day, and now it was hailing, thick globs of ice that smashed against the window-panes and turned the light to a sodden gloom.

She had seen List the week before, the first time since Christmas. Hoffmann had ordered her into the office, made her take off her clothes and parade naked as if she were a prize cow for breeding. He had stared at her with an architect's eye, at her shape and form, swollen now from the baby she carried inside her. He could see the stretch marks on her breasts and stomach, the veins that crossed her skin like a delta. His face was hard, and he gave no indication of his promise, his tender moments when they had been together. He can't, Dora thought, not with Hoffmann there. And Agnes, hovering like a harbinger. No, his indifference was protecting her. She'd wanted to nod, smile, *I understand*.

'Everything is in order?' He spoke in German. Nurse Hoffmann nodded.

'*Herr* Himmler has opened the facility personally.' She was beaming, as if *Herr* Himmler had singled her out. 'At Lamorlaye. *Mein Liebling*.' *My darling*.

List was smiling, nodding, whispered *Himmler*, as if it was an endearment, a secret bond between the two.

They must be lovers, Nurse Hoffmann and *Hauptsturmführer* List. *Lovers*. He'd let her down. Betrayed her. She was expendable, of course. Powerless. Why had she even begun to dream? She was crushed beneath the leviathan of the Reich, a pawn in its power play.

Dora bit her lip, held back the tears.

He couldn't love that Hoffmann woman with her moon face and squat frame. No. He'd summon Dora later, explain, apologise for his absence since Christmas. *The sea was too rough to sail.* Run his finger against her cheek. *Meine schöne Frau.* My beautiful lady. Press his lips to hers, *kiss me, Dora.*

He was using Hoffmann as a front. *Of course.*

But he hadn't called for her later and had sent no word since. Dora thought he must be ill. Or had been summoned elsewhere and couldn't tell her. The Germans moved their men around. *Top secret.* Or was busy. He was an important man, after all. Dora had often wondered how he'd found time to visit her so often.

'Well?' Nurse Hoffmann said again. 'Do you?'

There was something in Nurse Hoffmann's voice that invited a chat today, not just an answer. Much as Dora despised and mistrusted her, she longed for conversation, the ping-pong of talk, the possibility of human exchange. But she wasn't sure if this was a trap, to admit that she had feelings for List.

'How do you know I have a boyfriend?'

Nurse Hoffmann turned her face away, shifted her body so she stood, back turned to Dora.

'I know these things.' She threw the words over her shoulder, added, 'I used to see you. With the farmer.'

The farmer? Geoffrey? Dora felt a surge of guilt. He had not been her first thought, had been shunted into second place. She wasn't sure whether Nurse Hoffmann was tricking her into talking. Or bluffing.

'Oh,' Dora said, sounding casual. 'Where?'

'At his farm, of course. I thought, how nice you go to visit. He must be a lonely man. How *lucky*, you are close.'

She must have known where to spy on them, unseen from the house. What had Collette said, *Feldpolizei? Bad as the fucking Gestapo.* Who had told her about that spot?

'What were you doing at the farm?' Dora said.

'Watching birds.'

'That's unusual,' Dora said.

'My boyfriend is very keen,' Nurse Hoffmann said.

An unexpected confidence that made no sense. List had never hinted he liked birds. This must be somebody else Hoffmann was talking about, another lover.

'And do you miss him?' Dora said. If Nurse Hoffmann could trick her into talking, so could Dora.

'Yes,' Nurse Hoffmann said. 'I miss him very much.'

'He's not here, then?'

'He's going to Germany soon,' she said.

'Why?'

Nurse Hoffmann shrugged. *I can't say.*

Dora picked up a pile of dressings, placed them in a package. This wasn't true. List was in Alderney. Dora's instincts were right. He couldn't possibly love Hoffmann. She wasn't talking about him.

'May I ask you something?'

For all Nurse Hoffmann's intimacy, Dora knew her mood could turn. Nurse Hoffmann sniffed. She was *weeping.*

'The farmer,' Dora said. 'Do you know what happened to him?'

'Who?'

'My boyfriend,' Dora said. She felt the rip of pain. *Torn* loyalty.

Nurse Hoffmann brushed her tears away and shrugged. 'Sent to Neuengamme. For work.'

'Work?'

'*Arbeit macht frei,*' Nurse Hoffmann said. 'Redemption through labour.'

Geoffrey could still be alive. Neuengamme. Wasn't List something to do with that?

'Alderney?' Dora said.

'*Nein,*' Nurse Hoffmann said. '*Deutschland.*'

Dora felt sick. For one giddy moment she thought that Geoffrey was not so far away, that List could help him. But what would she have said to Maximilian? She'd have to admit she'd had a lover, and she wasn't sure how he would respond. She'd have to get word to him too, and that would be impossible, unless he called for her. And what would she say to Geoffrey? She wasn't sure she knew what to say to herself. What was List to her? If he treated her as his mistress, did that make him her lover?

'And the *Kommandant*?' Dora said, hoping her voice sounded casual, nonchalant. 'He hasn't been here recently.'

Hoffmann turned and plunged the long needle into the soldier's other buttock as he screamed.

'Now,' she said, pressing hard, 'that will teach you to use protection.'

Despite herself, Dora felt pity for the soldier. He was so very young. And the side effects from Salvarsan if administered badly were so very dreadful.

§

It was early evening when the real pains started. There was no one there, save for the soldiers in the ward next door. *Keep walking*. Pacing the room, holding on to a bed for support when the spasms hit hard.

A vice began to grip her pelvis, tighten, tug and wrench her apart, so she caught her breath. *There's nothing to fear*. It loosened its grip. *She would be fine*. The pain began to roll again, hammer blows smelting so her limbs felt on fire, stretching and moulding her ligaments. Dora knelt on all fours on the floor in the smaller ward, shut her eyes, screamed, waited as the blows cooled and faded. What if she had complications? The baby was premature, weak, could be stuck in the birth canal. The pains were too close together. It was moving too fast. Who can deliver it, take the forceps, free her? The cramp again, a tank with steel treads trampling her bones, crushing her spine. Dora cried out. She wanted someone there, to hold a hand. *It will be all right.*

The baby was pressing down, a hard, heavy skull at the base of her spine. *Not too fast.* She tried to ride the next pain, to breathe light as a fairy, puffs to blow the spasms away, but it was an army inside her, routing her flesh. She wanted to push, to expel the hard mass within. She hoped she was dilated, knew to be cautious, but the next advance took her breath away. Why was no one here? Dora shut her eyes. She could not think. The pain was tearing her limb from limb, a lump as hard and big as a football bearing down and down. And down.

§

The slap across the face jerked her back into consciousness. She could smell Agnes, a dank blast of foetid breath grabbing her shoulders.

'*Tot, tot,*' Hoffmann was screaming. '*Es ist tot.*' *Dead.* Dora could see her running out the door with the baby. *Tot.*

Agnes walked around Dora where she still lay on the floor.

'List's whore,' she said. 'He won't be able to protect you now.' She pulled a string out of her pocket. 'You've no brat, no special status, not anymore.' She flexed the string, pulled it taut. 'Get up.' She stuffed the cord back in her pocket, started to shout. 'Get out. You've buggered their plans.'

She smirked, walked out of the door.

Dora lay back on the floor, felt the placenta tumble from her, thick and wet as liver.

Nurse Hoffmann went on leave the next day and did not return.

'Gone.' Agnes clicked her fingers as she walked past Dora at the morning *Appell.* 'Like that. Seems you failed her with your dead baby. *Tot.* One word–' she ran her finger across her throat. 'That's all it takes. But you,' she pointed at Dora, laughed at her with black, crooked teeth, 'are sitting pretty. Aren't you the lucky one?'

Agnes would betray Dora as soon as look at her, but this could only mean that List had come true on his promise. She could feel her heart quicken and pulse, hard with hope.

'He's one for the ladies, so I hear.' Agnes stopped, faced Dora.

'Who?' A spasm tightened in Dora's stomach.

'Baron Aufsess,' Agnes said. 'Their number two. They say he's taking over. Knackfuss has got the chop. Seems Aufsess has taken a personal interest in *unser kleines arisches Mädchen*.' She chewed at a hair in her mouth, spitting it out on her tongue.

A ball of bile clutched Dora's throat and she began to retch, felt Agnes's hand clamp over her arm as she dragged her free of the line.

'List has gone too,' Agnes said. 'So no more special favours.'

'Oh?' Dora feigned indifference, but her tone was too eager. 'Where did he go?'

'Hah,' Agnes laughed, nodded. *I know your secret.* 'Back to Germany. To answer questions. Seems he let a whole lot of Jews escape last year.'

Dora shivered. Did that mean her? Had he known all along? Had protected her? Was facing a court martial because of her?

'Your *day* orders,' Agnes went on, 'are to stay in the *Revier*, *Kapo.* But at night, Cinderella, you dance.'

'Stop,' Dora said. She was breathless, faint. Her knees began to buckle. He had spared her the brothel for a time, but he could safeguard her no longer. Dora could see the bedroom again with its thick flock wallpaper and velvet drapes, feel the thrusts of the men, the weight of their bodies. She could hear the bray of the bedsprings and the cries as they disgorged themselves in her. She was nothing to them but loin and skirt, flank and belly.

'You need to get yourself another protector. Come.' Agnes put her arm round Dora, an unexpected support. Led her into the kitchen, carried her bowl and cup into the dormitory, sat her down on a bunk.

'Who is the nurse in the *Revier*?' Dora said. 'If Hoffmann's gone?'

'Seems you're in charge.'

Dora looked at Agnes, but her face showed nothing.

'Let them find their own nurses,' Dora said. 'I won't be party to it.'

They could do what they liked with her. Send her to the laundry by day like the other women, or have her mending uniforms, webbing. She wasn't going to be *their* nurse, sorting out their poxy soldiers.

'Believe me,' Agnes said, tearing her bread in two and placing half in Dora's bowl. 'Baron von Aufsess won't let you get away with it.'

'Let him shoot me,' Dora said.

'He has more imagination than that,' Agnes said. 'Why waste ammunition?'

Dora picked at the bread Agnes had given her, grateful for the little extra. The Germans had no scruples and Dora wasn't sure she was brave enough to step into the unknown. Was nursing a sick soldier by day so very wrong? Or comforting a lonely man at night?

§

There had been no word from List. No word about him, either. The officers did not speak about him. Why should they? He was *SS*, they were *Wehrmacht*. He had nothing to do with them, wasn't even based in Jersey. Even the *SS* officers on leave from France never spoke of him.

The seasons drifted free of winter, into spring and summer. She was used to the routine, punch-drunk and battle-hardened. A gown for the evening, sitting on a stool at the bar, waiting, inured.

She hoped for a protector. Someone to shield her. She'd look at each man, *Are you the one?* She couldn't think of *Vati*, or Uncle Otto, List or even Geoffrey, any of the men she knew and loved, as she lay with her legs open and some pink Nazi with yellow bristles thrusting and thrashing, the smell of their must cloying in her nostrils. She thought of London then, walked herself up and down Fitzjohn's Avenue, or recited the tube stations, Camden Town, Chalk Farm, Belsize Park. Or the U-Bahn. Friedrichstrasse, Hackescher Markt, Alexanderplatz. The Beethoven symphonies. 'Eroica'. 'Pastoral'. 'Choral'. Mahler. La-la-ing the themes in her head. Mahler. Mendelssohn. Jewish. Degenerate. She never wanted to go with another man in her life, knew the damage that was being done, the infections that would make her sterile. Void. Voided. Who would want her now? Used and abused. List wouldn't touch her.

She was no woman. She had no face, no features, nothing that spoke of her. Just cut and thrust. Mahler's symphonies couldn't help now, nor the streets and stations of home. She was a vacant, hollow frame lost in a no man's land.

'You're quiet,' Agnes said.

Dora had shrugged. With emptiness inside, what was there left to say?

There were two of them that night, SS, visiting, from Belgium. Drunk. Dora was nothing, skittles in an alley. The Mauser, cold in her groin, the hard steel inside her. Russian roulette. She wished there'd been a bullet. She could take no more. Her desire for death was sudden, overwhelming.

She'd have to be quick. Into the *Revier*. Her body was shuddering, uncontrollable motions that jerked through to her nerves and sinews. Hoffmann's office, the key from the drawer, the medicine chest on the wall.

Diamorphine. In case. In case the British invaded and they had to treat the wounded, though nobody admitted that. There was

Salvarsan, but arsenic was a slow death. It had to be fast. Two vials. Three, to be sure. The syringes were in another cupboard. She fetched the largest, and a new needle. It must be sharp. She took out the plunger, placed it on the desk with the barrel, reached for the pipette, a bottle of distilled water. Keep calm. Professional. She was light-headed, fizzy with relief. It would all be over. She laid out the tourniquet. Taut around the left arm so her right hand was free, when it was time.

She uncorked the first vial, staring at the white, odourless powder. Three vials. The solution would be strong. She filled the pipette from the bottle, picked up the barrel of the syringe. Intravenous. Would she have time to inject the whole lot before she fell asleep? Her hand trembled as she lifted the powder to pour into the barrel, small clinking tremolos, fine glass on fine glass, shaking.

Her elbow was pushed and the vial flew across the desk, the powder spiralling as it went. Agnes pulled her away, spun her round so she faced her, grabbing the barrel of the syringe that was still in Dora's hand. She was breathing hard, bellows of fury.

'They'd torture you first. Or send you to Germany. It amounts to the same thing,' she said. 'I've had my eye on you.'

Dora lunged across the desk, tried to grab the opened bottle. But Agnes was strong, pushed her away from it. 'Those goons tonight,' she said. 'I couldn't stop them.' She reached into her pocket, pulled out a cigarette butt and put it in her mouth. 'Sadists.'

There were some matches on the counter and she marched over to them. She went back to Dora, handed her the lit cigarette.

'For you,' said Agnes. 'Have it.'

Agnes never shared her cigarette hoard, Dora knew. She took a long drag. The smoke was hot and bitter. She started to cough, violent spasms as the smoke burned through to her lungs.

'That's your life, fighting back,' Agnes said. Dora's eyes had watered and Agnes's face was a blur. 'Still going to take it?'

The spasm subsided, and Dora took another puff of the cigarette. She wasn't a smoker, not really, not in the way that Agnes was. The smoke went to her head, made her dizzy.

'Better?' Agnes said.

Ash fell off the cigarette onto the desk.

'I know you lot all hate me,' she went on. 'But I have my reasons, and I do my best.' She took the cigarette, now no more than a glowing stub, pulled at it long and hard so the ash flared bright, then she pinched it dead between her fingers as the smoke blew from her nostrils like a dragon's snort. 'Now,' Agnes said. 'Help me get this lot back so they don't count a missing vial.' She cupped her hand, scooped the ash along with the powder into a neat pile.

'That's–'

Agnes looked up at Dora with a lopsided grin. 'We all do our bit for the war effort,' she said. Tilted her head back and laughed. This was the first time she had heard Agnes laugh. Dora opened her mouth, howled along, racking sobs and hiccups of grief and mirth.

'The war will be over soon,' Agnes said. 'Hold on.' She reached for a piece of paper, made a crude funnel, scooped the ash and diamorphine into it. 'This place is full of shit,' she went on, emptying the funnel into the vial. She replaced the stopper. 'Rage against them. Not yourself. Someone has to talk, when it's over, spill the beans. If they listen to a woman, that is.'

She hooked one hand under Dora's elbow and squeezed it. Tender, warm, human. Dora hadn't had Agnes down as a kind person, or a generous one, but she leant her head against Agnes's shoulder and Agnes didn't push her away. It was enough. The urge to live was as sudden as her desire for death had been.

§

The Hotel Maison Victor Hugo shuddered. They were in the courtyard, being counted. The planes were British, American.

So close. She could smell the cordite, see the thick, black smoke and hear the blasting. Normandy. Over the water. It was just after dawn and the sky above was red and stormy. Bombing. Bombing. Wave after wave. She knew the year. She could keep hold of those dates. 1944. It was summer. Was it June? Aeroplanes bellowing overhead. The German guns pounded back, their recoil jarring the earth around. Still the planes flew. Dora smiled, almost laughed. Looked at the other women who were smiling. And Agnes. Looking up at the sky as if she had been beatified. It would be over soon.

§

Another room was commandeered, turned into a ward. Soldiers with pneumonia and dysentery had been evacuated from the hospital to make way for the wounded from France. They were running out of medicines. Salvarsan. Prontosil. Saline. No supplies were coming in. The British had cut them off. Dora couldn't understand. Why would they do that?

Sick men with short tempers. Damp flannels on a fevered brow, cool water from a feeder. The kitchen was making the soup thinner, had cut the meals from four to three. Dora had twice the number of patients to look after, as well as having to clean the ward and make the beds, wash the bandages and boil up the instruments. She was inspected twice a day by whichever officer was on duty in the hotel. She had no special privileges now. Agnes was right.

The women's meals were cut from three to two, then two to one. Their soup was made even thinner. Dora could see the bones of her feet with the veins pumping proud. *By night, Cinderella, you dance.* Dora looked with envy at the soldiers' food, hoping they'd leave something in the bowl for her. She'd risk the dysentery for a full stomach. She wasn't sure she would ever get used to the way hunger gnawed, the way it hurt and hurtled through her.

The bombing went on through the sticky, stormy nights of July when the airless cellar steamed like a bath and the women sweated what little moisture they had. Through August when the nights grew shorter and the cruel pinch of autumn stalked the room. Dora could see the smoke on the Normandy coast form low, bulbous clouds, the sparks and fires burnishing them orange and green, blotting out the stars at night. Her head thundered from the noise, the constant *boom-boom-boom* of the guns, from the hunger that tightened round her temples, from the fear and the fury she saw in the soldiers' eyes. Fear made them impotent, angry. *Your fault, not mine.* Impotence made them cruel. There were twenty-one women left. Most had been sent back to France before the blockade, though Dora couldn't understand why. The last woman to arrive before the British cut them off was number three hundred and ninety-five.

The officers were listening to the BBC, openly tuning in on the wireless in the mess. They didn't notice Dora sitting in the corner. Jonah in the leviathan. Germany was in retreat, she learned. France was lost to the Allies. They couldn't win this war, not now. It would only be a matter of time before it was over. *Hold on*, she told herself. That's what Agnes had said. *Hold on.*

But it didn't end. The fallen leaves were dry and brittle beneath Dora's feet, the dawn a distant promise. Every morning dragging herself up and out into the courtyard to stand in rags while they counted them. She wasn't sure how much longer she could bear this. Knowing the war must end soon made the now unbearable. Hope, she thought, is the cruellest virtue. The damp November mornings gave way to the frosts of December.

They'd put a Christmas tree up in the hallway. 1944. Dora wondered how many fires could be made from its trunk and branches, how many people would have a moment's warmth, a cooked meal. She touched the soap in her pocket, hoping that List was safe. Perhaps he was as cut off as they were, as starving as she.

Perhaps he hadn't gone back to Germany. Perhaps he was still in Alderney. Perhaps they had surrendered, had rowed across when the sea was calm, with a white sheet blowing behind. *Spare us, spare us.* He'd tell the British, there is a Swedish woman. *Please rescue her.*

January rimed the door handles and the soldiers' bayonets. The fuel ran out and the *Revier* grew cold. Dora pulled extra blankets from the store, heaped them on the patients' beds, wrapped one round herself so the cold didn't nip her legs beneath the flimsy frock. Still she shivered in the night, swaddling the paltry blanket tight around her in a skein of rough wool. The soldiers grew depressed with the cold and the blockade, took to staying in their barracks rather than venturing out. Many nights, the women had nothing to do.

The rations grew smaller and smaller, and they ran out of medicines. The general hospital was running out of space, so they'd commandeered the *Revier*. She looked through the names of the sick or wounded, at their faces, in case one was List, rescued and transported to Jersey. Oh, she'd nurse him back to health.

Her father had taken charge. Brought in the wounded French to the German field hospital in Verdun, treated them as if they were no different. Was this the same? Would he be proud of her now? She didn't know. She wasn't sure, anymore, what was right and what was not. Did war do that? Blur the boundaries? Or just this one? She had been in the brothel eighteen months now. Her body had been pimped and polluted, her spirit crippled and abused. She stood crooked now, the world lopsided around her. She had been a nurse, once, her father a doctor. He'd won the Iron Cross. *Jewish.* She pulled the coarse army-issue blanket around her shoulders. Did that make her a liar and a coward?

Agnes took to hanging round the *Revier*. Sat in the ward playing cards with the soldiers, making dirty jokes, turning the place into a bawdy house.

'There are thirty-two patients here,' Dora said.

'Men.'

'This is a hospital,' Dora said. 'Not a brothel.'

'Cheers them up,' she said.

'They are the enemy.'

'You take care of their flesh,' Agnes said. 'Leave their spirits to me.' Sitting on a soldier's bed, smirking, mouthing *Kapo.* Doing the Germans' dirty business.

'We're two of a kind,' Agnes said. 'You and me.'

Perhaps we are, Dora thought. Perhaps.

§

Time crawled through the final weeks of that war, listless and aimless, made a nonsense of the days and hours. March limped along. April. Trees turned green and daffodils nodded on the front lawn of the hotel gardens. The officers hung around the mess while the soldiers kicked stones across the yard. They talked openly now. Mussolini dead. Hitler dead. And still it dragged on. The women carried out their duties, sluggish and ramshackle in their movements. The reprimands lost their sting, even though the beatings were harsher than ever. They have to take it out on someone, Dora thought. Women in the line of fire. The orders still came from the *Feldkommandantur*, but no one rushed anymore.

Only Aufsess kept his appetite for war, his loyalties to the dead *Führer.* He had no support, not if the talk among the officers was right. It was as if the beast was devouring itself. They waited for the British, but the British did not come.

She wanted to go home, to be in the apartment in Charlottenburg, to eat cake, drink coffee. *Real* coffee. The Saturday ritual with her aunts in Berlin, their words bouncing off the cornices in the tall white ceilings of their apartment as they nibbled chocolate and sipped at bone-china cups while Dora handed round the fluted silver sugar dish, with tiny tongs. She loved to listen to their

German, yearned to talk it again. She wanted to be snuggled up in bed beneath the fluffy *Federbett*, while her father read her stories. She was homesick. A pining as powerful as a lightning surge.

§

It was May, the leaves on the trees in the gardens freshly minted, the peonies in the hotel gardens about to bloom, voluminous and gaudy. *Vulgar plants*, Dora thought, but she was glad to see them, for it meant the winter was finally over now and it couldn't be long. Germany was in chaos, if what the officers said was right, no one was in charge. Berlin was in ruins, the Russians were at the gates.

And then the bells began to ring and ring and ring. They carried on through the day, into the evening. Dora couldn't think, wasn't sure she'd remember this day. The news had come through, relief among the German squaddies thick and tangible, drunk on happiness and home-made schnapps. Dora heard someone say that Aufsess and some of the senior officers were refusing to surrender. She wondered if he'd kill them all first. And List. Had he surrendered? She looked out of the window, saw British soldiers surrounding the hotel, knew the German game was up, as the bells pealed and the changes rang.

There was a half-bottle of brandy in the back of the medicine cabinet. She climbed onto a chair, fished on the top shelf and pulled the bottle out. Cradled it like a baby in the crook of her arm, walked away from the *Revier*. Down the stairs, through the hallway where the light from the landing shone through the motes of dust onto the floor, showing up the balls of fluff that had gathered in the corners.

Dora walked past the mess. The empty glasses were still on the bar, the ashtrays full and unemptied. A game of bridge had been abandoned, the cards faced down in orderly piles on the four sides of the card table. Her roster had been open on the *maître d'*s lectern. Dora took the page by the corner, ripped it free of the ledger, tore it in half, and half again. Threw the pieces on the floor.

She walked down the stairs, into the dormitory. Some of the women were sitting on the lower bunks, or squatting on the floor. Others had climbed on their beds and peered up through the light well. No one spoke. Too frightened to walk through the open door.

Dora held up the bottle. '*Pour la libération*,' she said.

There were fifteen women.

'Bring your tins.'

She poured the brandy. The women's hands were shaking and Dora had to hold the cups to steady them. The smell of the alcohol wafted up, pure and clean, making her eyes water. Her father had had a bottle of cognac that he'd brought out on special occasions, Martell 1877.

Dora began to cry, sobs of relief, and joy, of remembrance and sadness. *Think of the happy times.* The others cried too, put the brandy to their lips, sipped it on their empty, starving stomachs. *Sometimes, Doralein, we gave them brandy in Verdun. There was nothing more to be done.*

They wept, a phalanx of emaciated, ululating women, hiccupping.

La guerre est terminée. The war was over.

Dora went into a corner of the dormitory and sat with her brandy. She had dreamed of this day, how she'd dance in the street, throw balls in the air, sing and scream and jump. She'd imagined running around, hugging and kissing everyone she met, in a joyous frenzy of relief. Now that day was here, she felt weary and uncertain. She wanted to be alone. She looked over at the other women. They would be sent back to France, to their villages and families. She could hear them talking about it now, *Forget this war, get back to normal,* the brandy slurring their words. Let them get drunk. She thought of Uncle Otto. The last she'd heard, he had been interned, an enemy alien. She had no idea if he was still in prison. He could be dead. She would have no one. Were her aunts still alive in Germany?

Where would she go? Where was her home? She had no papers. Was there a record of them in London? Was she still a refugee? She had to find out what had happened to List. The Germans would know where he was. She'd find him. He'd said he'd take her away. Did he say he'd keep her safe? She couldn't remember. He'd look after her. He'd said she'd be his mistress, at another time.

And Geoffrey? She couldn't imagine that she had once loved him too. It was so long ago. She was a different woman then. If he had survived, she could never tell him about her war. Or anyone. How she had sex with the officers as if she were a whore, nursed the enemy soldiers as if they were her own. Never put up a moment's resistance. Too *cowardly* to stand up to them. She had looked forward to Maximilian List's visits. Her earlier love for Geoffrey seemed from another time. List was the man who loomed in her imagination, her memory. Geoffrey was a good man, despite his youthful indiscretions. If he was alive, it was best she never met him again. Best he forget her.

Her old life was over. She knew that, then. *La vie est terminée.*

CHAPTER FOURTEEN

JOE

Jersey: June 1985

What Joe couldn't tell Geoffrey was how Trude still ate at his heart. There were many ways to sin, many ways to break a spirit. He had believed Trude. Believed in her. Two souls lost in the moil of war. He squeezed his fingers into his eyes.

'Will you bid me goodnight?' he said. He was fatigued, a weariness that chiselled at bones and sinews, made it hard to put one step in front of another, one thought ahead of another. He felt those moments in his body as he relived them in his memory. He'd never revealed these sins, not in forty years. Oh, he'd told Geoffrey bits in the early days. Ernst. The lice. The hunger that reduced them all to animals scratching for life, thinking of nothing else. Once or twice he'd talked of cruelty, but not the sins. Geoffrey knew all about that too, had the same stories to tell.

A time came when there was nothing left to say and neither spoke of the war again. The memories were stashed away to gather dust, untouched, unvisited.

'Can you put yourself to bed this evening?'

'Turn on the light before you go.' Geoffrey's voice was weak.

Joe pushed himself up, flicked on the switch. The fluorescent strip flashed before it filled the room with a harsh white light. Geoffrey was gripping the armrest, grey bone through faded skin, knuckles now a range of frailty. His handkerchief was on his lap.

'That was a shocking story, Joe,' he said, softly.

He looked as if he had aged a decade in the last hour, his muscles sagging and his neck scrawny. Joe could see his Adam's apple rise and fall, the whiskers on his neck white and sharp. He'd have to shave him properly tomorrow. Joe could see he wanted to talk. He couldn't bid him goodnight, not right now.

'And you had it wrapped up tight inside you, all this time.'

'Like you bottled Dora's story inside of you,' Joe said. Geoffrey shook his head, *tut-tut*, dabbed at his eyes and wiped drool from his nose and mouth. Joe stared into the distance, at the damson light outside. Two old men, he thought, weighed down by the stones of guilt.

'I've thought about it a lot,' Joe said, after a while. He meant, it played on my mind. The nightmares. He walked back to the chair. Geoffrey looked alone, in pain.

'I didn't mean to kill the cook,' he said, lowering himself into the seat, elbows on the armrest. 'But no man has the right to judge who lives or dies. We were all starving. We knew the pain of that. The obsession. To deny a man food, that is a terrible crime.'

Geoffrey nodded.

Joe added, 'But I don't need to tell you this.' He had read about the trials in Hamburg after the war, the evils done in Neuengamme. Geoffrey hadn't wanted to stand witness, *to stand out*, as he said, but he'd followed them in the papers and on the wireless, day in, day out. *I knew him. Yes, that happened.* 'What had that old man ever done?' Standing with his bowl, so *meek*. 'I meant to teach the cook a lesson. I didn't mean him harm. No, Geoffrey, that wasn't my sin.'

Talking gave Joe energy again. He should stay, keep Geoffrey company. Geoffrey was upset. This was the longest conversation Joe could remember them having, a real heart-to-heart. There was a drop of Jameson left in the bottle. Joe reached for his glass, topped it up, showed the bottle to Geoffrey. He shook his head.

'I've had enough.'

'Denying the dead a proper funeral,' Joe went on. 'Not giving the poor souls back to the ground so their bodies could rise again. That was a sin.'

He took a sip of the whiskey. He hadn't drunk like this for forty years, could feel his brain swell and shrink beneath his skull, hammer for mercy.

'But it wasn't my sin,' Joe went on, 'and there was nothing I could do, except say a prayer.'

Geoffrey nodded.

It's past his bedtime, Joe thought. 'Will I help you upstairs?' he said.

'Presently. Go on.'

'The sin I committed was in believing there was a God in heaven on the first day of hell on earth. So I said the prayers, a requiem in my head, every night, in the Latin too.'

'How can that be a sin?' Geoffrey said.

Joe shrugged. 'It was a blasphemy, all the same. You see, I had *stopped* believing in a God. It was all a pretence. Lying, that I was a priest. I was no more a priest than you or Ernst.'

'If it gave them succour,' Geoffrey said, 'was that so bad?'

'They were dead,' Joe said. 'I couldn't help the living, only the dead.' He tipped the last of the whiskey into his glass, the liquid forming rainbows as it swirled and settled. The clock in the hall worked itself up, chimed once.

'Trude, now,' Geoffrey said after a while. 'You got her into trouble, trying to save Dora and myself. Do you count that as one of your sins?'

'Trude,' Joe said. He put down his glass and put a hand under Geoffrey's elbow, pulling him to his feet. When Geoffrey leaned on him now, his body was light as a bird. He'd lost flesh, his skin translucent, his veins blue rivers. Joe could feel the bones beneath, see the liver spots on his face and hands. When had Geoffrey got so old?

'You've been good to me, Joe,' Geoffrey said. 'And I thank you from the bottom of my heart.'

'You tell me that every night,' Joe said. He couldn't bring himself to say it, but he loved Geoffrey. Joe had wanted a wife at one time. He wasn't much to look at it, no more than a penny titch of a man with little moral fibre, but he was a grafter and that counted for a lot in a husband. But women were fickle, untrustworthy. He had never found another one to his liking and he'd grown content over the years, he and Geoffrey.

'Trude,' Geoffrey said.

It was a while before Joe answered.

'Now,' he said, 'there's the thing. I was green. An innocent. The cruelty of it. The cruelty of them.' Added, 'No, she was not my sin. I have no guilt for *her*. Not now.'

And it wasn't just Trude. Survival was a strange beast, seeing the man behind the uniform, we're all in this together.

Alderney: February – July 1944

Joe saw the steel on the toecaps, the blacking on the boots, and looked up. *Hauptsturmführer* Maximilian List. The *Kommandant*. Trude's killer. Joe had seen him in the camp and on the fortifications. Knew he had orders to kill them all if the British invaded. Round them up in the tunnel that led from the camp to his house and shoot. *Rat-a-tat-tat*. He'd never been this close to him, one on one, not since that interrogation with Knackfuss. He wanted to swing his shovel, smash his head in, bury him with the cook. Joe was breathing hard, could hear his lungs creak with the strain. He gripped his shovel, poised to lift it. He didn't have the strength, not to swing it like a caber and floor the bastard. He flung it on the ground.

'I hear you killed a man last night.' List's English was excellent.

Joe breathed in again hard, stared out to sea. 'I didn't mean to,' he said, not looking at him.

'Intention does not come into it. That man was in my charge.'

Joe's intestines churned, an empty stomach that burned bile. He wanted to spit it out, but that would get him a beating. He was in enough trouble as it was. He looked at the ground, at the lugworm casts in the sand. The little dunlins and sandpipers would have a feast if they came now.

'I heard you were a boxing champion,' List said.

Joe nodded.

'A runt like you, beat the *Wehrmacht* champion.'

How did List know? Joe had told no one, not on Alderney. Pierre had been right. *Let him win.* He had humiliated the Germans. They took their time, but they took their revenge. He knew then. Sylt was his punishment.

'I have a job for you,' List said. 'My men. They're bored in these long winter nights. You will teach them how to box.'

Joe looked at the *Kommandant.* Was that sarcasm playing on his lips? Was he being set up? Again? *Fail my men, and there will be consequences.* Joe could see Ernst run a finger across his throat. What choice did he have? He wasn't fit, wasn't *fed* like a boxer. When were they going to hang him? He could feel List's eyes bearing down, the presence of the man, too close.

'In the meantime, report to the kitchen. You are the new cook. The new *Kapo.*'

He nodded at the corpses waiting to be buried in the sand and Joe lifted his spade, ready to shovel again, List's clear grey eyes boring into him.

There it was. *Kruk-kruk-kruk.* Joe couldn't help himself. Looked up. Gannets. Not one solitary bird, but several.

'Do you know these birds?' List was training his binoculars on them as they flew over the waves.

'Gannets,' Joe said, despite himself. He didn't want to talk to this man, this murderer.

'Northern gannets. *Morus bassanus*,' List said. 'They have a colony on Les Etacs. That little rock, over there. Here is too noisy for them, with all the booming and the banging. Nobody fishes the water now, so food is plentiful, and that rock is safe.' He turned to Joe. 'There are benefits to war. We Germans love nature.'

There was life, in all of this, *life*.

'I like birds,' List went on. 'There are not so many in Alderney. We have disturbed their habitats. But Jersey now, there's a place for birds. Sea birds, especially. Puffins. Do you know about puffins?'

Joe said nothing.

'Answer me,' List said.

'They're a comical little bird.' His teeth were clenched, and Joe spat the words. 'That's for sure.'

'My girlfriend and I watch them all the time,' List said. 'Trude thinks they have a face like a clown. Would you agree?'

Trude. Joe heard no more. Trude was dead. Could this be a different Trude? It was a common name, surely, like Mary, or Joan.

'It's a small world,' List said. 'She's a nurse, you know.'

This man spoke of her as if she was alive, when he had killed her. Mocking her memory. He wanted to fly at List, strangle him so his eyes bulged from their sockets and his voice snapped in two.

'You murdered her.' He didn't watch his language. He had nothing to lose. 'Before my eyes.'

'You saw her die?' List said, calm as a glider.

That pistol *crack*, that thump as she fell. He'd heard for sure. They'd murdered her, her face too frightened to look up at Joe. He hadn't saved her. *Couldn't* save her. But no, he hadn't *seen* her die, except in his mind's eye.

'It was a game.' List was laughing. 'For our amusement.'

'Game?' Joe's voice broke like a boy's. He couldn't think. What kind of game was that? Trude? He loved her, thought she loved him. He would have told her he loved her, would have asked her, *Do you love me?* had they had more time. Had it all been a game with her? Was he her plaything? Had she *toyed* with him? He gave up everything for her. Would have married her.

'Would you like to look through my binoculars?'

Joe shook his head.

'Report to the kitchen when you've done this,' List said.

He turned, his heel scouring the sand. Joe watched him walk towards the dunes. Despite the jacket, Joe shivered and slumped to the ground, bones of marrow, the soft putty of his skeleton. List disappeared from view. He shuddered, the hairs on his arms standing up as if his grave had been dug and trampled over. An animal scurried in the sandy undergrowth, made him jump. Flashed. Gone. A dormouse? A field mouse? Perhaps a vole. A mole. There were molehills beyond the dunes, soft hillocks of chewed earth. Did moles chew? Or scratch? Worms chewed. He could hear them, a soft percussion in the silence, as the ocean breathed in and out.

The sun sat crooked in the sky. His sin. His *original* sin. He had believed Trude. Put his trust in her. All along, she was untrue. Why? Why *him*? He'd led her to the dell. Betrayed Geoffrey and the nurse. Were they still alive? The two labourers, they were dead. Four people, and the cook made five. Five people condemned because he had been too vain to resist. For what? She had promised him heaven but gave him hell. He was a murderer. A coward. A liar. He'd lived a lie as a priest and this was his punishment.

The cold muzzle pressed into his cheek.

'*Aufstehen!*'

Joe breathed in sharp, looked up at the guard holding the gun, his body foreshortened, silhouetted against the sun.

'Shoot me,' Joe said.

The guard kicked his thigh. '*Aufstehen.*'

Joe pushed himself onto his feet. He could make a run for it, head for the sea, force the guard to shoot him, kill him outright.

Joe looked at the beach. He was too scared to run, too feeble to decide. Stumbled back along the path with the Mauser pressing into his back.

A collaborator. A *Kapo.*

A cuckold.

Why couldn't he stay in the shelter of the marram grass, live on berries and fungus, sleep in the moss with the breeze of the sea?

§

Cook. His turn to field the suspicious, starving eyes of the inmates, the accusations. *You do all right for yourselves, you cooks. Bastard Kapos.*

Ernst had put his arm on Joe's shoulder. 'Remember,' he said. 'You're not guilty for what you did. You're the victim.'

'It wasn't just the cook,' Joe said. 'There was so much more. So many more.' Where could he begin? All his life. A lie.

'Don't look back,' Ernst said, shaking his head, wagging his finger. 'Think to the future. You and me, we're history's witnesses. Be strong, comrade. The past will look different in a few years.'

Joe lay on his bunk as the men moaned in their sleep. *This* was his cross. Guilt. Solid and heavy, boxing him in and shackling him tight. What was doubt now? Nothing but a flimsy cross made of palm fronds.

If he was to live, then he'd make amends.

§

Cabbage. Potatoes. Once or twice a sausage. Joe learned how to bake bread out of rough wheat, chalk and rye. He caught a rabbit once. Made a catapult and brought it down, but what was a rabbit among so many hungry men? He couldn't perform miracles. The thing was, there wasn't enough food, so the other *Kapos* and the guards turned a blind eye when the prisoners went foraging. Joe put his treasures in the stews, most of the time. Found a stash of wood ears growing from a dead elder tree. They called it Jew's ear in Ireland, but he wouldn't do that now. There was stinking onion and wild garlic, if you knew where to look. Rock samphire and nettles in the spring. He'd spotted wild carrots too. A little extra goodness, some flavour in the soup. Leftovers he smuggled back to the hut and handed round. Most of the time. A bite for Joe, first.

The *SS* had pigs and a cow. Joe wasn't the son of a butcher for nothing. He'd snatch a piglet if he could. Have it slaughtered, stripped and stewed before you could say *SS-Totenkopfverbände*, pickle the belly, salt the back. And when the cow had done her time, he'd graze her well and make her happy and lead her into her stall with a manger full of hay and a salt lick the size of Derry. She wouldn't smell the singe of death or listen to its bellows. 'For that would spoil the meat,' his *daidí* used to say. 'Sweet and tender like butter itself. Not some old ox with rubber muscles.' Though now, Joe thought, any old ox would do. Even a leather strap.

'One day,' Joe said, 'we'll feast for real.'

He and Ernst and the others. Those who survived. The numbers were getting thinner by the day. The Jews had been sent back. France. Germany. Who knew where? Even List himself. Rumour had it that some of the Jews had escaped in France, and they wanted List's head to roll. But nobody countermanded his order for Joe to teach them boxing and he took the *SS* through their paces. Some of the *OT* guards from Lager Nordeney or Helgoland took to hanging around. Stripped to their vests and underpants, hands strapped and gloved, he had them all skipping and running, sparring and punching.

It was early June, 1944. They were sitting outside, on the step of the hut, still damp from the previous day's storm. It was late, dark. The moon was full, but the sky was overcast, clumps of cloud blowing with the breeze. It had whipped the sea into a noisy froth.

Joe could hear it *slap-slapping* the shore and see white horses in the flickering moonlight.

'Sssh,' Ernst said.

The distant drone of an aeroplane. Joe and Ernst sat in silence as the sound came closer. Louder. Not one aeroplane. A squadron. Heavy bombers. They came from England, heading to France. And *boom. Boom.* The Germans fired up at them, heavy weaponry which shook the earth but fell short of their targets. Joe stood up on the step, peered through the wire fencing, saw the coast of France blasting orange and red, the smoke from the bombs furling mushrooms into the clouds. He fancied he could feel the heat from the fires that burned on the Normandy coast, breathe in the smoke from the blasts, taste the cordite on his tongue.

He smiled, the first time for months.

§

Gulls and guillemots. Shags and cormorants. Even before they climbed onto deck, Joe knew they were back in Jersey. He could see them through the hatch, flying low, silent in the storm. Too rough to sail to France. Or dangerous. If the skies swarmed with Allied bombers, the seas would be full of their ships. Early July the order had come from Berlin to evacuate Alderney, send the prisoners to repair the defences in France. They had filed out after *Appell*, down to the harbour and the boats. Joe waited on the wharf. The ship was called the *Minotaure*. The monster that ate humans, Joe recalled. Hundreds were shoved into the hold before the hatch was closed.

Joe was directed towards a neighbouring vessel. Crossed the gangplank, onto the deck, into the damp, dark space beneath. *Schnell. Schnell.* The vessel was much smaller than the *Minotaure*. Joe reckoned there must have been fifty prisoners or so crammed in the space with no air or water and a single bucket for their use.

The ship began to rock, rain hammered on the deck above, and Joe heard the wind tear through the harbour buildings. The weather had broken.

A crowd of civilians had gathered and watched the prisoners as they stood in the sun on the quayside in St Helier. Why would anyone want to gawp at them? Was misery so compelling? A spectator sport? Joe hoped no one recognised him. He kept his eyes to the ground, his face out of their gaze. But if they did spot him, he thought, could they not plead for him? *This man shouldn't be here. Let him go.* He looked up. He saw no one he knew.

Now the prisoners mustered, five abreast. There were other prisoners, too, some in striped shirts and trousers, others in rags, like Joe. He wasn't sure whether they were waiting to embark or had just come off some other ship. They were silent and sullen, dulled by starvation. But of the Sylt men, word got round. The *Minotaure* had gone down. Blown to smithereens. Ernst with it. Joe prayed he hadn't felt a thing. Drowning, they said, was a peaceful death.

It was evening before they moved. Some were sent east. Joe and the others, west. Past the wharves and the customs house, the yellow beaches criss-crossed with razor wire. The esplanade looked strange to Joe now, as if he no longer belonged. He knew every paving stone and brick, but he felt disorientated, anxious, each step a churn in his gut that made him light-headed and disconnected. *Homesick,* for the home he'd come back to.

They were turning right into Pierson Road. Right into St Aubin's Road. Oh, Joe knew the way. Ahead of them, a large building with white stucco and curly Dutch gables. *West Park Pavilion.* Joe'd been there for the Christmas bazaar and Pierre said they held grand dances, before the war. It was not so far from the hospital and the little park. Perhaps they'd stay here. Perhaps the war was over. *Over.* Joe felt hope for the first time, a fierce buoyancy that lifted his chin.

They were marched up the steps and into the main hall. Joe recognised the *SS* guards from Sylt, but there were others too, from the *OT* or the *Wehrmacht*. The prisoners had to stand in line, file past as a scrawny wretch doled out watery soup in tin cans. They were given orders to sleep on the floor. No room to turn. They'd be shipped out in the morning.

Joe lay awake all night. The war hadn't ended. This was his only chance to get away. Now he was back in Jersey, it made another day, another *moment*, in captivity, unbearable. He had to escape. *Two seconds*. That's all he'd need. Slip free of the guards. He knew the town. He'd find his way out. Didn't Pierre have a sister who lived nearby? Change of clothes, and he'd be on his way. He'd apologise for the lice, advise her to burn the garments. Go to the convent? No, he couldn't put the nuns in danger again. *Improvise*. He'd think of something. Head out to the country. *Speed*. That was of the essence. He'd leave the cook's shoes behind. He couldn't run in too-big shoes.

Up at first light. *Appell*. Always *Appell*. This would be the last *Appell* if it killed him. The *SS* guards from Sylt lined them up, marched them out. Two led the prisoners at the front, two at the rear, rifles at the ready. Two others, with shaggy Alsatians that pulled at their leashes, kept watch. Six guards for fifty prisoners. Not so many. Joe wondered where the rest had gone. He pulled back, a step at a time, out of the line of vision of the dogs and their handlers, worked his way, little by little, to the nearside ranks, checking with each move that none of the guards had noticed. *Links, links. Singen*. Sing, bastards. How about this? *Hitler has only got one ball*.

There was a lane coming up, off to the left, just by the bend in the road. *Göring has two but very small*. Little shops, small tradesmen. Doorways. Alleys. *Himmler has something sim'lar*. This was his chance. His only chance. He could feel the fire light in his stomach, his tendons tense, muscles stretched and at the ready. His big fight. His big *flight*. The guards were looking at the men in front of them or to their side. Joe paced himself, filling his lungs with oxygen. Timing was all. Five, four, three. One bungled step, and that would be the end. He straightened his spine, relaxed his chest and arms, up on the balls of his bare feet. Two, one. Pivoted, spun, flattened himself against the alley wall and held his breath as the rest of the prisoners, and the guards at their rear, tramped past. It would take them five minutes to reach the harbour. They'd do a roll call, discover he was missing. Five minutes there. Five back. He had ten minutes.

There was a horse standing further up the road, a chestnut. It pawed impatiently with its foreleg, hoof on the tip. It was harnessed up, standing between the shafts of a black delivery van. Joe guessed the time was about five o'clock in the morning. Too early even for tradesmen, though *someone* must be up, ready to go. Joe looked behind him. The street was empty. He hadn't been spotted. He ran to the van.

Pierre Besson and Co, Joe read. *Purveyors of Quality Groceries and Meat.*

'Well thank you, Lord,' Joe said to himself. 'You've answered my prayers.'

The back doors of the van were unlocked. Joe climbed inside, pulled them shut. It smelled of ammonia. Slivers of the dawn came through two small rectangular windows, one in the back, one in the front.

Easy. Joe laughed. *And Goebbels has no balls at all.*

There was the sound of clawing in the van. It took a moment for his eyes to grow used to the dimness. There were shelves either side. Rabbits, scratching the hard, wooden base of their cages. Above them, he could see baskets of eggs. *Eggs.* He took one, cracked its shell, poured the soft yolk and albumen into his mouth.

He heard the footsteps. Felt the sweat on his forehead. *Eejit.* The van would be the first place the soldiers would look. Open the doors, yank him out, shoot him on the spot. He had no idea where

Pierre was. The footsteps passed. Joe fingered the doors, but there was no catch inside. He was shut in.

They came close again. Joe heard the metallic scrunch as the handle turned and the door opened.

Daylight snapped in. Joe was sitting on the floor in full view with his mouth full of egg.

'Out,' Pierre said. 'Now. You. Out. *Raus*.'

'It's me,' Joe said.

'Out. Before I call the Gestapo.'

'It's Joe.' Added, 'Father O'Cleary.'

Pierre leaned into the van, pulling the doors to behind him. He stared at Joe, as Joe wiped his mouth.

'Father O'Cleary?'

'Help me, Pierre,' Joe said. 'For God's sake, man, help me. Don't hand me in.'

Pierre looked behind him, turned back to Joe.

'Crawl under the shelves and cover yourself with the tarpaulin.' He pointed at a canvas roll in the corner. Slammed the doors, locked them tight. Joe heard him walk to the landing board, felt the van rock as Pierre clambered up, jolt as the horse moved off.

Joe lay curled inside the tarpaulin. It smelled of pig and dried blood. The egg left a cloying taste in his mouth, was too rich for his stomach. The van was rolling and bumping over the roads. He felt sick, his guts were cramping up, his heart punching hard against his ribs. Up hill and down dale. He had no idea where they were heading. Up and down. Side to side.

Rocking. Rocking.

He woke with a jolt as Pierre opened the doors wide.

'Jump out,' he said. 'We're here.'

Joe pulled himself free of the tarpaulin. The sharp smell of the sea caught his breath. He heard the gentle *put-put* of waves in the distant cove, the cry of a circling curlew *crou-eee, crou-eee*. His eyes filled with tears, salty drops that dribbled down his cheeks and into his mouth. He began to shake, as if his rattled bones were sloughing off his skin, knocking at the ligaments that held him together. He sat down, pushed himself forward to the edge of the van.

'No,' Joe said. He wanted to run but his feet were as heavy as concrete, his frame frozen in a hurly-burly of terror as he saw again the dead boy's blasted skull spilled on the ground, the haunted faces of Geoffrey and the nurse as they climbed into the *Kübelwagen.* He heard the brutal chug of its engines as they drove out of the yard and up the hill. 'No, Pierre. Not here.'

'My God, Father,' Pierre said. 'If you weren't in such a lousy state I'd shake your hand at the very least.'

'Did you hear me?' Joe said. What kind of joke was the man playing? After all he'd been through. Pierre had brought him *here,* to the place he'd betrayed them all, to sip his guilt, slow and bitter as quinine. He could taste the mucous from his nose, the sweat from his lip. So near, so very near. He didn't have strength anymore. He had seized his chance to escape. He couldn't do it again.

'This is Geoffrey's farm.'

Did Pierre know?

'What happened to you?'

'It was my fault,' Joe said.

'What are you talking about?'

'That Geoffrey was caught. And the nurse. I opened my big mouth. Brought her to the farm.'

'Plenty of people have big mouths, Father,' Pierre said. 'And sharp eyes. Keen imaginations, too, some of them. There's nothing like an occupying army for settling old scores.'

Joe looked up at Pierre. 'It was me. I was here. I saw it all. They murdered a boy.'

'From what I understand,' Pierre said, 'you tried to save Geoffrey and the nurse. And you put yourself in the firing line. You weren't to blame. You weren't to know, if it's any consolation.' He pulled out a packet of cigarettes, lit one and offered it to Joe. Joe took it, smelled the coarse black tobacco, breathed in the heady smoke. He felt dizzy, grabbed the side of the door for support. Coughed.

'What happened to you?' Pierre said.

Joe stubbed out the cigarette on the floor of Pierre's van. He had no words for where he'd been, no shape to the story of what happened.

'I've done terrible things, Pierre.'

He'd got used to it. The humdrum horror of it. That was a terrible thing, too.

'I killed a man.' He was quaking, out of control, as if a palsy, or the devil himself, had taken over his body.

'Did you have a choice?'

Choice? Joe hadn't thought.

'There was no temptation, if that's what you mean,' Joe said. His spirit had hardened, atrophied. He saw corpses on the floor. 'And no remorse, either.'

He was tired, an unfathomable weariness that could slay him. He couldn't return, ever. He'd throw himself off a cliff, hang himself on a beam.

'Will you turn me in?' Joe said.

'No,' Pierre said.

Joe hesitated. Pierre supped with the devil when it suited him, Joe knew.

'Will you give me a chance to escape, if you change your mind?'

'I won't change my mind,' Pierre said.

'Only I couldn't go back. No. That I couldn't.'

He pushed himself forward again, dangled his legs over the end of the van.

'Lightning never strikes twice.' Pierre was smiling. 'This is the safest place you can be.'

Perhaps, Joe thought. He'd dreamed about a day like this, after all.

CHAPTER FIFTEEN

DORA

London: June 1985

Dora tugged at her skirt, smoothing its apron. She needed time to steady herself. She went upstairs to the bathroom, peered into the mirror. She had aged like her father, his lines criss-crossing her cheeks, his jaw, hers. *Vati.* What would he have done? She pulled at the toilet roll, blew her nose hard and flushed the tissue down the loo. Opened the cabinet and dabbed on some lipstick, went downstairs and walked back out into the garden.

'Apologies,' she said. 'An old friend.'

She piled the empty cups and plates onto the tray and took them into the kitchen. She hoped she'd stayed calm, looked indifferent. Maximilian List. Alive. He had a wife who looked after him. Children most likely. Grandchildren. Lucky him. He'd got away with it. Dora's head tightened and she could feel her anger bubble. Did his conscience play tricks on him? Did he ever think about what he'd done? Did he ever think about her?

She placed the tray on the draining board, looked out over the garden to where Barbara sat, leaning back in her chair, chin in the air. Hoffmann's daughter. She gripped the side of the sink. *List*'s daughter. Hoffmann and List. Dora's war, shrunk to two people. Stretched by two people, as if she'd been on the rack and they had turned the wheel until her tendons tore and her bones broke.

Her life in ghostly, ghastly tatters, while they lived out their days without a care. She had survived, Uncle Otto kept telling her that. Millions hadn't. But numbers meant nothing when faces brought it home. Their child, their progeny, sitting butter-wouldn't-melt in her garden.

Dora resented this woman for being alive, for being somebody else's daughter. She would have liked a child, a daughter, like her. But List and Hoffmann had destroyed any chance of that.

Did Barbara know anything? If her mother had lied about her father, and about being in Jersey, what else had she lied about? Barbara must have a birth certificate, or had she forged that, too? Lost in the bombing. Born in the countryside. No records. *It was so terrible here in Germany. Nobody thought about ordinary people.* Been widowed by it? *Poor me. I had to bring my daughter up all by myself.* She could see Nurse Hoffmann now, with her plain, round face and little mouth, weeping, *My boyfriend leaves for Germany soon.* She left not long after. Perhaps List took her with him. They made no secret of their affair, Hoffmann and List, that was for sure. *Mein Liebling.* My darling. Those words had stung Dora like a hornet.

Barbara was coming towards the house. Slim, elegant, a *professional* woman. Perhaps she had List's physique, his brains. Daughters often took after their fathers. The sins of the fathers. She wanted to be repulsed by her, but there was an innocence about Barbara and Dora believed her when she said her mother never spoke of the war. Not many people spoke about the war in Britain, and they were on the winning side. Too busy putting it behind them, moving on.

Even the victims, Jews who'd escaped before the war. Others who'd survived the camps. Why me? What more could have been done? Survivor's guilt, that's what Uncle Otto called it.

'But I *lied*,' Dora said to him once.

'And the truth would have helped you how?' he said. 'No one can be a hero against the tides of history. You can only swim with it and hope it doesn't drown you.'

'But I did it to save my own skin.'

'I ran away and left my sisters to die. Now, there's guilt for you.'

Why should Barbara feel guilt? Her war was nothing other than history. Still, Dora thought, what kind of a shock would it be to discover these sorts of things? To entertain the possibility that Maximilian List was your father? List was in the *SS-Totenkopfverbände*, Death's Head units, ran a concentration camp. Dora had heard nothing about what went on in Alderney, but a camp was a camp and Lager Sylt had been a satellite of Neuengamme, and there had been plenty about *that* camp in the trials after the war.

She heard Barbara climb the steps up to the kitchen and enter, her heels *click-clacking* on the wooden floor.

'Thank you for the coffee,' she said.

Dora smiled. 'You're welcome. I never really got used to tea, not in the afternoon.'

'I should leave you,' she said.

But Barbara made no move to go and Dora sensed she wanted to talk some more.

'What's the time?'

Barbara checked her watch. 'It's six o'clock. I've stayed too long. You have things to do.'

'Well,' Dora said, 'I can miss one night of bridge. It's not too early to have a glass of wine. It's not often I have visitors. Perhaps you would join me?'

She had a bottle of Riesling in the fridge. It had been on special offer. Not that Dora was poor, but she was careful with her money. Perhaps all refugees were careful with money.

'Thank you,' Barbara said. 'I have no plans for this evening. That would be nice.'

'Well, make yourself useful,' Dora said. 'There are olives in the fridge. Please will you take them out, put them in that dish.' She pointed towards a brightly painted bowl that she'd bought in Spain one year.

It was strange having another woman in the kitchen. Dora had always thought she'd resent it, but Barbara didn't seem to crowd the space. This is what it must be like to have a daughter, taking charge, knowing where the cutlery lived, or where the breakfast cereal was kept. Perhaps when she was older and she needed care, she'd allow a nurse in to prepare her meals. Could she afford that? Better than meals-on-wheels, cooked in some institution and delivered at ten o'clock in the morning. She had a neighbour who relied on them, and he always complained that they were cold and came at uncivilised hours. Well, she had a few more years before she need think about *that*.

'Will you pass the wine, too,' Dora said, 'while you're there.'

Dora rummaged in the drawer for the corkscrew, reached up to the shelf for two glasses. No. She'd use the *best*. Bohemian crystal. Uncle Otto had bought them on the black market on a trip he'd made to Prague.

'Shall we sit outside?' Barbara said.

'Why not?'

They threaded their way down the steps and across the lawn, placed two fine flutes on the table, and a bowl of olives. Dora opened the wine, poured. She raised a glass, and Barbara did too, smiling at each other, like old acquaintances, Dora thought.

'May I ask you another question?' Barbara said.

Now Dora wished she hadn't invited Barbara to stay. She'd be happy with chit-chat, *Do you have anything planned for the weekend? Are you going on holiday this year?* Of course Barbara wanted to carry on dredging up the past. Why else would she accept the invitation? Perhaps, Dora thought, she was asking for this. Deep down, was her unconscious grateful for Barbara's questions? Imprisoned by memory, hammering to be set free. That was a shocking thought, that she welcomed Barbara's probing. Dora felt small beads of sweat break out on her forehead. That hadn't happened since the change, and Dora wasn't sure why she felt so agitated.

'You said you'd seen my mother on the island. Do you know when she left?'

Dora bit her lip, felt something stir deep inside, as if a slumbering volcano was taking a stretch, a yawn, working its way to erupt. 'As I said, I didn't know her. I'd see her riding her bike, in her uniform. I really didn't notice when she went,' she said.

'But approximately? Was it in the spring or the summer of 1944?'

'No one could come or go after the summer,' Dora said. 'The island was under siege.'

'I forgot. Was it the spring?'

Dora had lost track of time, dates jumbled and jumped. 1944. 1945. She wasn't even sure about the seasons, at least, not the in-between seasons, those days when winter and spring fought it out. What had the weather been like? It was cold. They'd had Christmas, because she remembered thinking what an extravagance it was, to have a tree, when they were short of firewood. Or was that the year after? Was it the Christmas before, the time List sent her to work in the *Revier*? When had he given her the soap?

'I can't think,' Dora said.

'Please try,' Barbara said. 'It is so important.'

'Why?'

'My mother showed up in Hamburg in August 1944,' she said. '*Frau* List thought the baby was about six months old. That makes sense. But my mother doesn't look pregnant in the photograph with List that I showed you.'

'Sometimes women don't show much,' Dora said, especially, she thought, the fleshy ones.

'Hmm,' Barbara said. 'Not in my experience.'

Dora laughed, took a sip of wine. 'You are a midwife?'

Barbara laughed then. 'Maybe not.'

'When is your birthday?'

'The twenty-fourth of February.'

Nurse Hoffmann was not pregnant, Dora knew, or if she had been, it was early days. Was that why Hoffmann had disappeared? It would make sense, before she showed. Dora lifted her blouse away from her neck, waved it so the breeze came through.

'Perhaps you were a big baby,' she said. No baby was big in the war, but Barbara wouldn't know that. She was sure Hoffmann had left in March 1944. Cold. Windy too. What was it the English say? March comes in like a lion and goes out like a lamb. It had been windy, standing outside for the *Appell* in the driving, biting rain.

'That woman, the one whose photograph I first showed you,' Barbara said. 'Are you sure you don't know her?'

'I've told you,' Dora said. *Snapped.* 'No.'

'Perhaps she was a friend of my mother's. Please think.'

'Why are you dredging up the past?' Dora said. 'Why are you doing it? Why are you *really* doing it?'

Barbara sat back in the chair, ran her finger round the rim of the flute so it sang like a glass harp.

'It's been difficult for my generation of Germans,' she said. 'To live in the shadow of the war, with parents refusing to admit what happened. We took on their guilt.'

'You can't be blamed for the past.'

'No, but we are responsible for the future. We need to account for what went on, before we can forge ahead. That doesn't start in the archive. It starts at home.'

'But why is *this* woman important to you?'

'Because I have this crazy feeling,' Barbara said, 'since I found the photographs, that perhaps my mother isn't even my mother.'

'She brought you up. Cared for you. That's a mother.'

'Perhaps she adopted me.'

'Still your mother. Besides, she would have told you.'

'She lied about the war. Why shouldn't she lie about that? Women of her generation often lied about adopting a child.'

'Do you not have a birth certificate?'

'Only a replacement,' Barbara said. 'My mother said that all her papers were lost in the war, the originals, and the archives were bombed. She could have made anything up.' She breathed in. 'I think that woman might know. Perhaps my mother kidnapped me.'

Dora laughed, a short nervous *tee.* 'Your father isn't your father, your mother isn't your mother. You're not who you think you are. Goodness me, you don't think you're making too much of this? The English have an expression for that, making a mountain out of a molehill. Do you know it?'

'I'm serious,' Barbara said.

'Enough.' Dora's voice was firm.

'But the Nazis did,' Barbara went on. 'They kidnapped babies. Little blond, blue-eyed babies. To bring up as Aryans.'

'This is nonsense,' Dora said.

The wine was making Barbara talkative.

'Besides,' Dora went on, 'your eyes and hair are brown. Not very Aryan.' She gathered up her glass and the bottle of wine and walked towards the kitchen, sensing Barbara behind her. 'You have your mother's colouring,' she said over her shoulder. The end of the matter. She had been harsh. She wasn't used to company, not awkward company. She wanted to be on her own. Barbara would have to understand that. She put the glass and bottle on the table, as a flash of emotion charged through her. She was going to cry, could feel the tears welling, her nose running. She brushed her eyes with the back of her hand, reached in her pocket for a tissue, and blew her nose.

'I want you to leave, please.'

She heard Barbara breathe in, limber up. 'What is it you're hiding from me?'

'Nothing.' Dora's voice was loud and she could hear it quiver. 'Go away.'

'I am very sorry,' Barbara said, 'this upsets you. I had no idea.'

'No,' Dora said. 'You have no idea. There are some things best forgotten. I can't help you. I told you that from the start. Perhaps your friend in Jersey. What was his name?'

'Mr O'Cleary?'

'Yes. Perhaps he can tell you more.'

'He's not really a friend,' Barbara said. 'I've only met him once, and that was briefly.'

'Then go back and ask him,' Dora said. 'I can't think who he is, or how he knew me, or had my address.'

'Ah,' Barbara said. 'He doesn't know you. It was the old man who lives at the farm who recognised you. Mr O'Cleary just wrote to me. He's the caretaker. Maybe the carer.'

'The old man at the farm,' Dora repeated the words. *The old man at the farm.* Her breathing became shallow, short, light pants. 'Did you meet him? What did he look like? What was his name?'

Barbara blinked, put up her hands. Dora wanted to grab her, shake the information from her.

'Do you think you know him?'

Dora curled her tongue over her lip, her thoughts moiling like an ocean in a storm. 'I may,' she said, her voice in quavers. 'I may.'

'I only saw him in the distance. White hair. Frail. I think Mr O'Cleary said his name was Geoffrey.'

Dora grabbed the sink again, turned to face the garden. 'Are you sure?' she said, throwing the words over her shoulder.

'Quite sure.'

'Thank you,' Dora said. She stared through the window, her mind churning, inchoate shoals of memories jostling her thoughts and reason. She saw them swarming in front of her, synchronised, beyond her control. What did they call it? Group intelligence. Fish. Birds. Ants. Memories. She heard Barbara cough.

'Please let yourself out,' Dora said, without turning.

She waited until she heard the front door click shut, then poured herself another glass of wine, wandered back out into the garden.

Geoffrey was alive. She sat, repeating it, like a mantra. *Geoffrey is alive.* Barbara's questions swum in and out of focus. Dora had lost count of the days. Could have sworn it was March when Hoffmann had left, but perhaps it was earlier, in February.

She had to go to Geoffrey. She couldn't waste a moment. She'd go to the travel agent first thing, book a ticket to Jersey.

Jersey

The sea stretched as far back as the horizon and crags of rock jutted from the sand, sharp as sharks' teeth. When the tide was in, the waters looked calm and peaceful, belied the treachery beneath.

Green Island. That's what the locals called this beach. The Germans had called it something else, but Dora couldn't remember what. They'd cut it off with barbed-wire scrolls and mines, patrolled it night and day with dogs and short-haired soldiers. You'd never know that, looking at it now, Dora thought. Only if you'd lived through those times.

It didn't seem as strange coming back as she thought it would be. The houses were newer, fresher, more suburban than she remembered, as if they'd burst free from the chrysalis of her memory to become something altogether different. Not quite a butterfly, Dora thought, they were too ordinary for that, too pebble-dash and dull. Unless it was a plain butterfly, for instance, or a common-or-garden moth, the sort that chomped through cardigans and carpets.

Out of the corner of her eye, Dora caught sight of double gates. She stopped the car, reversed. They were shut, chained and padlocked. Through their railings, Dora saw the gardens, overgrown and gone to seed. It had once been the beauty of the town with its promenade to the beach, its elegant terraces and well-tended beds, roses and begonias, hydrangeas and camellias, filled with the scents of jasmine and honeysuckle. That was how she *knew*, all that time ago. She'd recognised its perfumes. The building looked closed, unkempt, as if it had been shut for months, if not years.

Dora moved the car forward, turned left, and left again. The gardens at the rear were as unloved as those in the front and the back of the hotel was boarded up. There was a side gate, from memory, that led to the courtyard behind the kitchens. Dora parked the car, walked round the corner. It was still there. She tried the handle. The gate was unlocked, though it dragged on its hinges and was heavy. Dora levered it open wide enough to squeeze through, pushed it shut behind her. It had been padlocked from the inside, but someone had wrenched the lock free. Children, most likely. Dora entered the small yard. The hotel was to her left, the street wall behind. The outbuildings and the old coal bunkers made up the other two sides of the courtyard.

In her memory, the space had been bigger. Time did that, played tricks. Now it had shrunk, was small and shoddy. Seedy, even. The stucco walls were stained with blotches of mould which crept up from the ground, the paintwork on the windows flaking, a dull, dead green. Some of the panes were broken, and the courtyard was filled with shards of glass, broken wood and old cardboard boxes. Plastic bags had drifted into the corners and sweet wrappings littered the ground. Dora guessed the rubbish had been thrown over the wall. A buddleia straggled close to a drainpipe and weeds had sprung up through the spaces between the cobbles. It used to be spotless, swept twice a day, the mould scrubbed clean and whitewashed away. It was hard to remember it now with the women lined up and the soldiers shouting out the numbers. Hard to remember how the square itself had taken on a life, had domineered and threatened.

Dora walked forward. A block of plywood had been nailed across the windows of the kitchen doors. It was rotting round the edges. Dora prised it free with the car keys. The glass panes beneath had been shattered. Dora put her hands through the gap, felt for the bolt, released it. The door swung open and Dora stepped down inside. The smell of must and damp, the fungal emptiness of the building, made her cough.

The kitchens were dark. They always had been, half below ground and overshadowed by the buildings in the courtyard. The little natural light they owned was now covered up and the day came through in the cracks and chinks. Dora waited for her eyes to adjust. The equipment had gone, the pots and pans, the cookers and cupboards. The quarry tiles on the floor were stained and littered, like the yard, with broken glass and scraps of paper. There were a couple of old wooden tea chests in the corner. To her left would be the dormitory with its stacks of bunks and the stench of drains. To her right, the boiler room. Opposite, the steep steps up to the interior of the building. Dora climbed them and pushed open the green baize door, into the hall.

The chequered marble floor needed a scrub. Her heels clicked as she crossed it, echoed in the hollow house. The vast oak staircase was still there, though the balustrades were dull and dusty, the ruby carpet threadbare on the tread, the stair rods covered in verdigris. To her left was the officers' bar, where she'd first heard the words of 'Lili Marleen' being played on the gramophone.

The verses swirled in her head. She knew the words off by heart, even now, after all those years. She walked along the landing, up and into the attics. Her fingers were shaky as she turned the door handle. She was all alone. What if the door slammed behind her and she couldn't get out? No one knew she was here and her cries would not be heard. But something was drawing her in, churning flashbacks into compulsions. *Come closer.* The windows in here were unboarded and the sunlight filtered in, as it had always done. The cries of the soldiers evaporated into the past, but the smell of their wounds seeped into this dead air. The beds had long since gone, but the nurses' office was still there, with its glass partitions. She could see her profile through the glass. Hoffmann. Nurse Hoffmann. Trude Hoffmann. The office was empty, the scales and instruments removed, the examination bed and medicine cabinet consigned away. The room was full of cardboard boxes.

Dora took out her cigarettes. This was where she had begun to smoke properly, whole cigarettes, real cigarettes. Senior Service. She could remember the day. And the time. It was in the evening, about six o'clock. 10 May 1945. The bells of St Nicholas in Greve d'Azette had been ringing all day, but they had stopped then. *Gone to tea*, the Tommy had said. He was a Geordie and Dora couldn't understand him, not at first. He'd given her that first cigarette. He'd called it 'a fag'. *D'you fancy a fag then, pet?* She'd had a twenty-a-day habit ever since. She took one out of its packet, placed it on her lips and fished around inside her bag for a match. Swan Vesta. She struck it against the coarse edge, lit her cigarette, tossed the match away as she walked towards the cardboard boxes with 'Campbell's Tomato Juice' stamped on the side.

The boxes were unsealed. Dora pulled out long strands of tinsel and twisted paper chains, rolls of crêpe and folded tissue bells. Christmas decorations. Box after box. It was a big hotel. Every room would need to be decked out. The English did that at Christmas, made dull rooms gaudy, tasteful spaces cheap. Tawdry. They even ruined the majesty of a fir tree, hanging it with pink baubles and stringing coloured lights through the branches.

She sniffed. The match had set fire to a scrap of paper. Its edges were blackening and curling and small orange flames flickered towards the unburned centre. Dora watched it flare and die.

This room was so very different now, but its ghosts were tumbling in. Collette's emaciated frame, Agnes's jowls hanging like dewlaps on a cow. The faces of the young women and girls who had come and gone.

Hotel Maison Victor Hugo, Jersey: February 1944

'You know what?' Agnes squatted on the bench beside Dora that evening, after the meeting with List and Hoffmann. She put her bowl on the table, slurping the soup over the side as she steadied herself. She licked her hands. 'Waste not, want not.' Grimace of a smile. 'He took my baby,' she said, leaning into Dora.

'What baby?'

Dora wondered if Agnes wasn't a little delirious, had caught a fever. She had no child that Dora knew of.

'My little blond-haired baby. He still had his curls.' Agnes's eyes filled with tears and her nose began to run. She wiped the mucous with two fingers, dragging it across her mouth, ran the back of her hand across her cheek. 'I never told you this. I never told anyone.'

Then why me? Dora thought. Agnes had made no secret of her contempt for Dora, and Dora didn't trust her now. But Agnes was no actress, and the tears were genuine. It could have been a phantom pregnancy, of course. Dora had read about them, though she'd never had a case.

'His name was Emile,' Agnes went on. 'He was born the twenty-seventh of April 1939. Just over a year before those bastards invaded.' She leaned to one side, rummaging in the pocket of her dress. 'This is all I have of him.' She opened a small square photograph and slid it along the table for Dora to see. The celluloid was cracked in the middle along the folds, but Dora could make out Agnes holding a small child with blond curly hair. She looked at Agnes, at her worn face, her cracked and missing teeth, her thinning, colourless hair.

'I fought like a tigress,' Agnes went on. 'When they snatched him. That's how I lost my teeth. *Bam* in the kisser with the flat end of a rifle. What they didn't knock out turned bad. Killed the roots, see.'

The baby could have been any baby, but the timbre of Agnes's words suggested she was telling the truth. Agnes may have been many things, but she wasn't a liar.

'I was never a beauty,' Agnes said. 'But this turned me ugly and old. I don't care. I live to get him back again.'

'Who took him?'

Agnes looked over her shoulder. The guard was slouching by the doorway, picking at his hand. Dora hawked, spat, an ugly glob of green phlegm.

'Himmler,' she said.

Himmler. She could hear Hoffmann simpering *Himmler,* as if he was a matinee idol. Even List held the name in awe.

'*Himmler*?' Dora repeated.

'Well,' Agnes said, 'technically, a henchman.'

'What for?'

'For his experiment. His programme.'

'What are you talking about?' Dora said.

'Breeding. Like cows. Or mice. Breeding fucking mice.'

'I don't understand,' Dora said. 'What mice?'

'Are you thick, or something?' Agnes raised her voice, but no one noticed. She leant into Dora again, her lips and foul breath close to Dora's ear. 'Breeding the master race. Pure Aryans. Why d'you think List didn't have to use protection, like all the other pillocks who pissed our way? Why d'you think you were given special treatment?'

Dora swallowed, shook her head. This was too much to take in. Agnes scraped the spoon around the sides of the bowl, scratching at the last morsel of food.

'You were picked,' she went on. 'That was what I was told. *Certificated* Aryan. I heard rumours, mind, that you were a yid, in disguise. And I thought to myself, good on yer. I'd never have known.'

She picked up the photograph, lifted it to her lips, then folded it carefully and put it back in her pocket.

'You were singled out to breed. With the *Hauptsturmführer.* The *SS.* A perfect little baby. They made sure you had proper food. I saw you, up in the *Revier.* Milk and all. Taken off whoring duties. Just in case one of the other morons contaminated you. See, I kept my eyes open.'

Agnes was right about that. But it was because List cared for her, loved her. *Protected* her.

'You think you're special, don't you?' Agnes went on, as if reading Dora's mind. 'Well, I've got news for you. You weren't the first, and if the *Kommandant* hadn't blotted his copybook, you wouldn't have been his last.'

'No.' Dora couldn't help herself. 'He cares.'

'Pah,' Agnes said. 'They're ruthless, these bastards.' She pulled out the photograph again. 'I had this rolled up my arse when they took me in,' she said. 'They never thought of looking there. Not that orifice.' She winked. 'You need your wits about you to out-do this lot.' She looked at Dora. 'You let your guard drop. Fell for the cheap glamour of power. Made sense for a while, got you favours. But it's crunch time now.'

She nodded, her dirty hair falling forward on her face. She lifted her hand, yanked it behind her ear.

'They snatched my baby. Took the fair-haired ones to give to families of the *SS*. Your baby's no different. Hoffmann's taking it to France, the moment it's born.' Agnes breathed in deep so her throat rattled. 'God help you then.'

Dora sat toying with her spoon, trying to understand what Agnes was saying. What she said made sense of the meeting with List and Hoffmann. And yet, Dora thought, Agnes hadn't been there in their private intimate moments. List was proud of his baby, was going to take Dora with him to Alderney. He wasn't a liar.

'I wasn't a whore, you know, before I came here,' Agnes went on. 'And when I leave, if I'm spared, and I will be spared, I'll see to that, I won't be one either.'

'Your husband?' Dora said. 'Couldn't he help?'

Agnes smiled, a crooked twist of her mouth. 'I didn't say I was an angel,' she said.

'Why France?'

'Himmler's opened this new facility, in Lamorlaye. *Lebensborn.* Mother and baby home. Mainly baby. And not for mothers like you.'

'Or you?'

'Certainly not for me,' Agnes said. 'They brought me here. July 1940.' She opened the photograph, closed it again. 'I saw what the set-up was here and I said to myself, I said, I can play them at their game. Because I will survive. Somctimes, looks pay.' She threw back her head and roared with laughter. 'Who'd want to screw me? I made sure they made me a *Kapo.* Keep on their right side, I said to myself. Keep alive. Because as soon as this war is over, so help me God, I'm out of here and searching for Emile.'

Dora had never liked the woman, but she'd never tried to find out about her, either. *Bitter men,* her father used to say, *have drunk poison.* She believed Agnes. But List? She wasn't sure that fitted.

'Nurse Hoffmann,' Dora said.

'What about her?' Agnes said. 'In it up to her neck.'

'And List?'

Agnes laughed, a genuine mirth, a rumble from the deep. 'You're bloody thick, you are,' she said. 'She's totally infatuated with him. Would kill you happily to get at him. She wants that baby. Her gift to him, if you like.'

Dora thought of their last conversation with Hoffmann. Sly, treacherous. Even if Agnes was wrong about List, she knew she was right about Nurse Hoffmann.

'What can I do?' Dora said.

'You're the nurse,' Agnes said. 'You'll know what to do, when the time comes.'

She folded the photograph again and tucked it into her pocket, climbed off the bench, lifted her bowl and wiped it with the hem of her shift.

CHAPTER SIXTEEN

JOE

Jersey: June 1985

Geoffrey was resting. He'd taken to having a nap of late, climbing the stairs and lying down under the eiderdown. Joe had offered to bring his bed downstairs.

'We never use the front room,' he said. 'Why not make it into your bedroom? You'd have the bathroom on the same level.'

If the truth were to be told, Joe knew he would feel happier if Geoffrey slept there. He was becoming more unsteady, as if his deafness had taken a turn for the worse and disrupted his balance. He was forgetful, too, confused. He'd called Joe 'Pierre' the other day, had put his reading glasses in the fridge. His bad leg was now stiff with arthritis and the doctor said it put wear and tear on his other joints, that he should have a new hip in due course, a new knee.

'Spare parts,' Joe said. 'You'll keep running forever.'

'I'm not a car,' Geoffrey said. His face had clouded and his eyes grew watery. 'I just want to run long enough for Dora. Not forever.'

Joe could hear him snoring in the room above. He should go out, take the bike for a spin. Why not search for the old labour camps, buried now under golf courses and luxury flats? Lay a wreath, perhaps. Make atonement. If they were to ask him what he'd done with his life, he could say, *I honoured the dead and paid for my sins.*

Joe could hear a car change gears, begin the descent to the farm. *A cheap rented car. That woman.* Joe braced himself. She'd ask him about Trude this time. He didn't want to set that memory free, but it had already escaped. Joe may have lived like an imposter, a quack priest peddling forgiveness and hope, but he'd never lied outright in his life, couldn't start now. He'd have to tell the truth. Besides, she might have news about Dora, and that was important for Geoffrey.

He pushed back his chair and went outside. She'd parked in front of the house, was walking up to the front door.

'Come round the back,' he said 'We stopped using that door after the war.' He and Geoffrey had not spoken about it, but they couldn't cross that threshold again, not after the lad had been shot. Joe swept it from time to time, kept it clear, Weedol between the cracks of the paving stones, but they never walked across it, not to go in and out of the house. She was wearing jeans, with a red blouse and white jacket. Joe had always thought it strange that jeans were fashionable, but the young woman looked good in hers, and as she rounded the corner of the house, the sun glinted on her black hair, turned it red. It did that, he knew, made ravens blue, crows green, blackbirds amber, depending on the angle of the sun and the time of year. Black was the richest colour he knew.

He opened the door, stood back as she entered the kitchen.

'It's warm in here,' she said.

'Well, see, it's the Aga,' he said. 'We keep it going all year.'

He pulled out a chair from the table and pointed for her to sit. He should take her into the front room, but they never used it these days, never had guests, and over the years it had become a storeroom, full of newspapers to be read one day and broken chairs to be mended. Joe would have to clear it out before he could turn it into a bedroom for Geoffrey, but in the meantime, it did no harm.

'I hope you don't mind the kitchen,' Joe said. His mother, now, she would never let a stranger in her kitchen, would only ever use the front room.

'This is fine,' Barbara said. 'Homely.'

'You're persistent,' Joe said. 'I'll give you that. Coming back again.'

'I'm on a quest.' She smiled.

He stood with his back to the Aga. It made him feel big, brave, to stand and not to sit with her, at her level. 'So it seems.' He added, 'Are you any further finding Dora?'

'Well,' she said. 'I may have found her.'

'And?'

Barbara shrugged. 'I don't know. She hasn't been helpful. She said the woman in the photograph wasn't her and she said she didn't know who you were.'

'Then why are you so sure?'

'I have a hunch.'

No, Joe thought, *that's not good enough, not for Geoffrey.*

'You see,' Barbara said, 'she seemed to know the old man who lives here. It quite agitated her. And though she denied it, I'm pretty sure she recognised the woman in the photo. I don't know what any of this means.'

'Has she not talked to you about anything?' Joe said.

Barbara shook her head. 'What is there to tell me?'

'Everything,' Joe said. 'Everything.'

'I am sure I have upset her.'

'You've upset us all,' Joe said.

'It's so difficult, to talk about what happened.'

'It is that,' Joe said. 'That it is.'

'I sent you a photograph,' she said.

'You did.'

'Did you know her? She was a nurse.' Barbara leaned forward, her blouse briefly gaping open, showing a white, lacy brassiere. She wriggled free of her jacket and draped it on the back of the chair. 'She was my mother.'

Joe leant against the Aga and stared at the young woman in

front of him. She didn't have Trude's physique, although she was a brunette, had her mother's colouring. He knew there were children who bore no resemblance to their parents. He'd known families where some were short and stout and others tall and lanky, same mother and father, or others where the children had blue eyes and the parents brown. It was just the way the genes and chromosomes toppled, some to the father's side, some to the mother's, some with too few bits and pieces in their make-up, some with too many. Oh, he'd seen his fair share of those.

'Mother?' Joe's voice quavered, made him sound as if he was fourteen. He stood staring at her, until she looked away. 'Tell me, now,' Joe said. 'Is your mother still alive?' He wasn't sure he wanted to know, his feelings tumbling and somersaulting.

'No,' Barbara said. 'She died a few months ago.'

'Oh,' Joe said, as a wave of grief passed over him, and relief, too. Added, 'I'm sorry to hear that.' He took a deep breath. 'And your father,' he said, his heart quickening once more, *ta-tum, ta-tum.* 'Who might he be?'

'He died in the war,' she said. 'Or so my mother said.'

'You never knew him?'

She shook her head.

Joe moved towards the table, pulled out a chair and sat opposite her.

'Did you know her?' Barbara asked.

Joe stood up again, walked behind her and stood by the sink, looking out across the yard to the cowshed beyond. 'I did,' he said, added, 'I loved her once.'

He heard her spin in her chair, push it back and walk up to him, leaning her face into his. '*You* loved her?'

'Is that such a strange idea?' Joe said.

'I'm sorry,' she said. 'That was tactless. It's just–' she hesitated and Joe waited. 'It's just I thought she was in love with another man.'

'Your father?' Joe said.

'I don't know if he was,' Barbara said. 'This is my quest, as you put it.'

'Then who is this other man?'

Joe knew the answer before she said it.

'He's called Maximilian List,' she said. 'Have you heard of him? I have a photograph of him too.'

Joe said nothing.

'But now you tell me that you also loved her.'

'I did that, yes.' He almost said, *And she loved me*, because that hope still smouldered in the deep of his dreams, unrecognised.

'You see,' Barbara said, 'List's wife said that my mother was infatuated with him and now I wonder whether they had an affair, or whether my mother was imagining it. And now you tell me that you–'

She walked back to the table and sat down. She was looking at him, and he her.

He pondered for a moment. 'And when did you say you were born?'

'I didn't. But my birthday is the twenty-fourth of February, 1944.'

Joe calculated. He hadn't thought Trude would get pregnant. What had she said? *Don't worry.* He hadn't given it another thought, hadn't wanted to give it a thought, that Trude would do unspeakable things, like those wicked girls with a tot of gin and a bicycle spoke. But here was her daughter. *Their* daughter.

He had been a bachelor all his life, had never dreamed he could be a father, *was* a father. He felt the blood rush to his face, colour his neck and cheeks, flushing like a middle-aged woman. *A daughter.* He rolled the word round. A *child. His* child. He looked up, at a loss for words, willing her to ask, *Could you be my father?* He'd find the words then, soon enough.

He felt nothing for this woman. Wouldn't a father feel love? He couldn't stop studying her, could see it made her uncomfortable, but she had an Irish complexion, that would be for sure, plenty of black-haired colleens with skin as white as porcelain, and hadn't he thought there was something familiar about the way she looked and carried herself? She didn't take after little Bridey, or any of the men, for they were small and wiry like himself, but didn't he have some great-aunts in Kerry who were tall and slender? Strong as oxen, mind. It happened, that a likeness skipped a generation, or two or three.

He'd grow to love her. And she him. Make up for those lost years, those little things that meant so much. Teaching her how to tie a shoelace, blow her nose. Things that fathers taught. And Irish dancing. Oh, she would have been champion.

'Excuse me,' she said. She reached for her bag, hoisted it onto her lap. 'Do you mind if I have a cigarette?'

Joe had stopped smoking after the war, but he understood its grip. 'I'll fetch an ashtray,' he said, walking to the dresser and taking down the chipped saucer he used for Pierre.

When she asked, Why don't I have a *daidí*? What was my *daidí* like? What did Trude tell her? What lies? She was capable of anything, Joe knew. Did she ever show remorse? For Joe surely felt it now. He would never have abandoned his child.

He placed the saucer on the table.

'Thank you.' Barbara was frowning. She was tongue-tied too, Joe realised. The shock of it all.

He would have been the happiest man, had he known. Had it been possible to know. He'd have cherished the little *babaí*. Still could. They'd work it out, he and Barbara.

But what if she rejected him? He'd heard the disbelief in her voice, the disappointment that *he* had been her mother's lover. He could feel his old anxieties swim to the surface, only he couldn't put a name to them, not now.

He opened the window. Perhaps Trude had loved him, just a little.

'Can we go for a walk?' she said, finishing her cigarette and scrunching it into the saucer. 'Along the shore? You can tell me everything.'

That I can, he thought. *That I can.*

§

Barbara had taken off her shoes and was walking barefoot, straying into the lapping water, watching her feet sink into the wet sand.

'There's no birds,' she said. 'Where are the gulls?'

Joe could spot them right enough, crouching on the branches of the wind-bleached spinney that reached to the shore, silent as corpses. 'They've taken cover,' he said. 'A storm's due.'

'How can they tell?'

'That's the beauty of them,' Joe said. 'They're more sensitive than we are. They sense any change in barometric pressure. Look,' he pointed at a hawk in the distance. 'That bird is usually high in the sky. But he's flying low today.'

'My mother used to tell me stuff like that,' Barbara said. 'She knew a lot about birds.'

Had Trude thought of him, perhaps, when she talked about the birds with Barbara? Did she see Joe in her mind's eye? *Listen, look*, standing behind her with his hand on the binoculars, training them into her sight, smelling her hair and the faint odour of her body, knowing her flesh was soft and yielding. Or was it List she had conjured up?

'But I never paid any attention.'

'That's a shame,' Joe said. 'Perhaps I can tell you all about them, sometime?'

'Perhaps,' Barbara said.

He wanted to say, *And will you come and visit me?* He'd like that very much but wasn't sure that's what he should say. It might presume too much. Was she even wondering if Joe was her father?

Was she waiting for the moment to ask him, in her straightforward German way? It was a difficult thing to broach, Joe understood that. The pair of them. Tiptoeing.

He stood still and watched her paddling at the edge of the water. She'd rolled up her jeans and was holding her shoes in one hand. She had bright-red toenails, he noticed, but it didn't make her look common. She didn't look like Trude, that was for sure. Trude's face was as round as a muffin, mousy with it. This young woman had a beauty about her which Trude never possessed. She was skinny, mind. Looked like she could do with a square meal. Perhaps she was one of those vegetarians, nothing but bone.

'Would you take food from a poor man?' he said.

She looked up and laughed. 'Do you mean, am I the sort of woman who'd take food out of a poor man's mouth?'

Joe felt the colour rise to his face. 'No,' he said. 'I mean, would you stay for a meal? That's if you eat meat.'

She laughed again. 'You have a strange way with words,' she said.

He wasn't sure if that was a criticism or a compliment, but it made him awkward.

'We don't have visitors,' Joe said, by way of an explanation. 'Apart from Pierre, and he doesn't really count.'

'Then thank you,' she said. 'A meal would be nice. I'd like that.'

If he boiled up another potato and put some pearl barley in the stew, he reckoned it would stretch to three.

'Then we'd best be going,' Joe said. 'I've got a lot to do.'

'I can help,' she said.

'No,' he said. 'I don't need a woman in the kitchen.'

He looked beyond her, out to sea, where thick black clouds were building on the horizon. A fork of lightning flashed in the distance. Joe began to count, waiting for the thunderclap, a second for every mile. They couldn't dawdle long. The squall would whip up the sea, gulp it down and spit it out. Joe knew the coastal storms well.

'I was wondering, though,' she said. She put her head to one side, and Joe was sure she was going to ask him if he was her father. 'How come you had Dora Simon's address?'

There was a roar of thunder. *Thor's anvil, all right.*

'Well, now.' Joe wasn't expecting this question. 'That's another story.'

He hadn't told that story to anyone, and wasn't sure he had a right to now.

'I'm listening.'

He was disappointed. He didn't want to talk about Dora. This was his daughter, and the war was a long time ago. Still, he could understand her curiosity. After all, it was finding Dora's picture that had started her off.

'If I tell you–' His words were reluctant. 'Will you promise me you won't say a word? To anyone. Not Geoffrey. No one.'

'Of course,' she said. 'But I'm curious.' She rubbed the sole of one foot against her leg, brushing off the sand.

'Well,' he said. 'Now, let me see.' He paused to gather his thoughts, jagged memories that had sharpened their edge now that he knew their significance. 'The war had been over a few weeks. It was June, I remember that.' A clear, soft sun and the land green and fresh, its ripeness not yet fulfilled. 'My favourite time of year. Do you like June, Barbara?' He hoped she did, father and daughter. He wanted to get to know her. This was as good a place as any to start, with the little things to share. And perhaps, he thought, he could distract her, take her round the long way so maybe she'd get lost and forget she ever asked. 'Do you?'

'Yes,' Barbara said. 'But go on.'

'Well, I was sad to leave the farm, I'll say that. I tried to keep the place in order. It was the least I could do. I thought, if Geoffrey comes back, he'd find it in good trim, more or less, and Pierre had been right. The farm was remote, and the Germans didn't suspect anyone like me would be there.'

'Weren't you lonely?'

Joe thought. 'To tell the truth,' he said, 'the nights were lonesome, in the dark, in the big house. But by day, I lived like a wild man in the copse with the birds and all for company.'

'But how did you survive?'

'I had a few tinkers' tricks up my arm,' Joe said. 'Hedgehogs. Rabbits. Baked underground. I hid out for almost a year.'

Barbara winced. *City girl, for sure.* Joe winked at her, tapped the side of his nose.

'And Pierre provided well,' Joe went on. 'Filtered off a little from the Red Cross. KLIM powdered milk. Sardines. Tea. I can see it now.'

There was another fork of lightning, sharp as a trident.

'Cigarettes. Cheese. Not the fresh stuff, the processed kind. KAM luncheon meat. Raisins. Sugar. Oh, and best of all, Lowney's Canadian Vanilla Sweet Chocolate.' Joe licked his lips, made a smacking sound. 'I can still remember the packet with its red lettering. I tell you, I hadn't seen food like this since before the war. I knew Pierre was up to tricks, but this was like the Monaghan gold of old.' Joe laughed. 'Oh, he was a right one for the tricks, was Pierre. I promised I'd never forget him, would pay him a visit. A holiday, perhaps. As a matter of fact,' Joe said, holding up his binoculars, 'Pierre got these for me. Zeiss. Spoils of war. I'd had to make do with an old pair of Geoffrey's, see, there was a crack in one lens and the dust–'

'The address,' Barbara said. 'How did you get Dora's address?'

'Oh, I digress,' Joe said. 'It's just there's so much of life to catch up on.' *You being my daughter, and all.* 'Forgive me. We were riding along La Greve d'Azette. Tell the truth, I hadn't believed, until that day, that the war was over and I'd be going home. The tide was out and the sand stretched for miles, with all those rocky needles sticking up. And there was the *Wehrmacht*, but this time the soldiers were walking along the beach holding hurling sticks, only Pierre told me they were mine detectors.'

Joe looked at Barbara, all neat and spruce. He'd introduce her to hurling, one day. Take her home to Ireland, perhaps.

'Oh, but the island looked poor, shabby. I thought it would take a while to get it shipshape, rid it of the camps, the railway, the fortifications.'

'Dora–' Barbara reminded him.

'Oh yes, Dora. It's just I've so much to tell you. Well, then, all of a sudden, there was this crowd in front of us. In the middle of the street they were, yelling. Pierre stopped and I stood up on the driving seat to look. I heard, quite distinctly, a woman's screams in all the kerfuffle. It was her, you see,' Joe said. 'Dora Simon. And after the soldiers got her away, I went to the Red Cross and asked for her address. I said I was a priest and I wanted to write to her. They gave it to me.'

'And did you write?'

'I meant to,' Joe said. 'But then there was all the business in Ireland when I went back home and I never got round to it. But you wouldn't know about that, how would you? I'll tell you some other time. I kept her address, though God knows why.'

A gob of rain splattered on Joe's head.

'You just said, you've so much to tell me. What did you mean?'

'Did I now?' Joe said. He could feel a blush firing up. 'Well, you know, if we are–' He paused, searching for the words. He never imagined he'd have to talk about this and wasn't sure how to start.

'We are what?' Barbara said. She had been smiling, but her face went solemn. 'Oh Joe, you don't think–'

'Will you come inside now,' he said. 'Or we'll all be soaked and catch our death.'

He turned and walked towards the path. He couldn't remember happiness, but this seemed close to it. But Barbara's face, now. Was it puzzlement to be read there, or anguish?

CHAPTER SEVENTEEN

DORA

Hotel Maison Victor Hugo, Jersey: June 1985

Dora was throwing out the contents of the boxes, so the tinsel and the paper chains spewed out across the floor. *Make a mess.* Derange the place, jumble up the tendrils of memory in a cat's cradle of madness. She took a long drag on her cigarette and stubbed it out on the dusty floor. She lit a new one and threw the match down. Her neck had tensed and the tendons in her arms and legs were stiff and tight. The match caught the tinsel, began to flicker. She threw the cigarette on the floor, watched the snake of smoke rise and curl. She fished for her matches again, lit the paper chains, saw the black, waving fumes as the flames slithered along their quarry.

Dora walked out of the room, back down the attic stairs. The bedroom was on the right, its door open. The red flock wallpaper still lined the walls and the burgundy velvet curtains festooned the windows. They had faded along the edges and moths had eaten holes in the pile. Net curtains hung close to the glass, yellowed by the sun, greyed by the dust. The fireguard with its folksy scene had gone and the fireplace had been fitted with a gas fire. Dora turned on the valve. The gas had been switched off. The Persian rug with its cobalt and ruby florets and scrolls that she'd stared at each night had been replaced with a mass of swirling green and orange Wilton medallions. She stood with her back to the marble mantelpiece, could see again the brocade sofa, the console table with its crystal decanter of scotch, the large double bed.

And lying on the bed, Maximilian List, one hand behind his head, the other beckoning her close. Smiling, *I was too hard on you. Come, see how I can make it up to you.* Dora stepped forward. *Will you make love with me, Dora? Like you cared?* Stopped.

'No.' She stared at the bed, but List had evaporated. She pulled at the mattress until it slid off the frame and buckled on the floor.

'What did you do to me?' He was nothing but bone and tissue.

'What hold did you have over me?' Skin and scales, a deadly reptile. 'I am free.' Dora kicked the mattress, over and over. 'Do you understand? You have no power over me. Not now. Not anymore.'

She walked over to the window. Her heart was racing, galloping hooves that thundered on her breast and kneaded her belly. Her fingers were boneless, out of control. She struck a match and held the flame against the net curtains. Another match, to the dusty velvet drapes. Another, to the next window. Three in all. Out of this room, across the hall. Six matches, two for each window. Down the stairs, into the bar. Nets were everywhere, the English obsession with secrecy. Flamed. The bar had the same swirling carpet as the bedrooms, but it had worn by the door, exposing its weft. It took seven matches.

Fire purified, cleansed. Fire was glorious, divine. Hadn't God revealed himself to Moses in a burning bush? Consumed Aaron's sacrifice in flames? Struck Elijah with fire? Lightning now. That was vengeance from the Lord. God didn't exist, but justice did, and righteousness, and wrath. There was nothing wrong with fire. Dora's fingers had traces of carbon from the matches. Phosphorus. Sulphur. Didn't the Christians believe that was hell? Fire and brimstone. Same difference.

She wiped her fingers down her skirt and skipped across the hall. Bonfires. The English burned a guy every November. Built a bonfire and placed the stick figure on top. Guy Fawkes, that was his name. Uncle Otto had taken her to Hampstead Heath. They'd stood and watched the bonfire, felt its warmth wrap them, seen the effigy shrivel to nothing and the fireworks shoot and drop from the sky. She could smell them now. Like her fingers. Swan Vesta. She was running low on matches. Would have to get some more.

Catharsis. That's what Uncle Otto said it was. *Catharsis.* A bonfire once a year to free the soul of stress and passion. The Nazis had had a bonfire. Burned the books they didn't like and danced like devils round the roaring flames. Black clouds of smoke swirled across the stairwell and Dora could smell its acrid stench. Forest fires. Burned the old, made way for the new. That was nature. Renewal. Redemption. The basement. Still the basement.

Dora opened the baize door, down the narrow staircase into the kitchen with its tiled floor and walls. She heard a rustle, saw a rat slither into a hole in the wainscot. The gas pipes that had once fed the ovens rested against the wall, tall copper pipes which had blackened with time. They looked like upright snakes, like the one Dora had seen in Greece, cooling itself in water, long and straight and black. She walked over to the boxes she'd seen, opened them. They were full of paper and old newspapers. Dora crumpled them up and spread them over the floor, a trail to the stairs, to the old pantry, to the boiler room. The empty copper pipes. Dora turned the valve. There was no hiss, but she fancied she could smell gas, even so. She walked into the old dormitory. *That* night crashed into her memory, thrashing from side to side, slamming against the hard, bone walls of her skull.

Hotel Maison Victor Hugo: February 1944

The dormitory was unheated and unlit, save for a dim bulb that hung in the centre of the room. At one end were some wash-basins and lavatories. None had doors or seats and the bowls were brown and smelly. The water was connected once a day in the morning when the women were required to wash. The baby was low down, pressing on Dora's bladder, and for the third time that night she had to push herself out of her bunk and pad her way to the lavatory. She was cold and pulled the blanket over her shoulders as she stepped across the room, groping in the dark for the door to the washroom. As she stepped inside, someone grabbed her from behind. Dora caught her breath, went to scream as the person spun her round and aimed a knee into Dora's stomach. Dora grabbed the cubicle wall for support. It happened so fast, but Dora smelled her, saw her silhouetted in the doorway. *Agnes.*

A thump like that could tear the placenta, kill the foetus. She waited until Agnes had drifted back into the dormitory, before she squatted down, shivering in the late winter cold, trembling from the attack. But it wasn't blood she felt. It was her waters. They trickled down her leg and puddled in the dank bowl. A cramp, no more than a grumbling, began in her abdomen.

It was Agnes who took her by the arm, helped her climb the stairs into the *Revier.* Nurse Hoffmann wasn't there. It was a Monday, her free day, when Dora was alone in the ward.

'Now aren't I being kind?' Agnes said. 'That's what a *Kapo*'s for. To look out for you.'

Dora lay down on the examination bed, grateful for the warmth of the *Revier.*

'Looks like you'll be by yourself,' Agnes said.

Agnes had planned this, waited for Hoffmann's day off before she set the labour going. Dora struggled with her duties all day. Agnes did her bit but left in the afternoon. Dora was on her own as the labour began, hour after hour of racking pain, crouching on the floor, until she felt the baby's head crown. She ran her finger round its neck, paused, blew out. The next spasm took her like a powerful wave, as one shoulder slithered out. *It was over.* Another wave, and the next shoulder. *She had done it.* The body plopped out between her legs, slick as a fish.

Dora caught her breath. She leaned forward and shut her eyes. List's baby. She wouldn't let Hoffmann have it. Or anyone. Boy or girl. Didn't matter. Hoffmann had led List astray, made him betray her like this, and the child. She knew, when Hoffmann said *mein Liebling.* She'd rather the baby dead than Hoffmann take it. No. She'd deny her that. Hoffmann had plans. She'd said so. *Lebensborn.* What future would this child have in that? What barbarity would it suffer? She wouldn't let it survive for some warped Nazi dream. She'd had to do enough abortions here on the women, what did it matter if another baby died? She and List would have more babies, once Hoffmann was gone, once the war was over. And if he heard the child had died, he'd come back to Dora. *I'm sorry, mein Liebling, for the loss of our little one…*

This was not how she had imagined it, with a face and hair and feet. This was not a mound of tissue, a bleeding swab of flesh. Tiny purple fingers. Plump little body. A strawberry mark on its neck. *Give me strength.* She groped for the head with her hands, placed her fingers on the tiny nostrils. Pinched hard.

Dora fainted, didn't hear them come in. She felt the sting on her cheek, smelled Agnes, a dank blast of foetid breath grabbing her shoulders and pulling her away from the baby as Nurse Hoffmann screamed and screamed, *Tot, tot.* Cut the cord and scooped the thing in a towel and ran away with it.

She heard no cry from the baby. She'd snuffled the life out of it. For her, it would be as if she had never given birth. She'd bury it deep in the folds of memory, forget about it.

CHAPTER EIGHTEEN

DORA

Jersey: June 1985

Dora left the dormitory. She stood by the kitchen door, lit a match and held it to the corner of the paper, waiting until it caught. She backed out, pulling the door to behind her.

Through the courtyard, out and into the car. She sat for a moment, her hands on the steering wheel, fingering her keys before she turned on the ignition, put the car into gear. Left and left again. La Greve d'Azette. She heard the *whoosh*, and looked up through her rear-view mirror at the Hotel Maison Victor Hugo, the flames lapping at the lintels and curling around the roof.

Her hands were clammy, sticky on the wheel. She drove on a small distance, pulled the car over to the side, opened the window, breathed the air. *In*, two, three, four. *Out*, two, three, four. There was an ice-cream van on the parade and a small queue had formed, holidaymakers in shorts and T-shirts, and children in flip-flops with sand on their legs. A little girl pulled the wrapper off her ice cream and walked towards the rubbish bin. She stopped, dropped the wrapper on the ground.

'Pick it up,' Dora called from the car. 'You don't want to be a litterbug.'

The girl looked at Dora. 'There's wasps,' she said. 'I don't like wasps.' She glared at her, ran away.

Dora opened the door, picked up the rubbish. 'They won't bother you,' she called, throwing the paper in the bin.

She walked along the promenade, leaving the car door ajar. The tide was out, exposing rocks sharp as stalagmites. It was a long way to the sea, but there were dips in the sand where water had pooled. A mother was holding a baby, legs dangling in the water, splashing its bare feet. Dora heard the child's chuckles. It had been an age since she'd heard that sound. She stopped and watched them, leaning against the sea wall, her breath in light, dizzy takes. *In*, one, two, three. *Out*, one, two, three.

The sirens of a fire engine sounded in the distance, and two police cars rushed past, klaxons screaming. Dora jumped. A couple were coming towards her, pulled a where's-the-fire? face as they passed, laughed.

Agnes had been one of the first to leave, once the war was over. She'd stood there, papers stamped.

'St Malo,' she said. 'First stop.' She looked at Dora straight. 'Like I said, two of a kind. You and me.'

They'd never talked about what had happened the night the baby died. No need to. Agnes was never one for small talk, and why bring it up?

'Good luck,' Dora had said, waved at her as she walked down the stairs. From the back, she was still a young woman.

Dora felt nauseous at the memory. She staggered back to the car, leaned over, vomited into the gutter until all that came up was bitter yellow bile. She steadied herself, sat down hard in the driver's seat, her heart pounding, her breath shallow. She needed a paper bag, something to breathe into, steady her, calm her pulse. Memory had been a cheat, all along. A foul, dirty streak in her imagination. She'd justified it to herself, over and over. But she and Agnes. *Conspired.* Murdered a child. She lifted her arm, bit into it, tearing at the flesh. Punctured her skin so the loathing that squatted like a pus-green demon within her could squeeze its way out. She deserved this pain. Lashed out at herself, at the vile loathsome creature she'd had to drag around for most of her life. Worthless. There was a knock on the windscreen. Dora let go of her arm, lifted her head. It was a policeman.

'You all right, madam?'

Dora stared at him. A wasp was spinning close to his ear and he swiped it away. He stared at her arm, colouring up.

'You been stung?'

Can't you see?

He looked down at the vomit. 'You had a bad reaction?' he said. 'Shall I call an ambulance?'

Dora shook her head. 'No.' Her voice was soft. 'There's no need.'

'Then I must ask you to move on,' he said. 'Only you're blocking the way for emergency vehicles. There's been an incident.'

Dora was hardly listening.

'Just move your vehicle back there, onto the slipway. You won't be in anyone's way then.'

She knew where the slipway was. Behind her, to the right, leading to the beach. She turned on the ignition, put the car into reverse.

Jersey: June 1945

The other women were returned to France by and by, once their papers were sorted.

'But there's always one, isn't there?' the sergeant said. He was friendly, this Geordie. 'You being a refugee, and that. Don't worry, pet,' he added. 'That telegram'll come through any day now. I can feel it in my bones.'

She sat hunched in the corner, holding her knees close to her chest, rocking. This soldier was her friend, but the other soldiers had eyed her up and down, spat it out, *Common whore. Go with anyone for a bob.* They didn't believe what she told them, that she'd been *forced* to sleep with the Germans. It wasn't part of war. War was to do with soldiers. Women went with soldiers, the loose ones, that was. The ones without any self-respect, any shame. *We know your type, hanging round Arthur's Hill or the quays in Gateshead.* She was alone. She alone had survived. She'd been found wanting, had betrayed all around her. What was the peace for, if not a reckoning? She wanted to wail, to scream, so the laments drilled deep and seeped from her body, keening as she breathed. The war was over. But there was nothing to live for, no one left in her world.

'Now, off you go,' the soldier was saying. 'Get some sea air. Do you the world of good.'

He spoke to her like a child, and Dora was as shaky as one, but he held her hand and led her to the door, pushed her forward and shut the door behind her with a smile.

'You'll be fine, like, pet.'

She was wearing a cotton frock that came from the Red Cross. It was too large and flowed over her body. She had new sandals too, that made blisters on her little toes. No matter. She stepped out of the building, walking free. Nervous. Excited. Strange. *Take it easy.* One step at a time. She hoped she wouldn't meet anyone she knew. What could she tell them? She wouldn't go far. Just to the slipway, and back.

She crossed the road, the sea on her left. The beaches were off limits, even though the Germans were clearing the mines. Three or four men, still in their *Wehrmacht* uniforms, were sweeping the sands with what the sergeant said were called mine detectors. Others were dismantling the barbed-wire barricades. Dora flinched as she saw them. Remembered. They were the prisoners now. They couldn't hurt her. Dora wondered how long it would be before everything had gone. She walked slowly, breathing deep. She'd be leaving in a few days, once the paperwork and the visa came through from Uncle Otto – oh, the relief that he was alive – and the Home Office. The beach was unlikely to be cleared before then. She longed to swim in the sea, to dive through the waves, taste the salt, feel the waters purge her, inside and out. Geoffrey had been with her the last time she'd sauntered like this. A different world.

Had he survived? She hoped so, though goodness knows what he must have gone through. She couldn't see him again. Not now. How could a man understand? She could tell no one, least of all him. The shame was too much. She couldn't love him, not anymore, not in the way they used to. She had betrayed him, been unfaithful to him. Had she loved List? He haunted her imaginings. She had lost him. It was the ones you lost who lingered the most. Had he loved her? Had he abandoned her? Used her? She had to bury this past, build a new life. If anyone asked, she'd say she spent the war in Jersey. No more. No less. Her secret. Her silence. Who would understand what she had to say? Who would not judge her?

Leave and never return.

She heard some men running behind her.

'Oi, you.'

She stopped, looked around, but she was the only person. *Me?*

'That's her.'

These were not men she knew. Dora understood, at that instant, that she had to get out of the way. She started to run, stepped out into the road, the Hotel Maison Victor Hugo in view. Not far. *Run.* Her sandals hurt and her legs were brittle. *Move.* The men were coming close. She could hear their breath, their shoes as they pounded the tarmac. She tried to scream, *Help!* but her voice stuck in her throat. She pushed her legs, one before the other, but they wobbled, weak, slow. She couldn't run, not a step.

One of the men grabbed her, spun her round, pushed her arms behind her and held them in a tight lock.

'Let me go,' Dora said. She kicked, caught his shin. He squeezed her tighter.

'Bitch. You're the nurse.'

Dora could see more people running towards them.

'Fucking Jerrybag.'

'No,' Dora said. 'Let me go.' She struggled, but the man held her tight. Five or six men closed in on her. One tugged at the shoulder of her dress, pulling it over her arm, bursting the buttons.

'*No.*' Dora was screaming. The gang was thickening. Men and women. Three or four deep. She couldn't see past them. Couldn't see through them. Peeling her dress off, tearing it. Screaming and shouting. Dora's knees began to buckle. She must not fall. She'd be pulled apart, limb from limb.

Someone grabbed her hair, yanked it back. She could hear the scissors crunch as the blades closed round her hair, feel their jagged points as they dug into her scalp.

'Please, please.' She couldn't move. She was held tight, jammed fast. Crushed. Trampled. Her chest was heavy. No breath. She was going to die.

'Jerrybag. Nazi whore.'

She could hear their jeers, feel their hands as they pulled and pushed her, ripping her dress and tearing it off her. She shook her head, struggled to break free.

'Call the *gardaí.* Let her go.'

She heard a whistle. The men released their grip, began to run away. Dora lost her balance, tumbled to the ground. Her dress lay in rags on the tarmac, coils of her shorn hair trampled in the dirt. She pushed herself onto all fours, tried to crawl, *hide*, felt someone pick her up, put a jacket around her naked shoulders. The crowd were disappearing in the distance.

'Come along, miss. I'll take you back.' It was the sergeant. He'd lifted her up, turned to the man with the Irish accent. 'Thank you, sir.'

Dora wanted to go home. Leave this hated place and its spiteful, mocking memories. Never visit them again. Ever.

CHAPTER NINETEEN

DORA

Jersey: June 1985

There were some public conveniences up the road on the left. Dora stepped out of the car, walked towards them. Her arm was throbbing, the bruising visible. Her mouth was dry and she could still taste the sick. She went into one of the cubicles, locked the door. Her stomach began to spasm and she sat down, groaning. Despite the weather, she felt shivery, as if she had a temperature, as if the stomach cramps and the throbbing arm were exorcising demons, salving a deeper pain within.

There were stickers on the back of the lavatory door, graffiti on the walls. *It will all end in tears.* Dora sat staring at the notice in front. *Now wash your hands.* As if handwashing would scrub away the filth. There was a knock on the door.

'Are you going to be much longer in there?' The voice was coarse, threatening.

Dora cleaned herself, tidied her dress and opened the door. A large woman was outside, scowling.

'Sorry,' Dora said. She went to the basin, turned the tap hard so it splashed her dress and the floor. She washed her hands and face, gargled with the water, spat it out, dabbed herself dry with a paper towel. She was empty, purged. Inside and out. She fished in her handbag for her lipstick, dabbed some on, took out her powder and brushed it over her nose. She ran her finger inside the shoulders of her dress and flapped it, cooling the sweat.

Took a deep breath, stepped outside. A wasp buzzed around her. Dora lifted up her hand, waved the insect away. Hitting out would make it angrier, but it was a sound she couldn't bear right now. That angry drone, like an aeroplane.

Dora had lost track of time back then. She had thought it was March when Hoffmann left. But it must have been the day she gave birth.

Even that little barrel of a woman, Hoffmann, would have shown signs of pregnancy. Dora had been a midwife, for heaven's sake, could tell if a woman was pregnant without her having to present a single symptom. And if Barbara was born in February, when Hoffmann disappeared, there was no way they could be mother and child. It must be some other baby that she had.

What if it was February when she gave birth? What if Hoffmann had taken *her* baby?

But her baby was dead. Dora was sure she'd killed it. It never cried, never made a sound. But it had happened so fast, she'd fainted, Agnes returned, Hoffmann snatched up the infant. What if it hadn't died? It was a plucky little thing, had clung on in her womb, had bounced back from the pelting Agnes had meted out.

Dora's waters had broken. Had she been due? Had she mistaken the dates? She hadn't menstruated the whole time she was in the Hotel Maison Victor Hugo. *It was the shock*, Dora thought. It did that, closed the body down. They never returned, not even after she'd had the baby. Dora swallowed hard.

Unless. What if the baby had survived and Hoffmann had taken *her* child? The dates could add up. Hoffmann and List had talked about going to France, entering the *programme*, as they put it. That would make sense. Take the baby to France, to Lamorlaye. Brought up as a *Lebensborn* child. List had left about the same time. What had happened to those babies? Perhaps they were fostered out, adopted even. Could Hoffmann have adopted it? Abducted it, even?

They could have taken the baby to Germany. The perfect Nazi child. Father: Maximilian List. Occupation: *SS* officer. Mother: certificated Aryan.

That baby could be hers. Dora could be the mother. A pneumatic drill started up in the distance, *grr-grr-grr*, hammered in her head.

She returned to the car, sat inside, holding the steering wheel. She hadn't thought about those days. It was a long time ago. The events fuzzed and blurred. She shut her eyes, as if that could conjure up her memories, piece them together, put them into an order, one after the other.

List had returned to Germany about that time.

She gave birth.

Hoffmann left.

Dora had been bred, like a cow, or mice. That's what Agnes told her. She was gripping the wheel, knuckles white through the skin.

If this child was born in February, then Hoffmann could not be the mother. If this child was born in February, List might not be the father. Dora sat still. Two fire engines rushed by. How could she have been so fixated on Maximilian List that she had missed the signs? Who was this person who'd clung to him? She must have been pregnant before she ever met List, before she had been arrested. The baby wasn't premature. It was full term.

Dora started the car, put it into gear, steered out into the road. What had pulled Dora into Barbara's life? She had never resisted it, from that first contact. She'd hummed and hawed, but every time she had agreed. She didn't believe in fate, in predestination, or anything like that. Yet there had been a fascination with Barbara, an intrigue. She had looked familiar from the start. There was only one man who could have been the father.

Dora could see it now: Geoffrey. She had his eyes, his complexion. She looked like Dora, too, a resemblance which Dora caught if she turned her head a certain way, looked on the oblique, like that Auerbach painting she'd thought of before. She had to find Barbara, tell her. Explain it all. She couldn't admit trying to murder her. But it wasn't murder. She was saving her from the Nazis and whatever barbarism they might have been planning for her. Where was Barbara now? She'd sent her away. Did she still have her address?

She had tried to kill the baby. She could never tell Barbara that. Her own mother. Could never tell Geoffrey that, either.

The road came to a crossroads and Dora stopped to get her bearings. The place looked so different, new buildings, super markets. Car parks. She pulled out the tourist map from the side pocket in the door, peered at it, at the road signs. It made no sense, but the coast must be to the right. The map was not detailed enough for the side roads, but that was the direction she should be heading for. She heard a clap of thunder, saw storm clouds on the horizon.

Geoffrey. She had to see him. She felt the same urgency now as she had forty-three years ago. Why had she waited so long? What a waste. What a terrible, terrible waste. Those sins, those secrets, didn't seem so serious now. She'd never loved List. She'd wanted his attention, the way a child wants to please a bully.

She turned down a lane, hedgerows either side so deep and tall they touched at the tips and made a canopy. Stopped. Dead end. It was Geoffrey she had loved. She turned the car, grating the bumper on the roots and verges. *Hurry*. She was in a hurry. She had to go to Geoffrey, beg his forgiveness, feel his caress, hear his murmuring, *Dora, Dora*.

She saw a small sign, Anse la Coupe. The road was narrow, turned sharply to the right, left and right again, and there ahead was the bluff, the copse that grew down to the shore, Geoffrey's hill field with the dell, below it the bay and, beyond, the sea, a deep, dark turquoise. She drove the car down the road, turned into the farm, parked in front of the house, unclipped her seat belt and stepped out.

The roses needed deadheading and the wisteria needed pruning. She'd do it later. Weeds were growing through the cracks in the path. Nothing that a bit of Roundup wouldn't solve. She'd have the place shipshape in hours. Up to the front door. The shoe-scraper had gone. Dora wasn't sure what that meant. She knocked on the door. There was no reply. Knocked again. Bent down to peer through the letter box, but it was blocked. Disappointment rose like a tide inside her and she had to fight back the tears. He was out. Gone away.

The back door. Dora ran round the side of the house. There was the shoe-scraper, by the kitchen door. The relief. It was on the left-hand side. What did that mean? Dora couldn't remember. Was the coast clear, or were there prisoners hiding in the attic? Dora knocked, tried the handle. The door opened and she stepped inside. The kitchen hadn't changed. There was the Aga, and the two Windsor chairs, the scrubbed pine table in the middle of the room, the blue and white pottery sitting on the dresser shelves. It was a little untidier than she remembered, with a dishtowel draped over the side of the sink and a pile of letters and newspapers on the end of the table. There was a calendar on the wall. John Deere supplies. The picture for June was a tractor.

The clock in the hallway whirred and Dora counted as it chimed. *One. Two. Three.* She'd set off at breakfast. Had it taken that long to come here? Perhaps the old clock was losing time, or gaining it. She called.

'Geoffrey?'

Silence. He was here, in the attic, or reading. She walked into the hall, and opened the door to the sitting room. It was empty, the air had the stale odour of an unused room, the furniture was not in order but placed higgledy-piggledy, and old newspapers cluttered the sideboard and the table. She closed the door, climbed the stairs, onto the landing. Ahead was the attic door. Dora tried the handle, but it was locked. There was no key on the outside. Perhaps it was bolted from inside? He only locked it when there was someone there. Dora called again.

'Geoffrey. Please open.' Leant with her ear against the door, but there was no noise inside. 'It's me.'

Nothing, not even the scuffling as a prisoner tried to hide. Dora looked along the landing. The door to his bedroom was ajar and Dora walked towards it, stood in the doorway. The curtains were drawn against the afternoon sun, cast a golden light across the room. Dora looked around. The wallpaper had faded and there was a damp patch on the chimney breast.

There was an old man in the bed, tucked up underneath the eiderdown. He was breathing heavily. Dora walked towards him. He was fast asleep. He had thick white hair, tousled on the pillow. Nasal fracture, badly set. His eyelashes were still kohl-black, though Dora could imagine that his dark eyes were now faded. In repose, his face hadn't changed, hadn't aged.

She leant over and kissed his temple. 'Geoffrey.'

He didn't stir. Best not disturb him. He must be tired. There was a photo on the bedside table. She picked it up. Clipped onto the frame was a picture, torn from a newspaper. A mugshot, her features grainy and indistinct in the newspaper image, the red cocktail dress showing grey.

She walked around to the other side of the bed, kicked off her shoes, unzipped her skirt and stepped out of it. She climbed into the bed beside him and sidled close, cradling his back. She reached over him with her arm and felt for his hand. She squeezed it. She felt him stir a little and squeeze it in return.

She pushed her face close to him, burying her nose in his back, breathing in his scent, of soap and sweat, the old fabric of his shirt. She felt the press of his body, its imprint on her own.

'Geoffrey,' she said again. 'I'm so very sorry.'

Dora's arm across his body cradled him as his chest rose up and down, up and down. She was home, sleepy. When he woke, they'd talk as if nothing had happened. He lay still, *putt-putting* in his sleep, she a soft companion to his softer silence, like the night they first met.

The storm broke outside and rain hammered at the bedroom window.

EPILOGUE

JOE

St Helier, Jersey: ten years later

Joe drained his cup and put it down. It wasn't like home, but he had his own room and had been allowed to bring in a single piece of furniture and a picture.

'Something familiar, to make your room more *personal*,' the manager had said. He'd taken one of the Windsor chairs from the kitchen and put the photograph of Dora and Geoffrey and Barbara into a frame which he'd found in the charity shop.

'That's nice. Are they family?'

'They are,' Joe said. Who would understand their story if he tried to tell it here?

It was shot with Barbara's camera.

'Take a photo of us, Joe.'

The three of them, sitting on the old bench outside the house. Geoffrey died of pining, Joe thought, for the years gone and the years that would never come. But he'd been happy for three weeks, the old man and Dora, side by side on the garden seat, looking at horizons they would never see.

Joe didn't begrudge her this time with the old man, but it hurt, all the same. Finding out that Barbara wasn't his daughter but Geoffrey's had pained, but only momentarily, for the thought flew out as fast as it had flown in, with no time to roost in his heart.

There had been no point in keeping the place on after Geoffrey died. He couldn't bring himself to move into the house, and the caravan no longer felt like home. The farm would tick over, but Joe wasn't sure for how long. He had twinges of arthritis, and what the doctor called bursitis, but, in truth, his heart wasn't in it anymore. Without Geoffrey, what was the point?

Once he heard Dora's story too, the farm was too heavy a burden to carry.

He got a good price for it. Learned, later, that the new owner planned to build a house on the dell in the upper field, all glass and white walls. It would have a grand view, right enough, with the ocean all the way round, the skies above and the shore below. Perhaps the new owner loved the birds. Joe'd taken his binoculars with him into the home, sat most days in the conservatory watching them. The home was in town, but all manner of tits and finches, gulls and cormorants came into its gardens.

Joe offered the farm to Barbara before he sold it.

'It's yours, rightly,' he said. 'Seeing that you're Geoffrey's girl.'

'What would I want with a farm?'

She'd moved to London, to be with her mother. Now they did new-fangled tests to find the true parent. He'd seen it on the television. The police used it to catch criminals. All they needed was a hair, or a bit of spittle. They didn't need to, in her case, though they did it anyway. She had the likeness of Geoffrey when he was younger. He could see it now. No wonder Geoffrey had thought she was Margaret. They had been the spit of each other. Joe'd made a will, left Barbara what remained of his money after he'd paid for the care here, and his funeral.

She'd been ill, Dora, after Geoffrey died. Off her rocker. They had words for it these days. Soldiers got it, in Vietnam, combat fatigue. Joe had never known it in a woman. *Well, there you go.* Post-traumatic stress disorder. Barbara said there was a lot of talk about it now. She'd had it too, as if she had inherited Dora's trauma and lived it all over again. Joe wondered if he hadn't had a touch of it, in his time, for his soul had died in the war, and wasn't that much the same thing?

Dora was happy, he understood. She had married a man called Charles. He hoped she hadn't made a hasty decision. It seemed a bit sudden to Joe. She'd sent him a photo of their wedding. It was in colour. She'd cut her hair, dyed it too, a soft, faded peach, and he saw again the woman she once was, freewheeling down the road to Geoffrey's farm, happy, carefree and in love.

He thought more and more about the war. Whichever way you looked, Trude was at its heart, pulling skeins of lies and death that threaded them together. What had driven her? Joe would never know.

Pierre visited every day.

'Two old codgers,' he said. 'That's what we are.'

They chatted about the old days, sat together for meals, played dominoes.

'You may as well move in,' Joe said. 'You're here often enough.'

Pierre was talking to a woman. Joe couldn't recall seeing her here before, but Pierre acted like he knew her. 'Did you have a good holiday?'

'It was grand,' the woman said. 'It rained every day.'

'I'd have kept you dry,' he said.

'Will you get away.' She was laughing. 'You old devil.'

She pushed her tea trolley forward. 'Would you like another cup?'

Oh, Joe knew those voices, made for laments. He looked up. 'You wouldn't happen to be from Cloghane, would you?'

The woman almost jumped from her skin. 'No I'm not,' she said.

'But you're from the Dingle.'

'I am that,' she said. 'Brandon.'

He could see the bay in his mind, the fishing jetty, the mountain, the sweep of the Owenmore as it flushed into the sea. It was a hop and a skip to Cloghane.

'And would you happen to know the O'Clearys, in Cloghane?'

She thought for a minute, finger on chin. 'Didn't they used to have a butcher's shop?' she said.

'Aye,' Joe said. Just past the church on the left, before you reached O'Sullivan's. He could hear the music from the bar in summer, the jigs and reels as the sun went down, the songs of grief and loss as the moonlight glimmered over the bay, as the whiskey turned the blood melancholy. He saw the brown stone cottages, the rough pitted road. Would it have tarmac on it now, street lighting?

'I never knew them,' the woman was saying. 'The shop's long gone. I only ever heard about them.'

'And would you happen to know what happened to the family?'

'One of them died, I think,' she said. 'Some went away. I think one of the girls may have stayed. Married. You know how it is.'

Little Bridey. His favourite sister. She could be a grandmother by now.

'And did you hear talk of a priest?' Joe said.

'A priest?'

His heart drummed fast and he wondered if he shouldn't take one of his pills. She was pulling a face, shaking her head.

'No,' she said. 'I'd have heard about a priest.'

That you would, Joe thought, if they'd had a care for him. It hit hard, all the same, that they never spoke of him again.

'Will you be having your tea?' she said.

Still, it was good to hear the Irish again.

'Do you work here now?' Joe said.

'That I do.'

Well, a little chip off the Dingle to end his days, a monthly call from Barbara and a letter from Dora once a year.

What more could he want?

AFTERWORD

At least 34,000 women were trafficked into prostitution by the Nazis in the Second World War. Some were placed in brothels in the concentration camps, others in military bordellos in occupied Europe, of which there were over 500. Despite evidence of sexual offences against women committed in the brothels, these were not included as a crime against humanity, as defined at the International Military Tribunal at Nuremberg in 1945–6.

The victims of sexual enslavement did not speak out after the war. There was little sympathy with, or understanding of, victims of sexual violence, and the women in the military brothels in particular would have been vulnerable to charges of collaboration. Many women suspected of sleeping with the enemy – for whatever reason – were subject to rough justice and humiliation by shaving or tarring and feathering.

There were military brothels in Alderney, Guernsey and Jersey. The main brothel for the *Wehrmacht* in Jersey was in the Hotel Maison Victor Hugo, which, before the war, had been a hotel renowned for its aromatic gardens and sea views. It burned down in the mid-1980s and apartments have now been built on the site. A second brothel, located first in the Abergeldie Hotel and then the Norman House Hotel, serviced the men from *Organisation Todt.* Women were included in an early contingent of Russian and Ukrainian *OT* workers brought to the Channel Islands in 1942, many of whom may have been destined for work in the brothels.

Witness statements collected by the Director of Public Prosecutions sent out after the war to investigate war crimes in

Alderney provide rare clues as to the women's identities and conditions in the brothels. According to British intelligence, they were 'licensed French women'. This included French colonial women and leaves ambiguous their status – while exonerating their abusers. According to the evidence of *Oberleutnant* Wilhelm Girrbach, the garrison commander in Alderney, the women were 'volunteers' engaged in Paris to clean and serve, but the promise of high wages attracted only 'criminal elements... streetwalkers'. Their use as coerced prostitutes is in no doubt: they were subjected to punishments, imprisonment, forced medical examinations, were 'ruthlessly' dismissed if infected, and were unpaid.

How many women were there at any one time is guesswork. The commandant of Alderney, *Oberstleutnant* D R Schwalm, who took up post on 23 October 1943, estimated their numbers at 'about 100'. He ordered them to be quartered together and imposed strict visiting hours. Most of the women in Alderney were evacuated after the Normandy landings in 1944. By the end of the war, there were five women. Details are lacking on the brothels in Jersey, but conditions would be analogous to those in Alderney. The numbers, including both brothels, are likely to be higher, although it is probable that the *OT* brothel was wound down when the majority of *OT* men and labourers were moved to the European mainland in 1943–4.

The *Lebensborn* programme, one of Heinrich Himmler's schemes, was a system of breeding, choosing women of 'pure Aryan' stock and encouraging senior *SS* officers to impregnate them. Babies born as a result of this scheme were to be raised in the *Lebensborn* homes or put up for adoption by suitable German families. Some 'Aryan'-looking children in the occupied countries were kidnapped and given to German adoptive parents. There were a number of *Lebensborn* facilities established throughout occupied Europe, including the one at Lamorlaye in France, opened in February 1944 and closed by the Allies in August 1944. The homes offered superior nutrition and hygiene standards and the most advanced medical treatment available for mothers and babies.

For Hitler, occupation of the British Channel Islands held not only propaganda value but was also critical to the coastal defence of Europe. The Atlantic Wall, built to rebuff invasion by Allied forces, was a system of heavy-duty fortifications stretching from Norway to south-west France. *Organisation Todt* provided the labour for the construction of these defences. As in the rest of Europe, a small part of the local workforce was employed as skilled labour, but the majority of workers (some as young as fourteen) were forcibly brought in from all over Europe. Some were also political prisoners from Africa or Spain, held by the French.

There were fourteen labour camps in Jersey, five in Guernsey and four (including a temporary camp) in Alderney under the jurisdiction of *Organisation Todt.* A fifth camp on Alderney, Lager Sylt, was under the authority of the *SS.* The commandant was Maximilian List, who earned his spurs in Neuengamme, of which Lager Sylt was a satellite. It was the only *SS* concentration camp on British soil. The inmates were largely political prisoners, criminals and Jews. An architect by training, List is alleged to have designed and had built the commandant's house on Alderney. He was recalled to Berlin in February 1944 to answer questions relating to an escape of Jewish prisoners removed from the island in 1943.

Anywhere upwards of 16,000 forced labourers passed through the Channel Islands under the occupation, 5,000 on Alderney alone. The working and living conditions were inhumane, starvation and brutality was routine, mortality and morbidity high. In Lager Sylt, in particular, they amounted to evidence of war crimes. There had been high-profile convictions in Nuremberg, but prosecution of other war crimes was left to the countries in which they had been perpetrated. The British, however, chose not to prosecute. Maximilian List, wanted as 'responsible for the brutal treatment meted out to the concentration camp prisoners by the *SS* guards…

[and] for the fact that many of the prisoners died of starvation', was never prosecuted. He lived out his natural life in Hamburg, dying in the 1980s.

Similarly, there were no prosecutions for collaboration or profiteering, although, as in continental Europe, women were scapegoated and harsh vigilante treatment meted out to those suspected of fraternising with Germans.

I have played with these ideas and events in my novel, including some of the key players in the Channel Islands, British and German, although their personas and circumstances are my invention. The character of Dora was loosely inspired by the story of Marianne Grunfeld, a Jewish refugee, born in Upper Silesia, now Poland, who escaped to London in the 1930s. Blonde, blue-eyed, an agriculturist, she took a job on a Guernsey farm in 1940, a few months before the German occupation. She hid on the farm until she was betrayed to the German authorities and deported to her death, presumably in Auschwitz. I hope I have not betrayed her memory. In my novel, I melded parts of this story with parts of another, that of a (Jewish) survivor of the Ravensbrück concentration camp who, with her fair 'Aryan' looks, had been identified for the *Lebensborn* programme, which she refused.

The detail of life in the brothel, and the existence of the *Revier*, or infirmary, is pure imagination. It is reasonable to assume that, where possible, women would have looked for a sympathetic officer to protect them from the worst excesses, much as Marta Hillers recounts in *A Woman in Berlin*. British intelligence reports that the brothel was scaled down, or closed, after D-Day and thirty women were sent to France for fear of revealing information gleaned from the Germans to the Allies; I have chosen to extend the brothel's life for the purposes of the novel. The evacuation report of 28 May 1945 referred, however, to thirteen women from Jersey, all displaced persons. Nine of them were French. It does not say what these women were doing in Jersey, or how they arrived there.

Given the regular and intrusive medical checks required, and the compulsory abortions performed, it would also have made sense to have an in-house clinic for the women in the brothel. I have taken another liberty with the historical truth by inventing such an infirmary, which also treated soldiers. In reality, soldiers who had contracted venereal diseases were treated in the general hospital, which had been requisitioned by the Germans. According to evidence, venereal diseases were rife.

I have no idea if certain women were reserved for officers, and others for the rank and file, but have assumed that would be the case. Although the *SS* were not present in Jersey, the Channel Islands had been earmarked as a place of rest and recreation and it is possible that Maximilian List, the *SS Kommandant*, or other *SS* officers, visited Jersey, although how often, and for how long, is guesswork. It is unlikely that Dora would have been allowed to nurse in the *Revier*; on the other hand, German wounded were evacuated to Jersey after the Normandy landings in 1944 and emergency hospitals and convalescence facilities would have been required. They needed nurses.

How Dora and the other women survived the emotional and psychological strain of sexual enslavement is conjecture. The scars of sexual violence run deep. Given how little was understood or recognised at the time, its trauma would grip for a considerable period.

Much of the detail of Joe's life in Lager Sylt is based on the accounts of its inmates and witness statements. After the Normandy landings, the prisoners from Sylt and the *OT* camps on Alderney were evacuated to rebuild the Atlantic defences in Europe. The *Minotaure* was one of the ships, containing prisoners, which sank in the process, on 3 July 1944, with the loss of 250 lives.

La Ferme de l'Anse is a fiction, as are its precise co-ordinates. That Joe found refuge in the farm is perhaps a little fanciful: a battery was built close to la Coupe in December 1944 and most houses left empty were either requisitioned by the Germans or looted by locals. On the other hand, some escaped prisoners did evade capture for the duration of the war. I wanted to give Joe a break – he had been the victim of enough abuse since childhood.

The following primary and printed sources were used for the research for the novel:

Addy, C. *Limpet Stew and Potato Jelly: Lillian Aubin Morris' occupation Recipes* (Jersey Heritage Trust, 2014)

Anonymous (Marta Hillers), *A Woman in Berlin* (Virago, 2008)

Briggs, A. *The Channel Islands: Occupation and Liberation 1940–1945* (Batsford, 1995)

Bunting, M. *The Model Occupation: The Channel Islands under German Rule 1940–1945* (HarperCollins, 1995)

Carr, G. *Legacies of Occupation: Heritage, Memory and Archeaology in the Channel Islands* (Springer, 2014)

Carr, G., Sanders, P. and Willmot, L. *Protest, Defiance and Resistance in the Channel Islands: German Occupation 1940–45* (Bloomsbury Academic, 2014)

Ginns, M. *The Organisation Todt and the Fortress Engineers in the Channel Islands* (Channel Islands Occupation Society, 1994)

The Island Wiki, www.theislandwiki.org

Jersey Archives (WO 208/3741)

Knowles Smith, H. R. *The Changing Face of the Channel Islands Occupation: Record, Memory and Myth* (Macmillan, 2007)

Le Ruez, N. *Jersey Occupation Diary: Her story of the German Occupation 1940–45* (Seaflower Books, 1994)

McLoughlin, R. *Living with the Enemy: What really happened* (Channel Island Publishing, 2015)

Moodrick-Even Khen, H. and Hagay-Frey, A. (2014). Silence at the Nuremberg Trials: The International Military Tribunal at Nuremberg and Sexual Crimes Against Women in the Holocaust. https://www.academia.edu/6712388/Silence_at_the_Nuremberg_Trials_The_International_Military_Tribunal_at_Nuremberg_and_Sexual_Crimes_Against_Women_in_the_Holocaust

National Archives (various files relating to the occupation of the Channel Islands, in particular, WO311/11, WO311/12, WO311/13, WO199/2114, WO/199/2116, WO199/2126, WO199/2127, HO45/22399)

Sanders, P. *The British Channel Islands under German Occupation 1940–1945* (Jersey Heritage Trust, 2005)

Steckoll, S. H. *The Alderney Death Camp* (Granada, 1982)

Sturdy Colls, C. *Holocaust Archaeology: Archaeological approaches to Landscapes of Nazi Genocide and Persecution.* (PhD thesis, University of Birmingham, 2012)

Watkins, S. *Hitler's British Islands: The Channel Islands Occupation Experience by the people who lived through it* (Channel Island Publishing, 2000)

Williams, A. T. (2016). Forgotten Trials: The other side of Nuremberg. http://www.historyextra.com/article/bbc-history-magazine/forgotten-trials-other-side-nuremberg

ACKNOWLEDGEMENTS

Top of the list, my agent, Juliet Mushens, for her wisdom and support, and Jenny Parrott, my editor at Oneworld, for her brilliant suggestions – and faith! Thanks are also owing to the entire team at Oneworld, including Harriet Wade, Laura McFarlane, Paul Nash, Thanhmai Bui-Van and Margot Weale.

My dear friend, Ursula Owen, herself a refugee from Nazi Germany, shared the story of her cousin, Marianne Grunfeld, who moved to Guernsey from London just before the Nazi occupation but was betrayed and deported to her death in 1942. This story was one of the sources of inspiration for my novel, though the story I told departs from the true and tragic history of Marianne. I hope she will forgive me, but I wanted also to tell another story of war, and another story of women and war.

I picked the brains of so many friends and colleagues and am grateful to them all – though each and every error is my responsibility. Bob Armstrong, the best butcher in south-west London, for his insights into slaughtering and slaughtermen; my nephew Luis Chamberlain (lightweight boxing champion, Scottish Universities 2005, British Universities and Hospitals 2005; gold medallist, boxing, British Universities Sports Association 2006–7; and a boxing half-blue at Edinburgh University) knocked me into shape; Professor Elizabeth Harvey for her references on forced labour and women; my very old friend Sylvia Kieling and her husband, Hans-Joachim, for correcting my German and sharing with me stories of growing up in postwar Germany; Emily le Feuvre from the Jersey Archives; Dr Laura Marshall Andrews, a truly extraordinary and innovative GP, for medical advice; Professor Caroline Sturdy Colls for her generous sharing of articles and chapters on the *OT* and *SS* camps on the Channel Islands; and Professor Paul Weindling for all his help on medical refugees in the 1930s and 1940s.

I owe a big debt to those who read, commented and advised on the first draft – Professor Cora Kaplan, critical thinker par excellence; Bob Marshall Andrews, arch-plotter who sorted me out; Anna Mazzola for her crucial insights; and Sara Sarre whose help on character, pace and narrative was invaluable.

My writing posse – what would I do without you? Cecilia Ekbäck, Viv Graveson, Laura McClelland, Saskia Sarginson, Lauren Trimble.

I am hugely grateful to everyone – and above all to my husband, Stein Ringen, for his love and support throughout, and, of course, my wonderful daughters and their families.

Hugs. To you all.

ONEWORLD READERS' GUIDE

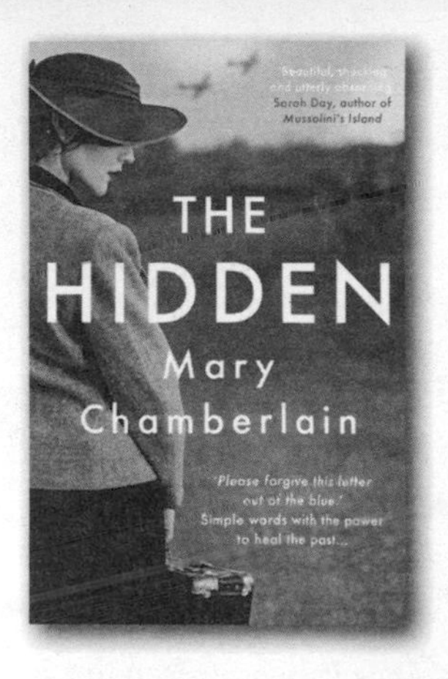

THE HIDDEN

Mary Chamberlain

This is a story of love and betrayal, shame and survival. Dora and Joe's worlds are abruptly upended by the sudden arrival of Barbara Hummel, who is determined to identify the mysterious woman whose photograph she has found among her mother's possessions. Forced to confront a time they thought buried in the past, Dora and Joe's lives unravel – and entwine. For, trapped on the Channel Islands under the German occupation in the Second World War, Dora, a Jewish refugee, had concealed her identity; while Joe, a Catholic priest, kept quite another secret… Mary Chamberlain dives into themes of love, betrayal, shame and survival in this breathtaking novel. The questions below are designed to enhance your discussion of *The Hidden.*

Questions for Discussion

1. The novel moves between time frames – is this a useful device? Would the story change if it were related chronologically?

2. What was 'hidden' in the novel? What does the novel tell us about memory and lies? What does it tell us of survival? And shame?

3. The story was told from two points of view. Would it have worked from a single point of view? Whose story did you enjoy the most? Did the stories stand in contrast to each other, or were there parallels in each?

4. What do we learn about Dora in the opening chapter? Does it prepare us for the story that unfolds?

5. Did Dora love Maximilian List? In chapter 7 Dora and her friends have a conversation about 'Stockholm Syndrome.' Do you think that is an adequate description of her relationship with Maximilian List? She made a decision not to try and find Geoffrey after the war. Why did she do that?

6. What would you have done faced with Dora's situation? Why could she not talk about her wartime experiences?

7. What was your reaction when you read how Dora tried to murder her own child? Did you agree with this choice?

8. Joe had buried his own traumatic past. Was it this, or loneliness, that attracted him to Trude? Or was he too naïve?

9. Later in chapter 12 Geoffrey says, 'Nobody wanted to talk about the war.' Was this a common experience after the Second World War (or any war)? On p.224 Joe says that 'victims leave no traces.' Geoffrey disagrees. What do you think about this?

10. There were a number of real-life historical figures in the novel – Maximilian List, Zepernick, Clifford Orange etc. Do you like it when writers fuse history and fiction? Does it detract from the novel or enhance its force? Are there ethical issues involved in using historical characters?

11. The occupation of the Channel Islands was a painful moment for the British in general and the Channel Islanders in particular, and is rarely referred to in popular accounts of the Second World War. Why do you think this is? The novel played with little known features of the Second World War – the sexual violence against women, the SS Concentration Camp in Alderney. Is there a purpose in revisiting the past, especially a traumatic one?